THE MALLORCAN BOOKSELLER

Pete Davies

Cover design by: Brian Tarr
(brian-tarr.pixels.com)

For everyone who has ever felt they have a story within them to tell. Sometimes you just need the inspiration to start writing and for me, it was the beautiful island of Mallorca.

ONE

"**I**s Anna in?"

He had plucked up courage to go and tell someone he trusted what had happened, but he still felt so stupid to have fallen for the scam.

With his eyes misting up as he walked through the small door of Sa Petita Llibreria, 'The Little Bookshop', he didn't recognise the young man behind the counter.

"No, she's not at the moment, but she should be back soon."

Bill felt himself start to crumble inside. He couldn't believe he'd fallen for it and now he felt tears in his eyes and again he felt so stupid and turned to go.

"Wait," said the young man. "It's Bill isn't it? It's me, Sam, Anna's son."

Of course it was! Bill couldn't believe he hadn't recognised Sam, who he'd known since he was a boy of around ten, but then the last time he had seen Sam had been at the funeral six months ago.

After the diagnosis, Luis, Sam's father, had gone within just a few months. The cancer had spread so quickly within his body that maybe it was a blessing in some ways, but anyway, why hadn't he recognized Sam? Of course! He realised that at the funeral Sam's hair had been short, much shorter in fact and now it was quite long, at least for a policeman, so Bill allowed himself to think that it was perhaps an acceptable mistake and hoped Sam didn't think him too rude.

"Mum should be back soon Bill, but it's pretty quiet at the moment, so shall we sit down and maybe I can help?"

And so it started.

*****

As soon as he had put the phone down, Bill had realised what had happened. He slumped back into his chair and wished his Val was there. He'd never been great with computers and she had always looked after that sort of thing.

But she wasn't there. Like Luis, she had succumbed to the same horrible disease, although sadly she didn't go quickly. Instead, she wasted away in front of him, although mentally, she was strong as an ox and remained so, right to the end, getting him sorted and ready for life after she had gone.

He had been scammed by a call centre into thinking his computer had a virus and now he needed to pull himself together.

"Right, what to do?" he said out aloud, but with only himself to hear.

He and Val had been living in Mallorca for over twenty five years, moving from the UK after taking early retirement when he sold his business. They had known Anna and Luis Martínez for about as long. He and Anna had both lost the person they cared so much for. First it was Val, two years ago and then Anna's Luis passed six months ago. So now he had to deal with this on his own.

*****

He set off for the short drive from Illetes into Palma, parked in the multi-storey carpark by the Teatre Principal at the end of the Rambla dels Ducs de Palma de Mallorca and made the short walk to Anna's bookshop,

Sa Petita Llibreria, where he found Sam.

Bill knew Sam was in the police back in London. He didn't know what he specifically did and thought he must just be across on holiday to see his mum. He thought Sam was pretty close to his mum, although it was a bit strange that he hadn't been around much since his father had died.

"So what happened?" said Sam.

"I was on the laptop at home, paying some bills, when something appeared on the screen. The screen froze and suddenly I'm hearing this voice coming out of the speakers, saying my computer was being attacked and that I should contact some outfit called Intertech Support immediately on the number on my screen."

Bill went on to explain that he had dialled the Intertech number and the person who answered seemed so helpful. He had followed their instructions and they had taken over control of his laptop and gone on to show him the problem was on one of his files.

"Sam, I feel so stupid, but he seemed so genuine."

"Did you pay them any money Bill?" said Sam.

Bill looked down at his knees and then said, "Yes, I did. I did tell him that I thought it was bloody expensive, but he said these things were hard to fix. He told me not to worry and that he could fix it all and give me a full twelve month support contract as a special offer."

"How much did you pay Bill?" Sam gently asked.

Bill looked at the ground and said, "Nearly £900."

Sam knew better than to react and anyway, at that moment Anna came through the door. One look at Bill told her something was wrong. She walked across and gave Bill a hug and he just clung to her for a moment.

"Oh Anna, I've been such a fool. I've been scammed, but it's not the money. I can cope with that. It's being taken for a ride and being so bloody gullible!"

She looked across at Sam and said, "What do we need to do?"

Sam always loved the way his mum reacted to any sort of drama. She dealt with what needed to be done in terms of giving a hug or words of encouragement and then went into a business-like mode, where she got on with what needed to be done next.

"Well first things first," he said.

"Bill, we need to get you to complete a denuncia, a crime report, with the police. They won't look at anything if it hasn't been officially reported. We can start this on-line and then go to a police station to sign it to make it official."

Bill nodded, but looked uncomfortable. "My Spanish isn't as good ......"

"Don't worry," said Sam, "I'm coming with you."

*****

After they had worked through the on-line crime reporting system, Sam and Bill set off walking towards the police station. Bill was still pretty fit for his years and made a point of trying to walk when he was playing golf, rather than take a buggy, so he had no problems with the walk that took them up and along Carrer de Jaume III, one of the main shopping streets in the city. At the end of the street they crossed the main Passeig de Mallorca where the 24 hour police station, that was also the Policia Nacional headquarters, was situated.

When they left Anna at Sa Petita Llibreria, she sat down and thought about her Sam. She had been worried when he had suddenly come home over three weeks ago and he hadn't really explained why he had left London. She could tell that something must have happened. He was edgy and a bit short tempered, which wasn't like him at all. She knew that he some-times needed a little time, after he came back to Mallorca, to be able to wind down and relax. This time though, things seemed different, but she tried to not fuss him or to ask too many questions and over the past few weeks she had seen him start to be, well, more like her Sam.

He now seemed to be enjoying just helping out in the bookshop and she hoped to persuade him to also now start taking an interest in helping her run the rest of the business. Since Luis had gone, she had started to think about the future and especially about how she would manage the family business. Whilst she still felt as fit as a fiddle, she had always been a planner and wanted to make sure that things were in place for either 'just in case' eventualities, or for when she just didn't feel up to doing it anymore.

Sa Petita Llibreria had always been a labour of love for the family. Firstly for Alberto, Luis's Grandfather, who had originally opened the bookshop in 1920 and then for Luis's father, Miguel, who then passed the baton onto Luis in the early '90's when he had become too frail to carry on. Anna and Luis were married by then and were living in Madrid when his father asked him to come home. She had known it was a request that her husband would never turn down. He had always considered his time as Professor of Spanish Literature at Universidad Complutense de Madrid, one of the oldest and most prestigious universities in the world, as having been 'his' time, but that he knew he would return to Palma when the time came for him to take over from his father.

Anna had enjoyed her time in Madrid. She had moved there with her job with the Foreign and Commonwealth Office after she found she was pregnant and no longer able to travel. Single and with a young baby, there wasn't much opportunity to socialise, but her friends encouraged her out on blind dates, something she hated, but went along with to please them.

She met Luis on yet another of the blind dates her friend Susan set up for her. They met for lunch at Café Comercial with a group of friends. It was one of her favourites, although with coping with young Sam, she didn't get the chance to go very often. She mostly went when her parents came across to see her from England and took her there for a treat. Susan knew she liked it there.

It was a lovely old world restaurant and bar that always had a great atmosphere and the décor was just lovely. She watched Luis from across the table and smiled when he too looked uncomfortable, but he also looked gentle and there was a caring look in his eyes. He looked older than her, maybe by around ten years and had never married and he didn't hide anything about why he had never married when one of her friends bluntly asked him.

"I have just never fallen utterly in love," he said.

"That's got to be ten out of ten for romance Luis," said Harry, one of Susan's friends. "Anna, did you hear that? He's got to be the man for you."

Anna had heard and she thought he seemed nice. He was quiet, thoughtful, caring and an academic. She had studied languages and history at university and their friends soon realised that this time, they might just have succeeded in finding someone to take Anna's interest beyond a nice lunch. The friends soon made their excuses after they had finished lunch and left Anna and Luis alone.

"Ah, we seem to have been abandoned," said Anna.

"I don't mind if you don't," said Luis. "Another coffee?"

*****

They spent the rest of the afternoon talking. Anna had not enjoyed herself so much for a long time, at least, not on her own as she suddenly felt guilty about the time she had left Sam with her babysitter.

"I really must go Luis, as I need to collect my little boy."

She had told him about Sam and he hadn't seem fazed at all. Sam was two now and she was ready to find someone for her. Not necessarily as a father for Sam, but because of her work she had never really had anything she could call a long term relationship. She liked him, but she was very much out of practice with dating, so hoped he would make the first move.

"Anna, I am not very good at this sort of thing, you know, dating, but would you like to go out again?"

"I would love that Luis," she smiled.

Over the next year their relationship blossomed. Luis was great with Sam and he never asked her about who his biological father was. Although Anna didn't feel she was hiding anything, she decided that it was something that needed to be out in the open. She told him that she had been in a very short term relationship with a man she really liked, but that his job made it impossible to be part of her life.

Luis accepted what she told him without question and as their relationship strengthened they decided to take things forward and moved in together. Luis had already taken her and Sam to his home in Palma de Mallorca, to meet his parents and get their seal of approval on their relationship. She had felt under pressure the first time she met them. Would they like her? Would they be okay about Sam? But they couldn't have been more welcoming and they were so kind. It was after they had been together a couple of years, when they were in Palma visiting for the weekend, that she heard Luis being quizzed by his father, Miguel.

"When are you going to make this beautiful English rose your wife?"

She had smiled at his father and listened as Luis tried to explain to him why they were happy as they were. She felt no great need to be married. She was happy, very happy and wasn't worried if Luis wanted to keep things as they were as well. So when they were back in Madrid and he suggested they go out for dinner one evening, she had thought nothing of it.

She got a little bit suspicious when he took her to their favourite restaurant, Café Comercial, where they had first met, but it really still came out of the blue when after the opening course, he had got down on one knee and proposed. It was so unlike him. Although he was used to delivering lectures and was a gifted public speaker, he was also a little shy and reserved when it came to showing his emotions in public and so it had taken him some courage to do this in the middle of a crowded restaurant.

She jumped up from the table and found herself yelling, "Yes, yes, yes!!!"

Maybe she hadn't let herself think she would really like to be married to this man, but it felt so good to be asked.

They were married later that year in one of the university chapels in Madrid and settled down to family life until Luis got the call from his father to take over the family business. She had loved living in Madrid, but soon fell in love with living in Palma de Mallorca. It was such a beautiful city with La Seu, the magnificent Cathedral standing high and proud above the city skyline.

They lived in the home that had been built by his grandfather, a beautiful villa near the coast, just south west of Palma and about a ten minute drive from Sa Petita Llibreria. Sam was five when they moved to Palma and he had quickly settled into his new life living by the sea. He was fluent in both Spanish and English by then and so settling into his new school, just a few minutes' walk away, was just like any other five year old moving to a new home and having to find new friends. But he was an out-going child who loved football and swimming and so quickly found new friends and had no problems adapting to the Catalan dialect more often used in Mallorca.

Luis and Anna set about starting their new life in Palma de Mallorca, running the family business and taking time for Luis to show Anna around his family homeland. His parents lived nearby and Sunday lunchtime was always a big occasion with family and friends.

The bookshop was primarily more of a hobby than a business and their main income had been from their property company. The family had owned land and property on the island for many years and with the on-going development of the tourism industry, Luis's family had been able to build a profitable business which had eventually passed to Luis when his father died. Even before Luis's diagnosis, the question for some time had been whether Sam would want to leave the police and take over the business.

There had been conversations with Sam over the years, especially when he joined the police in London, but Luis had always said, *"Let's be patient. Let him have time for himself, just as I did. I don't want to push this on to him, but I'm sure he'll come when we need him to."*

Anna now sat and wondered if Sam would indeed come and take over the business when she eventually needed him.

*****

The duty officer came out and spoke to them in English.

"How can I help you?"

Sam spoke to the officer in Spanish and explained that he was a police officer in London and that his

13

mother lived here in Mallorca and Bill was an old family friend. He briefly told the officer what had happened and that they had completed an on-line denuncia. A moment later the officer came back with some paperwork, looked through it and then asked Bill to sign the denuncia, explaining that this signified it was now an official crime report.

Bill signed the paper and said, "I'm so sorry, I've been so stupid and don't want to take up your time."

The police officer paused for a moment and seemed to physically relax his body.

"Señor, please don't worry. It is I who am sorry that you have fallen victim to this, what is the word, despicable scam?"

Sam nodded his appreciation.

"Thank you for your understanding."

"But I have not finished," the officer said.

The officer then spoke quickly in Spanish to Sam.

"Señor, I don't want to alarm your friend, Señor Patterson, but I can tell you that we have had a number of these scams reported in the last few months and in some cases, although not all, the victim has then been subjected to a burglary at their home, sometimes with extreme violence being shown."

Sam couldn't hold back a frown.

Bill said, "What is it Sam?"

The officer got up and said he would be back in a moment with a colleague.

"Bill, this isn't the first they have heard of this and our friend here has just told me that some scam victims have then been burgled. He's just gone to get one of his colleagues, so we might find out a little more in a moment."

As they waited, Sam sent a text to his mother to let her know what was going on and just as he finished, the officer returned with his colleague who immediately introduced herself.

"Detective Inspectora Lori Garcia. I usually work with the Unidad de Crimen Organizado, our Organised Crime Unit, but I am currently seconded to the Grupo Especial de Operaciones."

She let that sink in for a moment. Sam had heard of the G.E.O. They were a special operations group who dealt with terrorism and organised crime and were one of the elite teams of the Policia Nacional."

"Señor Martínez, I understand you are an officer from London and you also work in the same area as I do?"

Sam nodded. He was a Detective Chief Inspector in an Organised Crime Team and so he very much understood the type of work DI Garcia was engaged in.

"Yes Inspectora and thank you for taking the time to come and see us."

"Please call me Lori, it's Sam isn't it?"

Lori Garcia was a striking and attractive woman, who clearly had a presence and level of seniority that had the other officer standing upright and almost at attention to her side. She thanked the officer and dismissed him and then sat down with Sam and Bill.

"Your officer was very kind Lori," said Bill.

"Señor Patterson, that is good to hear and I will be sure to let his superiors know. Now, I'd like to make sure that you don't also become a burglary victim."

Sam understood that he was clearly been giving the courtesy of a more involved response from the Policia Nacional than perhaps a usual victim of crime might expect. He smiled and assumed she had done what he would have done in similar circumstances and just at that moment his phone buzzed with an in-coming text. He glanced quickly at it and saw he was right. It was Jimmy from his office. The message said, '*So why are the GEO asking about you?*' He looked back at Lori Garcia who smiled.

"Your office are telling you we have been asking about you?"

"Yes," he smiled back.

It was clear she had already done her homework as she knew Bill lived just down the coast towards Illetes. It was an impressive villa in extensive grounds and would therefore be a very attractive target for a follow up burglary. She didn't go into much detail about the violence that had been used making Sam think that these were no silent in and out burglars.

"Señor Patterson, can you go and stay somewhere for a few days, maybe a week, whilst we look after your house?"

"Oh, there's no need for that," said Bill. "I can take care of myself."

"Bill, this is serious. The people doing these burglaries don't mess about and they've hurt people who have got in their way and hurt them badly," said Sam.

Bill looked at Sam and then at DI Garcia and saw the look in their eyes. He was still pretty fit at seventy nine, but he knew they were talking sense.

"Look, come and stay with us. Mum would love that and so would I. We can catch up on old times," said Sam.

Bill nodded and smiled "That would be lovely". He knew that whilst he still got out and about and kept himself busy, especially with his golf as a member at Real Golf de Bendinat, he did sometimes feel very lonely.

"Okay, good, that's settled. Thank you Señor," said DI Garcia.

As they got up to go DI Garcia looked at Sam.

"Can we speak later?"

Sam nodded and as they all shook hands she continued, "These are nasty people Sam and are somehow tied into the call centres making the scam calls. We're putting a lot of messages out there for the public, especially the vulnerable, but we're still getting new victims coming forward every day."

*****

As Sam left the meeting with DI Garcia, he texted back to Jimmy, *'Nothing to worry about. Family friend been IT scammed.'* Almost immediately, his phone buzzed again. Jimmy. *'She sounded nice.......'* Followed by, *'You OK?'*

He had not had much contact from Jimmy since he had left London. Jimmy was a good mate, someone he'd known since he joined the MET Police nearly fifteen years ago and he knew Jimmy was giving him a bit of distance since it all went a bit pear shaped for him at work. He texted back, *'Yes she is nice..... if you like older women'* – he added a smiley emoji *'and yes I'm OK mate'*.

'Yes,' he thought, *'she is nice'* and she certainly looked like she knew what she was doing. First time he had thought about a woman since getting home to the island. He was pretty much over Kirsty, although he should be. It had been over a year since she had finally had enough and walked out on him. He couldn't blame her. He knew he had become withdrawn, moody and he'd stopped talking to her about the important stuff. They had been together for nearly five years and he wondered why they hadn't taken things further and maybe got married or had children. But they hadn't. He knew what it was and he didn't need the counselling to tell him either. He was suffering from post-traumatic stress disorder, PTSD and he wasn't dealing with it very well, not very at all in fact.

He had messed up on a firearms job three years ago. Distracted by a young child coming into his firing line, he had momentarily taken his eye off the target. That's all it took and his mate Jimmy took a bullet that he,

Sam, could have prevented. He couldn't get that Jimmy didn't blame him.

'Christ,' he thought, *'I don't know why not. I think I would!'*

The doctors had said Jimmy had been lucky. But how lucky is lucky? The bullet had gone through him and lodged near his spine leaving him in permanent pain and in a wheelchair. The guy who shot him just laughed in court when sentenced. Sam fell apart inside, but didn't tell anyone and did his very best to not let anyone see. In fact he had been promoted again since then, to Detective Chief Inspector. Something he had seen as a way of getting out of the front line, so that he longer went out on armed operations, but most of all, it had given him a way of dealing with the stuff going on his head about blaming himself for what happened to Jimmy.

The Job were pretty good with Jimmy and after he had recovered, he came back to work in the same team. Sam couldn't believe how well he adapted to being desk bound and he was still a bloody good intelligence officer, one of the best.

"Two choices mate," Jimmy had said to him. "Give up and wallow, or crack on with it. But don't ever think I don't hate it when the guys go out on a job and I get left behind. But I'd rather be here than lying on a slab in the morgue. Then again, it could be worse, I could have been promoted like you and still not been able to go out," and he'd smiled.

Cop humour. Jimmy was getting on with it. Sam not so well.

TWO

T he men approached the villa in silence. They had parked up away from the main entrance and split up. Two to the front and two to the rear.

Senichi Sargsyan took the lead. Known as Sonny, he knew he could have left this to his men, but he enjoyed the adrenalin of the moment and it let them know he was still very much the boss.

The recon team had reported that there was just an old woman in the house at this time of the day and the CCTV was wireless operated. These were easy targets, with little risk and a low likelihood of the police getting anywhere near them.

The radio crackled and he heard that the CCTV frequency jammer was now on and after acknowledging the team at the rear were in position, Sonny gave the order over the radio to move in and cut the CCTV wiring. He climbed the garden fence and walked to the side door nearest to him which easily gave way to the force of the jemmy.

Entering the villa, he found the woman in the living area.

"Mrs MacDonald, I need you to tell me where your safe is."

The woman looked terrified. A slight woman. She

looked in her 70s and was smartly dressed and clearly had the look of having money.

He thought this was going to be another easy one until the woman straightened up and shouted at him, "Who the hell are you and what are you doing in my house?"

Sonny smiled. She had courage this one. He slapped her hard across the face and she screamed and fell against the sofa.

"You'll have to do better than that mate," she snarled at him.

His smile turned to a quizzical frown.

"One way or the other, Mrs MacDonald you will tell me where the safe is, but we have enough time anyway before anyone comes back, so with or without your help I'm sure we will find it."

He sat down across from her and waved for the other three men to start looking for the safe.

"Take that picture and that one as well," he said, pointing at two pictures hanging in the living room.

Sheila MacDonald tried to get her senses together. From the East End of London she had seen many things in her life and so wasn't completely overwhelmed by what was going on. He spoke with an East European accent, but there was something in the man's eyes, the one sitting calmly across from her, that was unsettling her. It was such a cold look that she decided there and then that the best tactic to get out of this would be to just give him what he wanted and get him out of her house as soon as she could. Hopefully that would be enough.

"It's in the main bedroom. Behind the picture of the waterfall."

Sonny smiled.

"Now that was almost too easy Mrs MacDonald. I was expecting more from you, being a tough East End

London woman."

"*How does he know that?*" thought Sheila.

He let it sink in for a moment, smiling at the confusion and uncertainty in her face.

"I know you're wondering how I know these things Sheila. It is Sheila isn't it? Well, you need to be careful who you talk to on the telephone."

He saw the puzzled look on her face and then the recognition. She had been on the computer when a box flashed up saying there was an IT problem. She had spoken with someone in an IT support call centre and they had fixed it, but it had been ridiculously expensive. She hadn't yet told John, who was back in London, as she was worried she might have been scammed and felt a bit stupid, so she wanted to tell him when he got back.

"You bastard!"

She couldn't help herself, but wished she had as he got up and came towards her. She crouched in a ball. She thought he was going to hit her again, but he didn't, so she relaxed. But then he dragged her roughly off the sofa and into the main bedroom and dropped her by the safe.

"Open it Sheila," he said, again in a calm voice.

She knew the combination. The safe had her jewellery, some cash and some documents in there. '*Not worth dying for,*' she said to herself. She opened the safe and sat back on the bed, her head throbbing from the pain.

"Thank you Sheila. See, that was easy."

One of the men gathered the contents in to a bag and just as he did, the alarm activated.

"Oh Sheila, what have you done? That was not a good thing to do."

Again, the calm, disturbing voice. She was worried now. He had been wearing a balaclava, but now he'd taken it off.

He could have just shot her. He knew that was what his men were thinking. She tried to put up a fight as he punched her face, again and again. She was tough, he had to accept that, so he didn't stop even when he felt her go limp and eventually Alex Krikorian, his second in command, had to pull him away from her.

"Sonny, she's dead. We need to go," said Alex.

Sonny looked down at the beaten and bloodied face of the woman and felt nothing. He turned and at first he glared at Alex, but then he nodded, yes, they needed to get out as the cops would be on their way. The recon team had calculated the response time in the event of an alarm and they still had time to get away without a panic.

He motioned to the other men to move out and they were out of the area by the time the police were arriving on the scene.

*****

Back at his Operations Centre, a suite of offices in a smart office block, away from suspicion, Sonny took stock of the morning's events. Another easy job on the back of the call centre scam that he had set up with Jaz. This was a great bit of collaboration that was bringing in some easy money and Sergei had been impressed with his initiative.

He was responsible for all of Sergei Grigoryan's operations in the Balearics. These included extortion, money laundering, drugs and prostitution and more recently this side line of high value burglaries.

He had known Sergei since he joined the Armenian Army, when he was eighteen. Sergei was four years older and had taken Sonny under his wing and he had become one of Sergei's most trusted lieutenants after they got out of the army and started up in business. Beginning in their home town just outside of the main city Yerevan, Sergei had grown the business with a philosophy of trust and loyalty, reward and punishment. Sonny had often been called upon by Sergei to deal with a punishment 'issue' and had gained a reputation as being someone not to cross.

Sergei expanded the business in the US and into Europe, with Country Heads looking after the business for him. It was three years ago that Sergei had sent him to Palma to 'take over' from the previous boss. This meant putting a bullet in the head of the idiot who had got too greedy and was skimming too much off the top of the business.

Sergei ran the entire organisation back in Yerevan. He ran it like a corporate business, with a command team, clear performance targets and defined outcomes. Whilst he demanded total loyalty, he also rewarded his people very well, but in return, loss of his trust resulted in a level of punishment befitting the level of responsibility. Hence, when his previous In-Country Head in the Balearics had been discovered stealing from the corporation, he had been permanently dismissed.

*****

He stood in the Chapel of Rest at the funeral director's offices. John MacDonald was holding his wife's hand and could feel the tears streaming down his cheeks. Fortunately, they hadn't seen the police photographs and the funeral directors had worked miracles and so when he and his sons saw Sheila, their wife and mum, she seemed at peace.

She looked beautiful. She was dressed in the really pretty dress they had bought in one of the boutiques on Passeig de Born. He was always happy to go dress shopping with Sheila as he loved the way she just glowed when she came out of the changing rooms. He would never do this again. He felt empty.

His two sons were there with him, supporting him,

but he was struggling to contain the hurt and pain of losing her. He hadn't been there. He hated the fact that she had died alone, without him. They had always been together and he rarely went away on business without her, but this was only going to be for a couple of days whilst he popped back to London for a Board Meeting.

"Dad?" said Chris, his oldest son. "Are you Okay?"

"Yes boy, I'm just missing her. Not sure what to do now to be honest?"

"Drink Dad?" said Jack, his younger son.

"Yes, son. It might not help, but it certainly won't do any harm."

*****

John MacDonald had also been born in the East End of London and he'd married his childhood sweetheart Sheila.

Chairman of Trent MacDonald, John was a highly successful businessman who had built Trent Mac-Donald into a multinational engineering company. But whilst he was used to dealing with crisis management and operating in challenging countries, he suddenly felt very tired.

As he walked slowly across to the two cars they had travelled in down to the Chapel of Rest, he saw his two sons and recognised the look in their faces. *'Why the hell had this happened? Why would someone need to harm a woman in her seventies when they have clearly got what they wanted?'*

As he got into the Range Rover, John glanced back to his son Chris.

"Get hold of Greg."

*****

Greg Chambers was sitting in the Cittie of York, a pub in Holborn, London watching a young man, a City Trader, who was with three other people in one of the line of snugs in the pub. They were all dressed in smart suits and had been flashing their cash at the three other pubs they had been to so far during the afternoon.

The Trader had been identified as a potential liability by his company, not just because of a suspected drug habit, but because of a reckless streak in his trading. His employers, an old established company at the Stock Exchange, had engaged 3R, Greg's company. This wasn't his idea of the type of work he usually took on and he certainly wasn't enjoying it, However, they were a very good client and had called in a favour, not least because the Trader was the son of one of the senior partners.

As Greg looked back at his target he remembered when the pub had been called Henekey's back in the day, but it had been renamed in the late 70's. He'd used the pub a lot during the 90's and recalled either reading or being told that the original refurb had taken place in the 1920s, probably at a time when pubs were generally being restyled with a more modern look, so it must have been quite something to see the pub being given such a classic late Victorian interior. He smiled. His mind was wandering around these facts when his phone buzzed with a text, *'Call me ASAP'*.

It was from Chris MacDonald, John's oldest son. John Mac was one of his oldest clients, actually, he was his oldest client and he had taken a chance on Greg, when he set up 3R when he left the Service. It was usually Mac who rang him, so he wondered what was wrong. He had seen enough of what was going on with the Trader, so it was time to wrap this up. He texted back *'5 minutes Chris'*.

In one of the pubs the Trader and his friends had been in, before they got to the Cittie of York, Greg had seen him exchanging some small packets with one of the others in the group, a smaller guy dressed in a smart light blue suit, who was obviously getting the drugs and supplying the Trader with coke or something similar.

It had been too busy in the other pubs for Greg to be able to create a situation where he could safely engage with the Trader. Now he took a moment and looked around the pub, checking out the clientele for any possible risk. Nothing.

'Okay, time to sort this,' he thought.

He picked up his pint. It was a pity to waste one of Samuel Smith's finest, but needs must. He changed his walk into a slight stagger and walked across to the booth where the four guys were sitting and did a very good impression of tripping and throwing his beer over the young Trader.

"What the hell!"

"I'm so sorry," said Greg, slightly slurring his speech and he started to try to mop down the young man's clothes, deftly reaching in and removing the wallet from the Trader's inside jacket pocket.

"Get off me you drunken piece of shit."

"Now that's not very nice. You should learn to respect your elders."

"Oh, piss off mate and be bloody grateful I don't take you outside and teach you how to respect your youngers."

"No need for that young man," said Greg and he started to walk away.

"Good. Bugger off. Right, another boys? On me."

As the Trader got up, Greg started for the door, but as the Trader approached the bar he put his hand to his jacket pocket for his wallet. After a mix of drink and drugs during the afternoon and evening, he did well to put two and two together and realise Greg had dipped his wallet.

"Guys, he's stolen my bloody wallet!"

They all scrambled outside into the road and one

of them saw Greg who looked like he was just turning into an alley just up from the pub. Greg was waiting for the action to start and allowed them to see him before moving into the alley, where he then hid in the shadows right at the front of the alley.

He knew they'd be unprepared and would just run straight past him into the alley. He would then have them blocked in the alley and sure enough, in they came with the Trader at the front. *'Is that a bit of courage or just drink and drugs bravado?'* he thought to himself.

"Oh, there you are. Hiding in the shadows are we? I think you have got something of mine," said the Trader.

"Yes and I suppose you want it back?"

The Trader paused, recognising the drunk, who had spilled beer over him, was no longer apparently sounding drunk.

"Listen mate, I don't know what's going on here, but just give me my bloody wallet and you can walk away, no hard feelings."

Greg smiled back.

"I can walk away? What about you? Do you want to walk away or what about your friends? Guys, do you want to walk away and leave me and young Matthew to have a chat?"

The Trader looked stunned. *'How does he know my name?'* Then thought, *'He's looked in my wallet that's all.'*

"Yes, very clever mate, you've looked in my wallet, so just give it back before I come and take it back off you."

The Trader was looking at the guy in front of him. He looked in his sixties, well built and looked pretty fit, but there were four of them.

"So Matthew, you're probably thinking this is one old guy on his own and there's four of us. But really, are there four of you? What about you James, or you Martin? How would scrapping in the street appear to your employer?"

The two guys looked at each other and then at the man in front of them.

"How do you.....?" James began.

"What, how do I know you work for a large trading company in the city?" said Greg.

Even as they nodded Greg continued, "Because they are a very old established firm who value their reputation and will go to some lengths to protect it. Now if you run along now, I might just leave your names out of my report."

He saw the two guys visibly lower their shoulders, any idea of a fight had been knocked well and truly out of them with just the mention of protecting the organisation's reputation.

"Guys, what are you doing? He's bluffing."

"Matt, this isn't worth it. You need to sort this out. Your old man will go bananas," said James.

"Good call James. So you two can go, whilst I stay and have a chat with Matt and his friend here."

"James, Martin, guys, come on, we can do this. My dad will see you're okay. We can't let this bastard get away with this."

They said nothing as they quickly walked out of the alley.

"Hey mate, you haven't spoken to me yet and by the way, you're scaring no one here," said the guy in the light blue suit pulling out a flick knife from his back trouser pocket.

Greg watched him for a moment, looking for signs of fighting capability. The knife was in Cummins' right hand but he was standing straight in front of Greg, in a passive position, rather than adopting any sort of open and athletic stance.

"I wondered when you'd speak. Billy isn't it? Billy

Cummings, entertainment fixer and sometime low life drug dealer to Traders with too much bloody money and no bloody sense."

"Are you old Bill?" said Cummins.

"You may well wish I was in a minute Billy," and Greg didn't give him any time to think as he sprung at Cummins, deflecting his knife hand away with a left forearm block that shook the knife out of Cummins' hand, before he hit him hard with a driving right punch to the stomach that took Cummins off his feet and dumped him on the ground.

The Trader just stood there, frozen.

"I don't know who you are, but my dad would never have agreed to this and you won't know what's hit you when he's finished with you."

"I think you will find that your Chairman has already spoken to your father about this Matt and he understands his position in the firm is dependent on you changing your ways. As of now, you are on sick leave and there is a room booked for you at a very private and very expensive drug rehab centre just a few miles away. Count yourself damn lucky that the Chairman still thinks enough of your father to have agreed to his request to get you specialist treatment. But understand this. If you leave the treatment programme or lapse in any way, they will terminate your position with the company. There are no further second chances. Is that understood?"

"Yes," said the Trader quietly.

Greg saw that Cummins was starting to sit up and he bent down to help him up or so it looked to the Trader, but then he heard Cummins scream as Greg bent his right arm back and in a grotesque motion snapped the arm with a sudden and vicious twist of the forearm.

"Sorry Matthew, I didn't hear you."

"Yes, yes, I'm sorry, I understand and I'll do it and

please don't hurt me."

"Oh good," he smiled, "I'm so glad you agree, now come on and we'll leave this piece of shit to crawl back under his rock somewhere."

Just at that moment, a Range Rover pulled up at the front of the alley and Greg walked the Trader towards the car and sat him in the back seat.

"This is Tommy. He'll take care of you. He's from Barbados and is very friendly, but he's also an ex-para, so please do not do anything to annoy him. The back doors will be locked until you arrive at your location. Once there he will escort you to the reception and you will be booked in and then allowed to make one phone call to speak to your father. Do you understand?"

"Yes."

All the fight had been taken from the Trader. He looked at Greg.

"Thank you."

"It's your father that needs your thanks Matthew. He went out on a limb for you with the Chairman, so don't mess this up and you'll get your life back," said Greg.

Greg made the call as he walked back into the alley and picked up Cummins' knife and found the nearest drain cover to drop it down.

"It's done Sir Henry. One young messed up trader on his way to rehab."

"Thank you Greg. I know this was a messy one, so one favour deserves another. Let me know anytime you need to call it in," said the Chairman.

*****

As he continued walking towards the underground station Greg rang Chris MacDonald.

"Chris, what's up?"

"Hello mate. Listen, there's no easy way to say this, but Mum's dead. She's been murdered."

Greg took just a moment to let it sink in.

"Where are you Chris? Is everyone there, your dad especially?"

"We're at the villa and yes we're all here. Greg, she was beaten to death." Chris's voice faltered.

Greg looked at his watch. It was now 5.30pm.

"Chris, I'm so sorry. I'll be with you as soon as I can and Chris, we will get whoever has done this to your mum."

He messaged Tommy to meet him at his apartment after dropping the young Trader off at the rehab clinic and to be ready to take him to LHR or Gatwick, depending on where he could get the first flight to Palma de Mallorca from.

He then had a thought and dialled a number.

"Greg, I wasn't expecting you to call in your favour quite so quickly," said Sir Henry.

"Neither did I Sir Henry," said Greg.

"What do you mean?" he said. "It is actually a favour you need? I was only joking just then."

"I wish I was too. I need to get to a client in Mallorca and quickly. His wife has been murdered. Strictly speaking, I'm breaking client confidentiality here, but I'm sure he won't mind in the circumstances, but it's John MacDonald's wife I'm talking about."

"What? You mean John from Trent MacDonald?"

"Yes, I don't know any more details at the moment, but it's important I get out there quickly."

"Good God! Greg, I'll call the team now and they'll get things ready and you will get a text confirming the airport and time."

"Thank you Sir Henry."

"Now give my sincere condolences to John and his boys and listen, you call me direct if you need anything Greg and I mean anything."

"I appreciate that and I will," said Greg.

Five minutes later he got the text telling him where

to go and two hours later he was in the air in a Gulfstream G550, Sir Henry's company jet, with the co-pilot asking him if he wanted anything to drink. He sat back in his seat and thought about Sheila MacDonald.

He knew she was from the East End of London and had had a tough upbringing as a young girl, but she had met and then married John, a local boy who was just setting up a small engineering company under the railway arches near Southwark.

She had supported John through thick and thin as he first built up a national company and then a multinational conglomerate when he merged with Trent Holdings to create Trent MacDonald. She held a special place in Greg's heart as he knew that it was Sheila who had encouraged John to take a chance on Greg's new company, 3R (Risk Reduction and Resolution), when MacDonald Engineering was still in its early stages and they were having problems with protection rackets at some of their sites.

THREE

I t seemed a long time since he was growing up in Slough, but Greg Chambers had done two things well. One was studying at school and the second was learning to fight and fight dirty when needed.

He got a scholarship to Cambridge to study languages and philosophy, something that he knew made his parents immensely proud, but he found the huge wealth divide of the students both frustrating and challenging. He could handle the occasional barbed comments from some of the stuck up privileged kids, either with an equally sharp retort, or a stinging right hook if necessary. However, it also helped him understand how to build relationships based on trust and friendship, rather than rank and money.

At Cambridge he enjoyed the physical contact sports, playing rugby and learning to box. Not that he wasn't able to handle himself, as he had had to learn to look after himself growing up on the Britwell estate in Slough, so he already had a pretty handy set of street fighting skills, not all of which fell within boxing's Queensbury Rules.

He enjoyed the university environment, winning his sports blues for both rugby and boxing and it was his friends back home, rather than his parents, who first noticed his accent was changing. He hadn't planned this or even realised this was happening, but he accepted it, realising that it might benefit a Slough boy wanting a career in the City.

That all changed when he was in his third year at Cambridge. He had been doing the rounds at the career recruitment meetings and had been given some good signs by some of the big players in the City. It happened after he had been doing some laps around the running track and was just starting his warm down when he saw a woman watching him. She was a few years older than him, maybe around twenty seven or twenty eight, dressed casually in check trousers and a smart figure-hugging cream polo neck top, with flaming red hair down to her shoulders. A twenty one year old being looked at by an attractive woman was usually sufficient to get any guy's interest and Greg was certainly no different. He couldn't stop himself having a second look, just to check he wasn't mistaken and *'No, she's still looking at me!'*

The woman smiled. *'God, she knows I've looked again,'* he thought. He felt himself going red and just hoped that the sweat he had worked up from his run was covering his embarrassment. He wasn't short on experience with girls, but they were girls, not strikingly attractive older women.

She started to walk towards to him, still smiling and he instinctively flinched when she said,

"It's Greg, isn't it?" in a wonderfully flowing Irish lilt.

"Er, yes. How do you know my name?"

"Oh, I was looking at the rugby team sheets and someone mentioned you were out here running, so I thought I'd say hello."

She smiled again and he relaxed and so it began.

*****

This was no chance meeting. It took a little while until he realised what was happening and that Fiona, the name she gave him, wasn't actually chatting him up. She took her time, slowly but surely getting his trust. She took him for drinks in some smart bars and then a nice meal. They talked about everything and nothing. She asked him what he wanted to do with his life, what he thought about free speech and what he would do for his country if we, god forbid, had another war.

He loved talking to her. He loved being with her. He loved her accent. But he was also puzzled and found himself getting frustrated why he saw no encouragement from her to take things any further, to something more physical. Then he found out why. She had taken him for a walk along a quiet pathway, by the river when she made the proposal.

She was a recruiting officer for MI6 and he had been spotted at one of the events with the big city traders – she later explained the intelligence services had people within these companies who they asked to keep an eye out for people with potential. Greg had been spotted by someone used by MI6.

He didn't say yes straight away. Something which he was later told went in his favour. But then having made up his mind he went through the selection process. He had no idea how he was doing and was given no sense of his progress either. Other people in the process fell by the wayside and eventually he was told he had passed. He knew that working for military intelligence wasn't like being James Bond with fast cars and beautiful women on his arms, although secretly he hoped there might be some of that at some stage!

He started as a desk officer. Sitting at a desk for eight hours a day researching information that came in from across the world. Information was assessed and graded on its level of credibility by reviewing any supporting corroboration or the past history of the source, the person who was giving the information. Information that was assessed as actionable was classed as intelligence – meaning something further needed to be done and a desk officer's job also included providing some options for his team supervisor to then consider and take further.

He enjoyed the work, understanding that intelligence to a field officer, those people who were the ones actioning the intelligence, often alone, was vital for their safety and the security of the operation. He knew he had been earmarked as a future field officer and so was content to bide his time and learn his craft, knowing that a field officer often got in trouble as a result of a poor intelligence assessment. If something was missed, this could leave a field officer exposed to risk, a risk that could mean expulsion from the country they were operating in, or potentially something far worse, including losing their life.

After a couple of years, he was posted to Berlin with a role initially looking into potential terrorist factions. A relatively low risk assignment, he combined desk work with some basic field work. He shone in this role and was given greater responsibility in the field and over the following three years, his responsibility grew to the stage where he was both planning and leading field operations. The Berlin Station Chief, John Woodward, a very experienced field officer in his own right, recognised Greg's skills and attributes for field work and put him forward for undercover training. So three years after arriving in Berlin, Greg found himself posted back to London, reporting for specialist U/C training.

The programme started with a class of ten field officers. Greg knew three of them. Not well, but at least by sight and to occasionally chat to. They had met during their initial basic training and would occasionally see each other at the MI6 offices at Vauxhall Cross on the Embankment. The first part of the programme was a mix of classroom and field exercise work and then each Undercover Training Programme trainee was assigned to an experienced U/C training officer for a further two weeks intensive one to one training, with the final assessment on suitability being directly down to the U/C training officer.

*****

Greg performed with distinction during the first six weeks of basic U/C training. Sitting with the Programme Director known to him only as Patrick, he was feeling confident about the next stage of the training.

"Greg, you've done bloody well so far."

Greg noticed a pause.

"I sense there's a 'but' coming sir?"

"More a note of caution. We teach and practise for the real thing. For the time when you are out there alone and it all goes belly-up."

Patrick paused and then said, "But it can never, I repeat, never get near to that sense of isolation when you are deep into your cover and you need to react to whatever goes on."

Greg saw the look on Patrick's face. This wasn't just any sort of bollocking, but a genuine *'listen to this and listen carefully'* message.

"I see you as someone a little like myself. I'm not old school, I'm a council school kid like you."

Greg heard the polished English private school accent and Patrick saw him taking in this information and he smiled.

"Yes, funny how we seem to lose it when we're at a posh university like Cambridge. But I can tell you there have been times when it's been quite handy to revert to my home accent."

As Patrick carried on talking, he now quietly spoke

with an East End accent.

"Because sometimes you can use it to get your message across quite well."

Greg felt the hairs on the back of his neck stand up as he heard the menace in Patrick's voice.

"Anyway, where was I Greg?" as Patrick settled back into his polished British accent.

"Well, other than scaring the shit out of me Patrick, I think you were about to tell me who my training officer will be."

"Yes, quite right. I'll let her introduce herself, but you are right at the top of the class, if not at the top Greg. So, I've given you the best U/C trainer to work with, but be aware, she takes no prisoners and you will need to work bloody hard to reach the standard she demands."

Greg started to say something when Patrick stopped him.

"Lesson One. Don't interrupt. Listen, listen and then listen again. The reason she's so bloody good at this is because she is alive. So everything she says is for one reason and one reason only – to keep you alive. Understood?"

"Yes sir," and he said it as he genuinely meant it.

He knew working as a U/C officer carried with it a high risk tariff and that mistakes could cost not just his life, but those of others. But the best U/C trainer? Wow! He had come a long way since scrapping behind the garages on the Britwell.

*****

He had been given a location and time to meet his trainer. It was The Blackfriar in Queen Victoria Street, just north of the Thames. A nice old pub close to the river. He'd been there before a few times and liked the marble in the main bar area. As he walked in, fifteen minutes early, he looked around and took note of the two men at the bar standing chatting and a group of three young women who looked like they were meeting after work. He ordered a pint of Doombar at the bar and then as the barman poured his drink, he excused himself saying he was just going to the toilet. This gave him the opportunity to look around the rest of the pub. Satisfied that he had a good look, he came back as if from the toilets and as he did, he saw a woman sitting on a stool at the bar by his drink.

"Hello Greg."

It took him a moment to register. It was a different accent and her hair was different too, both the colour and the style.

"Fiona?"

"The very same."

She smiled. It was the same smile as before.

She gave him some time to settle as she went on, "So you've done well, very well, to get here and I've heard good things about you from John in Berlin too."

"Thank you," he paused. "So, an Irish redhead becomes an English blonde with a genteel accent?"

"Greg, Lesson Two, I heard about your Lesson One, now Lesson Two is never go on appearances or accents. Look at the eyes and the hands. They are much harder to conceal even with coloured contact lenses. You can still learn a lot from someone's eyes."

Greg nodded and then said, "Right, before we start Lesson Three, would you like a drink?"

Two weeks of intense and at times exhausting training followed. She was a hard taskmaster as Patrick said she would be. She pushed him until he was near breaking point and then pulled him back to look at what he was learning about himself. She could be tough and ruthless and then the next moment, she looked at him in a way that made him feel like she loved him. But as the training went on, he began to see small acknowledgements from her of his work. He knew she was now rebuilding his self-confidence as he needed to believe he was not just good at this stuff, but that he was bloody good!

He kept Patrick's Lesson One close to his thinking all the time, *'Listen, listen and then listen again'* as he took on board all that Fiona was teaching him. He wanted to ask her about her experiences but she would always say, "Not now, later, when we're done."

During one of the sessions on developing a solid background cover, she quizzed him about his previous relationships and asked if he had anyone special in his life at the moment. He told about the girls who had been in his life so far and that any sort of relationship pretty much stopped when he left Cambridge. He knew she was asking a loaded question when it came to any current relationship, as it was company policy to report any relationship for vetting.

"No, I haven't had any sort of relationship since then. There never seems to be time and there's the hassle of the vetting and how do you tell someone *'I work for MI6'*?"

"But presumably you've had sex since then?"

He had expected the question, but still felt himself shift uncomfortably when asked. He went to answer.

"Stop," she said. "What the hell happened then? You get a little bit embarrassed and you start showing off all sorts of body language. Get a bloody grip Greg! This is not a joke. Everything I'm doing is for a reason and you need to be always on your guard."

"But I thought you were just asking...," he started to say.

"You should know by now Greg, I never just ask anything."

He could see she was furious with him and he understood why. It worried him that he could so easily make such a fundamental slip. *'I thought I had this. Stop being so bloody cocksure of yourself and sort yourself out.'*

He looked back at her and she had relaxed.

"Okay, I think you've got the point. So let me tell you one of the best lessons Patrick gave me, *'If you want to fall in love, then it's time to get out of U/C work.'* So for you Greg, it's no strings, no ties and no commitment and if you find yourself falling into something that you want to be a longer term thing, then get out of U/C quickly and find yourself a nice field officer job somewhere, as you just cannot afford to have what is a massive vulnerability sitting in the back of your head. Got it?"

He nodded. She was making it very clear that he could not afford the luxury of falling in love if he was to be an effective and more importantly, a safe and alive undercover officer.

"Got it," he said. "No strings, no ties, no commitments."

*****

As they approached the final exercise and after another occasion when her smile and eyes lingered just a fraction longer than perhaps necessary, he dared to think that there was perhaps something there, as he had felt between them when he first met her in Cambridge. But then shook his head, *'She's good. Really good at this. So shut up Chambers and get on with your job.'*

*****

Patrick addressed the trainees who remained after the eight week programme. There were five of them. Two of the three people he had previously known were still there, with him and two others, so three men and two women.

"Ladies and gentlemen. It may not have escaped your now advanced investigative and observational skills that there are now only five of you left."

There was a smattering of half laughs and grins from the group.

"I did say that we would announce whether you had passed the programme at the end, however, like much within the U/C world that was only a half truth. So, here's my final lesson to you. Not everything is all that it seems."

He then paused and looked at each of them in turn with a smile slowly appearing on his face.

"If you are to live and operate safely within this world of deceit and deception, then remember that if you can do it around a half lie, then it will ring true so much the better."

The five trainees looked around at each other and then to Patrick, whose smile for once actually portrayed his true feelings.

"Yes, you have passed. So well done and I wish you all well."

With that he walked out leaving five envelopes on the desk.

After the five finished congratulating each other, Greg picked up the envelopes.

"What do you think? Pay cheques or new postings?"

He passed them out to the others and then opened his letter. It was from Fiona.

Dear Greg,

Many congratulations on passing the programme.

Meet me again where we first met.

7pm tonight.

Fiona

PS Get the train

Not much was said after that. Each of the newly qualified U/C officers said little, knowing they may not see each other again, but that if they did, it may be in challenging and dangerous circumstances.

Greg looked at his watch. He didn't have much time

to get to Cambridge. He assumed she was going to brief him on his next assignment, but why go back there? He had been hoping to get away for a week to rest and recuperate as there had been a rumour that they would all get a week off before being posted.

He packed an overnight bag with the usual preparations of rapid deployment – passport, money in assorted currencies, one change of clothes and toothbrush and toothpaste – he smiled as he thought back to another of Patrick's Lessons, *'Never forget dental hygiene'*.

He was cutting things fine by the time he got to King's Cross and had to run down the platform to get the 17.39 train just as it was about to leave. Less than an hour later he was getting in a cab at Cambridge station to get to the running track at Wilberforce Road. He got there ten minutes early to find Fiona sitting in a magenta red open top sports car.

"Hello, fancy meeting you here," he said.

"Get in," she said sternly.

He dropped his bag into the back seat and got in.

He hadn't closed the door before she leaned across and grabbed him and kissed him. He kissed her back. Hard at first and then slowly, allowing the passion to settle between them for a moment. Then she broke away.

"Right, that's got that out of the way, let's go and get some dinner."

She drove fast and sure. It was a classic car, A Triumph TR6. His dad had always loved this car but had never had the money to get anything like this. This was a properly restored and gleaming example. It was a beautiful summer's evening and he thought things couldn't get any better until they just did when he got into the car. God, she looked gorgeous in a summer dress and wraparound sunglasses. He had no idea why this was happening but after three weeks intense training with her, he knew better than to ask. *'Listen, listen and listen again.'*

*****

It didn't take long to get to the small country hotel.

"Come on, dinner's booked for eight and I want a drink and a bath first, in that order."

They checked in under his name and the thought struck him, he still didn't know her surname. They made their way up to the first floor to a beautiful room with a bottle of champagne sitting on the side table with two flutes. Fiona walked straight into the bathroom and started to run the bath before coming back out and taking him in her arms. This time he kissed her, slowly as they held each other tenderly, feeling their bodies touch and enjoying the moment of gentle intimacy.

"Why now?" he whispered.

"Let's not worry about that now," as she eased herself away from him. "Pour me some bubbles and I'm going for my bath."

He clearly wasn't going to get any explanation until she was ready. So he did as he was told, opening the champagne and then taking a glass of champagne into the bathroom where she was already submerged into a Victorian style bath tub.

"You seem to have got this all planned then."

"Well I would have thought you would have learned by now that planning is a key part of any operation," she smiled.

"So I'm just an operation then?" He feigned a look of disappointment.

"Okay, don't go all sad on me. Yes, I really like you," she said. "But here's the thing, I've been telling you for the last two weeks, *'no strings, no ties, no commitments,'* so I'm being serious that we need to just enjoy this moment and then walk away. And before you ask, no, I don't do this with every trainee, in fact I have never done this before. Call it a failure of my professionalism or just my lust and passion getting the better of me. Whatever, it is, I know there's something there between us."

"Now pass me the towel."

Greg stood there for a moment, still taking in what she had said, when he heard her say again, "Towel please, I'm getting cold standing here."

He fumbled around for her towel as he was distracted looking at her, standing naked in the bath. He held it out and wrapped her in it, kissed her and carefully lifted her out of the bath.

"Thank you kindly sir," she said.

He then showered and changed and they went down for dinner.

They talked easily and the hours drifted by as they just enjoyed each other's company. He felt so relaxed and she looked the same. She was radiant. Her blonde hair, not red as she had been when he first met her, falling softly onto her shoulders. They enjoyed a nightcap and then went upstairs to their room. The door had barely closed when they kissed and fell onto the bed, laughing and undressing.

Fiona suddenly stopped.

"Greg, I need you to understand that in our world, it's got to be 'no strings, no ties, no commitments'. I have booked this room for a week, but after that we go our separate ways. I don't mind if you want to go earlier if you'd rather, but this is it. Are you okay with that?"

He stroked her hair. He knew what she was saying and why she was saying it. They couldn't afford to get involved for both their sakes. So a week it would be.

"I know. So we need to make the most of this week."

"I'm glad you said a week," she smiled.

"No more talking," said Greg.

*****

They walked, talked, went for some wonderful drives and later, back in their room they made gentle and then passionate love. He so enjoyed her company and he knew she liked him, really liked him. It was an idyllic time for them. The people in the hotel thought they must be newly-weds, but as the end of the week drew ever closer, they both felt their moods and spirits changing, knowing things were coming to an end, whilst trying to live just for the few last moments together until finally, the last day came.

"So how do we say the goodbye? I'm not sure I'll be all that good just giving you a hug and walking away."

At that moment his pager buzzed.

"Timing. How did they know?"

He looked at Fiona.

"You called the office didn't you?"

She nodded.

"Yep, time to go to work Greg."

They kept the mood as upbeat as they could as she drove him back to Cambridge Station.

"Do you know where I'm going?"

"Yes," she said.

"What about you?"

"I have got some easy job apparently, but that's as much as I'm going to tell you. No more words Greg, let's go our different ways, but keep this week as something special. Stay safe for me."

He saw tears in her eyes. It had been glorious and in another life, then what might have happened? He could imagine them settling down, two children, mortgage or maybe mortgage and two children. But just as suddenly, his thoughts stopped. That wasn't his life. She had trained him to go and do a job and to be as safe as he could be.

"Fiona, this was so special and I promise you......"

"Shush," she said. "No promises."

She pulled up outside the station and leant across and kissed him for a final time.

"You take care."

"I will and you too," said Greg.

He got out as though he was just catching the commuter train to London and would be home later that day, except that he wouldn't. He closed the door and she drove off without looking back.

FOUR

Fifteen years later he left the Service. He knew his time in the field was coming to a close because there weren't too many places he could now go where someone didn't know him.

Not much good if you are supposed to be an undercover officer and he knew he didn't want a desk job in some back office somewhere in the world.

When he retired he decided to utilise the skills he had developed throughout his career. He set up 3R (Risk Reduction & Resolution), a private security company and for the past twenty years he had been particularly successful working with insurance and corporate companies on high value projects across the world.

3R were now considered security industry leaders when operating around sensitive issues where they could provide solutions to negate a threat or to prevent and mitigate loss. Their work often involved recovering high value stolen items without necessarily going through any judicial process. However, they also had expert operatives to gather covert intelligence and deliver identification packages of targeted criminals to law enforcement agencies.

He smiled at his last thoughts. This was his '3R presentation speak' to clients. He had built a strong reputation around performance and confidentiality and when called upon he also had the option to use what he called 'Dynamic Intervention Action'. DIA was a way of describing the area of 3R's work that involved the proactive use of force and whilst not necessarily always entirely lawful, Greg's direction to all of his team was that any use of force was always necessary and proportionate to the threat.

As business increased, he had used his contacts with other retired intelligence and Special Forces colleagues to build a significant network across the world. He had never married, but he did have a daughter Terri, from a summer long relationship with Josie, an Aussie girl he had met in London when he had been office based for six months in 1989, as part of an R&R posting, after a bit of trouble in the Ukraine. He had steadfastly held to the mantra of *'No strings, no ties, no commitments'*, until he found out that Josie was pregnant. She had gone back to Sydney before discovering she was pregnant, but thought he should know about the baby. She told him that it was up to him if he wanted to be in his daughter's life, but with the distances involved she'd understand if he just walked away. Typical Aussie pragmatism.

He did want to be part of young Theresa's life, but realised that sending money just wasn't enough. He found ways of getting to see her in Sydney as she grew up and Josie was great about him being part of Terri's life, even when Josie married a local guy, ten years later. He had to admit that the guy did a really good job as the live-in step-dad, whilst never treading on Greg's shoes. But even being a part-time dad meant he now had a weak spot. A commitment which left him and now Josie and Terri potentially vulnerable and that it no doubt meant his days undercover were numbered. He kept going for another five years or so, before he made the decision to step away from a job he loved.

He smiled as he thought about Terri. She was so like her mum. Outward going, fun to be with and tall and blonde. She was thirty now and had joined the army when she was eighteen as an officer cadet at university. He had hoped she would join the British Army if she joined any army, but she said she was an Aussie and so it had to be the Aussie Army.

In 2013 she had been one of the first to volunteer when women were eventually allowed to be part of a combat unit. She had seen action in Iraq, first during Operation Slipper, as part of the Australian contribution to the International Security Assistance Force and before all Australian combat forces were withdrawn at the end of 2013. Operation Slipper was superseded by Operation Highroad, by which time Terri had made Captain and was again part of the Australian 'train, advise and assist' mission.

By 2016, she had to decide to either stay and stay for good, or get out and look for another challenge and when he knew what she was thinking of doing, he had had no hesitation in asking her to join him and run the operational teams at 3R. This was no token nepotism either, because Greg knew his daughter would never accept that in any shape or form, but it was because he knew she was damn good at what she could do and he needed that skill set in 3R.

That had been four years ago and Terri was in Egypt at the moment, working with a major client on reducing high value losses from their depots near the Canal. It would be late there with the time difference, but he needed to brief her on what had happened. She answered almost immediately, her Australian accent coming through loud and clear.

"What's up Dad?"

He quickly filled her in on what had happened to Sheila MacDonald.

"Jesus Dad! Poor John. What do you need me to do?"

"How much longer do you need out there?" he said.

"I can hand this over to Asim, the local guy here, first thing tomorrow. He's really solid and I trust him," said Terri.

"That's great. Then get yourself to Palma and I'll see you there."

He sat back for the rest of the flight taking some time to rest, knowing he might not get much chance to do the same over the coming few days.

*****

Sam walked into Contrabando, a tapas restaurant in Llucmajor. He had come out to see Miquel who he hadn't seen since he got back from London and he had been regretting not ringing his friend earlier.

"So amigo, why has it taken you so long to come and see me?"

"I know Miquel. I'm a crap friend, but hey, I'm here now," said Sam.

They spoke in Mallorquin. Miquel had been his best friend for as long as he could remember. They had gone to junior and then secondary school together, played sport and started going to bars and meeting girls together. Yes, Sam understood why Miquel would be more than a little annoyed at him not getting in touch.

Miquel put two glasses of red wine on the bar.

"No matter. Salud amigo. Now tell me all about London. Has Kirsty finally got fed up with you and thrown you out?"

Miquel saw the look on Sam's face.

"Oh God, what have I said Sam?"

"Don't worry amigo. I'm over it. It was a while ago, so Christ, I should be over it by now. It's a long story and I should have told you before, but anyway I'm back for a few weeks and helping Mum in the shop."

"Well it's good to see you. What do you think of the

wine? It is one of my new specials, good eh? And if you are here for a few weeks, I must get you to meet up with my cousin, Carmen. She's back from the States where she's been working and doing a Masters or is it her Doctorate? Far too clever for a London cop, but she likes you. You remember her from school don't you?"

"Miquel," groaned Sam. "Please, no blind dates. I remember Carmen, but wasn't she younger than us? She's no doubt a lovely girl, but I don't know if she's my type."

He did remember her. A little girl following them around because Miquel had been told to look after her by his Aunt and make sure she didn't get into any trouble. She must have been about five years younger and so at that age, she mostly got in their way, but she could be bribed with an ensaïmada pastry to sit still for a least a few minutes whilst they played football.

"Okay, so tell me about London," said Miquel.

Sam went quiet and Miquel looked at him.

"What is it my friend?" he said quietly.

"They think I've got PTSD, you know, after the shooting I was involved in a couple of years ago, when my partner got shot."

Miquel just listened. He knew about the incident from Anna, Sam's mother, but he'd never heard Sam talk about it and he hadn't asked him either. He didn't know a whole lot about Post Traumatic Stress Disorder, but knew enough to realise how and why this was affecting his friend. Sam had been like a brother to him for thirty years and whilst he found it painful seeing his friend hurting inside, he knew he had needed to wait for Sam to be ready to talk about it.

People were still coming in and out of the restaurant, but Sam was oblivious to them. He just poured his heart out to his best friend. About the guilt, not being able to sleep, the mood swings, the aggression when he lost control and how he couldn't open up to Kirsty. He didn't need his friend to say anything. He didn't want or need any platitudes and or any kind words to pacify him. Just letting him say the words out aloud, the words that he needed to say to himself, was enough.

Sam was at last talking about how he felt. He had been close before, when he was talking to the counsellor the force had provided for him, but he'd never been able to fully let go and certainly not to Kirsty who then felt hurt herself that he couldn't. He didn't know how or why he had suddenly come out with it to Miquel, but guessed it was what the counsellor had been telling him. He had needed to mend first. To mend mentally before he could let it out. He felt guilty that he had allowed himself to be distracted by the little girl coming into his eye line and for his partner, Jimmy, then being shot.

The post incident management debrief, had called it an 'operational incident' with no blame attached. The only person blaming anyone was Sam, who was blaming himself. Miquel was hearing and seeing his friend opening up before him and he seemed to be starting to acknowledge what had happened and to begin to replace blame with acceptance. The hurt wouldn't go away, that he hadn't been able to protect his friend Jimmy, at least not straight away, but maybe the pain of living with it every day would now start to subside. As Sam stopped talking, Miquel just stood up and hugged his best friend. The restaurant went silent. The people at the tables hadn't known what was going on, but they all realised something had happened and they gave the two men just a moment in silence.

Sam let go of his friend and mouthed the words 'Gracias amigo' and the diners returned to conversations and their tapas, content that whatever it was, they had just been witness to something good. Miquel smiled back. It might take some more time, but with some more help, he saw his friend was going to get through this.

*****

At 11pm the Gulfstream touched down at Palma de Mallorca and coasted to the VIP reception area and as Greg walked through the Arrivals gate, he saw Chris MacDonald waiting for him.

They sat in the back of a Lexus RX Hybrid and at Greg's request the driver took them at speed to the Mac-Donald villa.

"Greg, I don't know what the hell has happened, but she was beaten to death. Thank God Dad didn't see her before they'd had time to at least clean her face. She was an old woman. Why would anyone need to do that?"

He couldn't stop talking and Greg just let him get it all out. He could see there were tears in Chris's eyes. He was having to look after his dad and care for him and he hadn't had time to take in the immensity of what had happened himself. Twenty minutes later and they were stopped at the main gate to the villa. There was a police car there. Greg didn't expect to be allowed into the crime scene, but it was more just to get a sense of the place, as well as to get the officer on the gate to make arrangements for him to see the officer in charge in the morning.

The officer took his details and they then set off for Cap Rocat, the hotel where Chris's dad was currently staying and Chris had already booked him a room. They got through the hotel security set up, useful having that here thought Greg. He didn't want John or the family being bothered by the Press at the moment. A few minutes later he saw John waiting for him in the bar, together with his younger son, Jack. Nodding a hello to Jack, Greg walked straight over to John and held him in his arms.

"John, I'm so sorry," he said quietly. "I'll make sure we find who has done this."

"Thank you my friend," said John, "I've lost my beautiful girl and cannot start to begin to imagine the terror she went through Greg. I want you to find the person who did this."

"I promise I will."

Greg started to say something else, when John stopped him.

"Greg, I want these people to suffer and pay for this and I don't care what it takes to do this. Am I clear?"

"Yes John, I understand."

He then spent time with John and his two boys letting them tell him what they had found out so far. It seemed on the face of it a random burglary. Not necessarily unexpected at what was a high value property. John had the villa built some twenty five years ago and Greg felt it must now be worth somewhere in the region of £10 million. The police had identified the places of entry, one front and one back and it looked like there had been four people involved. The CCTV wires had been cut and given that the wall safe had been opened using the keycode, it was reasonable to assume they had forced Sheila to give them the code.

'So why kill her?' was the question Greg was thinking. Yes, if she saw their faces, that would be a good enough reason, but it was more likely that they wore masks, especially before they could get to disable the CCTV.

*****

The following morning, Greg awoke to find a text from Terri saying she would be landing at around midday and she had arranged for one of their local contacts to pick her up and take her to her apartment. When she joined 3R she decided she needed somewhere of her own to crash between jobs. He smiled. There wasn't enough sun for her in London, so she had found a place in Palma. It was in Portixol, right by the seafront and right now it was a perfect base for them to be able to get to John's villa in around ten minutes and close enough to the city to keep checking in with the police.

His phone rang. It was a message telling him the investigating officer, DI Garcia, could see him in Palma at 10.00.

*****

Sam parked up in one of the side streets at the bookshop. He was using his mum's old Seat, so it wasn't likely to catch the eye of any local toe-rags looking for an easy hit. The sun was shining and he looked up at the blue, cloudless sky. Yes, there really was something about living here. He knew his mum was worried about what would happen to the bookshop and the business, but he hadn't made his mind up either way at the moment and he realised it was something that he needed to give some serious thought. Given his policing background, he was usually very spatially aware of his surroundings, but he had been distracted with his thoughts and didn't see the two young African guys come out from the side alley before he was almost on them.

"Señor, are you lost? You are a long way off the tourist routes," the taller of the two said to him.

Sam cursed himself for not seeing them before. It was pretty clear that these guys were looking to turn him over and see how much money they could get from him. To them, he looked like a 'lost' tourist and presumably they wouldn't be too worried at the level of violence they might need to use.

"No, I'm not lost, but thank you for your concern," said Sam.

"For a fee we can help you get to where you want Señor?" said the smaller one helpfully.

"Guys, I think you are mistaken. I don't need your help. So best you turn around and go about your business."

Sam wasn't hopeful that this tactic would work and he was right, it didn't. The taller guy pulled a knife from behind his back.

"We've warned you mister. The fee just went up. Just give us everything you've got and you can get out of this without getting hurt," said the taller one.

Sam could see that there were some people up ahead on the main street, but even after glancing into the alley and seeing that something seemed to be happening, they scurried along not wanting to get involved. *'These guys must be doing this all the time,'* thought Sam and that wasn't good for the tourist trade.

"Okay, I don't want any trouble," said Sam.

That said, he also wasn't inclined to use the saying, *'Is there anything I can reasonably say or do'*, a well-used mantra in UK policing before officers would take pre-emptive action. After all, this was their call. They were the ones looking to pick on and rob an unsuspecting and defenceless tourist. Except he wasn't either a tourist or defenceless.

Yes, he was primarily now in a desk job as a DCI, but he'd been in firearms and tactical teams for long enough during his career to be able to handle himself.

The taller one was standing to Sam's left and was the nearer one to him. He was the one holding the knife, so was presenting the bigger threat. He had the knife in his right hand as Sam started to walk towards him, making as if to go for his wallet from his inside right pocket with his left hand. He saw them both relax, but he was particularly interested in watching the one with the knife. He saw the tip of the knife dip down as the guy relaxed his right arm. The momentum of Sam walking forwards gave him the impetus to swing his left arm out and down hard onto the man's right forearm taking him off balance. The move had left Sam into a crouching position and he followed the forearm strike with a vicious right belly punch that dropped the tall man like a stone, sending the knife clattering to the floor. The smaller guy had been waiting for the tourist, who seemed to have given in, to just hand over his money and his brain struggled to react quickly enough to help his friend.

"Now I don't mind what you do now. You can pick him up and walk him away or try your luck. But don't take too long to make up your mind," said Sam.

Sam recognised the dilemma the guy was having over honour and living to fight another day. His friend had been hurt and he hadn't done anything about it. He saw the smaller guy start to go to his friend, but then he made a slight adjustment to his body, hoping Sam wouldn't see and as he did this, he missed the fact that Sam had opened his shoulders, giving him more room in his fighting arc. As the smaller guy took a step forward, Sam's rolling right hook caught him square on the temple and sent him flying to the floor. He tried to get up but Sam was quickly on him and picked up his right arm in a gooseneck, a police approved hold, and applied pressure onto the hand to gain compliance.

"Now stand still and this won't hurt. Do you understand?" said Sam, who was keeping a watch on the taller guy who was still retching on the ground after his belly punch.

"Get off me," screamed the smaller one.

Sam looked towards the main street again and this time was surprised there were some people standing there watching. They weren't making any attempt to intervene or stop what was happening, but he could see some of them were even smiling.

"Does this happen a lot?" he shouted out, first in

English and then in Spanish.

An older man, about fifty who was carrying a small brief case and looked like he might be on his way to work, shifted forwards.

"Si Señor, these two are always trying to catch out tourists and even some of us locals."

"Muchas gracias Señor," said Sam.

He looked at the guy whose hand he still had hold of. Sam thought the guy was being compliant, but he was still keeping an eye on the taller one, as the knife was not secure. It was still lying on the ground.

Sam spoke to the smaller guy, "Probably best that you don't do this for a while amigo."

He was about to release him, when the guy twisted sharply and tried to lash out at him. He felt the tension rising in himself. *'Why? He'd given him a bloody chance and what?'* The man saw a change in Sam's face, as it tightened and he saw Sam staring coldly at him. The man flinched. The body reacting to the imminent threat of pain. Sam still had the 'gooseneck' on the man's wrist and he dipped his own wrist down and heard the man scream as his wrist snapped. Sam dropped him to the floor as he saw the taller one trying to reach the knife on the floor. He bent down, as if to help pick the taller guy up off the floor, but as he did so, he grabbed the man's right arm at the elbow and twisted it sharply away from his body. An unnatural movement of the body that could only do one thing, break the elbow. The taller man screamed, even more than the first and ran, not waiting for his friend.

Sam stood for a moment. He'd lost control. Again. It was like someone else could just take over his body and start lashing out. He then heard a soft voice. The man who had spoken before was still standing at the end of the alley, calling him.

"Señor?"

Sam walked towards him.

"Señor Martínez isn't it? Are you okay?" said the man.

"Si, Señor," said Sam, "do I know you?"

"I am Señor Alfonso Cabrera. I work for your father and mother, or sadly should I say, I now work for your mother. I manage her business."

"Of course Señor, I'm sorry I didn't recognise you, you were at my father's funeral. Thank you for your help today and by the way it's Sam."

"Sam, are you okay?"

"Yes, I'm fine thanks," said Sam.

He wasn't sure if Señor Cabrera had seen that he had seemed to lose control or not. He no doubt knew that Sam was a cop back in London and that it probably wasn't usual practice to go breaking people's wrists or arms, except maybe in self-defence, whereas this had been more like direct retribution.

"It's me who should be thanking you Sam. We have been having more and more problems from some of these gangs. We have an African community in the city, most of whom are just ordinary people trying to make a living and get by, but there are some who give them a very bad name. They can be very violent and intimidating," said Alfonso.

"Well, hopefully these two won't be doing anything for a while. Alfonso, if you could not mention this to my mother, I'd appreciate it. She worries about me and I wouldn't want to give her anything to add to her worries."

"Understood Sam," said Alfonso as they started walking. "Forgive me if this is not my place, but I know your mother would like you to take over the business at some stage, so if you would like me to show you the books I would be happy to do so."

"Maybe sometime Alfonso. I know she does and I

don't want to let her down, but I have a career back in London, so maybe not just yet," said Sam, who wondered how much time it took Alfonso to help in managing Sa Petita Llibreria and a couple of properties he knew his parents owned.

They carried on walking in silence towards the bookshop. It bothered Sam that he had lost control. This was what had brought him back home to Mallorca, this losing control thing. He'd been so close to hitting his boss back in London and over what? Nothing. Well nothing of importance anyway, a slight disagreement, but he'd lost it and had his boss up against the wall and he'd had to be restrained by his own men.

They had all understood, but that didn't make it any easier for them to deal with him. He had become moody and withdrawn since Jimmy was shot. He had felt it happening. He had tried the counselling they had offered as he knew his behaviour was having a big impact on Kirsty. She had tried her best, but he just kept pushing her away until she couldn't take it anymore. He was lucky Mike, his boss, was someone he had joined with and their careers had crossed over the years, especially as they had both specialised in firearms. So yes, he was lucky. Mike at least had an understanding of what he was going through and he was instrumental in seeing that the incident went down the road of Sam needing an extended period of sick leave, rather than any sort of disciplinary action.

"Time for us to part our ways, but I hope to see you again soon Sam, maybe when I take you through the books?" Alfonso smiled as he left Sam standing at the front of the bookshop.

"Was that Alfonso?" said Anna opening the door for him, "I didn't know you knew him?"

"We met by chance. I recognised him from Dad's funeral and we were just chatting."

"About the business?" said Anna.

Sam smiled. She wasn't going to give up on this.

"Well yes, he was offering to show me the books and talk me through the business."

Anna smiled. Alfonso had worked with them for many years and before that his father worked with Luis's father. A good man who had been so kind in making sure the business kept running when Luis had died and she had been dealing with all of the funeral arrangements. But now wasn't the time to press Sam on the business.

Anna said, "Have you heard anything from the police about Bill?"

"Not yet. I'll ring DI Garcia now and I'll see what I can find out."

Anna said, "I also heard this morning that the police are at the MacDonald's place. A police car has been there all night and there's a lot of activity going on. I've tried ringing John but he's not picking up any of my calls. Do you think it might be connected?"

Sam knew the MacDonald family through his parents. They had two boys, Chris and Jack who he used to see when they came out for the school holidays. He was the same age as Jack, whilst Chris was maybe four or five years older.

He made the call and Lori Garcia picked up the phone quickly.

"Sam, nothing happened at Señor Patterson's villa, but we have had another high value burglary. We're running checks on the family's bank records for any recent transactions that may be connected with the IT scams and there's something else," she paused. "They killed the householder, a seventy year old British woman whose husband was away on business back in London."

"Lori, I appreciate this might be breaching confiden-

62

tiality, but was it Sheila MacDonald?" said Sam.

"Sam, how the hell did you know?" she trailed off. She knew this was an island and news got around like wildfire sometimes, but this had been kept really tight because of the severity of the attack. "I don't want this getting out before I want the press to know, but there's no easy way to tell you Sam, she was beaten to death. It was a savage attack and whoever did it, it looked like they used their bare hands."

Lori Garcia went quiet.

"So how did you know Sam?"

"My mother got a call this morning from a friend who was trying to get hold of Sheila. They're family friends Lori. I've known the two sons all my life and the MacDonalds have known my parents for many years."

Sam turned and looked at his mother. Concern was written across her face. He didn't know if she had heard what Lori had been saying, but she clearly knew something was seriously wrong.

"I'm sorry for your friends' loss Sam," said Lori.

"Thanks Lori," he paused, "so what about the case? Have you got any leads?"

"We haven't got much to go on. There were four of them. The CCTV picked up the vehicle as it stopped at the front. It was stolen and it's been found burnt out with no possible forensics. They wore hoods and there was no real effort to hide themselves, so we can tell that they were definitely men, but that's about it. We've got feelers out with the local officers and their informants, but no one's saying anything because this looks like una pandilla del crimen organizado. What you call OCGs, organised crime gangs."

Sam took in what she was telling him.

"Yes, you're right Lori, so if it's an OCG operating here, then what's your intel telling you about possible options?"

"We've got a few OCGs operating across the Balearics, but nothing with this usual style or M.O," said Garcia. "I'm seeing the MacDonald family representative later this morning and I will call you back if I have anything for Señor Patterson later, but Sam, if it was just a call centre scam with your friend Bill, I hope you appreciate that I won't be able to do a lot more on that whilst we have a murder and these other violent high value burglaries to deal with."

"But surely the burglaries are linked to the call centre scams aren't they?" said Sam.

"I don't know that for sure Sam and until I do, I need to focus on what I do know."

He could sense that she was getting irritated. He could understand why. He had been in the same position, back in London, when you get a well-meaning friend or relative to a crime victim who is a cop and they just keep firing questions at you.

"Okay, look, I'm sorry Lori. I know you are doing all you can. I understand that, so I'll back off and let you do your job."

"Muchas gracias Sam. I appreciate that and I will keep you posted, I promise."

As soon as he came off the phone his mother looked at him.

"Sheila's dead isn't she?" said Anna.

"I'm so sorry Mum. There's no easy way to say this. Yes, she was murdered during the burglary, but they don't know why yet. Here sit down for a moment."

"Oh Sam, how can people be so evil? And what about John and the boys?"

She was crying now, tears flowing down her cheeks. He didn't know how much this was because she might have been bottling things up since Dad had died, so he just sat by her, holding her hand until the tears slowed.

"We need to get to see John and his boys and see how

we can help," said Anna.

"Yes, of course," said Sam.

Even in a crisis she was thinking of someone else.

FIVE

Sergei held his weekly management calls via Zoom. He told himself that he wasn't micro-managing and that it was important to keep a check on any issues going on around the organisation.

But he also knew it put pressure on those In-Country Heads who weren't performing, although it gave those who were doing well, an opportunity to dwell in the limelight and encourage the under-performers to set things straight. Better that he thought, than him having to take a more forceful approach with them.

He gave them full responsibility for the operations in their region, but with that he demanded total loyalty and anyone found taking too much off the bottom line would answer to him, generally being removed, permanently, from their position.

Today's call was going well, with very few issues arising. There were some problems in the US, but there always were, particularly around the politics of New York, where it seemed the Governor had a particular desire to show what he was doing to tackle organised crime in the city. Andranik, the In-Country head had a tough job, but Sergei wasn't about to tell him that in open forum. He rewarded him well and in return expected him to resolve the issues to keep the business, the extortion, drugs, prostitution and money laundering on track.

"Okay, Andranik, these sound like excuses you are giving me. So, sort this out by the end of the month or we'll talk again," said Sergei.

Andranik knew better than to try to argue.

"Yes Boss, of course."

"Right, let's move on. Sonny, what's happening in the Balearics?"

Sonny was relaxed, unlike some of his colleagues. A trusted confidante to Sergei, Senichi "Sonny" Sargsyan had his trust and much to the annoyance of some of the other In-Country Heads, he was never challenged in these sessions.

"All good here Sergei," said Sonny, "the sun is shining and business is good."

Unlike the others, Sonny called Sergei by his first name, something Sonny knew annoyed his colleagues and yes, he found he enjoyed seeing them squirm during these sessions.

"Good," Sergei paused, "so what about this woman in the burglary?"

Sonny was momentarily taken aback. Sergei never questioned him and what the hell did he want to know about this woman for, the MacDonald woman?

"Regrettable Sergei. She was old and she held out a little more than expected on giving up the key code for the safe, but it's okay, we've had no backlash from the local police," he started to laugh as he said, "they're still running around like headless chickens."

"That's good then," said Sergei, "let's wrap this up for today. Sonny, call me after we come off Zoom."

The other In-Country Heads had never heard Sergei question anything Sonny had done and they sensed that this was clearly a message to Sonny that even he was subject to Sergei's will. Whilst it made them smile, they also recognised that it also demonstrated Sergei was absolutely ruthless when it came to running his OCG and no-one, not even his Golden Boy, was exempt from his attention.

Sergei waited for the call. He knew he had dented Sonny's pride by calling him out in front of everyone, but he was annoyed. He had been told of the woman's death in Mallorca, or to be more precise, the nature of the woman's death. He knew Sonny's penchant for violence and for much of the time this was a very useful asset when he needed certain things re-enforced with his team. However, that was something that remained all within house. He had been happy for Sonny to pilot this idea of follow up attention for some targeted high value victims from the IT scams. He'd let Sonny negotiate the deal with the Kaur woman in India and it had been seeing some useful returns in terms of cash and some of the fine art was a useful bargaining chip with the Italian Mafia, especially the Camorra in Naples. His mobile rang, it was Sonny.

"Sonny, thank you for calling. How are you?"

'Pleasantries,' thought Sonny, *'but what's coming?'*

"I am fine my friend. What did you want to talk about? I gather there's something troubling you for you to call me out in front of everyone."

"Call you out? Not at all. I was just asking a question," said Sergei.

Sonny knew better than to push Sergei too far. He didn't want to antagonise him and felt he made his point by saying he felt he had been called out.

"Okay, good. It's not a problem though Sergei. There have been no issues," said Sonny.

"The point I'm making Sonny, is that it seemed to be an unnecessary death that had and still may have the potential to arouse unwanted attention from the police, something that as you know I ask you to ensure we keep to an absolute minimum."

"It was regrettable Sergei and I have dealt with the person responsible."

Sergei knew Sonny was throwing him a line here. Arman, his inside man within Sonny's team, who had told him what had happened, had been most specific about the nature of the killing because he knew it raised the likelihood of the police digging deeper into the incident. However, to challenge Sonny further risked revealing Arman's identity.

"That's good to hear Sonny as I wouldn't like a repeat of this. I don't think I need to remind you that I have a clear policy of keeping under the police radar in the countries where we operate," said Sergei.

"Yes, absolutely Sergei, it's an appropriate tactic and you can trust me when I say I make sure we comply with that strategy over here in the Balearics. I'm sorry, but if it's okay, I need to go now as I have to get to an appointment," said Sonny.

"Thank you for your reassurance Sonny and yes, I won't keep you any longer."

As Sergei came off the phone, he shook his head. He had known Sonny for many years and looked upon him almost like a younger brother. But it mattered not. Sergei could feel that Sonny was testing him. Testing his authority. If he sensed any sign of weakness he knew that Sonny would not hesitate to make his bid to depose him and take over the OCG. Sergei smiled. Brother or not, he would not allow Sonny to get too big for his boots, so he was glad that he had Arman keeping a watchful eye on what was going on in the Balearics.

Sonny on the other hand, came off the phone with the thought that Sergei must be really annoyed with him. But with an unsettled feeling that Sergei knew more than he was letting on. Sergei hadn't challenged him about the woman's death, when he had said he had dealt with the person responsible, when in fact he had killed the woman and not one of his men. He sat down and thought through the conversation again. Sergei wasn't showing signs of weakness in running the OCG, at least not yet. Sonny was ready to make his move when he saw any chink in Sergei's armour, but that wasn't going to be soon. He knew Sergei retained a very strong grip on his organisation and was not one to be crossed. He knew what was going on across all of the regions they operated in. Sonny knew that Sergei had his own spies out there, but he hadn't thought he had anyone in the Balearics. He paused. That was careless, of course he would have someone. He should have thought about that before. Something to think about and he needed to find out who this was and re-align their loyalties.

*****

Greg got the MacDonalds' driver to take him into the city to meet DI Garcia. It was an easy drive in from Cap Rocat and at this time of the morning most of the commuters had already got to work and not many tourists were on the road yet. Last night, the police officer at the villa entrance had told him to go to the Policia Nacional HQ in Palma where DI Garcia was working from. He always liked to know who he was meeting, but the officer couldn't tell him much more than she was an experienced detective who worked on organised crime. That was reassuring, to hear that she was a specialist, and he hoped she'd have some positive news for him. The driver dropped him at the police headquarters on Carrer de Simo Ballester, just off the Passeig de Mallorca. It was a 24 hour police station and it was busy, so he waited patiently in reception till 10.00 when a smartly dressed woman came out of a side door and looked at him enquiringly.

"Señor Chambers?"

"Si," said Greg, "Inspectora Garcia?"

"Si Señor," said Garcia, smiling as he had called her 'Inspectora' using the correct feminine form. "Do you speak Spanish, or I can talk in English if that helps?"

"My Spanish is a little rusty to go into the detail of what happened, so I would appreciate English if that's okay and thank you for your courtesy Inspectora," said Greg.

She nodded and then motioned for him to follow her as she walked through the building to an interview room on the same floor. The tables and chairs were screwed down to the floor. This was a room that, whilst also used for talking to victims and witnesses, was primarily used for interviewing offenders and as such was well away from public view.

"First of all, may I say thank you for seeing me Inspectora. I appreciate that you will have a thousand and one things to be doing and seeing a family representative would not have been high on your priority list," said Greg.

Lori Garcia smiled. *'He's quite charming,'* she thought and no doubt he was used to using his charm to open doors to information he might not otherwise be privy to.

Greg saw her smile and understood she would be no easy push over for information. *'She looks a smart cookie this one,'* he thought. *'Indeed, a very smart cookie.'*

"I have provided specialist services to John MacDonald for over 20 years through my company, 3R," handing over his business card before going on, "and he has asked me to be your family liaison contact for him if that's acceptable to you?" said Greg.

"Yes, of course Señor Chambers. I have no problem with that. I looked you up with the details you gave the local officer at the villa. There isn't much about you on your website except that you provide, as you say, specialist services. So what exactly are these specialist services?" she asked.

"Well as my card says, we help clients with risk reduction and resolution. This might be in relation to stock loss, corruption and site and team security, right up to kidnap situations."

Lori Garcia looked firmly at Greg.

"Señor Chambers, if I read between the lines I assume that you have the capacity to engage in a number of different interactions with the people your clients are dealing with."

Greg nodded and started to say something, when Garcia interjected.

"What I do not want Señor Chambers is any sort of renegade activity going on as I continue my investigation. Do I make myself clear?"

Greg had pretty much expected her to make this sort of statement and he could understand why, so he just nodded.

"Yes, of course Inspectora, I'm here purely for information gathering and to make your job easier."

"Information gathering is good. Making my job easier? Now that worries me, but let's see if we can't get along. Okay with you?"

Yes, a tough cookie. Better to work with her if he could, than against her.

"Absolutely."

His estimation of her went up further when she told him she was seconded to the Grupo Especial de Operaciones. The GEO were a crack unit and he had worked with them during his time with the Service. She briefed him on what they knew so far, which wasn't much but it seemed that he had sufficiently gained her trust for her to tell him about some of the details that hadn't yet hit the ears of the press.

He tried a few 'yes' questions. A technique to get people used to answering questions.

"So the van was stolen? Do you have anything more on that? Location? Any CCTV?"

"Yes, stolen the same day as the burglary. It's an electrician's vehicle and they were working in a shop doing a refit and it was parked outside, keys in the cab. It was opposite El Corte Inglés on Avinguda d'Alexandre Rosselló, you know? On the ring road, so we're checking the street CCTV."

He asked a few more easy 'yes' questions which she was happy to answer.

He then asked, "Any other similar crime types over the past few months?"

She gave him a half smile.

"Good technique Señor Chambers. Something from the security services I imagine? Please don't abuse the courtesy I have afforded you. It was bad enough having a London police officer trying to get information from me, without you doing the same."

She stood up. The meeting was clearly over, but she seemed more amused than annoyed at him, so he took one more chance.

"Thank you Inspectora, I really do appreciate your help. Two final things if I may? When do you think you will be able to release the crime scene and where might I find a London police officer in this beautiful city?" said Greg.

She smiled again. *'Yes, charm personified.'*

"Maybe late tomorrow, but work on the following day and Sa Petita Llibreria, The Little Bookshop, it's down near the theatre."

*****

Sam looked up at his mother, Anna, who was sorting through some books at the front of the shop. He had been curious about how much money the bookshop took in takings, as since he had been there he hadn't seen too many people come in to actually buy a book.

"Do you actually make any money from Sa Petita Lli-breria Mum?" he asked.

"Oh no dear, we haven't made a profit since the internet took off," she smiled, "but it never mattered to your father. We had enough coming in from the other side of the business to keep food on the table and so this really became a hobby for us," said Anna.

"Quite an expensive hobby isn't it? What with the rent and taxes?"

"Oh we don't pay rent Sam. We own the building, in fact we own this block."

She turned away and carried on with what she was doing. Sam had always thought that his parents never seemed to worry about money. He didn't think they were wealthy, but probably comfortable, but hearing his mother tell him they owned not just Sa Petita Lli-breria, but the whole block took him by surprise.

"So Mum, exactly how much property do you own?" said Sam.

"We dear, we. It's family owned and so it belongs to you just as much as me."

"Okay, but what do we own?"

"Well Alfonso has got all the details, but there's this block, then there's another one across the other side of the city, up near El Corte Inglés and then there are some villas, some apartments and a few retail units here and there."

"Mum! That's an enormous amount of property," said Sam.

"Well yes, that's why your father was keen that you take it over when it became too much for us, but if you remember, you've never been all that interested when we mentioned it before and your father wanted you to have your time doing what you wanted to do, just as he did, before you took over the business."

"I'm sorry, I didn't know," said Sam. "Are you worried at all about the business? I mean is it doing okay? Do you have any money issues? I have some savings and can help."

"Sam, that's really nice and kind of you, but I'm fine. Your father and I have had Alfonso and before that his father, to help us manage the business and it provides very well for us and it can do so for you as well. Speak to Alfonso and he can give you any information you want."

Sam sat back in his chair. So this wasn't just a bookshop business. He had known his parents had some other property, but nothing like what his mother had just outlined. If anything this troubled him more than before, because as much as he didn't want to think about it, his mum was almost seventy now and might be wanting to take a step back from managing what he now realised was a significant business portfolio.

*****

John MacDonald couldn't settle. He hadn't slept very well until he had finally fallen asleep late into the night, so he hadn't seen Greg leave the hotel. He had taken a late breakfast down on the lower terrace with Jack and he was now pacing up and down waiting for news from Greg. He felt the anger arising inside him again. Whoever did this would not get away with it. He would make damn sure of that. He heard and then saw one of the hotel buggies coming down the slope to the lower terrace. Greg and Chris got out of the buggy and they all sat down at a table overlooking the sea, with Jack ordering more coffee.

On another day thought Greg, this would be a spectacular place to sit and take in the views and enjoy the company of a man he had much to thank for, but sadly that wouldn't be today.

"We've got a good person working on the case John. She's a Detective Inspector called Lori Garcia, an Organised Crime specialist and currently attached to the Grupo Especial de Operaciones, the GEO. I know those guys, worked with them. They're not quite Special Forces but they are a really good police version, so they can definitely handle themselves."

"Okay, but what about leads? You say she's Organised Crime? Why is she dealing with it?" said John.

"Good question. They've just started looking at the CCTV for where the vehicle was stolen from, up near El Corte Inglés. The fact there were four of them on the job suggests this wasn't a local outfit stepping up their game, especially going for a villa of this size. It looks much more likely that an OCG would have the channels to offload what they might find. I need to give her a bit of time to get into the investigation John, so I'll go and meet Terri. She's due to land around midday and then we'll start doing our own digging. Apparently there's a London cop who is also looking at something Garcia is dealing with, so I want to find him as well and see what his interest is in all of this."

"A London cop?" said Jack. "That might be Sam Martínez. You know Dad, Luis and Anna's son."

"Yes, good shout Jack. Nice people Greg. The boy would come and play here when we were over for the summer. Sheila always liked Anna and her husband was a good guy too. Died recently. Cancer, poor bugger."

"Maybe one and the same. She told me to go to Sa Petita Llibreria?" said Greg.

"Yes, that's their bookshop, down by the theatre," said John.

"Okay that's helpful. Now look, I appreciate you sorting me a room last night, but I think you guys need some space from me, so I'll be staying down at Terri's place."

He could see that John had probably had enough for now so it was probably a good time to go.

"I could do with a lift to the airport if that's okay, but I'll be back in touch later today guys."

Chris spoke first, "No problem, I'll sort the car for you and say 'Hi' to Terri from all of us."

SIX

G reg got dropped off just short of the airport, at the off-site car hire unit.

He wanted a small van, something relatively inconspicuous and they had a white Peugeot Partner van, perfect for what he wanted. He was finishing off the documentation when Terri called him.

"Dad, I've only got a carry bag, so I'm through security and will be out in just a few minutes."

He saw her as she came through the Arrival doors. He hadn't seen her for a month as she had been in Egypt and he had been meeting clients in the Far East, so it was good to catch up. He smiled as he noticed heads turning as this beautiful woman, his daughter, strolled through the Arrival doors, sunglasses on the top of her head, carrying a smart holdall and looking a million dollars whilst just dressed in jeans and a smart top. She knew of course, the impact she had on some people and whilst she was happy to use what she called her 'strewth' look in her work if she needed to, he knew that Terri was much more than, as the saying went, 'just a pretty face'.

They hugged and she wanted to know everything about what had happened. He briefed her as they walked to the multi-storey carpark and as they approached the van, she stopped.

"Hellfire Dad, can't you hire anything other than a bloody white van!"

He laughed. She was not keen on his choice of vehicles, never convinced at his rationale that white vans didn't stick out in the sort of places they often worked in and around.

"It's perfect. But don't worry, I've got you something more up your street. We can pick it up on our way to your place," said Greg.

"Good, but let's hope your choice of something I'd like is the same as what mine would be."

She smiled. It was good seeing her dad again, but she could see the strain on his face. He had known the MacDonalds a long time and she knew how much of a part they had played in making 3R a success.

She wasn't disappointed when they got to the car rental unit. She slid into the open top Merc SLK and waved as she called out.

"See you back at my place."

He didn't think he was too far behind her. However, she could park in the underground carpark, where she had a spot allocated with her apartment, but he had to find a space in the public parking area close by. He found one quicker than he thought and walked the short distance to where her apartment was, just around from the small marina, but as he put the key in the door, she opened it. She had already showered and changed and was standing ready to go.

"Okay, you said we had two things to do, first was check out this London cop in the bookshop and then second was to look around where the van was stolen. So why don't you drop me off at El Corte Inglés and I'll see if I can't find something more than what the local cops got from the street CCTV?" said Terri.

"Good plan."

They went in the van, so Greg drove and he pulled

across the Ma19 de Levante Motorway, the main road heading towards La Seu and the city centre, before he turned right up on to Avinguda de Gabriel Alomar and within a couple of minutes he was pulling up by El Corte Inglés and Terri got out of the van.

"Catch up soon," said Terri, before she disappeared into the crowded pavement.

She walked towards the little railway station, the one where she knew you could get the train to Sóller and Port de Sóller. She loved taking friends on that train. Such a great trip, but not today she thought. She crossed over the Alexandre Rossello, the main road and it didn't take long to find the empty shop unit, where the van had been parked when it was stolen. There were some guys still working inside. She tapped on the glass front door.

"It's not open, can't you see?" yelled one of the workmen in Spanish.

She could get by in Spanish, which was helpful as they had clients in Madrid and a couple of Spanish speaking countries in South America.

"Entiendo a mi amigo. I understand my friend. I just want some help please," said Terri.

The workman turned at the sound of her voice and seeing this strikingly blonde young woman with a wide smile and a short summer dress, he jumped up and ran to the door. So shallow, she thought, but it worked, so why knock it?

"I'm so sorry. Are you American?" said the workman.

"No mate, but don't worry, not a bad guess. I'm from the Gold Coast, Australia."

"You are a long way from home Señorita," smiled the workman.

"I'm looking for the guy who had his van stolen yesterday."

The workman looked disappointed and looked towards the other workman.

"Juan, she's asking about your van."

Juan, an older man had been routing some wires through the wall. He turned and saw Terri and smiled.

"Señorita, you don't look like a cop?" said Juan.

"No, I'm working for the client whose house was burgled by the guys using your van. Just wanted to check some things with you," said Terri.

"But I've already spoken to the cops yesterday and to some more detectives today. Can't they tell you?" said Juan.

"I can see you're busy Juan, but it won't take a minute."

She tried the wide smile again and bingo, it worked again. Shallow times two, but hey it works. She went through what had happened and the timings of when he had parked the van and she got him to show her exactly where it had been parked and what vehicles had been parked near the van. He almost seemed disappointed at having to go back to work when she thanked him for his help and walked towards the door.

"Thank you Señorita and I hope you catch the burglars."

Interesting, thought Terri. The police have still not released the fact that this was a murder as well as a high value burglary. Did that mean this wasn't an isolated case and maybe the local police commissioner was getting a bit jumpy at reputational damage to the island? After all, the economy is pretty much built on tourism and negative press could harm the numbers of tourists coming to the island.

*****

She started by walking across to the central reservation in the middle of the road. It was a raised grassed area and she stood looking around her, trying to identify potential CCTV locations other than from just the main road cameras. It was feasible that one of the nearby offices or shops might have cameras that would give a different angle than the street CCTV, one that just might have caught a good image of the thief. There were a couple of possibilities. One was El Corte Inglés itself, which might be a bit difficult as viewing their CCTV would probably entail overcoming data protection issues that a major chain like El Corte Inglés would have to comply with. However, the second possibility was a small shop that looked like an independent retailer. It was a bit further away, but bingo, it was of all things, a camera shop. She walked in to see a young man, maybe about nineteen or twenty. She waited for any sort of reaction. The young guy almost jumped up to greet her. This should work she thought and out came the wide smile once again.

His dad owned the shop, but he wasn't in at the moment, so he was in charge. Given the opportunity to spend time with a woman he was probably still at the stage of dreaming of, he didn't seem too bothered about data protection and with no one else coming into the shop, he only needed a little gentle persuasion to encourage him to want to show her how the CCTV cameras worked. He had helped his dad fit the cameras quite recently, just after someone tried to force their front door and they had decided to upgrade what was already a good system into a really good High Definition CCTV system. She had to admit, the equipment they had was superb quality, from the HD cameras to the super high quality DVR, the digital video recorder. He beamed when she praised the system, telling her that it was his idea to go for the 1080P HD and super DVR set-up because of the increased processing capability.

Terri had thought it was a long shot, especially with the empty shop unit being across the street, but one of these cameras could clearly pick up the parking area outside the shopfront. She gave the young man the times of the theft and crossed her fingers. It took him just seconds on the digital systems to bring up first of all, the images of the van parked outside the shop and then after it had been stolen. He seemed to be in his element now and she just kept smoothing his ego as he went into geek mode as he broke the images down into smaller time chunks. Then he pushed two buttons and went to the back of the shop, returning a few moments later with a DVD and a set of photo images showing the van, then a van with a male approaching the vehicle from the rear, then getting into the driver's seat and the van moving away. This was followed by a close up of the male. It wasn't crystal clear, which she accepted because of the distances involved, but it gave a reasonable outline and a pretty good full face picture as he looked to his left, over his shoulder, before opening the driver's door and getting into the cab.

"That's the best I can do Terri," said Pablo, the young man. "I hope it helps and oh, if you give me your email, I can send you the images as jpegs."

"Pablo, you have been an absolute star. I could kiss you!"

Pablo flushed up. And stood there, waiting hopefully rather than expectantly. Terri had said it figuratively, but saw the look on the young man's face. *'Ah well, best not disappoint,'* and she leaned over the counter. Pablo closed his eyes and she kissed him on his forehead. He opened his eyes and a look of disappointment crossed his face. Terri smiled at him.

"Mate, you never want to close your eyes on your first kiss," and she kissed him full on the lips. "There you go Pablo. One to tell your mates and no doubt you've got the CCTV images to remind you as well," she winked at him, glancing up at the cameras in the shop as she walked out the shop and texted Greg, *'Ready when you are. All good here, got some good images. Will start walking towards the theatre'* and she finished it with a smiley face emoji.

*****

After dropping off Terri, Greg had carried on the same road that took him around the city centre, eventually bearing left down Carrer d'Alemanya before taking a left into Baro de Pinbar and then straight onto Rambla dels Ducs de Palma de Mallorca. He knew there was a car park at the end, by the Teatre Principal, so headed there keeping an eye out for Sa Petita Llibreria as he drove. The road was fairly busy, which was helping as it meant he had to drive slowly and it gave him a better chance to look out for the bookshop. He was almost at the carpark entrance when he saw it, on his right and pretty much diagonally across from the theatre. He signalled left and pulled across the road into the multi-storey car park and found a space.

He felt the heat when he got out of the aircconditioned van. It was probably somewhere around 30-32 degrees, but with the sun bouncing off the light coloured buildings around the theatre, as well as the pavements, it was making it feel more like 37-38 degrees, so he was glad he didn't have far to walk before he got to the front door of Sa Petita Llibreria.

As he walked through the door, he heard an old fashioned bell ring above his head announcing his arrival. He took in his surroundings and saw what appeared to be a sales counter at the rear of the shop, floor to ceiling shelving all around the sides of the shop, all crammed with books and then two units in the centre of the shop, double sided, about eight feet tall, four feet wide and again the shelves were full of books. He heard a movement ahead of him and a woman appeared from behind the counter.

"Fiona?" said Greg.

Anna stopped in her stride. She hadn't seen him for what? Thirty five years or more?

"Greg, is that you?"

"My God, you look wonderful." He moved forward and they hugged, as old friends.

"What are you doing here?" said Anna.

"Where do I start? Listen, can we go for a coffee or have you had lunch?" said Greg.

"We can go when my son gets back, he's just popped out and Greg," she paused. "It's Anna. I left Fiona behind a long time ago, so it's Anna Martínez, ex-Foreign Office, okay?"

"Yes, yes, of course."

He understood immediately. It was often the case that field agents took up a new name or went back to their original name when they left the Service, so he wondered if Anna was her original name or a new identity.

"And your son you say? Would that be Sam Martínez, a London police officer?" said Greg.

"Why yes, but how did you know?" said Anna.

"Long story, but I need to talk to him urgently about something I'm working on, but hey a son, that's great."

"Yes, he's only been back a few weeks. I lost my husband six months ago to cancer and it's been lovely having Sam home."

Greg saw her eyes were red and thought she might have been crying.

"Oh Anna, I'm so sorry," he said.

Just at that moment Sam came back in through the door and saw his mum talking to a man. *'A customer, finally,'* thought Sam who hadn't seen anyone in the shop all day.

"Sam, this is an old friend of mine from my days in the Foreign Office."

"Hi Sam, pleasure to meet you. I'm Greg Chambers and I was looking for you and who should I find but Anna here, who turns out to be your mother!" said Greg.

"Looking for me, why?" said Sam.

"I got your details from a mutual contact, DI Lori Garcia. She suggested it would perhaps be useful to speak to you about a burglary at my client, John Mac-Donald's villa yesterday."

*****

"How much do you know Greg?" said Sam quietly.

"I'm guessing you know about Sheila?" said Greg tentatively.

Sam nodded and even knowing Anna's real background, Greg could see that this was why she was shaken.

"I'm so sorry for your loss. Presumably they were good friends of you and your husband Anna?" said Greg.

"Yes, I'd known them for many years and the boys used to play together in the school holidays."

Greg saw Sam move closer to his mother and wrap his arms protectively around her.

After a moment Sam spoke first.

"So does Garcia think there's a connection between Sheila and the IT scam with Bill Patterson?"

"You've got me there Sam," said Greg thinking the inquisitive nature of the police officer in Sam was showing through straight away. "I know nothing about an IT scam or Bill Patterson. You'd better fill me in, but first, let's get the kettle on. Anna, are you okay I'm so sorry, it must be a hell of a shock."

"Yes, I'm okay," said Anna thinking, 'yes, a hell of a bloody shock, one to hear about Sheila this morning and then two, seeing you after thirty five years!' "I just need a moment, so tea would be lovely."

Sam smiled and went to make some tea. His mum was always great in a crisis. He didn't know where she got it from. From what she said her job hadn't been all that exciting and she had grown up in a genteel middle England family from Surrey. She had been the same when Dad was diagnosed with the cancer. Immediate shock, followed by a steely determination to sort things as best as they could. He came back with three mugs of tea.

"I didn't get a proper chance to introduce myself Sam," said Greg. "I run a small company called 3R and we specialise in risk reduction and resolution, essentially negating or reducing risk for our clients. They are mostly insurance companies and corporates who have problems with things going missing, or their people being threatened. It happens a lot with some of their foreign ventures."

Sam nodded and so he went on.

"I have known the MacDonalds for around twenty years. They were pretty much my first client. John was just about to move into the big time with Trent MacDonald and I sorted out a small problem for him. I have a lot to thank Sheila for too, as she was the one who persuaded John to take a risk with my small outfit, so this is pretty personal for me. I got the call from John's eldest, Chris, last night and came straight here."

"What does he want you to do?" asked Sam cautiously.

Greg paused and saw them both looking at him.

"Get justice for Sheila."

Sam decided it might be better not to ask what form of justice that may take in front of his mum, unaware that she had a very good idea of what Greg meant by his use of the word. In fact she probably had a much better idea of what Greg meant by risk resolution. Instead, Sam switched to telling Greg about what happened to

Bill and the potential threat Garcia had thought could follow in the form of a follow up burglary, given that Bill lived in a £3 million villa.

"How do we move from simple IT scams to high value burglaries?" said Greg.

"I guess Garcia's thinking there's a connection between the scammers and an OCG over here. Not the usual connection I know, but you can see it makes sense. The trouble is finding anything out about the scammers is bloody difficult," said Sam.

He had put a call into Jimmy back in London to see if he could get anywhere with identifying the scammers. But the issue was there were so many of them and they operated on multiple fronts. Jimmy was looking at intel on similar MOs to see if the scam and burglary tactic was being seen anywhere else across the UK and Europe, but he'd found nothing so far.

"Okay," said Greg. "You've given me a great lead there Sam. I'll get on and check the MacDonald's IT and bank payments for the last few weeks and see what that brings up. Anna, maybe we could do that coffee or lunch soon? It would be so good to catch up."

He also thought it best to not start asking Anna any questions in front of her son until he knew more about what she had told or not told her family.

SEVEN

J asvinder Kaur was sat at her desk in a smart set of offices in BKC, the now de-facto central business district in Mumbai.

Looking over the monthly figures of her operation, she was pleased with the data she was seeing, especially from her pilot project. Her company, Direct Solutions, now employed over one hundred and twenty staff and ran four call centres, with offices in Mumbai and Chennai and the business was growing fast.

The youngest child of Gurnum Singh, Jaz, as she was known, had been well educated, finishing her business degree in the US. She had found that being brought up in a family where your father was the boss of a criminal gang, had brought with it a good deal of advantages. There were only occasional downsides, sometimes disputes with other gangs and very, very occasionally, the unwanted attention from the police when they felt they needed to demonstrate they hadn't given up on holding organised crime at bay.

One of four children, but the only girl, she had learned to fight and stand up for herself as she was growing up. Her parents soon gave up on the idea of any sort of arranged marriage for their daughter. She was headstrong and after returning from the US with her Masters in Business, she made it clear that she was going to make her own way. Whilst her brothers, who were happy to go into their father's 'family business', made fun of their little sister, they also knew she had the same ruthless streak as their father running through her.

Four of her call centres were fully operational legitimate businesses trading under the name of Direct Solutions, providing first point customer contact services for a variety of companies in the UK and in the USA. She had been successful in building this side of the business. Turnover was growing fast and so now investors were sniffing around, she knew she needed to keep the business under her sole ownership to avoid prying eyes. She didn't mind the company getting a profile in the media as she enjoyed the limelight that came with it, so was happy to be pictured in the social media handing over cheques for local community projects. It provided the cover she was looking for with Intertech, her other business, where she ran six further call centres, but the ownership of these was buried deep within a network of spurious company names, that would make it very hard, if not impossible, to track ownership of Intertech back to her.

The call handlers in these centres had been carefully selected. She had recruited the early ones, but now her managers knew what she wanted and they did the job well. There were plenty of people out there who wanted a well-paid job and she made sure this paid better than the salaries in her legitimate business. However, she did expect them to earn it, by cheating and deceiving vulnerable and unsuspecting people through the IT scams and with no qualms or morals. The profit sharing incentive she rewarded them with also ensured total commitment from her team and she smiled at how she was putting her learning from her business degree to such good effect.

The scam was simple. Victims would see a pop-up appear on the screen of their laptop or desk computer that without the right course of action, could block the screen. The victim then sees an IT Support telephone number, which when dialled is answered by the Intertech call centre call handlers, who pressure and intimidate the caller to pay money, often significant sums of money, to solve their IT issue.

Also based in Mumbai and Chennai, her Intertech business was providing a far higher turnover and profit ratio than Direct Solutions. She checked the figures again for Intertech, yes, business was good. After overheads, she was clearing over ten million rupees a month in net profit, about a £100K in sterling she calculated and it was growing. She smiled again and wondered what her brothers were making under their father? It certainly wouldn't be anything like that. One final thing. She should check the pilot that was going on in the Balearics. She wasn't sure at first that it was a good deal to get involved with. It was a strange tie-in, linking Indian call centres to an Armenian OCG, but the figures showed it was working.

Her Intertech call handlers took the addresses of the people they were scamming and then during their downtime, they researched them. They produced a summary for their supervisor, outlining the estimated property value, likely number and age of the occupants and any access details for the location, such as security cameras. They could also add to the report by including additional information they may have gained whilst speaking with the scam victim, such as whether or not they liked fine art or sculpture.

In reality it was a small return for her business. She was getting around two hundred and fifty thousand rupees, about £2.5k sterling, for each address, however, there was a strange element of trust that was growing between her and her Armenian partner in Mallorca which she found interesting, almost refreshing, like honour amongst thieves. If the address paid off and the Armenians got a good haul, they would give her another ten percent of what they made, starting at one hundred thousand rupees, so it could be quite lucrative, but again if nothing came of it, she only returned half of her fee. As with the main scam, the call handler and their supervisor also took a percentage of the fees, however, she never asked them to repay their money if the Armenians didn't get anything. Generous, yes, but the staff did know that too many addresses without a good return on investment could result in them being dismissed, so the incentive was there to do a really good job.

The pilot had been going three months now and was due for a review, so she should probably go back to Mallorca to see Sonny. It was a good time of the year to get out of Mumbai for a few days anyway. No doubt they thought it was hot in Mallorca, being their summer season, but it was still nothing like the incessant humidity of Mumbai. She had been in Mallorca for a long weekend's break earlier in the year and had met him in a smart bar one night. Five to ten years older than her, he was big, very imposing and he hadn't been slow in coming forward and that always suited her, at least when they first met. She wasn't into long term relationships as she saw them as an unnecessary distraction. When she needed company, she generally looked for European businessmen staying in the up market luxury hotels for one night stands, sometimes two if they were good.

Sonny had been a good two night stand and it was probably because they spent some of the second day together that she found out enough about his business to understand the potential for a tie-in. He had told her that he thought she just owned a call centre business, so he had been surprised when she made the proposal. The figures she projected had made sense to him and she knew he was keen to show his boss that he could manage a bigger In-Country operation, maybe even North America. The prospect of taking the partnership into the States was enticing, but enough of work she thought to herself, time for some rewards. She looked around and saw Ekam and motioned for him to get the car ready to take her home. She wanted to celebrate with a meal out and maybe some fun.

*****

Later that evening Ekam took her to one of her favourite hotels. As an attractive and rich young woman, it was never difficult to engage with one of those guys you could nearly always find having a meal alone and then a drink in a hotel bar after a day with their clients. She was always cautious with these encounters, but once she'd make it clear she was available and they'd got back to his room, she liked to take control, but this one tonight had taken her by surprise.

At first she thought he just liked things a bit rough, or maybe he thought she was actually one of the high class hookers operating in some of the top end hotels. But then he started to slap her and hit her hard. She tried to fight him off, but couldn't and it only stopped when Ekam heard her cries of pain as he waited outside the room door, something he always did once Jaz had texted him the room number. Ekam didn't bother knocking. He was a big, athletic man and he leaned back and kicked at the door lock, the weakest part of the door and the door gave way. The man was still semi-dressed and looked up in surprise as Ekam stood there. Jaz scrambled out from under the man and ran to the bathroom.

"Who the hell do you think you are coming in here?

Look, I'm sorry if she's your wife or something, but she offered herself to me on a plate, what can I say?"

He didn't say anymore as by that stage Ekam had walked across to where the man was now standing by the side of the bed. He didn't stop walking, but his right arm moved slightly back and then he punched his fist forward quickly into the man's stomach. The man was around the same age as Ekam, about forty and looked reasonably fit and well built, but the punch took him to his knees. He then had no defence to what followed as Ekam hit him again, this time to the head, with a hard punch to his temple, followed by a low left hook that straightened him back up again. The man was trying to talk and trying to defend himself at the same time, but with blood coming from his nose and his head spinning from the punches he was completely disorientated.

"Look, I'm sorry, I'm sorry. It was just a bit of fun, can't we sort this out, I have money."

Ekam had been given responsibility for looking after Jasvinder Singh when she was born and he was just eight years of age. He was her companion and lived with Jasvinder's family.

When they left him at this strange and much bigger house than he had ever seen before, he was told by his parents that it was a great honour and that they would never forget him. He cried for a week, but he had a bed to sleep in and food every day, something he didn't always get at home.

He learned many years later that his parents hadn't given him away, but had asked Jasvinder's father, Gurnum Singh, to take pity on them and to take their son and give him a better life than they could afford. Once he knew, Ekam had wanted to find and then help his parents and when he finally could, he was truly content with a life he had dedicated to looking after Jasvinder.

He would do anything for her and in this case, the man in front of him had hit her, hit his beloved Jasvinder and he would be punished. As she came out of the bathroom, he saw some reddening around her cheeks. He checked with her that she was otherwise okay. She nodded at Ekam, who then looked at the man.

"Sit down and do not move."

The man did as he was told and Ekam quickly made a phone call.

"Balnoor will be here in just a few minutes. He will meet you downstairs."

"Thank you," said Jaz.

Her voice was quiet. He could see she was shaken, but couldn't bring himself to put his arm around her. He had not touched her, even to comfort her, not since she was thirteen and starting to turn from a girl into young woman. He knew he could never have or at least never show feelings of love for her, as to do so would threaten his very ability to be able to defend her. Instead, he waited whilst she quickly let herself out of the room, pulling the smashed door behind her, before he turned to the man, who looked like he was expecting him to say something, so he was taken aback when Ekam punched him again in the stomach.

"Just let me go, please," he pleaded, before realising he hadn't been punched. He had been stabbed.

"Christ, you've stabbed me!" said the man. His hands went down to the wound and he tried to stem the blood, looking in vain for help from the man who had just stabbed him.

He started to move to the hotel phone until he saw Ekam rip it out of the wall and then pick up the man's mobile phone and walk to the other side of the room and turn and hold it out, as though offering it to the man. The man tried to stagger towards Ekam.

"What are you doing? Just give me the damn phone.

We can still sort this out. Please help me."

"Come, come for your phone. Or has it occurred to you that by keeping moving, you are keeping the blood flowing into, or rather, out of your wound? So in effect my friend, you are now killing yourself," said Ekam.

It was as though Ekam had punched the man again. He stopped suddenly and looked down at his wound. He couldn't stop the flow. He looked around for something he could use as a bandage. *'Why hadn't he thought of doing that before?'* He started to scramble at the bed to get one of the sheets off to make a makeshift bandage. Ekam let him do it. He knew the length of the knife had gone deep into the man's stomach and that no bandage would stop the bleeding sufficiently to keep him alive. He would be dead in another five minutes or so. He wanted the man to feel the helplessness Jaz had felt when he was attacking her, but this time he would have no one coming through the door to help him.

Ekam sat down in the chair and watched the man frantically trying to apply a bandage. By now the man's strength was going and he had forgotten Ekam had his phone. He had started sobbing and was begging for his help.

"My friend, you had my angel delivered to you on a plate. She chose you and she would have let you have her. You cannot know how much I have dreamed of doing the very thing that she gave you," said Ekam.

The man looked up at Ekam.

"So you're a jealous shit, who is too much of a coward to do anything about it. Ha! That's it, you're just a coward, you bastard!"

"Sticks and stones," said Ekam and he smiled. "Not long now my friend. If you're lucky your body will go into shock and you won't feel any more pain. If I had my way, you would be screaming in agony by now. Maybe I'm losing my touch?"

The man wasn't listening, his eyes were opening and closing. The blood loss was now reaching a critical stage. Then he slumped to one side. Ekam checked for a pulse. It was faint. He started to clean the room and bathroom, removing any evidence that he and Jaz had been there and by the time he had finished that the man was well and truly gone.

He made one more call to one of Gurnum Singh's men who he knew looked after this hotel. He needed the CCTV for the past six hours 'accidently' removed and for the Duty Manager to remove the reservation he had made for dinner in Jaz's name. By the time Ekam was being picked up by one of his drivers as he left the hotel, the man he had called had made all of the arrangements asked of him, leaving the police with no leads of any significance to go on when the body was found during the early hours as the hotel security did their rounds. They could only surmise that the man may have been murdered because he wouldn't pay for the services of a high class hooker.

As the car took Ekam back to Jaz's home, he got a text from her 'Come and see me when you get back.'

He wished he could read more into this than he knew he could. She had always looked at him as another older brother. That should have been enough for him, given his upbringing and the difference in their positions in life, but it wasn't. However, he knew what was had to be. His job was to protect her and he had done that tonight.

He knocked gently on her door and heard her voice.

"Come in Ekam," said Jaz.

She was feeling settled again now. Jaz knew that she actually liked the risk of what she was doing, picking up men for sex in hotel bars. It gave her a rush, a thrill and it wasn't just the sex, it was the chase of picking a man she didn't know. It was the same with her business. She actually found the legitimate business pretty boring, but the Intertech side of things was much more exciting. She didn't care about the people being scammed. *'They shouldn't be so stupid and gullible,'* she thought. She knew she had much of her father's ruthlessness in her and so it was with the man tonight. She hoped Ekam had punished him, had hurt him, really hurt him and yes, she hoped, no expected him to be dead.

"Did he take long to die?" she said.

"Long enough to feel pain and helplessness and to know he should never have hurt you," said Ekam.

"Thank you, I made a mistake, I'm sorry I put you in this position Ekam."

He had never heard Jasvinder Singh apologise for anything, to anyone. Ekam flushed at the thought she had apologised to him. She must feel something for him, he thought, but of course, she has her position and cannot show anything. He felt so proud.

"It is my honour to protect you Miss Kaur, there is nothing to apologise for, I wish you a peaceful night's sleep," said Ekam as he stepped out of her room.

She smiled. He had looked after her since he was eight years old and he had always called her Miss Kaur, even as children. *'Like a guardian angel,'* she thought as she settled down in her bed.

EIGHT

Sam turned and looked at his mother as Greg Chambers walked out the door of Sa Petita Llibreria.

"Okay Mum, come on now, spill the beans. I'm out the door for a couple of minutes and a charming and handsome Englishman is here when I get back," he smiled as he described Greg.

"I said he's just an old friend. He was looking for you, not me, so I think he was as surprised as I was to see him. Gosh it's been over thirty years. Now stop looking at me like that young man," said Anna.

"Like what Mum?" said Sam.

"You know only too well. Stop digging. He was a friend from when I was in the FCO," said Anna.

"Well he doesn't seem the Foreign and Commonwealth Office type to me. Especially not running a business called Risk Reduction and Resolution! What was he, Security Services or something?"

"Now, how would I know?" said Anna. "He worked in one of the embassies I think." She immediately regretted going down a storyline that had no truth in it. Always, always, make the lie plausible. That was what they told her in her training. Silly mistake and she was right, Sam wasn't giving up.

"So where was this? Was this when you worked in

Madrid or before, as you've never really told me about that?" said Sam.

"Put the kettle on again dear, let's have another cup of tea," said Anna deciding now was as good a time as any to tell him about at least part of her previous life.

With two new mugs of teas in front of them she told him about being recruited into MI6 at university and where she had subsequently worked. He knew enough about the Official Secrets Act not to pry into the details, knowing she was giving him as much as he needed to know. He sat back, taking it all in.

"Mum, you were a bloody spy!" said Sam, "My God, I never knew. Did Dad know?"

"Well of course you never knew dear, that's the point of being a spy," she smiled, "and no, your father never knew either. As far as he was concerned I'd been with the FCO since leaving university."

"What about Gran and Gramps? Did they know?"

"Oh heavens no," said Anna. "Can you imagine Gran knowing I was a spy? She would have been so worried about me and I'd have then been fretting about her worrying."

"So I guess you probably had to stop when you had me?" said Sam.

"Yes, it was a time when there was no chance of them accepting me back into the field once I had you, so I decided to take a desk job and there was a job going in Madrid," said Anna.

She was now worrying that he would start to push her on who his biological father was. She had always said she had been involved with someone and it hadn't worked out and by the time she knew she was pregnant, he had long gone. That was the story she had stuck to and it had been the one that Luis had been okay to hear, so she hoped he didn't push on this, not just at the moment anyway.

Sam was trying to take it all in. His mother had been a spy! She'd told him a little bit about being in the field, being a U/C operative, which he knew was a bloody dangerous pastime and that she had also been involved in recruiting field officers and U/C training. So she must have been damn good at what she did, especially to be a U/C field officer and trainer, as he understood a little bit about the U/C world and how much the officers trusted their trainers, literally with their lives.

"So, presumably this means that Greg is also ex-MI6 or one of the other Security Services?" he said finally.

"Yes Sam, it does."

*****

Greg met Terri in Plaça Mayor and they walked down to Plaça Cort and went to one of her favourite coffee stops, Cappuccino Grand Café in the boutique hotel, Hotel Cappuccino. They sat outside on the front terrace and ordered some coffees and Terri also went for Gató Mallorquin, one of the traditional local cakes she really liked, as she hadn't eaten since getting off the plane that morning.

"Hell of a coincidence running in to an old girlfriend then Dad, one in every port then?" she teased him.

"She wasn't a girlfriend," he said a little too firmly. "She was my U/C trainer and a bloody good one at that," said Greg.

"Definitely a girlfriend then!" said Terri and waited.

"Look, there's nothing to tell. It was thirty odd years ago, long before I met your mother, so can we move on please," said Greg.

His daughter just stared back with a knowing look, with a smile slowly appearing.

"Okay, okay, chill Dad, but you know I will get it out of you at some stage," said Terri.

He had no idea why he had bitten when she had quizzed him. Why was he getting, what, defensive?

'*This is nonsense,*' he thought.

"Yes, you probably will, but can we get back to what we're here for?" said Greg.

They ran through what each of them had discovered. A couple of hours before they had nothing concrete to go on, but now they had two solid leads to follow up. A good start that was looking promising. He sent the images Terri had got from her helpful young man at the camera shop through to DI Garcia, with a note asking her if she could get anything on the guy getting into the driver's seat. Then he rang John MacDonald and asked him to check his and Sheila's bank records for the past month for anything irregular going out of the account.

"What am I looking for Greg?" said John.

"Maybe a payment to someone who looks like an internet company. It's possible, just possible, that Sheila may have been subject to an IT scam sometime before the burglary took place. I'll fill you in on the details later, but let's only go down that route if, and only if, we can see a payment going out of one of your accounts, so check both your debit and credit cards. One possible payee name is Intertech, but don't limit your search to just that name as these people use multiple identities," said Greg.

"Okay, but she didn't say anything to me about any IT problems, but then again, she dealt with all that stuff on the home computers and she'd be more likely to ask the boys about something than me. I'll get on it. Meet tonight? 7.30pm, bring Terri and we'll eat afterwards," said John.

Greg smiled. It wasn't really a request, but more of an instruction.

"Yep, see you later."

*****

DI Lori Garcia was getting nowhere fast. They had

put feelers out in the criminal community and were tasking all their OCG informants, but so far they'd had no positive results. She knew the OCGs who were operating in the Balearics, but with no leads, she was struggling and was getting pressure from above to bring some good news. Presumably her boss was getting hassle from the local politicians too, because nobody liked high profile crimes on the islands and you couldn't get much higher than the murder of an ex-pat Brit.

There had been nothing from the street CCTV around El Corte Inglés, so when she got the text from Chambers she was both annoyed and pleased. Annoyed that her people hadn't been as effective as he seemed to have been, but pleased because at least she now had something! She was always wary of offers to help from privateers, but she had to admit, this guy seemed to know his business. By his manner, he was probably an ex-Cop, no, thinking about it, he was more likely ex-security services. That may be a good or a bad thing, as he may be more inclined to go beyond the boundaries of the law and it was that element that made her wary of people like him, because it usually brought with it other collateral damage. She stopped herself, she was going into a negative zone, when all he had done so far was given her something to go on. She texted him back with a *'Gracias. I'll get back to you'* and then sent the images through to her Intel team to start work on.

She transferred the images onto her desk top and took a better look at them. The Intel guys could no doubt do something to improve the resolution, but it was still worth her taking a moment to have a closer look. It was a damn good image of the guy stealing the van. Side on, as he looked over his left shoulder as he got into the driver's door. Admittedly it had been taken from across the main road, so it was quite a way from the van, but they must be bloody good cameras. *'Why the hell didn't my team find these?'* she thought. *'That will be a good one to try to explain to the boss.'*

She parked that problem for the moment. The key thing was she had a start. He looked white European, about 6'2", maybe 6'3", athletic build, maybe 85 kilos. He was wearing a grey polo shirt and black chinos, watch on his right wrist. Good, at least that's something different about him. Potentially, but not definitely left handed. She hoped the hi-tech team could do something more with the face because he looked to have quite an angular jaw line, so maybe he was East European?

She got some answers an hour later. She was impressed. They had done a pretty good job, made easier the guy said by the quality of the camera that took the pictures. She had a close up. Not good enough for colour of eyes or anything like that, but it did show something, possibly a tattoo just below his left wrist, where your watch strap would usually do up. The tech guy told her he had tried to get into the mark, but couldn't get it into any finer detail.

"Best guess then. Is it a tattoo?" said Garcia.

"Best guess? Yes," said the tech guy.

That put him being left handed in some doubt then. If the tattoo meant more to him than wearing his watch on his left hand then it must be important. She knew a lot of the tattoos that came out of Russian prisons held a lot of kudos to those who had them, so maybe it was something like that. Now she had to be patient and wait for her Intel team to run it through their systems, but in fairness, she should really put a call into the 3R guy, Chambers.

*****

Sam was sat at the desk in Sa Petita Llibreria. He was putting together a mind map of what he knew and didn't know about the two cases involving Bill

Patterson and Sheila MacDonald. He had learned the mind mapping technique during one of the leadership programmes he had attended at the National Police Training School in Bramshill, deep in the Hampshire countryside, before it had closed and everything had moved to a rather dull, but apparently more cost effective site in the Midlands. Essentially it was a bit like a spidergram, where you put headings down on a blank sheet of paper and then grew links from each heading with something that was connected with the heading. People sometimes did this in a circular fashion, but his thinking was a bit more linear and so he started with a heading at the top left and continued down the page and then wrote the links to the right hand side of each heading. He started in the order he had heard the story, with Bill as a heading, followed by the other headings of IT Scam, then Possible Burglary, Murder of Sheila MacDonald (SM), OCGs and finally 3R.

He was then adding in comments to each of the headings from what he knew when Anna came back in after going to see Alfonso an hour before.

"What are you up to?" said Anna.

"Just figuring out what we know and don't know about what's been going on. I've just about finished with the 'what we know' and I'm starting on the 'what we don't know' bit if you fancy joining in?" said Sam.

She joined him at the desk and they both started coming up with things that they didn't know.

Sam said, "We need to get a lead on who the scammers are. Jimmy did some work but hasn't got very far, although he thinks they may be in India, but it's more a professional guess because we know so many scammers operate from there."

"Has Greg come back with anything yet?"

"No, he hasn't and to be honest Mum, I don't know if he will, after all he's working for John MacDonald and has nothing to do with what happened to Bill," said Sam, who also still wasn't a hundred percent sure how far he could trust this guy.

"I think you just need to ask him Sam," said Anna. "I'm sure if there's any sort of link to Bill, then he'd be happy to tell us how far he has got."

"Well you've got more confidence in him than I have, that's for sure, but hey, there's nothing to lose is there," said Sam, "but first, look it's four o'clock and time for tea and then I'll call Greg."

Despite all her years in Spain and Mallorca, he knew one thing his mother still very much enjoyed and indeed had persuaded her many Spanish and Mallorquin friends to enjoy as well.

"Tea and almond cake it is then," said his mother.

*****

Greg got the call back from Chris MacDonald quicker than he expected.

"Greg, we've found a credit card payment from last week. Dad knows nothing about it. It's for €899 and payable to the company you mentioned, Intertech. So what does that mean? Was she scammed?"

"Yes, it looks like that Chris," said Greg "and there's a strong possibility the scammers sold your mum's details to an OCG, I mean an organised crime gang, who are probably responsible for what happened to your mum."

"Bloody hell, the bastards!" said Chris. "What do we do next Greg?" He paused, "You know Dad is after blood," he added quietly.

"Yes, I know, but we're a long way from anything like that at the moment. It's going to take some tracking down to find this Intertech. They usually hide behind a multitude of shell companies, but we may have better luck with the OCG, so I'm going to hook back into the London cop and of course Lori Garcia."

"Okay," said Chris. "Dad says you're coming for dinner around 7.30. I've booked a table down at the terrace and I hear Terri is on the island and is joining us?"

"Yes, she is, we'll see you later," said Greg who knew Chris had a bit of a soft spot for his daughter. He was slightly older than her and had been through a messy divorce, caused primarily by him never being at home as he was forever travelling around the world for Trent MacDonald. Then again, Terri was also always travelling, so maybe they might be a good match?

Greg then sent a text to Lori Garcia and Sam Martínez. *'Confirmed, SM made a CC payment to Intertech for €899'*. Almost immediately Sam pinged him back, *'When can we meet?'* which was quickly followed by an incoming call from Garcia.

"When was the payment made?" said Garcia.

No hello or pleasantries thought Greg. She must be getting a lot of flak from her bosses. Whilst he didn't always link up quite so much with law enforcement agencies, he recognised she was a good cop and would probably be happy to mutually cooperate with him, especially as he was the one who had brought two massive leads to the table.

"Last week, Tuesday to be precise, so five days before the attack on her villa. When were the other burglaries you mentioned, in relation to the scams?" asked Greg.

"Similar. The burglaries were between five and seven days after the scam. Look, I'm really grateful for your help Señor Chambers," Garcia paused.

"Please call me Greg and before you go on Inspectora, I do understand you will want me to go through you and not to undermine anything you may be doing in your investigation."

"Okay, Greg it is and you can call me Lori, except perhaps when I am with my team. Then it may not be appropriate, is that alright with you?"

"Yes of course Lori, thank you. Listen, I am meeting the MacDonalds tonight at 7.30, do you have time now to perhaps meet up for a quick exchange of ideas. Happy to do that at the station or if it's more convenient and you can book off duty, maybe we could do it over a glass of wine?" said Greg.

She looked at her watch. It was just coming up to five.

"I like the second idea better. Can you be at Bar 13%, it's a little wine bar on Carrer de Sant Feliu for 5.30?" said Garcia.

"Yes, look forward to it," said Greg.

He then turned and looked at Terri who had been checking messages on the 3R jobs she was managing.

"Can I drop you back at your place and I'll come back and see Lori?" said Greg.

"Lori now is it? So is this a date or an intel meeting?"

She was teasing him, so he just looked at her shaking his head. After dropping her back in Portixol, he made his way back through the traffic. Much of it was leaving the city as workers made their way home, so it didn't take him long to get back to the main underground carpark by La Seu. He then made his way past Passeig de Born and up through the side alley to 13%, the small wine bar where she said to meet him.

It was still really hot, so it was a bit of a relief to get inside and out of the sun. At 5.30 he saw the door open and he didn't recognise her first of all. She hadn't changed and so was still in a business style blue jacket and trousers, but she had let her hair down and was wearing big, fashionable sunglasses and looked a lot less detective and much more woman. She walked confidently up to him and he stood up to greet her.

"Ah, such the English gentleman Greg," she smiled.

He smiled back, not too sure what to say, something which puzzled him as he wasn't usually short of a word when he needed it.

"I'm sorry if this isn't appropriate Lori, but you look amazing."

"Ah, the dilemma of keeping business from pleasure Greg, but thank you, that's nice of you to say. So, what shall we drink? A rosado I think?" said Lori, signalling to the waiter and then ordering two large glasses of local Mallorquin vino rosado.

He had arranged to see her to talk through the case. That had been the main but not the only reason. Ever since they had met he had wanted to spend time with her to find out more about her. He hadn't been in any sort of a relationship for some while now and other than the odd date here and there, he had realised he had got out of the habit of wanting to spend time with someone, other than for work, so this felt good. He knew he still needed to focus on the case. John wanted results and so did he too. He would find those responsible and make sure they paid for murdering someone he cared a lot for, but for now, on a sunny Mallorquin evening, it was good to just sit, talk and drink some very nice wine with an attractive woman.

They talked about who they were and their backgrounds. Lori also seemed in no rush to talk about the case. He knew she was probably under pressure to get results, so taking a moment to kick back and relax was probably something she hadn't done in a while either. She looked relaxed and animated as she talked and he found himself just looking at her. So when she stopped, it took him by surprise.

"Greg, where are you? Have you been listening?" she smiled.

"Yes, yes, I'm sorry, I was listening honestly, but you've got me," he paused then said, "distracted".

She smiled again. She knew she didn't need to ask him what was distracting him. She was old enough and wise enough to know when a man is looking at you as a woman and not as a detective. She certainly didn't mind that. It had been a tough three or four weeks on the island working on these cases and not really getting anywhere. So, to talk about something else and with someone who, yes, she was attracted to, was a nice thing to do, even if nothing came of it. She lived across on the mainland and he seemed to work all across the world, so anything permanent was unlikely, but she hadn't felt like this for a while, so why not enjoy it?

What he liked was that she was very easy to be with and to talk to. Occasionally their hands briefly touched, as they were both 'hand wavers' as they talked. To start with there was the usual slight embarrassed apology, in case one of them had been too forward, but that soon slipped away and gradually they came together and he found himself taking hold of one of her hands as they talked and she responded by closing her fingers around his.

"I wasn't thinking this would be like this," said Lori. "Hmm, I confess I'm slightly confused, but in a good way."

"Yes, strange for me too," said Greg, "and in a good way, a very good way. And I don't see a problem with this Lori, if you don't? After all, we're on the same side and we're already collaborating on the case."

"I don't see a problem either, but I don't know what my bosses might think. Listen, it's pretty obvious I think that we've got an attraction, let's just enjoy it and see where it goes shall we?"

A common sense approach. Just like when she was in her work mode. He liked that.

"That's good for me. Now, I need to go and see the MacDonalds. They're staying at Cap Rocat. Can I call you tomorrow and see where we're at? In the meantime, I'll call Sam Martínez. He seems like a really good guy. Another strange thing Lori, I know his mother from way back when she was in the Foreign and Commonwealth Office," said Greg.

He thought it best to not go into Anna's story as that was something private for her to decide who she told and that clearly had been no one for thirty years or so.

"Cap Rocat? Nice and yes, I like Sam too and he's younger than you," she teased him. "Okay, I'll call you in the morning and then you can take me to dinner tomorrow night."

They parted with a kiss on both cheeks and as he drove back to Terri's apartment he wondered what had just happened with Lori. He certainly hadn't been expecting that when he sat there waiting for her, but he was really glad it had. He then smiled to himself. He knew Terri would get it out of him, probably before they got to the MacDonalds for dinner. But then again, it might just deflect her from asking questions about how he knew Anna, so *'every cloud....,'* he thought to himself.

NINE

Lori walked back towards police headquarters, up Passeig de Born and then left into Jaume III.

She caught herself smiling. She hadn't done that for a while, smile, so it was good to think about something other than work for a moment, but it was time for a quick call into the Intel team to see where they had got to in identifying the image Greg had given her. She called Alberto, the OCG Intel team leader.

"Inspectora, I told you I would call you as soon as I had something," said Alberto.

"I know Alberto, but first thing tomorrow morning I am going to have my boss wanting to know what progress we're making. Now you can either join me on the conference call tomorrow or you can let me handle him. Which is it to be?" said Lori.

"Okay, okay, Señora. I know you're just trying to help keep the wolves away from me, but I can only give you some options at the moment. I think you were right in your original thinking, that the guy looks East European. The tattoo is difficult to get any more from, but it looks from the size and positioning, on the left wrist, that it could be Russian, Ukrainian or maybe even Armenian."

"Why Armenian Alberto? I know we've got some

Russian and Ukrainian OCGs with a strong presence here on the Balearics, but why are you thinking about the Armenians?" said Lori.

"It's just a hunch, mostly based on the fact that the Russians and Ukrainians know to keep a low profile and we haven't had any change in their team players to suggest anything different in the operating style. That leaves the Armenians as a maybe. They are run by a guy called Senichi Sargsyan, known as Sonny. Now he is a very nasty piece of work and so this might just be the sort of thing he might do. But please Inspectora, don't take this as anything more than a professional guess at the moment," said Alberto.

"Alberto, I understand, but I do like your thinking. I know this Sonny Sargsyan and yes, with no new players in the other OCGs, this also suggests no change in their operating style. We know the Armenians have been trying to up their game on the islands, so this could be a new tactic, but how the hell have they got a tie-in with an Indian IT scam? Don't answer that. That's just me talking out loud. Look, it's nearly seven o'clock and time you went home to your family. I'll call you in the morning."

"Muchas Gracias Inspectora Garcia," said Alberto.

He liked working with her. She was firm, but always very fair and she had a very good reputation as a senior detective. She should be higher up the chain he thought, but then again, we need her type operating at this level to catch these guys. She always expected high quality work, but she was always quick to recognise it as well and to make sure you got your share of the credit. Time for home she had said. Tomorrow he would work on checking out the Indian link.

It was too soon, she thought, to tell Greg of the possible link to an Armenian OCG. She needed more on this and quickly, but for now, it was also time to get back to her apartment and put her feet up. The GEO had set her up in a small one bed place close by to the headquarters. It was ideal for work, but also for getting about in the city. She hadn't eaten yet and thought about killing two birds with one stone. She called Sam Martínez.

"Inspectora Garcia, how can I help?" said Sam.

"I've got some updates. Have you eaten yet?" said Lori.

He hadn't eaten and he liked the idea of an opportunity to get an update from her. The text from Chambers had made him think they were absolutely right to move Bill when they did, but he was still a little puzzled that she would take him further into her confidence. He suggested a place to meet just down from Sa Petita Llibreria. Lori had enough time to shower and change before she set off to meet him. The sun was still shining and it was a lovely warm summer evening. She wore a summer dress and had kept her hair down. He was a nice young man and so why shouldn't she dress up a little to meet him. *'He's much too young, but it's not often I get to go out with two nice attractive men in the same day,'* she thought.

An hour later they were sitting at a table. Sam had thought she was an attractive looking woman when he first met her, but seeing her out of her work style clothes and with her hair down made him sit up. *'Maybe I need to text Jimmy with an update?'*

"Inspectora Garcia, it's good to see you," said Sam.

"Sam, please, call me Lori and you're smiling, that's nice to see," she said.

He almost blushed, so came up with an alternative story.

"Yes, despite all the crap that's been happening, what with Bill and now even worse with Sheila MacDonald, I am feeling good. I'd like to try to help Bill get his money back, even if it's just through his credit card company and I'm happy to help if there's anything you might need from me, even if it's a polite *please stay out of my way*," said Sam.

"Well, as you can see from Señor Chambers' text about Intertech, there seems to be a connection, so I think at last that we're now making some progress and to be fair, I need to thank Greg," she corrected herself, "Greg Chambers, for his help in also finding the image of the guy who stole the van."

"That's great news," said Sam, also noticing her slight slip, referring to Chambers as 'Greg'. That's interesting he thought.

"I think you probably appreciate Sam that I wouldn't usually share such information, however, you operate in my line of work and these guys could be running a similar scam in London, so it won't do any harm and it might actually do me some good to get your viewpoint on this."

"I understand and I appreciate your trust. So have you got anywhere with the image?" said Sam.

She told him about the tattoo on the left wrist of the van thief and her intel officer's professional guess on the possibility of the OCG being Armenian. He liked the rationale her intel guy was using. It made sense. Many OCGs kept low profiles in and around their own areas and kept the dirty work reserved for places away from where they were based, but this wasn't necessarily the case if an OCG was looking to extend their business operation.

"By the way, I met your Greg Chambers today," said Sam, "and bizarrely, he knew my mother! I don't know who was more surprised, Greg, my mother or me."

She noted him use the word '*your*' and wondered if he had seen them, but she let him go on.

"To be honest, I wasn't sure if I'd take to him, but

he seems an okay guy. What do you make of him? I'm assuming he's ex-security services of some sort," said Sam.

"Yes, I think you may well be right, said Lori. "I spent some time with Greg late this afternoon and yes, he seems as you say, an okay guy, the very essence of an English gentleman I think."

"An English gentleman? Hmm, I don't know about that Lori. Once a spook, always a spook," said Sam.

"Spook, what do you mean? A spy?" said Lori.

"Yes, sorry, that's what I meant."

"Well Señor MacDonald doesn't seem to be the sort of man to do business with anyone he doesn't rate highly, so I'm assuming that is a good endorsement," said Lori, who decided she should move the topic of conversation off Greg and back to the images. "Anyway, we need to show the images to Señor Patterson, just in case he has seen anyone like that near to his villa before you moved him out to your mother's place."

"Good idea to cross reference things," said Sam. "Never assume and never overlook the obvious. Text book stuff from my Hendon Detective Training School days and probably yours too Lori," said Sam with a smile.

"Yes, when in doubt, look for the evidence and when you have found it, look again and see what you have missed. Professionally it was embarrassing to get two key pieces of evidence from Greg, well one was from his daughter, but it would be worse if I was sitting here now with nothing to go on," said Lori.

"Daughter?" said Sam.

"Yes, his daughter flew in today from Egypt. She's like his Operations Director, ex-army and she seems just as resourceful as her father," said Lori, "because she's the one who came up with the images."

"Daughter huh? Didn't know about her," said Sam

just as the first course arrived at the table. Lori had shown a preference for local Mallorquin wines, which suited him as his father had brought him up to support the local Balearics wine industry. They shared a bottle of Macià Batle1856, a very nice, easy drinking vino tinto and just right to go with their choice of food.

They talked as they ate. It was an easy relaxed conversation. She found him easy to talk to and she told him about her father, who had worked for a small vineyard for many years back on the mainland and so she too liked favouring the smaller wine producers. Sam told her about his parents and why he was back in Mallorca. She understood the pressures of their work, including carrying a firearm, as she was always armed. He also knew the pressure Lori was probably under from a high profile case involving the murder of a wealthy British woman on the island.

"I can imagine you are getting a fair amount of hassle, I mean pressure, from your bosses about the murder?" said Sam.

"Well you'll know what it's like Sam," said Lori. "It was tough enough with the string of burglaries, but now with the murder, they really want a result and I don't blame them. They put me on secondment to the GEO because of these types of cases and I've got a set of highly trained and very tough cops ready to take on these OCG guys. I just need to point them in the right direction. They sent me over here when the first high value burglaries occurred. Always single occupants, usually aged over seventy, high value villas, but other than frightening the victim, which was obviously bad enough, they weren't physically harmed until Señora MacDonald. I think because they were shaken up, none of them made mention of anything to do with a computer scam, although to be fair, they probably still thought it was genuine and it was the last thing on their mind after they were burgled. We've now got my investigators re-contacting the victims of all high value burglaries since January and getting their bank records checked against payments to Intertech. The problem I've got is getting into Intertech. They seem very well protected by a myriad of shadow companies and dead ends, so I can't get near to finding where they operate from and who runs them."

"It's a tough one. I've had my guy back in London run the name through our records and he's hit the same brick wall as well. We need a plan, so let's sleep on it and see what we come up with," said Sam.

She looked at him quizzically and he started to blush again, realising how what he had just suggested could be interpreted.

"Is that an invitation Sam?" she asked him quietly, looking over the rim of her glass into his eyes?

"Er, no, no. And not because I don't find you very attractive, because you are. It's because I didn't mean it like that. I meant we should go our separate ways and then sleep on it," he stammered.

"So you don't want to sleep with me then Sam?" said Lori, still looking at him.

By now, he didn't know where to look, until he looked back at her face and saw her starting to laugh.

"I'm so sorry Sam," she said. "I was only teasing you. Please forgive me."

He started laughing too. She was good fun and he enjoyed her company.

"Listen, do you fancy going for a drink somewhere and maybe rattling some cages?" said Sam.

"I'm sorry Sam, what do you mean 'rattle some cages'?" said Lori.

"Well, you've told me what this guy looks like, East European with a tattoo on his left wrist. Let's go and check out some of the local bars where I know they have doormen from that part of Europe and see if we can't flush something out," said Sam. "No confrontation, just observation and intel gathering".

She thought for a moment.

"I like your 'rattle some cages' idea Sam. Where do you suggest or shall I ring my Intel team for some suggestions?" said Lori.

"I might have worked in London for fifteen years Lori, but I grew up in this city and still know my way around. I might be a bit rusty on who runs what in terms of protection, but I'm sure we'll find a few possibilities to try out," said Sam.

"Okay," said Lori, "let's do it."

*****

Sonny had gone into the city to check on some of the bars and clubs where his team collected their Support Package fees in return for his team ensuring their property came to no harm. Admittedly, the bar and restaurant owners could feel that their clients were safe and that anyone getting unruly or violent towards anyone was quickly dealt with. However, the Support Package also worked the other way and there was sufficient evidence of burnt out properties in this part of the city to show what happened if an owner decided not to pay their 'fees'.

Whilst Sonny was happy that the money he was bringing in from these places was a fair and reasonable return for the investment of his team's time, he was also keen to move to a more upmarket area of the city. This was not going to be easy, because he had to think about who currently ran those sites and there were many who paid nothing because of a strong policing presence in that area, especially around the tourist places.

So part of his visit was to look at whether he could persuade some of the owners to take their own establishments upmarket in terms of trade and clientele. He was even happy to help with favourable loan terms and a reduction on fees to help them get their business off the ground and so far he had received some interest from two owners where he saw some real potential to develop their business.

As he was sitting in the Security Room of one of the bars, Zero Zero, just off the main Ramblas street, he noticed a man and a woman on one of the CCTV cameras. He could see the man's face, but not the woman's. They were talking to one of the doormen, Artur. What struck him was that they didn't look like the usual type of customers who frequented this bar. Sometimes admittedly, they had stag parties and even some tourists strayed off the main streets and into areas they were best off not spending too much time in, but there was something about these two, but he didn't know what it was. They didn't seem to be causing any issue, so he left it to Artur to deal with.

Downstairs in the entrance to the club, Sam and Lori were playing the part of two punters wanting to get into the club. They were both speaking in Spanish and pretending to have a bit of an argument with each other. Sam wanted to attract the doorman to try to get him to lift his left arm, so he could see if he had the same size tattoo as the guy who stole the van. Lori was playing her part well as a passionate and angry woman and he was trying not to laugh at her excellent performance, but the noise she was making was starting to annoy the doorman.

This was the third bar they had tried with East European looking doormen and they'd had no luck so far. Just as Lori looked like she was running out of steam, ranting at Sam about him having been looking at another woman in the last club they had been in, Sam noticed the doorman start to get off his stool. It was still a very warm evening and he looked like he got a kick out of showing off his body, as he was wearing a short sleeved shirt that was just a little small for him, so it exaggerated his muscular body. As he moved, it gave both Sam and Lori the opportunity to look at his left wrist and there it was, a matching tattoo for the van thief. Seeing the doorman move seemed to make the wild Spanish woman calm and Lori started muttering apologies, but blaming her boyfriend for his wandering eyes.

Seeing the woman calm down seemed to settle the doorman and he said in English, "So, are you coming in or not? Ten euros each at the door."

"Si, si, gracias," said Lori and they walked past him into the club entrance.

It was approaching midnight and the club was starting to fill up. They got a drink at the bar and took a walk around the club checking for other security guys. There were two more standing close by and neither looked like the van thief, so they paused and sipped at their drinks.

"I think you enjoyed yourself back there Inspectora," said Sam smiling.

"I haven't had so much fun since I can't remember Sam. You know what that's like Sam, the higher up the ranks you go, the less chance you get to go out and about with the team."

They were standing at the back of the club, looking around the room when she saw three men coming down some stairs.

"I think we've just struck gold," said Lori.

Sam saw Lori looking across at the men who were by then moving through the club towards the entrance.

She had immediately recognised that the man at the front was Sonny Sargsyan, the Armenian OCG boss. She didn't have time to tell Sam, so she just beckoned to him to follow her as she quickly moved to catch the men up. Sonny was waiting at the entrance to the club as the other two men moved towards a black Porsche Cayenne.

"Señor Sargsyan, I didn't know you were involved in this place," said Lori.

The two men stopped what they were doing and started to move back towards Lori and Sam before Sonny motioned to them to stop.

"Inspectora Garcia. What a pleasure to see you," said Sonny, immediately realising she had been the woman he saw in the CCTV cameras.

Lori tried not to show that she was the one taken aback, but he had seen her reaction, even if it was only a brief flicker of her eyes.

"What? You didn't think I would know the GEO had someone on the island? Come Inspectora, or can I call you Lori? We knew you were here from the moment you set foot on the island. So have you been getting anywhere with these dreadful crimes, especially the murder of that poor British woman? Who would do such a thing?"

She saw he was smiling. The bastard was trying to get a reaction from her and he was doing a pretty good job as she struggled to maintain her composure. Sam didn't know who this guy was, but assumed he must be linked to the Armenian OCG. Was this the boss? He was certainly full of himself and was enjoying goading Lori, who Sam could see was having a hard time not reacting, but then he saw her eyes narrow as she stood right in front of Sonny.

"Yes, indeed Sonny, who would do such a thing?" said Lori who, without warning grabbed Sonny's wrist and turned it over to show the same shaped tattoo she had now seen on both the van thief and the doorman.

Sonny went as though to strike Lori. Sam stepped

forward, but Sonny stopped as Lori quickly released the wrist.

"Never touch me again woman," said Sonny who was the one this time struggling to hold his anger in.

"Can't promise that Sonny. I got what I wanted. It was the tattoo. Your guy who stole the van. We got a picture of him and his tattoo, so know this. I am coming for you and so the next time I touch you it will be to put handcuffs on you, got it?" said Lori.

'Bloody hell,' thought Sam. *'She's fearless. He's an OCG boss and she's fronting him out and in one of his bars!'*

Sonny tried to show that he wasn't rattled, but it was pretty obvious to everyone and there was a bit of a crowd gathering now as people had turned up to get into the club and were seeing this little side show for free.

"I've no idea what you are talking about Inspectora, but I wish you and your boyfriend a very good and safe night." He turned and looked at Sam. "I'm sure we will meet again, whoever you are."

Sam stared back. He had the advantage, at least for the moment, so better to 'rattle the cage' one last time before withdrawing.

"No need to go looking mate. My name's Sam Martínez. I'm also a cop, but from London and I can guarantee you'll be seeing me again," said Sam.

Sonny was seething. But they were two cops and there was a crowd. This was not the time, so he tried to laugh things off as he walked towards the Porsche.

"I look forward to seeing you again Señor and Señora, but perhaps next time without a crowd to give you some, what do you call it in London? Dutch courage?" said Sonny as he slammed the car door and the driver sounded the horn to clear a path as the car moved away.

They looked at each other. Sam spoke first.

"Well, I think we definitely rattled his cage."

Lori had gone quiet.

"Are you okay Lori?" said Sam.

"Si, si. He's the one Sam. I saw it in his eyes. He has evil running through him, he makes my skin crawl," said Lori.

He saw she was shivering. It was still warm, maybe in the mid-twenties, but the guy really had made her skin crawl, so he put his arm around her and she moved into his body for warmth.

"And look at me, being escorted down the street by a very handsome young man. The end to a perfect night," said Lori with a smile returning to her face.

Sam heard the word *'end'* and gathered that Lori cuddling up to him was as far as she saw this night going. He wasn't sure why he was even thinking like this. He didn't think he was ready for any sort of a relationship yet, even if she had been interested in him and he certainly hadn't thought of the two of them in any sort of romantic way. He smiled. He did really like her. She was full of fun, passionate about her work, very attractive and he had really enjoyed the evening in her company. Maybe things were changing for him. *'Good luck to whoever captures your heart Lori Garcia,'* he thought to himself.

"Okay, I might be being over-protective here, but can I walk you back to your apartment?" said Sam.

"That's really kind of you Sam, but there's no need," said Lori, just as a car pulled up alongside them and the passenger door opened. "We've had some backup looking after us tonight and this one is going to make sure I get home safely."

"I like your style Señora Garcia. Bona nit," said Sam reverting to Mallorquin to say 'Goodnight'.

"Yes, good night and we will speak tomorrow," said Lori and kissed him on both cheeks.

TEN

As the Porsche sped away from the Club, Sonny was drumming his fingers on the arm rest.

He'd have the head of that bloody idiot, Gevorg, who had stolen the van and why the hell was a London cop in Mallorca and working with the GEO? That wasn't something he would want Sergei to find out about. He needed more than ever to find Sergei's grass and see to it that he had an unfortunate accident. He tapped Alex, who was sitting in the front passenger seat, on the shoulder.

"Bring Gevorg to me tonight. I'll be down by the boat," said Sonny.

Alex looked at the driver. They knew Sonny well enough to know what a late night trip out on the boat meant for Gevorg. They drove on to Sonny's villa, a large six bedroomed place with gardens running down to the waterfront and a jetty, alongside which was moored a sixty foot Sunseeker Predator.

As Sonny got out of the car at the front door to the villa he said, "Don't take too long and if he kicks up, hurt him."

Gevorg didn't want to come quietly. Any audience with Sonny was something to usually be wary of, but being told to see him after midnight was not the sort of news he wanted to hear. As he started to back away from Alex, the Porsche driver stepped up behind and pistol whipped him with his Glock. They bundled him in the back of the Porsche and ten minutes later they were ushering him at gunpoint towards the boat where Sonny was sitting on deck with a drink in his hand.

"Guys, guys, there's no need for that. Gevorg, I'm so sorry, I only want a chat about future possibilities. I think the guys got the wrong end of what I was saying when I said to go and pick you up. Guys, I'll deal with you later," said Sonny.

They all knew it was a charade, even Gevorg. They'd taken his gun off him, so there wasn't much point in trying anything. He just hoped that whatever he'd done and he didn't know he had done anything wrong, Sonny would make it quick.

Sonny did make it quick. He liked Gevorg, but it was obvious that Garcia had something on Gevorg and so it was far better to get rid of the very thing she would be looking for and hope it blocked her progress. He couldn't even just transfer him to another part of the business because then Sergei would find out and ask too many awkward questions. He even apologised to Gevorg. It really wasn't personal and yes, it would be quick, which was him being, well, kind. He killed Gevorg with a single bullet to the head using a suppressor so as not to wake the neighbours. Then as Sonny stepped off the boat and walked back up the gardens towards the villa, Alex and the Porsche driver eased the Sunseeker away from the jetty and out towards the bay. Just past the tide line should be far enough thought Alex, far enough that the body wouldn't float back in with the current.

*****

Terri had driven in her open top Merc. She said she wasn't turning up for dinner with the MacDonalds at Cap Rocat in a white van. It hadn't taken them long as she had driven fast for the five miles or so it was to the hotel from Portixol. She looked stunning in a summer evening dress as she stepped out of the car. Chris was waiting for them at the main entrance and Greg thought Chris's eyes were going to pop out of his head when he saw her.

She could always light up a room and it was good that she was going to be able to bring a moment of relief to John and his boys after the tragedy of losing Sheila. John as always, was business-like and kept his emotions in check, well almost anyway. The boys weren't faring so well. Losing your mother was bad enough, but the manner in which she had died had hit them hard. Jack, the younger son was withdrawn, definitely not himself and Terri soon noticed this and spent time with him, gently talking to him and bringing him back into the conversation. Chris wanted to know the minutiae of what was happening, whereas John operated at a higher strategic level and so was more interested in the overarching plan. Greg did his best to satisfy all of their questions before they eventually sat down to eat. Terri then took over and made sure the conversation flowed, to keep the boys talking. John saw what she was doing and turned and spoke quietly to Greg.

"She's a lovely girl Greg and she's done a great job taking their minds off their mother tonight. I still can't believe Sheila's gone, so thank you from the bottom of my heart for what you're doing and please ask me for anything you might need to help you, whether that's money, transport, expertise or whatever," said John.

Greg had known John MacDonald a long time now and knew he was never given to showing any great signs of emotion, so seeing him like this was difficult. He was taking it very hard, which was only to be expected, but it was making Greg think about what John's expectations were. As it stood, it seemed pretty clear that if John had the killer in front of him right at this moment, then there was a good chance he would kill him with his bare hands if he could.

John was an old school East Ender and vengeance was *'an eye for an eye'*. Greg had, on rare occasions, had to resort to what he referred to as a permanent resolution to deal with a problem confronting his clients, including Trent MacDonald. He was therefore prepared to fight fire with fire if things came to it. However, he was also very aware that Lori Garcia, on the other hand, would follow police protocols to bring the killer before a court and this might cause a conflict of expectations. This was something that was best not discussed now, but he might have to resolve this at a later time.

They left at around midnight with a plan to see everyone back at the villa tomorrow as the police should have finished their crime scene investigation by then. It was a beautiful clear night and he felt the warmth in the air as Terri drove them back to her apartment. They had just turned into the underground carpark when his phone buzzed with a text. It was Lori. *'Met up with Sam Martínez tonight and we rattled some cages. Found Armenians with same tattoo. Speak tomorrow'*.

"What's that Dad?" said Terri.

"It's Lori, she's been rattling cages apparently with Sam Martínez," said Greg.

"She's two timing you then Dad!" said Terri in mock shock. "Rattling cages doesn't sound very Spanish."

He ignored her attempt to get him to bite with the *'two timing'* comment, although he did feel something of a slight pang of, what, jealousy? Maybe envy? *'Good God'*, he thought, *'I've only been out for a drink with her and I'm behaving like a fifteen year old.'* So he focused on the *'rattling cages'*.

"Yes, I wonder whose cages they've been rattling?" said Greg.

"Well she's only just texted you, just call her. You can tell her you're missing her too."

"Will you just stop on this 'setting me up for a romance' with every woman I meet," said Greg, "Or do I need to start on how Chris had his tongue hanging out all night and you let him drool all over you?"

"No, sorry Dad. Doesn't work on me," she smiled. "The thing is, I know he was drooling, but hey, he needed to think about something other than his poor old mom. So are you going to ring her or what?"

He gave in and called her. Lori saw his name come up on her mobile and picked it up and then stopped. *'Easy girl. Don't be too quick to answer. Don't want him thinking you were hanging around in your bedroom hoping he might call,'* she thought, smiling to herself as she then picked up his call.

"Greg, I hope I didn't wake you or were you still with Señor MacDonald?" said Lori.

"No, you didn't wake me, we're just on our way back to Terri's place." Terri motioned a wave. "She says *'Hi'* by the way and is looking forward to meeting you. So whose cage have you rattled?" said Greg.

"Well tell her that I'm also looking forward to meeting her, maybe tomorrow? Yes, so young Señor Martínez took me around some of the more dubious clubs of the city after I had dinner with him."

"Dinner and then nightclubbing? I leave you alone for two seconds and already I am your second choice, presumably because he's younger than me?" he teased.

"Well definitely younger, but not maybe as handsome." *'What am I doing?'* thought Lori, *'Concentrate!'*

Terri looked sideways at her dad. She hadn't heard what Lori had said, but whatever it was had made him smile. *'We're in the middle of a murder investigation and my dad is smitten in love. Ha!*' she thought, *'Good for him.'*

"Well I'm pleased I scored on at least one of the points. So whilst you were out on the town with your young man," he felt more assured now having heard her response, "how did you manage to ID someone with the same tattoo?"

"I haven't had so much fun in quite a while. We were trying to get a response from the doormen, to get a look at their left wrists, to see if the tattoo was some sort of sign about being a gang member and we got a success at the third club. Same tattoo and the guy was Armenian. That wasn't all, but who should I see coming out the back offices but the boss of the OCG, Senichi Sargsyan. He's known as Sonny. We had a bit of an exchange and I think I got to him as he wasn't happy when he left," said Lori.

"Bloody hell, I hope you were careful Lori? You know as well as I do, these guys don't mess about, even when it comes to cops," said Greg.

She went quiet and he thought he might have offended her. Did he sound too over protective or even patronising? Christ, she was an experienced OCG cop who didn't need him telling her to be careful.

"Lori? I'm sorry, I didn't mean to be patronising or over protective, I'm sure you had it covered."

"It's okay Greg," she said quietly, "I do know what they are like. My husband was a cop and he was murdered by an OCG back when our boys were just little kids."

He paused, "I'm so sorry," said Greg.

"Look, can your daughter drop you off at my apartment? I could do with some company tonight," said Lori, adding softly, "just company."

"Yes of course, I'll be about 5 minutes or so."

She told him the address and he asked Terri to head

for the city and explained on the way.

"Talk about putting your foot in it," he said.

"Dad, you didn't know. Don't beat yourself up. You had one drink with her and she isn't necessarily going to blurt out her entire life story, but she clearly thinks enough about you to ask you to go and keep her company," she winked at him as she spoke.

"You are incorrigible Theresa Anderson," he said, "I'm far too much of a gentleman to take advantage of a woman in need."

As she dropped him off at Lori's apartment block, Terri leant across and gave him a kiss on the cheek.

"Love you Dad," she said quietly.

"Love you too my lovely girl," said Greg.

*****

Lori let him in and stood for a moment. She had been crying. He held out his arms and she fell into them.

"Thank you for coming," said Lori. "I was fine when I got back here. I'd had a great evening. First with you and then Sam, who is really good fun, but I think it was being away from home for the last few weeks and then just thinking through what that thug Sargsyan had said to me. It brought it all back, about my husband I mean. It's so long ago, but it's like yesterday. They killed him outside our home." She went quiet. "I just needed to have someone close by me tonight".

He slept alongside her, holding her gently in his arms. She had changed for bed and wore a white cotton summer nightdress and she looked wonderful. Her breathing was fast and uneven to start with. He stroked her hair and back of her neck and gradually he heard her breathing become more relaxed as she moved into a deep and relaxed sleep. It was hot in her room and there was no air conditioning either, so he had taken his shirt and trousers off before getting into bed with her, but Lori hadn't reacted, presumably

131

because it was warm and he hoped more so, because she trusted him. He thought about what had happened during the day. He had only been here for just over twenty four hours. He was making some good progress on the case and he had met two beautiful women. Anna, from thirty years ago and Lori today and here he was now in bed with one of them, albeit in a caring role. He smiled, *'the very essence of an English gentleman'.*

Lori woke before he did and it took her a moment to remember what had happened and why Greg was in her bed. Then she smiled and looked at him. He hadn't hesitated when she asked him to come, even knowing that it was because she was thinking of her husband and didn't want to be alone. She felt better this morning. The grief came over her every now and then, but for most of the time, she could control the pain of what had happened. She had been a police officer too at the time, a patrol officer, as the shifts made it easier for her to look after their two boys who were six and eight then. Afterwards, she took time off to look after the children fulltime before she made the decision ten years ago to become a detective and to take on the OCGs that had murdered the father of her children.

She was now held in high regard within her team and her reputation had helped secure this current secondment to the GEO, tasked with disrupting OCG activity across the Balearics.

She slipped out of bed and went to the kitchen and made coffee, bringing it back in to the bedroom. She leant over Greg and kissed him on the lips, waking him.

"Good morning Señor Chambers."

"Good morning Inspectora Garcia."

"Thank you," she said quietly. "You were a perfect English gentleman".

He just squeezed her hand and smiled. Now was not the time to pull her back into bed and make love to her.

That was what he wanted to do, but it wasn't perhaps what a *'perfect English gentleman'* would do.

"Why are you smiling?" said Lori.

"I'm thinking about what someone, who wasn't a *'perfect English gentleman'* would do," said Greg.

She looked at him coyly.

"Señor Chambers, I am shocked that you would think of taking advantage of a woman."

"But Lori, I was only thinking about what that other person would do. Remember, I am a perfect English gentleman," said Greg, smiling, as he leaned up, took hold of her hands and kissed her gently on the lips.

She didn't know if she was pleased or disappointed that he didn't do or say anything more after kissing her. She thought for a moment and decided she was pleased. She didn't want to rush into anything, but she got the feeling he liked her as much as she liked him. She hadn't really had anything she could call a relationship since her husband had died, despite her boys telling her to get back on the dating trail, so why was this different? She pulled away from him, slowly letting go of his hands.

"Okay, I'll shower first and then make some breakfast. Then we must work," said Lori.

"Yes, Inspectora!" He grinned. "I think we're going to have a busy day".

ELEVEN

Sonny looked at the latest data to come in from Intertech. There were some good options, particularly around the south and east of the City.

He picked two and passed them across the table to Arman.

"Get these looked at and come back with a recommendation. If the police are getting a bit too interested, then we should give them something else to think about."

"Okay boss," said Arman and paused.

"What's up?" said Sonny.

"I'm just thinking Boss, after last night and that Garcia woman, are you sure it's a good idea to hit another place? Wouldn't it be better to let things die down a bit?"

Sonny looked at Arman, who immediately regretted offering his advice. Sonny was a dangerous man to cross, but he had only been trying to help.

"Thank you Arman, but if I want your advice, I will ask for it," said Sonny.

As he admonished him, Sonny was reflecting that perhaps killing the MacDonald woman had not been one of his best decisions. It wasn't the fact that he had killed her. He had seen and been a part of too much killing in his life to be bothered about taking another life, but it was now causing him an unnecessary distraction.

Two things were niggling him. The first was Sergei. He had never known him to pull him up in front of the rest of the team before. That was embarrassing, but also a concern. As much of a friend as Sergei was, even though he was his boss, he knew Sergei was completely ruthless when it came to running his organisation. He had taken out one of his cousins only a month or so ago, when he suspected the cousin was skimming a little too much off the bottom line. So despite them being so close for twenty or more years, he knew Sergei wouldn't hesitate, well true, he might hesitate, but not for long, in deciding to replace Sonny and 'replace' in his world was pretty permanent.

The second thing was the police. That Garcia woman from the GEO, the one who was looking at the MacDonald murder. One of his informants in the local police was saying she was like a dog with a bone and after meeting her last night, it looked like she wasn't going to let go quickly. He looked back at Arman, he saw him flinch perhaps expecting a backlash from Sonny, *'but maybe,'* thought Sonny, *'maybe, he has a point.'*

"On reflection my friend, you may have a point, so thank you for your advice. Still check out those two targets, but we'll make a decision when we see how things are going," said Sonny.

Arman flushed with pride. For Sonny to come back to him and thank him was a big deal. He still needed to mind his step, Sonny could call you his friend and still either kill you or give you a hug and a bonus. He was working hard to move himself up the organisation and if Sonny was willing to backtrack on what he had originally said to him, then he may have done himself some good in going up in Sonny's estimation.

"Thanks Boss, just trying to help", but by this

time Sonny was already walking out the door, leaving Arman to wipe a small bead of perspiration away from his forehead that he felt appearing when Sonny first 'thanked' him.

Sonny had gone to find Alex and he found him looking over the deployments for the evening, now that he was one man down.

"I need you to find out why we have a London cop on the island working with Garcia," said Sonny.

"Okay Boss. It was Sam Martínez wasn't it? Maybe he's half Spanish and back to see his family or something?" said Alex.

"That's a fair point, but why the hell is he then going around nightclubs with Garcia? Did he look like her boyfriend? It looked more to me like they were putting on a show with the doorman, as though they were looking for something or someone," said Sonny.

"I don't know Boss, but I'll get on it," said Alex.

"Find me later Alex. This is important," said Sonny.

Alex knew his boss well enough to know that urgent meant urgent and he would need answers by later today.

*****

They were sitting at the breakfast table.

"I think it's time I went home Anna," said Bill Patterson, "before I outstay my welcome."

"Don't be silly Bill, you'll never do that, but I do understand. It's always nice to be in our own place and our own bed," said Anna, "but I think we should check with Sam and the police first don't you?"

Sam walked into the room saying, "Check with Sam about what?"

"Whether you will release me on bail and let me go home officer?" said Bill.

"Well you have been on good behaviour, so I suppose that counts for something," said Sam, joining in the spirit of the conversation, before adding, "I was thinking a week to be on the safe side Bill. I know nothing further has happened in the last few days, but we shook a couple of cages last night, me and DI Garcia and so I'd rather you didn't go home today. Is that okay?"

"Shook some cages huh? Did you get anywhere? And before you answer, yes, I'll stay, I just don't want to be a burden," said Bill.

Anna sensed he probably didn't want to go home just yet anyway, so smoothed things over saying, "Well that's good, because I've already got tonight's dinner sorted. Now what exactly do you mean, you 'shook some cages' Sam? I hope that doesn't mean you were doing anything dangerous?"

Sam looked at his mother and shook his head. It still slightly exasperated him that she looked upon him as a young boy and not an experienced London major crime cop used to tackling organised crime gangs, but he smiled.

"I know, I'm just an interfering mother who worries too much," said Anna.

He gave her a hug.

"No, it's nice to have someone worry about me, but please don't worry too much, okay?" said Sam. "But to answer your question, I was out last night with DI Garcia and we think we got somewhere in identifying at least the group who may be responsible for Sheila's murder and so they may be tied up somehow with the people who scammed you Bill."

"Well that's bloody good progress in just a few days," said Bill.

"Yes, it is and Mum, we have Greg to thank for two very significant finds, including one by his daughter. Did you know he had a daughter?"

"No, but then again it was a long time ago Sam. So go on, what are you looking at?"

"Well it seems that Sheila was also a victim of an Intertech scam, so that's why it's still a good idea you remain here Bill, just for a few days more," said Sam.

"Well I certainly won't argue with that point," said Bill.

"And then Greg's daughter has managed to find an image of the guy who stole the van that was involved in the burglary. Now obviously guys, this is confidential and we can't go spreading this around, but it helps make the point as to why you should continue to stay here Bill," said Sam.

Anna took it all in. Greg had only been on the island a day or so and had managed to get two great breaks for the police. She knew he would be good when she recruited him and it looked like he hadn't lost any of his old skills.

*****

Just at that moment, Greg was finishing off breakfast with Lori. They hadn't stopped talking since they had woken up. He felt good, really good and better than he had for a long time if he was honest. It was all right working your butt off 24/7 but what was the point if you didn't have anyone to share it with. Yes, he had Terri, but he didn't want to be an anchor around her neck as she should be out finding herself someone too. She kept her love life close to her chest, so he had no idea if she was seeing anyone, but he did worry he was asking too much of her and that she might be missing out if she was too engrossed in 3R and not looking after herself.

He suggested to Lori that it may be more appropriate if she went into work and he met up with her later. She agreed, in part she said, because she thought she might not be able to stop smiling and people might get a bit suspicious.

"So are you a grumpy boss then?" he teased.

"No, but I work with a team of very good detectives and one of them will surely spot something and make two plus two equal five, when we haven't got past three," she paused and whispered in his ear, "yet," and then kissed his cheek.

"Okay, I like your thinking. In the meantime, can the MacDonalds get back into their villa this morning?" said Greg.

"Yes, of course." She had just checked her emails and there was one there from her CSI, the crime scene investigator. "They've got some prints, but because there's nothing around the point of entries, she thinks the offenders wiped it clean and so they are probably either Señora MacDonald's or her husband's," said Lori.

"Well good news anyway that they can get back into their place. Hopefully that might settle John. He's very wound up at the moment. Only to be expected I know, but I don't want him stressing too much as his heart is a bit dodgy at the best of times. I'm also going to have a catch up with your other man, the 'younger' one," said Greg.

"Oh good. Give him my love," she teased him back. "Now come on, let's go before I'm late," and she picked up her keys, grabbed her sunglasses and headed out of the apartment and into the bright morning sunshine.

*****

Greg checked his watch. It was just past 8.00, so he rang Terri.

"Hi Dad, everything okay?"

"Yes, Lori just needed company and yes, before you ask, I do like her and we're going for dinner tonight," said Greg.

"Good plan. A lady likes to be wooed. So what's the plan for today? Shall I pick you up to grab a change of clothes?" said Terri.

"Please. I'll be at the junction by the police HQ," said

Greg.

"Ten minutes, depending on traffic."

She took seven and he jumped in the Merc and they talked as she re-joined the morning commuter traffic going out of the city. She filled him in on a couple of key jobs, the one in Egypt she had left to come and help him in Mallorca and another one in London. "I've got some calls to make to check these are going okay, but otherwise I'm free for whatever you need me for," she said, before branching off right into Portixol and then leaving the car outside her appartment in a free parking space zone.

"If that's Tommy doing the job in London, can you get him out as soon as you can? I think we're going to need some back up," said Greg.

"I'll get it sorted. We're almost done with the London thing, so he can bring Simon as well." They carried on talking as they walked into her apartment. "You mentioned to the MacDonalds about seeing them at the villa today? What time are you thinking?"

"They can get in this morning. Can you ring Chris whilst I'm in the shower? Tell him we'll be across to update them, probably sometime this afternoon. I want to try to do lunch with Anna today if I can. She was a big part of me getting into the Service, so I want to make time for her for a catch up," said Greg.

"I'm on it," said Terri.

*****

Jaz Kaur boarded the 08.50 British Airways flight from Chhatrapati Shivaji, Mumbai and turned left as she boarded and took her seat in Business Class on the Boeing 787, before settling down with a glass of champagne. It took just under ten hours to get to London Heathrow, where she would then spend a couple of hours in the Airport stores and the BA Lounge before her next flight on to Palma.

She was looking forward to a restful few days holiday, as well as seeing Sonny again. He was definitely a bit of a rough diamond, but he could also be remarkably gentle and caring, especially when they made love. She liked that about him and yes, it was a surprise, given the way she heard him sometimes talk to his people. He ruled by pure power with the threat of punishment always sitting very close to the surface. This was so far removed from her style of managing people, but then she was overseeing a team of IT scammers and not, well, how best to describe them? A bunch of hardened thugs was the best description she could come up with. They all looked like ex-soldiers of some sort and even Ekam, who was sitting back in Economy, was wary of them.

*****

Greg felt refreshed after his shower. Terri had got through to Chris MacDonald and he'd said his father was pleased they could move out of the hotel and get back to the villa.

"I said we'd see them there around mid-afternoon. I kept it loose and he's cool with that," said Terri. "I spoke to Asim and he's got Egypt well in hand. I'm thinking of making him Regional Manager as he's doing so well out there."

"It's your call, but it sounds like a good choice to me," said Greg. She knew what she was doing, but he also knew that sometimes she wanted to keep him in the loop, mostly he thought, so that he didn't feel left out. "What about Tommy?"

"Yep, all good. He's booked on the 12.55 out of LHR and he's bringing Simon. Tommy's happy their job is almost done, so they're okay leaving it to James. He's new to us as you know, but already I can see he's going to be a very useful addition to the team. Now I've booked a four bed finca a little way out of the city, so Tommy and

Simon can stay there. There's a chance we may need to decamp there if things get a bit messy with this and it'll be ideal anyway for us to use as an out of town base."

"Great. Next question, these guys are going to be carrying, so can we access anything out here?" He was talking about weapons. Transporting firearms on commercial planes was almost impossible now and a good job too he thought, because if it was hard for him, then it was just as hard for criminals and terrorists.

"I haven't shown you my addition to the flat have I?" said Terri.

He looked quizzically at her and she led him through into her bedroom. She had built in cupboards which he had seen before, but after she opened both the doors, she reached through to the back and motioned for him to see what she was doing.

"So I got Tommy to come across and do some of his handy work. You'd better know how to access this, just in case I'm not here, so it's a concealed button just down here and hey presto!"

She touched the button and he heard a gentle swish of some hydraulics kicking into action and the back of the cupboard opened up to reveal a space where he could see racks filled with rows of different firearms.

"I thought four of each would probably be enough and it took me long enough to get each one of these out here," said Terri.

"Terri, this is fantastic and a great bit of handy work by Tommy. I'm impressed. So that was why you kept coming out for weekends last year? What did you do? Bring them in one by one?"

"Pretty much. I had to take a whole different bunch of routes and I used that ex-RAF guy, Daniel, the one who has helped us before. He's the private charter bloke who owns his own plane? Well the bank actually owns most of it, but anyway, he's put in some very discreet hideaway compartments, especially for us, to help with transporting certain items we might not want to be found by any Customs guys," said Terri.

"Small army comes to my mind," said Greg smiling as he looked at the array of weapons before him, "you are as resourceful as ever."

"Glad you like it," said Terri.

He cast his eyes over the firearms power she had gathered together. It was pretty impressive. There were Glock 17s, Tasers and SIG MCX 5.56 carbines with 30 round box magazines. This was the sort of stuff the Counter Terrorism guys were using in London. Top rate kit. Four of each and she also had one rifle, which he pointed at.

"Australian Sniper's special. I did some work with it in Afghan," said Terri.

"Bloody hell Terri. Dare I ask if you've had cause to use it yet with 3R?" said Greg.

"Nope, but I've kept my eye in with a ton of practice. The tele-sight I've got for it is great for long distance vision though, so I've used that on some of our jobs. I'm talking up to a mile Dad, it's bloody brilliant," said Terri.

"Impressive."

He had to remember sometimes that his beautiful and very caring and loving daughter was also a very highly trained ex-combat soldier, who had seen active service and action during her time in the Army.

He knew she had killed people in combat situations, as she had spoken to him about it and also how he'd dealt with coming down after enemy engagement. He had been pleased that she had come to him, as he felt he had done a pretty good job over the years in building a loving and trusting relationship with her. He didn't necessarily have all the answers about dealing with the pressure that came with active combat, but he certainly knew that talking about it had helped him, so if she was willing to talk to him, then that was good.

"So what's your thinking for today?" said Terri.

"I got the full story of Lori and Sam having their little chat with the local Armenian OCG guy. So if I was him, I think I'd be either deciding to lay low for a while or to show some muscle. I don't get the impression that these guys are in any way scared of the police, even the GEO, so I want to chew this over with Sam and get his viewpoint," said Greg.

"You like him don't you?"

"Yes, he's a good lad. Maybe you could take him out for dinner and get some more of his story, especially what he is doing out here in Mallorca and not back in London, as it's pretty clear he's not out here on holiday," said Greg.

"Good for me, he's a pretty good looking guy and I don't want to be the only one not having some fun."

Greg went to say something, but she was teasing him again, so he stopped himself and just looked at her.

"What?" she said. She then picked up the car keys, "Are we ready? Can't wait to meet the mysterious Sam."

TWELVE

S he had decided this was another day for the Merc rather than his preferred little white van.

Ten minutes later Terri had parked in the multi-storey carpark by the Teatre Principal and they were walking towards the Sa Petita Llibreria.

Anna and Sam were sat at the front counter as they walked in.

"Anna, Sam, this is my daughter Terri," said Greg.

"I've been so looking forward to meeting you Terri," said Anna. "Let's get some chairs and sort some coffee out."

Introductions over, Sam got the coffee on and brought some extra chairs from the back and they sat down around the desk. He'd been taken aback meeting Terri. Tall, blonde and Australian. He hadn't been expecting her to be Australian, but neither was he prepared for how good looking she was. Anna noticed his reaction, as did Greg and the two looked at each other and smiled.

"So it sounds like you and Lori had some fun last night Sam?"

"Well yes, she certainly put on a performance. I don't like that guy Sonny, the one she had a set to with. He looks a nasty piece of work. So here's a question. What are you guys thinking of doing and what, if anything, can I do to help?" said Sam.

"And me, I want to help too," said Anna.

Greg paused, "Sam, you're a serving Met DCI. I'm not sure this is necessarily something you should be getting involved in is it?"

"Fair point, but there may be stuff I, sorry Mum, I mean we, could do? Background stuff, that sort of thing? I suppose it depends on what you have in mind? What's your client want from this?" said Sam.

"Maybe best I don't share specifics Sam. I don't want to put you in any sort of difficult position, so let's just say we're here to help the police in any way we can to bring those responsible for murdering Sheila to justice," said Greg.

"Okay, so that's nice and wide," said Sam. "There's two points of interest here aren't there? Someone at the OCG who actually murdered Sheila and two, the scammers who gave them Sheila's data."

The Senior Investigator Officer role was coming out in Sam, putting the facts down and setting out strategies. Greg liked that about him. He didn't want Sam compromised professionally by being too involved, but he was a really useful extra head to think through the strategic and tactical planning to make this work.

"It looks like we've got headway with the Armenians here," said Terri, "but where we are struggling is with the scammers. They're probably in India, but that's as far as we can guess at the moment."

They tossed around some ideas but they kept hitting the brick walls of shadow and dummy corporations around Intertech that prevented them establishing who may be behind the organisation running Intertech.

"Sam, you said you'd asked one of your guys to check them out? Is it worth going back to him to see if he can dig deeper?" said Terri.

Sam was starting to like her and like her a lot. She had an energy about her that lifted everyone, even though they were facing one hell of a problem in moving things forward with Intertech.

"To be honest, I don't think it would help. Jimmy is one of the best and if he's done something on them, then he's done it," said Sam.

"Greg, what about Jonny Woodward?" said Anna.

"Anna, he was never Jonny to me," said Greg.

"Oh well, I knew him at uni. He might be able to help."

Almost in unison, Sam and Terri said, "Who the hell is Jonny Woodward?"

"You tell them Greg, I'll go and give him a call," said Anna.

Greg looked at Sam and Terri.

"Sir John Woodward is a former Deputy Head of MI6. Your mother certainly has friends in high places Sam."

"How does she know him Greg? I mean, I know she was a field agent, but hey, I'm a Met DCI and I don't know the Met Commissioner from Adam!" said Sam.

Greg ignored the question. He was pretty open about his past, because it helped with the credibility of 3R. Therefore quite a number of people knew he was ex-MI6, so it had been different for him when he told Terri. But he definitely wasn't going to get involved in how Anna explained her past to her son.

Sam carried on.

"And you were MI6 as well, weren't you?"

"Look Sam, I was, but you need to be asking your mother these questions, not me."

Sam sat back. He went to ask another question but thought better of it. What exactly had his mother been? Just at that moment Anna came back into the room.

"He sends his regards," she said looking at Greg. "I'll

get a call shortly apparently, so Terri could you maybe help when I speak to whoever John is getting to ring?"

"Yes, of course," said Terri.

"Sam, you've probably got some more questions for me. Some I should perhaps have told you about before now. It's maybe not the time to explain why I didn't, but I will do later." She didn't wait for him to say anything. "And yes, you may have guessed already, but I wasn't just a low level U/C officer, I worked deep under cover and trained only those who would work in similar roles."

Sam couldn't contain himself, "You were a deep U/C officer?"

"Yes my dear and I trained Greg."

"And she was a bloody good trainer too," said Greg.

Sam just looked at his mum. She had always just been his mum. Well, never "just" his mum, but she had been so caring, loving and yes, most of all gentle. That was it, he thought. It was her genteel nature that he couldn't relate to the profile of the woman she had once been during her days in the intelligence service. He shook his head as she went on.

"It was all a long time ago. But when I fell pregnant with you I was effectively side-lined from the Service, that's what happened then, although I gather it's better these days."

"These days? Are you still involved?" said Sam.

"No, no, of course not. I just chat every now and then with a couple of old friends."

"What, including Greg?" said Sam.

"No strings, no ties, no commitments," said Greg quietly.

"What's that?" said Sam.

"He said, 'no strings, no ties, no commitments'," said Anna.

"It was a U/C mantra Anna, your mother, drilled in

148

to me," said Greg, who was now looking directly at Anna.

She caught Greg looking at her and gave him an imperceptible shake of the head. *'Please don't say anything now,'* she thought.

"And Dad knew nothing?"

"No, he didn't. I met him after I had left the Service and with the Official Secrets Act, it wasn't something I could tell him and anyway, it was all in the past," said Anna.

Terri could see Sam was trying to get his head around his mother's past, so decided to move the conversation on.

"Sam, can you take me out for dinner tonight. My dad's got a hot date with his lady cop friend, so I'm at a loose end," said Terri.

Sam nodded, "Of course, of course, that would be great," still trying to take in what his mum had been telling him.

Anna's mobile then rang. Whilst Sir John, having been retired a number of years, had no continuing operational authority, he still maintained a significant network of contacts and he had called Martin Carruthers, the Intelligence Head for Asia Pacific within the Service.

"Hello Anna, Sir John has asked me to speak to you," said Martin.

"Thank you for calling so quickly Martin."

"You will probably appreciate that this is usually outside of the work remit of the Service. That said, these OCGs are working across borders and impacting on the safety and economical security of UK citizens. Therefore, destabilising the activities of these criminal gangs, who are threatening the national interest, is now worthy of consideration."

"Martin, is that a long way of telling me that you can

help me?"

"Yes Anna, I thought that was clear."

Anna smiled. "Crystal clear," she said.

"Now it may take a little while for me to get hold of the person best placed for you to talk to. He will ring you direct," said Martin who didn't wait for her to respond before ending the call.

"He's going to get someone to call me, but he can't say when," said Anna.

"Excellent. Now why don't we go for that lunch I promised you Anna and we can talk over old times," said Greg.

"Yes that would be lovely," said Anna, thinking he may have just as many awkward questions as Sam.

*****

Sonny was having lunch at one of his regular side street cafes when Alex joined him.

"How did you know I'd be here?"

"Boss, it's Thursday. You nearly always have lunch here on Thursdays," smiled Alex.

Sonny looked down at his Pa Amb Oli, his favourite dish at the cafe. Alex was right. Probably not the best tactic when you're running an OCG when other people sometimes wanted to muscle in on your territory. That said, the risk was pretty low on the islands. Everyone had their set areas and it was rare that boundaries were breached. *'Maybe we are all just a bit too comfortable here?'* he thought.

"So what can you tell me about this London cop?"

"His family own a bookshop, Sa Petita Llibreria, it's close to the big theatre."

"So is he a cop or a bookseller?" said Sonny.

"Both Boss, but I can't find out why he's been out in Mallorca for so long. It's over three weeks, so longer than the vacations I think they usually take in the police," said Alex.

"Are we sure it's a vacation and not an investigation?"

"Well according to the guy we've got at police HQ, there's nothing to suggest he's got anything to do with an investigation out here."

Sonny thought on this. It was better if it was just a vacation. One zealous cop, with that woman Garcia, was enough to be dealing with without having him involved in some way as well.

"Okay, good work my friend, but can you get someone in London to work through his name as well? I know they've got a lot of cops there, but there won't be too many with the surname Martínez. In the meantime, where does he live?"

"His mother has got a place just south of the city," said Alex.

"Go and pay his mother a visit. Leave a calling card to let this Bookseller know that we know where he lives and I think we need a distraction for the cops too. Who was the last one on the list from the scammers?"

Alex checked his phone. "Patterson, Boss. A Bill Patterson, lives alone. Villa is also south of the city, not far actually from the Martínez place. Estimated value €2-3 million."

"Okay, get a team around to Patterson's place. I don't care if he's there or not, do the usual and take what's of value, but trash the place as well," said Sonny.

"Will you be coming to the Patterson place Boss?" said Alex.

"No, I have plans for dinner tonight," said Sonny.

*****

Anna suggested they try to get a table at the Marc Fosh restaurant for lunch. It was one of her favourites. Luis used to take her there for dinner for special occasions, but they would sometimes lunch there too. Even with a Michelin star rating, they had a three course lunch menu for less than thirty euros.

They had walked from the Bookshop to the restaurant, which was only a few minutes' walk away in Carrer de la Missió, just exchanging small talk about Sir John Woodward.

They sat down and ordered the sea bream with the recommended bottle of Albariño.

"Anna, how old is Sam?" said Greg.

"Why do you want to know?" said Anna.

"Why the hell do you think?"

Anna went quiet. "Look, I told you 'no strings, no ties, no commitments'."

As soon as he had stepped through the door to the Bookshop, she had known the time would come when Greg would start asking questions about Sam. It was funny, but she had been dreading it, but since spending time with him this morning she had remembered the feeling she had when she was with him when they first met. For the first time since Luis had died, she felt alive. It wasn't Greg, in as much as she knew she didn't have the same feelings for him as she had all those years ago, but it was him who had reawakened her and she felt good and so it was right to tell him about Sam.

Greg continued.

"If the answer is what I think it might be, then I understand why you didn't tell me. Or at least, I'm trying to understand. So let me just ask this straight. Am I Sam's biological father?"

He was careful in phrasing his question, as he knew he had no right to suggest he was Sam's father.

"Yes, you are," said Anna.

She came out with it so quickly, without hesitation and that took him a bit by surprise.

"Bloody hell, I mean, does he know? I guess not," he answered himself before she did. "Do we tell him? Do you tell him? God, I've sent him out with his half-sister for dinner! We'll have to tell them," he was gabbling.

Anna took his hands.

"Greg, calm. I know you have Terri, but you haven't actually ever been an everyday parent have you my love?"

He stopped and smiled.

"You just called me 'love'."

"You will always be my love you idiot. I loved you so much during that week together, so you will never lose that place in my heart," said Anna. "Both of our children are grown adults you know, so they will cope with what we have to tell them."

"You're right, of course," he paused, "so this is probably a daft question, but why didn't you tell me?"

"Yes, it's a daft question, because you know the bloody answer is the Final Lesson I gave you. 'No strings, no ties, no commitments.' You were just being deployed on a really tough assignment and it would have messed with your head too much and you must know what happened when you found out about Terri. How long was it before you retired out of the field?"

She was right of course.

"I managed five years, but I probably only lasted that long because she was in Australia with her mother," said Greg. "You've done a fine job bringing him up Anna. He seems like a great guy and does you and your husband proud."

"Thank you and yes he does. Now that was much easier telling you than I thought it might be, but telling Sam?" she paused, "I just need to do it don't I? He's just found out I'm an ex-spy, so I might as well throw this at him as well," said Anna. "And you'll tell Terri?"

"Yes, just so we don't have any mishaps, as they seem to like each other."

"Maybe they sense a connection?" said Anna.

They spent the rest of lunch talking about old times,

enjoying the time together. Greg was relieved that she felt like an old friend and that nothing was being compromised by any suggestion of there being anything else between them. Just as they were finishing their meal, Anna's phone buzzed. *'Expect a call in 30 minutes.'*

THIRTEEN

"What have you guys been up to," said Greg.

"We grabbed a bite to eat and then Sam has been showing me around," said Terri.

"We also took a look at the club where Lori and I met up with Sonny. I was hoping we might be able to ID his Porsche, as it would be handy if we could find out where he goes," said Sam, "but there was no sign of it, or anything that looked like one of theirs either."

"Trackers. Good thinking. But have we got any? Should've thought of that before. Terri, has Tommy left yet?"

"Chill Dad, it's already in hand."

"What would I do without you?" said Greg.

"Not just a pretty face then?" she smiled.

"We got the text, so we should be getting a call shortly," said Anna.

"What do we hope to get from this?" said Greg.

"Let's start with the basics. If we can get a location on Intertech beyond just India, I'll feel we're getting somewhere. After that I want to narrow this down to city, area, street plus the people side of things, who is running it, where the money is going and so on," said Sam.

"Not much then mate," said Terri.

"Don't ask, don't get."

"Fair enough," said Terri.

*****

It was a blocked call. A soft Scottish accent, male. He called himself Rob.

"Okay Anna, what do you need help with?"

No pleasantries, no engagement. She briefly told him about the scam.

He listened, no interruptions and then said, "I'll need what you have so far on Intertech. That will give me a good start."

"Great, can I pass you to Terri and she can tell you all about it."

There was a pause and then Rob spoke.

"Anna, it needs to be just you okay? I'll only speak to you. That was my agreement with Carruthers. It's not that I don't trust Terri, whoever he or she is, but I do trust you based on what he's told me. Just give me the basics of what Bill told you, okay?"

Anna knew better than to argue the point. He was clearly very protective of himself and she understood why. She wasn't all that au fait with the internet, but it was pretty clear that people like Rob could do as much damage, if not a lot more, than any highly skilled field agent. Therefore, it stood to reason that the people they were after would be very keen to identify the likes of Rob and any subsequent interaction would not be a gentle affair.

He took some brief notes as she told him about Bill's credit card payment to Intertech, including the payee details, Bill's personal details and his address. Then, as she finished he seemed to lighten up.

"Well, this should be fun then. I'll call you in an hour."

There was no reason to ask for his number. As well as zealously guarding his own personal security, he would be masking his digital presence with multiple phones and sim cards constantly being changed.

Anna briefed them on the call.

"He said he'd call back in an hour."

"Okay great. I'm going to go and see the MacDonalds and bring them up to speed," said Greg. "Terri, can you drop me off at your place and I can pick up the van?"

"Sure, I've got the guys coming in from London, so I need to get them sorted with a vehicle and settled in at the finca. I'll get them looking around the clubs tonight, to see what they can spot," said Terri, "and don't forget, you're taking me out for dinner tonight Sam."

"Yes, looking forward to it. Tapas at one of my favourite places. Pick you up at around eight?"

"Good for me," said Terri.

Greg and Terri left leaving Anna thinking of the best way to tell Sam about Greg.

"Mum, what's up? Look, I'm not angry or anything about you not telling me you were in MI6, honestly. I'm in awe actually, so proud of you."

"Thank you my darling son. But there's something else, something I'm not sure will make you so proud," said Anna.

"What do you mean Mum? I'm sure you may have had to do things whilst undercover that you might not be proud about, but it was a long time ago and things were different. I get it Mum, I've run U/C jobs and I know the lines can get crossed and blurred sometimes. Look, you don't have to tell me anything you don't want to."

"It's not what I did in the Service Sam," she said quietly. "It's about your father. I mean your biological father."

"What's that got to do with this, with you being in the Service? You told me my father, rather my biological father, was someone you cared for, but who was a short lived fling."

Sam tailed off and looked at his mother, who looked back at him, she had tears in her eyes.

"I wish now I had told you, but I never thought I would see him again."

"It's Greg isn't it?" said Sam.

"Yes. We had a very special time together and I loved him very dearly, but it couldn't last, I couldn't let it because he was being deployed."

"Did he know?"

"No, he had no idea. It was just too dangerous to tell him something that could potentially put his life in danger."

"I don't understand. How could knowing about me put his life in any sort of danger?" said Sam.

"I know you've managed U/C officers Sam, but being one, especially those officers we put deep under cover with no support or back up, was so high risk that I couldn't afford for him to have any distractions of any sort."

"How long were you together?" said Sam.

"Just a week, straight after his training. After that I never contacted or saw him again until he walked through the door of Sa Petita Llibreria."

"Wow! What a story. I don't know what to think at the moment Mum. I mean Dad adopted me, so I suppose it doesn't alter anything, but even so, it's been quite a day and tonight I'm going out with my half-sister."

"I'm sorry Sam. Maybe I should have told you all of this before, I honestly don't know, but as long as you know that your father brought you up as his own. He didn't know about Greg and he never asked. He was so kind to me and taking you on as his son was just like him, so caring and so loving." The tears in her eyes returned.

"I miss him too Mum. I wish I'd been here more in recent years, but work seemed to take over."

"Oh Sam, he absolutely understood, never think other than that. We both did. His parents had let him go and find a life in Madrid and he was so proud you did the same, going to London and doing so well in the police," said Anna.

It had thrown him. That was for sure. But he couldn't and didn't want to judge his mother on decisions made over thirty years ago. He smiled. Good job he found out Terri was his half-sister though, as he had been going to text Jimmy that he'd found a tall blonde Aussie bombshell to go out with. Actually he thought, still smiling, *'I'll still text him and then tell him later.'* Then he looked at his mum and gave her a hug.

"Love you Mum."

"Love you too Sam."

*****

Rob flexed his fingers and set to work. An on-line scam vigilante, Rob had set up Digital Counter Action three years ago. A team of highly skilled scammer jammers, who work in isolation across the globe, with the purpose of identifying scam websites with a view to seriously disrupt the activities of those involved.

Some worked because of a deep sense of righting the wrongs of the scammers, whilst the others just took obscure pleasure from seeing the scammers squirm and run into chaos.

Rob fell on the side of those who really didn't like anybody being taken advantage of. He was happy to pass on his intel to law enforcement agencies and this had led to him connecting with Martin Carruthers. He had never met Carruthers because he retained a deep distrust of all things linked to authority, but he also knew where his influence ended and where people like the intelligence services and the police could take things further with the low lifes he was trying to take down.

Many of the scammers were clever, but they often employed people who were careless and who unwittingly left virtual doors open to those who, like Rob, knew what they were doing. Anna had given Rob the phone number Bill Patterson had dialled. It was a simple task to then phone the number and start the process of pretending to be someone who had just seen a pop-up appear on their computer screen.

"Hello, this is Raj at Intertech Support, how can I help you today?"

The call taker sounded genuine and Rob both smiled at the simplicity of the scam and then inwardly winced that people like Bill, who was the same age as his grandad, could be taken in by the concerned voice at the end of the line.

He allowed Raj to gain remote access to his dummy computer by typing in the URL, the unique reference link, into the address box. Rob played along, half listening to Raj with his calm and helpful comments, although it was something he had heard hundreds of times before, whilst at the same time putting his technology into action and reverse accessing Raj's computer.

'Okay,' he said to himself, 'Let's see what we can find out about you and your scamming friends.'

"Hello Sir, are you still there?" said Raj.

"Yes, still here."

Rob had missed the last thing Raj had said, but he wasn't worried as that was often what had happened to real victims as they were usually so disorientated with what was going on.

"Sorry Raj, I'm in such a state about this. I think I've lost some really important files and so I'm not really functioning."

"Don't worry Sir, or may I call you Steve?"

"Yes, Steve is fine," said Rob.

He had set up the dummy account in the name of Steve Hobs of 15 Apple Tree Close. It never failed to amuse him how often the scammers missed the irony of the names he chose. Raj took him through what was often the usual precursor check of the Windows Event box. This was designed to show him, Steve the victim, a list of faults and errors on his computer. Rob had made sure he had showed his parents how the Windows Event checkbox worked and that they knew all computers will show faults and errors and bugs, even when working perfectly. He let Raj go through his explanation about what the faults meant and how he would need to put a fix into his computer.

"Okay, so how do we fix this and how much will it cost?"

"We have a special offer on at the moment Steve and I can offer you the fix and a twelve month support package for a one-off payment of £899."

Rob waited. Mostly for effect to make Raj think he was taking all of this in, but also because his software had gained reverse access and he had just managed to open up the CCTV cameras the scammers had in their building. So he wasn't now just listening to Raj. He could see there were about twenty call takers in the room and by restarting the conversation he was able to identify which one was Raj, whilst all the time Raj was completely unaware of what was happening. Raj was a young guy, maybe about twenty five thought Rob. He was sitting with one of his legs hooked up over the side of his chair. Every now and then Rob could see him making signs to the guy sitting next to him. He seemed to be telling his neighbour that he had hooked a good one. Rob smiled.

"Oh my god Raj, I don't have that sort of money

to hand, but I need my computer back up working quickly. I'm self-employed and can't do without it."

Rob waited for the next line in Raj's script and he wasn't disappointed.

"Listen Steve, I shouldn't do this, but," and Raj paused for effect.

'Good touch,' thought Rob.

"Let me give you an additional ten percent introductory offer and you can do it on your credit card for no additional charge. Will that help?"

Rob had to hand it to Raj. Even though he could see him laughing with his neighbour, presumably at the soft touch he thought he had on his phone, Raj was managing to sound very sincere as he tried to scam him for nine hundred quid. Rob then kept Raj talking as he downloaded a section of files he had found on Raj's computer. He had found them quite easily. No password or any sort of protection. *'They are so bloody confident that nobody can touch them,'* he thought. He had been looking for anything with a Mallorca address and these looked like they had the details of the people they had scammed, together with the payment details.

Rob then noticed that even as Raj was trying to close the deal with him, he was looking at his social media accounts on his desk top. This gave him the opening to drill deeper into Raj and find his bank of personal photos, Bingo! He was looking at Raj standing outside a building with a group of his friends – some of whom Rob could see also worked in the call centre. It only took a moment to look at Google Maps at the location from Raj's computer IP address to see that it was the building from the one in Raj's pictures.

Rob had one last thing to try to access. The call centre payment files. He could see them, but they would probably be password protected, so the next step was get Raj to access these files by agreeing to pay the nine hundred quid, which he would pay using the credit card details Carruthers had given him to use for such events. Even though it wasn't his money, he hated giving the scammers anything, but it was necessary to continue the deception for the time being.

"Okay, Raj, I don't think I've got any option but to pay. So how do we do this?"

"Steve, you won't be disappointed."

Rob smiled and thought, '*No, I won't, but I bet you and your boss will be soon enough.*'

Raj then brought up the payment box and Rob saw him enter a password, just as he had expected to happen and he noted it down. Raj then went ahead and asked for Steve's credit card details before he then processed the payment. Once it had gone through, Rob saw Raj take off the lock on Steve's screen and as if by magic, everything was working again.

"It should be all good now, so thanks for calling us Steve and don't hesitate to get back in touch for any further support on this number."

"Thanks Raj for all your help. You don't know what a big help you've been," said Rob with a smile.

Whilst Raj thought his victim had signed off, Rob was in fact still monitoring the CCTV in the call centre room and he'd now started working on the payment files using Raj's password. He quickly trawled back and found the entry on the day Bill Patterson had been scammed and found the operator had been someone called Sajid. He remembered seeing a Sajid who had been tagged in one of Raj's photos and so it didn't take him long to then find Sajid in the call centre room. Sajid was talking to someone called Andrew. Another scam, another victim being taken for a ride. He listened in a little longer and decided to search for the payment file Sajid was working in. Andrew had been completely taken in and was at the payment stage. He had agreed to pay an introductory rate of €799 on his credit card.

"What's the payment address Andrew?" asked Sajid.

Andrew gave an address in Port de Sóller, Mallorca and was about to read out his credit card details, when Rob cut off the call. Sajid didn't know what was happening and tried calling Andrew back, but Rob had already dialled the mobile he had seen on the payment screen and so blocked Sajid's attempted call back. He saw the confusion on Sajid's face and smiled.

"One less victim for you to crow about, you useless piece of shit."

At that moment Andrew answered his mobile.

"Hello, hello, Sajid is that you? I think our call dropped out."

"Andrew, please don't be alarmed. I'm here to help you. I've terminated your call with Sajid as you were just about to be scammed for €799 when there is nothing wrong with your computer that a quick two minute fix won't solve," said Rob.

"Now just a moment, I don't know who the hell you are," said Andrew.

"I appreciate that Andrew, so please call the police in Palma and ask for Detective Inspector Lori Garcia. She is currently investigating these scams. Please do not answer any more calls on this mobile until I speak to you again. This is because the scammers will try to reach you again."

"I'm not sure who the hell I should trust, but call the police you say? Okay, I'll do that, but you will fix my bloody computer won't you? The damned thing's frozen," said Andrew.

Rob smiled. Despite nearly being taken for almost eight hundred euros, all poor old Andrew was really worried about was clearing his screen.

"Yes, of course, let's do that now should we," said Rob. "Tell me what your screen is showing at the moment?"

Andrew described the Intertech pop-up that was blocking the screen. It was simple enough to get him to click a couple of keys and the pop-up disappeared.

"Is that it? But they wanted €799 for that."

"It's a scam Andrew, there was nothing actually wrong with your computer. They had just put a jammer onto your screen causing it to block and to show a phone number for you to call. I just happened to be in the right place at the right time," said Rob.

"I have no idea what you have done or how you've done it, but thank you so much for your help. How can I thank you? And who are you?" said Andrew.

"No need to thank me Andrew. You can call me Rob and yes, it's okay to give the Inspector my name, but just the Inspector please because this is an-going operation. Oh, and Andrew, if Sajid rings again, please do not give the game away," said Rob.

"Yes, yes, of course and thank you again," said Andrew.

Rob took one last look at Sajid who was looking very confused, unable to fathom out how he had just lost a €799 payment, before returning to the payment files he had found. These would be really useful in discovering where the money went, although he'd need some good old fashioned digital legwork, but he should soon be able to create an organisational structure of who was running this call centre operation.

He rang Anna.

"Okay Anna, we're in. It's a call centre in the Andheri West district of Mumbai. They have about twenty people working there and the guy who did the deal with Bill Patterson was someone called Sajid. Nasty piece of work, but whilst I was looking at their CCTV I managed to ruin his day, by screwing up a deal he was about to do for nearly eight hundred euros with a guy called Andrew from Port de Sóller."

Anna just shook her head and thought *'I'm feeling all of my sixty nine years when this young man can do all of this so quickly!'*

"Rob, this may be simple stuff for you, but wow, am I impressed!"

"No problem Anna. If I can help take these scumbags down, then that's all I want to do. Okay, so first things first. Andrew is going to be ringing your Inspector Garcia, or is it Inspectora in Spanish? Please can you get a message to her to tell her the call is kosher? Then give me the rest of the day and maybe a bit of tomorrow to work on gathering as much data as I can to ID the boss of the outfit, together with an organisational chart showing how it all interlinks. That should give you guys something concrete to work on in terms of who is running this and where they are based."

"Rob, that's fantastic and you're right, it is Inspectora," said Anna, "and Rob, thank you for this, but also for helping whoever Andrew is. It sounds like he needed your help and got it just in time."

"It was my pleasure. I told you it would be fun," said Rob.

*****

Greg took the call from Anna just as he was arriving at the gated entrance to the MacDonald villa and he phoned Lori straight away.

"Hello, how is your day going Señora?" said Greg.

"Ah, Señor Chambers, yes I am well. I suppose you are ringing about your English friend, Andrew from Port de Sóller?" said Lori who was sitting in a room with her team.

"Can't talk then? So yes, I am calling about Andrew. I don't have any other details, but we've had some help in tracking down the scammers. They are in India and we've got the area they are operating in. Probably not a resource you could legitimately use Lori, but we've been given access to a professional scambuster. I think that's the sort of term they use anyway."

"Can you trust them?" said Lori.

"I think so. They come from a very solid source."

She thought for a moment. She didn't really want to know any more, not officially anyway. He was right, she couldn't use these type of people, but getting the intel from them was the next best thing.

"Maybe we should meet?"

"Yes, 8.30 okay for you. I'll pick you up," said Greg.

"Si, Señor Chambers that will be fine. We'll speak later."

She put her phone back down on her desk and caught Nino looking at her from across the other side of the desk.

"What?" she said.

"So is that a meeting with a victim's representative, or a dinner date?" said Nino.

"None of your business. Get back to work Sergeant," said Lori trying to hide a smile.

FOURTEEN

John MacDonald was happy to be back in the villa. He hadn't really been able to settle in the hotel.

Cap Rocat was a marvellous place and he was so glad they were protected from any prying eyes, especially the Press, as he didn't think he could have dealt with them, but it felt good to be back at the villa.

The difficult thing was that it had brought it home to him all over again that Sheila was gone. She had been stolen from him and he felt empty. He was glad he had his boys there as there were a hundred and one things to do regarding her death, including starting the difficult job of sorting out Sheila's things, but he also hadn't had a chance yet to sit down with the small team of staff they had to help run the house.

Nearly all of them had been with them since they built the place, so he knew they must be feeling bad as well, especially Consuela, who kept the house in such immaculate condition and who had become like a part of the family. She had been standing in the kitchen when they got there. She seemed like she was rooted to the spot, unable to move. He could see her bloodshot tear-stained eyes. He took hold of her and gave her a hug and she sobbed. That started him off as well and he wept unashamedly. Chris and Jack came in with the luggage and came and hugged them both.

The boys looked upon Consuela as their Spanish grand-mother and she held them tight. The release of emotion seemed to help all of them.

"Could you get some tea on please Consuela?" said John.

"Si, Señor John."

As beautiful as the inside of the villa was, it was the garden that had been Sheila's pride and joy. She had spent so much of her time lovingly designing and land-scaping the land around the villa. She was a hands-on gardener, working alongside Pepe and Juan, her two long-serving gardeners who helped turn her dreams into reality. He would watch her from the villa and just love the enjoyment and delight she took from keeping it looking so wonderful. The guys were still there. He could see them working away at the bottom of the garden, keeping it looking good for her, even though she had gone. They turned and waved at him. The welcome was warm, but they looked as lost as he was without Sheila.

*****

Greg pushed the intercom and Chris answered.

"Come on in Greg."

The electric doors started to open and Greg drove the van up the driveway and parked beside the Lexus. Chris came out to meet him.

"Good to see you Greg."

"How's your dad?"

"He's doing okay, considering. We've all had a few tears. It just seems very odd being here without Mum. Dad was often away on business and we would be here just with Mum, so her not being here just doesn't feel right," said Chris.

They walked in and got the greetings out of the way. John wanted to know what was happening.

"We've been focusing on the scam today and we've

got some good progress there. It's coming from a call centre in India as we thought, but now we have a specific area within Mumbai. The guy who is working on it is coming back to me with more on the organisation set-up. That way we can look to ID the money trail. If we're going to hurt these people we need to get to the money John and if we can, put them out of business," said Greg.

"I won't bother asking how you managed to get this information Greg, but it's a bloody good start."

"Networks John, just like in your business. I'm seeing Lori Garcia tonight and I should get an update on what she's doing with the OCG." He saw John looking puzzled. "Sorry, bloody acronyms, the organised crime gang, the guys who did the burglary and...."

"Murdered Sheila," finished John.

"Yes. Lori's going to disrupt what they're doing on the island and look for the fallout. Identifying who actually killed Sheila may be hard John. Not impossible, just hard."

John looked at him.

"I do understand Greg and I do appreciate, really I do, what you and Terri are doing. But let me be quite clear here. When an organisation is not forthcoming in providing the person or persons responsible for an act that has caused harm or distress, then it is the senior management who must bear total responsibility."

John stood up and walked away from the table and out into the kitchen. Greg looked at Chris and Jack.

"Well I think I got the message on that one," said Greg quietly.

*****

Sam had been speaking with Jimmy during the day about any intel on the Armenian OCG structure. They were known to be operating in a couple of areas in London and in some of the major cities across Europe, as well as the east coast of the United States. Jimmy could only find a limited amount on Sonny, although he thought that when he had taken over the Balearics about three years ago, it had been the result of a change authorised from the top, from Sergei Grigoryan, the big boss back in Yerevan, Armenia. He was just coming off the phone to Jimmy when he heard his mother shouting.

"Sam, Sam, it's Bill. We need to get home," said Anna.

"What's happened?" said Sam.

"I'm not sure. He's very confused and I think he might be hurt."

"Come on, let's go. You can tell me the rest on the way."

There wasn't much traffic about, so he made good progress as she told him more of what Bill had said.

"He was out in the garden and heard someone knocking on the front door. I think he said there were two of them. They were asking for me and then they thought he was your dad, but when he told them who he was, they started asking him questions," said Anna.

"Have they gone Mum? Did Bill confirm they have gone?"

"Yes, yes, but they hurt him."

"We're nearly there Mum, but what sort of questions, did he manage to say?"

"Why was he there? How did he know me? Did he know you? That was about all he could say," said Anna.

"I think we need to tell DI Garcia about this. Can you ring her and I'll get in and check on Bill?" said Sam.

She knew immediately that he didn't want her going into the house before he checked it out. She made the call.

"Inspectora Garcia, it's Sam's mother, yes, I'm using his phone. Look we're at my house. I think we've had some unwelcome visitors and Sam has gone in to check on Bill Patterson. He thinks it may be the Armenians."

"Señora Martínez. Please wait outside as Sam asks. We will be there very soon," said Lori.

Lori had stood up and Nino, having heard the gist of the call, was already getting his keys, sidearm and protective jacket.

"Nino, with me and get Pérez to take his team and start heading south towards Portals Nous and I'll get the address for them in a moment."

She found the address and radioed Pérez the details just as Sam phoned her.

"Sam, what's happening?" said Lori.

"We're okay. Bill's shaken up and has had a couple of nasty slaps to the head. He managed to see they were in a dark blue BMW, either a 5 or 7 series, he wasn't sure. No registration plate, but it looked pretty new. He thinks there were just two of them in the car, the two who came to see him. Fortunately for us, he's a tough old boy, ex-military, so he's done bloody well to take all this in."

"I'll get all this intel out and we'll be with you in about ten."

Pérez would have taken two cars, but with the additional information on the BMW, Lori got him to deploy the rest of the GEO team and put in a wide area search. She had a team of twenty in total, with six cars and a motorcycle. Half of the cars were in full police livery and the others were unmarked, including the bike that they could use as loose surveillance vehicles, together with some of the team in plain clothes, ready for foot surveillance if required.

"Pérez, you find me this BMW," said Garcia.

"We're on it Boss," said Pérez.

His team hadn't had much to do on this operation so far, other than helping with the door to door stuff after each of the burglaries. They had been waiting for something to happen and he knew the adrenalin would be starting to flow.

"Easy does it guys, I want Alphas 2 and 3 to hang back on the main routes back into the city and Bravos 2 and 3 to start following us," said Pérez.

The team acknowledged on their radios. All the Alpha cars were high performance SEAT estates in full police livery, whilst the unmarked Bravos were a BMW 440, a Skoda RS and a Mercedes 350. They all carried gun boxes with an assortment of firearms and ammunition and the officers carried side arms every time they deployed.

Garcia was a couple of miles ahead of Pérez's team. She and Nino were in the VW Golf GTi she had on hire and they quickly got to the Martínez villa that was just a short distance outside Illetes. Garcia saw Anna Martínez waiting for her.

"Sam's gone back inside with Bill, but told me to stay here so as not to compromise any potential forensics."

"Is Señor Patterson okay Señora?" said Garcia.

"Yes, I think so, but I've called an ambulance just in case," said Anna.

"Good, so yes, please stay here with Nino."

She called out as she walked into the house and Sam responded.

"Yes, we're okay Lori, we're in here."

She found them in a living room at the front of the house. Bill looked up and smiled.

"Señora Garcia, I seem to be becoming a bit of a nuisance, I am so sorry."

"No Señor, there's no need to worry. We have an ambulance on its way. Just to check you out," as he started to protest. "Sam, I've got a team out looking for this BMW. What do you think we're looking at in terms of a timeline?"

Sam checked his watch.

"It's got to be thirty minutes by now."

"I've got some of the team hanging back nearer the city watching the Ma20. Sonny has got a place out towards S'Arenal, but I can't see them going there. But there's a few houses and apartments we know they use, so we can start checking those too," said Lori.

"They wanted to know where my mother was. It looks like they thought Bill was my dad, but when he told them who he was, they seemed to lose interest in Mum and started to give Bill a hard time, asking him a bunch of questions, 'What was he doing here? How was he tied in with me? Why was a London cop asking questions?' And of course, he couldn't answer some of their questions and so they started hitting him," said Sam.

She could see he was agitated and was getting angry. She needed him to stay calm and in control. This isn't the time for his PTSD to come out, she thought. He had told her about what had been going on in London and she realised he'd hit a pinch point with what had happened to Bill and he was close to lashing out. She kept her voice low and quiet and kept him talking to give him time to regain his control. After a couple of minutes, where he had been talking almost non-stop, he was now slowing down his speech and breathing more easily. He looked at her with a knowing half-smile.

"You know you're really good at that stuff."

"As long as it has helped, that's the main thing," said Lori. "Okay, here's the ambulance. Señor Patterson, let's go outside and get you checked out and I'll get back out looking for the BMW. Sam, I've got a local unit coming here just in case they need to take him to hospital. They will follow and make sure they are all okay whilst at the hospital too. In the meantime, keep in touch."

In a moment, she was back at the wheel of the GTi and turning left out of the driveway and heading back towards the city as Nino filled her in on the scope of the search.

"So nothing?" said Lori.

"Well not yet, the Alphas didn't see anything coming in on the Ma20 towards the city, so I've got one of the Bravos sitting further up towards the Valldemossa junction and I've sent the bike up towards the finca they use on the Inca road."

"What about CCTV? I know it's a needle in a bloody haystack without an index plate, but we need that car."

"I'm on it Boss. They've been looking, but I've kept it to the specific areas it was likely to head for, otherwise it would be just too much," said Nino.

"No, you're right Nino, that's a smart bit of thinking. Okay, what next? Suggestions?" said Lori.

She had learned many years ago that she didn't know all the answers and including the team was a damn good way to keep the ideas flowing, as well as keeping them motivated and involved.

"This wasn't a planned intervention Boss, so they're going to have to report back to Sonny on this. Let's find him and then we might find the BMW."

"Let's do it and Nino?" said Lori turning to look at him. "It's about time you went for that exam and got yourself up that promotion ladder to Inspector, you deserve it."

"Yes Boss, understood," said Nino.

He liked her. She was a good boss and always made sure her people had a chance to speak and get their fair share of praise. He saw how the team responded and it was something he'd taken on board. He put out another call for a general update and the team came back with their negative responses to their search for the BMW. Nino rang the GEO team leader, Sergeant Fernando Pérez and they talked through options on how to best track down Sonny. They knew he changed cars regularly, but the Porsche Cayenne the boss had seen him in was a new one to them.

"Let's run the plate through CCTV and see if we get any hits today and get the Bravos to sit up along the likely routes from his place in S'Arenal back into the City," said Nino.

"Right, we'll keep on this for tonight Nino. They might be a bit hacked off that we haven't spotted the car, but they are up for this," said Pérez.

"Tell Fernando that if they get the chance, the guys and gals should put a bit of pressure on the doormen around the Armenian clubs too," said Lori.

"Did you get that?" said Nino.

"Loud and clear Nino. We'll push some buttons and see what happens," said Pérez.

Nino rang off and glanced across at Lori as he drove.

"Well that should be interesting Boss. What's your thinking?"

"Sonny will know we have nothing on them, otherwise we would have arrested somebody. But we know these OCGs don't like too much police activity as it scares the customers away from their clubs and street girls," said Lori.

"Is this what your young London cop called 'rattling some cages'?" said Nino.

"Exactly," she smiled. "Okay, now drop me off at my apartment please Nino."

He thought about saying something to tease her, but thought better of it. It didn't do to test her patience and hey, if she was having some fun, who was he to stop her? What had happened to her husband Felipe was well known throughout the force, so if anyone deserved a bit of happiness in her life, then she certainly did.

"Have a good night Boss and I'll keep you posted if anything comes up, otherwise I'll see you in the morning," said Nino.

"Thanks Nino. I've a good feeling about finding this car. See you tomorrow."

*****

Sam checked that the paramedics were happy with Bill. He needed to go to hospital as they had hit him hard around his head. Lori had also called the Forensic team and they were arriving just as the ambulance was leaving with the police escort taking Bill to hospital with Anna going along to keep him company. Sam showed the Forensic guys the layout of the house and left them to it as he rang Greg.

"Sam, I'm sorry you had to find out this way, you know, about me, your mum and you. I didn't know either."

Sam had completely forgotten about his mother telling him about Greg.

"It's okay, it's okay, we can talk about that later. We've had a problem Greg. Some unwanted visitors came to mum's house looking for her and found Bill instead. He's taken quite a beating. He's alright, but he's on the way to hospital with my mother."

"Bloody hell Sam."

"Yes, I know. This looks like payback for me rattling his cage. Stupid really, I should have thought about the possible repercussions."

"No point looking back at the moment Sam, let's focus on the here and now and what we could, should or want to do about this," said Greg. "So what happened?"

Sam ran through what Bill had told him.

"He's done very well to give us an idea on the BMW. So we now have an image of the van thief and two cars including the Porsche to look for," said Greg. "I'm going to get my two guys to poke around the clubs tonight. Different faces they might not be expecting to see, so

177

if they see any of the vehicles we might be able to get a tracker on them. I know they might be surveillance savvy, but then again, complacency may be our friend and their enemy."

"What did you mean Greg, when you said what we 'could, should or want to do'?"

"You're a serving police officer Sam. I am a freelance consultant. You operate within the law and I operate, well, let's say within the spirit of the law," said Greg. Sam went quiet and Greg continued, "Bringing these guys to justice may be difficult. My client wants those responsible for his wife's death to suffer harm, both in a physical and financial way. This may compromise those values you hold as a police officer."

"I understand," said Sam, pausing. "You're right. I am going to be sitting on the same side of the fence as Lori in terms of what I want to happen to these guys. I'm happy to help you where I can, but I'm not going to be able to help if you start crossing the line of what I see as the right thing to do within the confines of the law."

"I'm fine with that Sam. Just thought it better to have that conversation out in the open," said Greg.

"Me too," said Sam. "Now, I'll go and check on Bill and Mum and then I've got a dinner date with my half-sister."

Greg smiled. It didn't sound like there was going to be a problem for Anna, with Sam finding out about him. He still had to get his head around it himself, but if he was going to have a son, then someone like Sam would be just the ticket.

"Good, I'm glad. Take care and let's catch up tomorrow," said Greg.

FIFTEEN

Jaz Kaur felt the pilot start the descent before the Airbus A320 finally touched down at 19.15 and she met up with Ekam as they walked through Arrivals at Palma de Mallorca International Airport.

She then went and waited at the sliding doors that led out into the airport, whilst Ekam collected their baggage. Jaz looked over to him and saw he was on the phone, probably to the private hire car company. He joined her with a baggage trolley loaded up with his one trolley bag and her three full size bags. She smiled, a girl needed a few changes of clothes, but he didn't make any sort of fuss. She looked at him. He was so loyal and she trusted him absolutely. He had definitely saved her from being seriously hurt when that guy had attacked her. Ekam turned and caught her looking at him.

"Yes, Miss Kaur, do you need something?"

"No," she said gently, "I was just thinking how lucky I am to have you in my life Ekam. You are so kind and loyal. You would make someone a very nice husband, so why haven't you married?"

He was taken aback that she should think of his well-being. Him, just a lowly servant to her. He couldn't tell her that he would never marry because he had only ever loved one woman and that was her, so he laughed it off.

"Oh Miss, I could never marry. Who would look after you then?" he said smiling.

"Well that's okay then, as long as you're happy," said Jaz, before returning to her more usual business-like self. "Now where's the car?"

"It's that one over there Miss, follow me," said Ekam, as he started walking to a dark blue Mercedes E Class.

The driver opened the rear door for her and then he helped load the baggage with Ekam, who then took his seat in the front with the driver. They were staying at the same hotel as in March, the Hotel Glòria de Sant Jaume, a smart five star place in Sant Jaume, just north of the Plaça del Rei Joan Carles I and on the way she texted Sonny to say she had landed and would be having dinner at 9pm if he wanted to join her. A text bounced back almost immediately with '*Yes*'.

*****

The doctor had decided that Bill needed to stay in for observations overnight, so Sam took Anna back home before getting ready to go out for dinner.

"Are you sure you will be alright if I go out tonight Mum? Lori has put some officers on the front entrance for tonight."

"Yes, I'll be fine, so stop fussing. I'll put the alarm on as well when you go out and Sam, we haven't really had a chance to talk about what I told you about Greg, but thank you for your understanding," said Anna.

"It's fine Mum, just the two shocks in one day. First I find out you were a spy and then boom! I find out my biological father was also a spy," he grinned and hugged her. "Anyway I won't be late. It's not as if it's a romantic evening out, not now I know she's my half-sister!"

"Now you're teasing me, so you can just stop that," said Anna grinning back at him.

Terri saw them come through the Arrivals Gate. Tommy with his rolling relaxed gait with a big grin on his face and Simon with a more upright, chest out walk.

"Hello darling," he said in his beautiful and gentle accent from his homeland of Barbados.

"Hello my big Bajan hunk," she said.

"Terri," said Simon.

"Simon, good to see you."

They couldn't be more different, both in looks and character. Tommy was big, African Caribbean and always had a smile on his face. Simon was Welsh, talked softly and you had to dig deep for his sense of humour, but when you found it, he was just as much fun as Tommy.

"I've got a KIA Sportage for you guys," said Terri handing Simon a set of keys.

Tommy said, "Just as well you were choosing it Terri and not Greg, as we'd have been in...."

"One of his favourite little white vans," the three of them said in chorus.

They followed her to the finca that was just a kilometre off the Ma20 ring road around the city. As they had turned off the motorway onto the Ma11, the Sóller Road, they had noticed a red motorcycle parked up at the side of the road, with the rider sitting astride the bike watching passing traffic. Tommy and Simon looked at each other.

"Funny place to sit and watch traffic?" said Tommy, and Simon nodded in agreement.

They pulled in behind Terri's Merc into the driveway. This was a lot better than some of the accommodation they sometimes had to stay in, so as they got out of the car, they nodded approvingly to Terri.

"And it's got a pool guys, although I'm not sure how

much chance you'll get to use it as I've just got off the phone to Greg." She always referred to her father by his name at work. It was more professional in front of clients and again just easier all around when she was working with her guys.

"Did you see the biker?"

They nodded.

"He's a cop out looking for a BMW, new model, 5 or 7 series, dark colour with two armed and nasty Armenian thugs who have just head slapped a harmless old man."

"What do you want us to do Terri?" said Simon, ex-Special Forces and like Tommy, more than capable of handing out different levels of retribution when required.

"Okay, tonight is just a seek and find Op. Take a trip into town and trawl the clubs, I know, a tough job, but you can do it guys," she said smiling. "Look for any Armenians with a tattoo on their left wrist, plus you've got the image I sent you of the van thief, as well as the Porsche index plate. If you get any chance to get a tracker on either car, then do it. Just one thing, the investigating officer has a bunch of handy ninjas working with her, they're GEO, so you may well spot them on the lookout. Do not engage, well, if at all possible do not engage guys, you know what I mean. We're on the same side, but best they don't know about you if we can manage that, okay?"

"Yep, no problem. We'll be quiet as mouses," said Tommy.

"Mice," corrected Simon and Tommy just looked at him.

"Good, now help me unload this gear into the back of the house. Maybe best to do a bit of gardening to hide the gun box, look I've even brought you guys a nice new shovel," said Terri, with a grin.

"You're just too good to us Terri," said Tommy, handing the shovel to Simon. "Your turn to dig mate."

They checked the firearms before locating a suitable hiding place within the garden to bury the gun box, leaving out two of the Glocks and a Taser.

"Okay guys, speak tomorrow. I'm now off for dinner with my new half-brother."

The two men looked at her. She had got in the Merc and driven away before they could say anything. They looked at each other with the same thought, *'Half-brother, what on earth was that all about?'*

*****

Sam picked Terri up from her apartment and drove to Llucmajor, to Contrabando. As they walked in the restaurant, he noticed the people at the tables close to the door looked towards her. She did look stunning. Miquel saw them and came across to greet them.

"Sam, welcome my friend and you must be Terri. It is a pleasure to meet you and welcome to Contrabando."

They sat down at one of the window tables and Miquel brought cocktails on a tray. Terri looked at the drinks and then at Miquel.

"It's a Martínez, Terri. Gin, sweet vermouth and maraschino cherry liqueur. Enjoy!"

"You've got a drink named after you?" she looked at Sam.

"Well, I can't claim it's named after us, but I have to admit I do like it."

They chose some tapas and Miquel suggested the wine and as they waited Sam asked her to tell him about her father.

"Strange day for you Sam. What with finding out about your mum and then about my dad, or rather our dad."

"Yes, definitely. The thing with Greg is, well, in some ways it's less of an issue. Mum had never really talked

183

about my biological father. She didn't exactly hide anything and she had told me what had happened when I was old enough to grasp it. She'd had a relationship with a guy who she would never be able to be with. I think I might have thought he was either married or his parents wouldn't allow it, you know, that sort of thing and it wasn't Greg's name on my birth certificate. I gather now it was a name with a made up background that someone in MI6 had put together for her. So finding out he's my actual biological father is strange, but now I know they both were spies, well it sort of makes sense."

"If it's any consolation mate, he's a pretty good bloke in my view," said Terri. "My mum went on later to have a long term relationship with a guy back home and finally married him. He's been a great step-dad, but Greg has always been there for me and worked with my mum to be part of my life, so when I decided to leave the army it was too good an opportunity to pass up not to work with him."

They talked about each other's jobs and Sam found her easy to talk to and found himself telling her about what had happened with Jimmy and how it had affected him.

"So how are you feeling now?" said Terri.

"Pretty good actually, which surprises me a bit. I hadn't realised how close to the edge I'd got. I just need to watch it when I get in pressure situations." He went quiet. "I can sometimes lose it a bit then."

"What do you mean?" she asked gently.

He told her about the two guys who had tried to mug him as he walked from the car and how he could have just disarmed them and let them go, but he'd wanted them to try again and then he'd made sure he hurt them.

"Don't lose too much sleep over them though Sam,

but I get where you're coming from. Are you getting any help, any therapy?"

"I've tried, but I think now that I wasn't ready. Go back a week and I couldn't talk like this to anyone and now I've off loaded to both you and this guy here," as Miquel came back to see them.

"Yes, you did amigo and it was about time he opened up Terri. He's had me worried for a while, but hey, enough talking and more eating. I have the rest of your tapas for you," presenting them with plates of grilled vegetables with Romescu sauce, pork loin with homemade sobrassada sausage and honey and finally, pork cheeks with sweet potato purée. "Buen provecho amigos. Enjoy your food my friends."

*****

Greg had collected Lori from her apartment and they had walked into town for some dinner. They found a quiet restaurant away from the usual tourist area and a good distance from the clubs where Pérez and his team would be working tonight. Conversation was easy and Lori felt relaxed and comfortable in his company, but she was also still trying to get her head around her feelings for Greg and how to not let things get in the way of what she was supposed to be on the island to do.

"Lori, is it just me or is this, well, just a bit awkward. I mean the timing of this?"

She looked at him and smiled.

She felt that he liked her, but was it all just too much like a holiday romance? She was working away from home and so was he and they had been brought together because of the situation, so why not just live for the moment and enjoy a bit of romance with an attractive man? But he was now asking if it was a bit awkward.

"What do you mean Greg?" She wanted him to lead

on this. To tell her how he felt about her and what he might want to do.

"Look, I really like you," said Greg.

"I sense a 'but' coming here Greg."

"Yes, but I think it's for the right reasons," said Greg taking hold of her hands. "Could this be something that is more than just a few days and nights together whilst we are working on this case?"

It had been so long since she had felt anything like this about someone. She felt her heart throbbing and thought it must be so loud that he's got to be able to hear it. She smiled. It was like being a teenager again *'and I'm nearly forty eight,'* she thought.

"You're smiling Lori. Is that good?"

"Yes."

He didn't say anymore. He didn't think he needed too. They held hands and just looked at each other, before he suddenly got up from his chair and leaned forward towards her, hesitating a moment until she moved towards him and he kissed her tenderly on the lips.

*****

Jaz saw him enter the hotel bar, El Patio de Glòria. She had been looking forward to seeing him and she was glad he didn't have his two bodyguards walk in behind him. This was a lovely hotel and she didn't want people looking at him and wondering who he was. He greeted her with a gentle kiss on both cheeks and they went in for dinner. They talked a little business and then like a couple out on a date, they talked and laughed together about memories of growing up and first loves. She then noticed he went quiet after he had been talking about his friend Sergei.

"Sonny, is anything wrong between you and Sergei?"

"Are you asking as a business partner, or as someone who might have some feelings for me?" said Sonny.

She paused and said, "It might surprise you, as it actually surprises me a hell of a lot, but I'm asking as someone who does have feelings for you."

He had first met her over three months ago when he had noticed her sitting alone quietly in a bar. She wasn't like a lot of the women he often went for. Yes, she was still very pretty but she wasn't having to make a noise so people looked at her and yet, the way she was sat at the table still screamed out loud to him, 'Hey, look at me.' He lived in a harsh world where violence was part of his everyday life, but that all seemed to disappear when he was with her. He didn't know why and he didn't really want to think too hard about it in case the bubble burst and he never saw her again, but he had been looking forward to her coming back to the islands, especially with how things had been going with Sergei.

"Thank you," he said taking her hand.

"Let's go back into the bar and you can tell me all about it over a drink," said Jaz and she led him through to the bar and ordered two brandies, the fifty year old Suau that she knew he had really enjoyed last time they had dined there.

She listened as he explained what had happened and how following the death of the MacDonald woman there was an increasing amount of police activity. Although he didn't tell her outright that he had been responsible for the MacDonald woman's death, she heard enough to make the assumption.

"So who is this London cop and what's his involvement?" said Jaz.

"I don't know what he's doing over here. We can't find out if he's just on holiday and across to see his mother or if he's working on a case, but the fact he heads up a major crime unit in London makes me suspicious."

He told her about how his men had gone to the Martínez house, to send a message by shaking the mother up, only to find the Patterson guy, who had been one of her scams and was on the potential burglary list. His guys had roughed him up a bit getting the information out of him that he was a family friend, but it was just all getting too much of a coincidence. He was thinking now that he wanted to make sure the Martínez cop got the message loud and clear to back away from any investigation he might be involved in.

"Sonny, do you really think intimidation will work on this guy? It's a pretty high risk tactic if it doesn't come off."

She was making a good point, but he had always met any sort of conflict head on and it had worked pretty well so far in his life.

"He's out here on his own, so if he wants his mother alive and well, he needs to back off and then I can just focus on the Garcia woman and she's got nothing except a guy with a tattoo who stole a van and she won't get far in finding him."

She didn't react to his last statement. She thought she knew what he had meant and if it meant keeping the business safe then it was something she might well do herself.

"Okay, if he is on his own, then he's got no back up or support, except the police here and they are already stretched, so I can see why you're thinking that way," said Jaz. "So when will you do it?"

He looked at his watch. It was 10.30pm.

"I'm expecting a text any moment."

SIXTEEN

They had waited until the lights had been turned off in the villa. Alex Krikorian and his team had then taken up their positions.

He had a view of the Martínez villa and of the two local cops sitting in their marked police car blocking the front gate. Alex checked the team comms and then told everyone to sit quiet and wait. He was expecting a change in police crews, with the new one covering the night shift.

It wasn't long before he saw another police car with two officers arrive. Alex saw the four officers get out of their vehicles. He could hear them talking, presumably the day team were briefing the new officers that the Martínez woman was back at home from the hospital, but he couldn't quite pick up what was being said. The officers then got back into their vehicles and the day crew left, leaving the night crew in their car, but for now, they weren't blocking the villa entrance. He texted Arman, who was closer to the police cars, to see if he had heard what was said. Arman texted back, 'They're expecting the son home from dinner sometime soon.' Realising that this explained why the new cops hadn't moved their car forward to block the villa driveway when the day crew drove off, Alex knew he needed to move quickly to take advantage of this opening.

Sonny saw the text arrive. *'We have a window with low risk.'* He smiled at Jaz as he texted back, *'Do it.'*

"Good news then?"

"Yes. Now, shall we go to your room?"

"I'd like that," she said, standing up and taking his held out hand.

*****

Alex motioned to his team to execute the plan. All had military experience, with good skills and above all, good discipline. Arman and his crewmate moved out from their position and made their way up towards the police car. Approaching from the rear and hugging either side of the small road they could stay in the shadows and away from the street lights. Arman waited until his partner was in position close to the rear of the driver's door. They could hear the officers talking and barely paying attention to their surroundings. It was sloppy and careless. He smiled. They'd have to explain their negligent actions in the morning. Alex had said no bloodshed if it could be avoided. Killing cops wasn't a great idea as it always got them over-excited and it brought too much activity that might disrupt their business. He took his jacket off, leaving him in just a short-sleeved shirt and left his gun by the jacket. His partner would take care of things if things didn't go to plan, but he needed to show he was unarmed and didn't pose a threat as he pretended to be a friendly drunk on his way home. He nodded to his partner and moved out of the shadows and started singing softly, staggering towards the middle of the road. The policeman in the passenger seat heard the noise and immediately went to get out of the car. The driver's eyes followed his crewmate and so he didn't see Arman's partner move quietly towards the driver's door. The timing was perfect. Arman started talking to the police officer and his partner, knowing the central locking was now off the car, pulled open the driver's door and hit the driver on the side of the head knocking him out cold. The policeman heard the noise behind him and his turn back was involuntary and costly, as it gave Arman time to cover the space between them and the officer was unconscious on the floor before he knew what had hit him.

They picked him up and put him back in the passenger seat. Arman collected his jacket and gun by which time Alex had joined them by the car. They weren't sure if there was an alarm or CCTV, so Alex flicked the jammer switch. Now wearing black balaclavas, they made their way to the villa. The windows around the villa were old and wooden and not up to modern security standards. Arman made short work of gaining access by forcing one of the locks with a screwdriver and a bit of force and they were quickly inside the house. They had seen the lights on in one of the rooms upstairs before they had been turned off, so it seemed a good assumption that the woman was in there. The staircase was old and marble and Alex was thinking it was good that it wouldn't creak or groan, but just as they got to the first floor they found they were on wooden floorboards and before he could warn the others to walk at the sides, he heard the creak as one of them found a loose floorboard.

Anna had been waiting for Sam to come home to tell her about his evening, but couldn't stay awake any longer. She was a light sleeper, but she heard the floorboard creak.

"Sam, it's okay, I'm not really asleep. Come and tell me about your evening."

The door opened and she expected Sam to turn the light on, but even in the darkness she suddenly saw there was more than one person in the doorway.

"Who the hell are you? What are you doing here?"

"Señora Martínez, we need you to come with us. Please do this quietly or I will have to make you," said Alex.

"Well you've got another think coming if you think I'm coming quietly," said Anna, trying to back away, before realising she had been out flanked along the other side of her bed. She felt an arm come across her right shoulder towards her face. She went to block it, but he was strong and then she smelled something sweet, something she hadn't smelled for many years. Even as she lost consciousness, it came to her. Chloroform. She was easy to carry and one of the team went and got the Ford Transit van they had stolen earlier in the day. The officers in the car hadn't even stirred by the time the van was on its way out of the driveway and heading towards the city.

*****

Sam dropped Terri off and then as he approached the villa he saw the police car. He could see it wasn't across the driveway which was a bit odd, but then he thought that maybe they were waiting for him to return. He looked in as he passed the car and saw the policeman in the passenger seat was sitting back with his head towards one side. He slammed on the brakes and jumped out of the car and opened the police car and saw they were both out cold. He shook one and then the other. They weren't dead and first the passenger and then the driver started to come to. He saw the panic in their eyes and then without waiting, he rushed towards the villa, leaving the policemen trying to pull themselves together.

The front door was open. He was yelling for her, but he knew there was probably little point. He was cursing himself for leaving her. Was she dead? He was running from room to room and the audible alarm activated as he tripped the motion sensors. The police officers were with him now, guns drawn, but it was all too little and way too late. He lost all sense of which rooms he had been in to check and it was the officers, both wide awake now, who had meticulously gone from room to room, who grabbed him and told him she had gone. One was on the radio calling in what had happened, whilst the other was now outside and he was the one who found how they had got in. Then they carried out a preliminary search of the immediate grounds to make sure she wasn't there. The rest could wait for when they got a full team out there, probably with a dog thought Sam.

The noise stopped as he turned the alarm off and he sat down on the step outside the villa. He'd let her down. Tears were welling up in his eyes. He should have been there. He felt the anger building in him. '*No, not now, not now,*' he thought. He didn't know if he was saying this out aloud, but he saw the policemen looking at him and then they were stepping back as he went towards them. Then he heard his phone ring and he stopped.

"Sam, I am so sorry. I will be with you very soon," said Lori, who had just had the call from the police control room supervisor. "I know you must be angry and upset, but please, please, do not do anything until I get there."

Again, her calming voice. He looked at the two officers and forced a smile and allowed his body to relax and he saw them take their hands off their side arms. He didn't know what he had been about to do and that worried him. '*Was he going to hit them? Really? What the hell good would that do?*'

*****

Lori looked at Greg. They had just been about to say goodnight when she got the call. She yelled at him to go with her as she ran to her car.

"They've taken Anna!"

"What? Who? The Armenians?"

"Yes, I think so. Sam's there now. I don't know what's happened yet, but I'll find out soon enough," said Lori.

It only took ten minutes to get to the villa. On the way Greg rang Terri and broke the news and got her to find out where Tommy and Simon were. No leads, no descriptions. Just keep watching and see if anything stands out.

The police officers at the villa knew they had screwed up and badly. This wasn't the time for reading them the riot act. Instead Garcia got them to tell her everything they could about what had happened. She was surprised that they had only been knocked out, one with a punch and the other with a smack on the head with a gun. Surprised in as much that kidnapping was a high stakes crime, therefore this suggested those responsible had clearly taken into account the likely rebound effect if they had seriously injured, or even killed the officers. Neither of the officers had seen the second offender and only the officer in the passenger seat had seen the one who had been acting like a drunk.

She could see what had happened. The officers had come on at the shift change and hadn't picked up on the seriousness of what they were dealing with. It had happened before and would no doubt happen again and she needed to take responsibility if the message hadn't been clear enough. But all of this would have to wait for the inevitable debrief when, as often was the case, the bosses would be looking for a scapegoat to hang out to dry. What she needed now was to know what one of the kidnappers looked like. She sent the one who had seen the 'drunk' back to headquarters and got Nino to find a police artist and get them back into the office and working on an image. This was too urgent to wait till the morning. She needed this picture out and about as soon as possible.

She had asked for and been given the lead on the investigation. She got it, primarily because of the connection with what she was already looking at, but this was also the second high profile incident involving British ex-pats in a week and the local politicos would be looking to allay blame. Therefore off-loading it to the GEO made sense to the local police command team, so it came with a warning that everything rested on her shoulders if things did not go well.

Nino was already setting up a Kidnap Control Room. Kidnaps were ugly things to deal with, but usually the ransom was linked to money or the release of someone else. Garcia suspected that this was a strong-arm intimidation tactic by the Armenian boss, Sonny Sargsyan. But why would he think she would back off? As she thought through what had happened, it occurred to her that Sonny may be focusing on Sam and he was the one he wanted to back off.

"Sam, I think Sonny thinks you are somehow involved in the MacDonald investigation," said Lori.

"What are you thinking?" said Sam.

"You told him you were a Met cop when we were playing our little charade at his club. He might be thinking that you are out here on some sort of Met investigation and he wants to scare you off."

"How would that benefit him?" said Sam.

"He knows I haven't been able to make much progress so far and so he might be thinking he can deal with any threat I can offer. We can't find the guy who stole the van in the MacDonald murder, so there's probably a good chance Sonny has sent him off somewhere out of the way, or maybe even got rid of him altogether – that way we never find him and then can't connect Sonny to the murder," said Lori.

Greg hadn't said anything so far. Lori had been talking with Sam as the victim's son, so she needed to get on and do her job. The first hour of any serious criminal offence like kidnap was really important. Called the Golden Hour, it was a critical time where law enforcement teams could get things very right or very wrong, so he didn't need to be getting in her way. He saw the way she went about her business and was impressed. Sam was also listening to her. She was good, very good at her job. Sam, like Lori, was an experienced SIO, a Senior Investigating Officer. He had heard her set the overarching investigative strategy and it was sound: to ensure the safety of Anna, secure and gather evidence to the crime and to find and arrest the offenders. She had put this out over the radio, so there would be a recording of the transmission that gave the whole team absolute clarity of what was expected and in what priority.

Greg said, "Sam, your mother was bloody good at what she did. I know it's a long time ago and she's a few years older now, but I don't think she would have forgotten how to deal with something like this. You probably don't know this, but before I worked with her, she was taken prisoner during an operation and by all accounts she handled everything they threw at her and came out of it in one piece when she was released. I only say this because I want you to know she is some tough cookie."

Sam looked at him and nodded a thank you. He still worried that it was a long time since she had been in the spy game and to him, she was his sixty-nine year old mum who some bastards had taken as a means of getting to him.

"You know that conversation we had before Greg?"

Greg nodded, "You ready now?"

"Yes," said Sam quietly.

Lori looked at Sam and then at Greg. "Now listen to me guys. I do not need you two, or presumably three with Terri, running around the island in some sort of vigilante action group."

Greg started to try to say something, but she held up her hand.

"No, I'm serious on this. Do not get in my way. I will keep you completely in the loop and I'm not completely stupid, so if I think there's anything you can do that maybe I can't, then I will tell you. Do you understand?"

Greg and Sam looked at each other. They knew she was right and Sam would be saying exactly the same if he was in her shoes. It didn't make it any easier to hear though, although they both heard the potential was there to help in some way that she seemed to be hinting at. She stood waiting for their acknowledgement.

"Yes, agreed," said Sam.

"Greg?"

"Yes, yes, of course, I was just thinking how we might start helping," said Greg with a smile.

She had needed to say it and she knew they probably expected her to say it as well. Whether or not they took any notice of her? She very much doubted it.

SEVENTEEN

The sweet taste of the chloroform was still in her head as she woke the first time. She lay still, just sensing her environment and mentally checking her body for injury. Nothing.

She was lying down on her back on a bed with her hands bound in front of her. Better than behind her she thought and far more comfortable. Her feet were free, so she made the assumption that her kidnappers, and she guessed it must be the Armenians, weren't experienced in kidnapping. She knew that you didn't want your victim having the freedom to move around. You wanted total control of them. From there, kidnappers could then relax things if the victim became compliant. She thought back to a different time. *'You used to train this stuff. So come on think!'*

She started again. This time working methodically through each of her senses. She had done taste with the chloroform, so she took time to work through what she could see, hear, smell and feel.

She looked around the room. It was about ten foot by twelve. One bed, a single with what felt like a light duvet, the sort you would have for summer. Difficult to see anything below her eye line because of the lack of light. There was a window. It was small. Too small for anyone to crawl through. She looked again squinting through the darkness trying to get her eyes to adjust. She could just make out what looked like a bar or a rod running vertically down the centre of the window, so no chance of getting out of there. The door was opposite the bed. No niceties like a bedside table or toilet. That might be useful if she needed to ask to go to the toilet unless they'd left a bowl, but she couldn't see one. She knew that kidnappers didn't usually like their victims to have no toilet options at all. If they were forced to go in the corner of the room the smell soon became abhorrent in the rest of the premises, directly impacting on the kidnappers. Therefore, it was far easier to give them a bowl or just take them to a toilet, especially for someone like Anna who posed a low threat. She paused for a moment and realised she still felt tired or maybe it was the lingering effects of the chloroform. She fell asleep again.

*****

She was usually good at estimating the time when she woke, but her head was fuzzy. She lay there listening. At first it seemed quiet. No apparent traffic noise, but then she heard something. It seemed quite far away, a car or maybe a truck because the road noise was louder. It was dark in the room and she could see through a small window that it was dark outside, so presumably the road noise was echoing with the night air. It was loud enough to think that the window must be at least slightly open. She listened again. Maybe a radio or television. No talking or dogs barking. Kidnappers didn't all sleep at once and generally they had a TV to take away the boredom if they weren't the ones on watch.

She eased herself off the bed. She wasn't wearing any shoes as she had been in bed when they had grabbed her. However, she was a runner and so her feet were pretty tough. She felt the floor with her toes. Some sort of tiling. That suggested she was maybe in a finca or something like that, where they would have used tiles on the floor. She could just see out of the window if she stood on her toes. First thing she noticed was the air, so the window was slightly open. Looking out, she saw no other buildings, but to her right, she could see a corner of the rear of a car. She wasn't sure what it was. It didn't look to have any slope, so perhaps it was a saloon and in this light, it looked dark in colour. Was it the dark coloured BMW Bill had seen? She went back to her bed. The level of darkness told her that it was still the middle of the night and she should try to sleep. *'Remember, you've done this before. Relax your breathing and deal with things in the morning.'* Luis had always marvelled at how she managed to get herself off to sleep so easily. It had been something she had trained herself to do when she was in the Service as she never knew when she might get her next opportunity to sleep. She smiled and closed her eyes, *'Oh my darling Luis, at least I haven't got you worrying about me.'*

*****

Alex had tried a few times to ring Sonny but hadn't got a reply. He knew where he was. He was with the Indian woman at the Glòria, so he probably shouldn't try to disturb him anymore he thought to himself. He sent a text. *'It's done'* and about an hour later he got the call back from Sonny.

"Any problems?"

"No. Simple in and out job and no issues with the cops," said Alex.

"Well done Alex. We'll leave them all stewing until the morning and then see how co-operative Señora Martínez is when she wakes up," said Sonny.

He put the phone down and turned back to look at Jaz.

"Now where were we?"

*****

Lori was still busy going through the actions for her initial investigative plan with her team. Greg and Sam left her to it and went through to the kitchen and Sam made some coffee, before leaving the cops some space in there and going through to the family dining room.

"I've dealt with a fair number of these things Greg, but I can honestly say I now know what it's like for the families involved and it's a damn site worse than I ever imagined," said Sam.

"I get that, but Anna, your mum, is going to need you to be right on your game Sam. We need to think through what we can do to support Lori. I think we can both see that she's got everything in hand here, but there's going to be other stuff that we can do that might be beyond the police's operating parameters."

"What are you thinking?" said Sam.

"Sonny is the key here. But if we, and I include Lori in this, if we can't find out where they are holding Anna, then we're screwed," said Greg.

Sam looked at him. "So, instead of going after Sonny, you're thinking we go for the snake's head? Go for Sergei Grigoryan?"

Just at that moment Lori came into the room. "Ah, found you." She stopped and looked at them. "What are you up to? You were talking about something and I have specifically told you to do nothing to get in the way of what I am trying to do."

She was, well, not angry, but definitely annoyed. They had agreed not to do anything and the first minute her back is turned, she finds them plotting something.

"It's just an idea," said Greg. "But I promise we won't act until we have spoken to you. We won't get in your way and we'll just scope things out for the time being."

This was probably the best she was going to get from

them, so she nodded and then said, "Sam, can we have your phone for a while? There's a good chance they will ring you and I want to be able to patch any calls through to the control set-up to record the conversations and try to track the phone they are using. And before you say anything, I know there's only a slim chance of tracking any phone calls in, but it's a Standard Operating Procedure as you well know."

"Yes that's no problem Lori and I've seen how you have been running things and I am very reassured, so thank you," said Sam.

He knew the SOP and yes, it was only a slight chance, but it was vitally important to make sure you covered the basics. He had seen too many mistakes made when SIOs hadn't done this in the Golden Hour and they had bitterly regretted it later. He handed her the phone and she left them, closing the door behind her.

As soon as the door closed Greg rang Terri. She had Tommy and Simon walking the streets in Palma, doing the rounds in the clubs watching for any suspicious activity and taking pictures of anyone who looked like Armenian Security and any cars they were using. They hadn't seen any dark blue BMWs that seemed to be connected to the gang, but they had seen Sonny's black Porsche Cayenne parked up close to one of the clubs with the driver sat in it. He was still there an hour later and so it looked like he was waiting for someone, presumably Sonny.

"The guys need a tactical decision on whether to deploy the tracker on the Porsche Dad. There's a risk they may be surveillance conscious but if they are, we haven't seen any evidence that they scan the cars before they leave the clubs. That suggests they aren't scanning, as they wouldn't wait till they got back to their safe house before checking. Worst-case scenario? Two possibilities if they find it. One is low risk and

Sonny just gets a little bit more paranoid but the second one is they think it is Sam or the police trying to find Anna. I reckon we go for it, if only because it would be exactly what they'd think the police would try to do."

Greg was thinking about the possible outcomes for Anna. He needed to detach himself from the emotions. *'Easier said than done,'* he thought.

"You're right Terri. Even if they find it, Sonny is only going to expect the police to have done something like this. If he was that surveillance conscious he would have dumped the Porsche by now but I think he's the sort of guy who likes being seen out and about in it," said Greg. "Just so you know, I won't tell Lori what we're doing. Best she doesn't know I think."

"You know I don't usually question you Dad, but what happened to transparency and trust? What's she going to think if she finds out?" said Terri.

"I knew there was a reason I asked you to join the firm. We need one sensible head running the show. You've got a really good point there, so here's what we'll do. Get the guys to fit the tracker on his Porsche if they can and then text me. I can then break the news as a fait accompli."

"Reckon she'll fall for that?" said Terri.

"Not in a million years," laughed Greg out loud, making Sam look at him.

"I'll get it done," said Terri, "and then I'll get back to you."

"Who won't do what in a million years?" said Sam.

"I might as well tell you now. We're trying to get a tracker on Sonny's Porsche," said Greg.

"And you're not asking Lori first?"

"Do you think she'd go for it?" said Greg.

"No, neither would I in her shoes. But I'm not, so I think it's a bloody good idea, both to fit it and not to ask her first," said Sam.

Terri was still on the phone and had been listening to them.

"Okay, so that's Sam on board. I'll get it done and then come and pick you up."

*****

Lori brought back Sam's phone and gave them a quick round up on what was rolling out from her preliminary plan. She wasn't hopeful in stumbling across the hideout and was more intent in getting everything lined up ready for when the call came in to Sam. They assumed it would now be in the morning, so Lori suggested Greg and Sam get some sleep. As Greg was leaving to go back to Terri's, he paused and looked at Sam and Lori.

"You know something? It occurs to me that Sonny and his friends may not know about my part in this and that might be a good thing and something we can keep under wraps. It'll mean me staying away for a bit and we'll have to do things by phone. What do you think?"

"Presumably the same goes for Terri and your boys?" said Sam.

He was about to answer when Lori interjected.

"Boys? Who are these boys Greg? Is this a little surprise for me? When were you going to tell me?"

"Just some help for me and Terri that's all. There's just the two of them," said Greg.

She glared at him whilst Sam looked apologetically at him too, realising he had let the cat out of the bag about Tommy and Simon. Terri had mentioned them in passing when they had been at Contrabando and he hadn't thought about how it might look to Lori.

"Please Greg, no more surprises. I'd rather know, good or bad, than find out later," said Lori.

Just at that moment he got the text from Terri that the tracker was fitted. He decided it was best to tell her

204

now.

"Would it help if we could get a tracker on Sonny's Porsche?"

She was about to say 'Yes', but stopped herself.

"Greg Chambers, you are impossible!"

"Yes, but am I forgiven?" said Greg.

"Not really, but yes it might help, but make damn sure you share the Tracker data."

"Si, Inspectora, of course," said Greg. "Now Terri's on her way to pick me up, so goodnight to you both." He shook Sam's hand. "I just know Anna will be handling this okay Sam and we will get her back, I promise you." He then gave a quick look to the door to check it was closed and then gave Lori a hug and a gentle kiss on the lips.

Sam looked at them both, "Have I missed something?"

*****

Greg left the villa and hadn't been walking long when he saw the white Merc approaching. Terri stopped alongside him and he got in.

Some hundred metres above them, one of Alex Krikorian's men was hidden away in some bushes looking down on the villa and the approach road. He dialled a number.

"Yes?"

"Alex, I've got a white guy, fair hair, age maybe fifty or sixty, who has just left the villa and is getting into a white open top Merc coupe, looks like an SLK."

"Driver?" said Alex.

"Female, long blonde hair, about thirty, looks like a model."

"Can you get the number?" said Alex.

"No, sorry, but the tops down if that helps?"

"Yes, okay, now probably best you get out of there Garik and well done."

Alex immediately made a call to one of his team.

*****

"Any problems with the tracker?" said Greg.

"No," said Terri as she accelerated away. "The boys said it went really well. Tommy said the driver was too busy looking at the talent walking by to notice anything. Then they got a real break with a bunch of locals walking by, on their way up to Sant Miquel and they gave Tommy some really good cover. It was then easy for Simon to distract the doorman, giving Tommy enough time to drop down at the back of the Cayenne and get the tracker on a good bit of solid metal."

"Good. Any movement so far?"

"No, we've got it running on a web-based platform, so we can share it live with Lori, so that should keep her happy," said Terri.

He looked at her.

"Web-based platform?"

"Dad, you really need to get more into this stuff. Okay, we can all see it on our phones and we'll get a signal when the car moves off."

"Good and why do I need to know how this all works when I've got you to figure this stuff out?"

"Ha! Anyway, how do you think Anna will hold up? I know what she used to be, but she's a fair bit older and been out of the game for quite a while," said Terri.

"I've told Sam that she'll be fine, but I just don't know. She was a really good field officer when I knew her, but that was a long time ago. I reckon she'll know what to do, but it's whether or not she can physically and mentally hold up that worries me most."

"How long do you think we have Dad?"

"Two, three days. He's using her as a pawn. He's got to know the police won't negotiate, but maybe he thinks Sam is on some sort of Met investigation? We could buy some time if he thinks Sam will back down."

"The tracker is a long shot as he doesn't need to go anywhere near her does he?"

"No, he doesn't," said Greg. "But, and I appreciate that it's a big but, the Porsche could still go there for some reason."

"Yes, you're right, I'd missed that point. Tommy is leading on following any signals that come in, but one thing we need to sort out for the morning is this call coming in from Rob the Tech guy. He's expecting to speak to Anna and he certainly wasn't going to speak to anyone else," said Terri.

"Okay, let's think about this. So we've got Anna's phone at her house and that should have Sir John's number on there. I'll ring him tomorrow, using her phone and explain and get the message through Carruthers to Rob. That should reassure him and get us the information as I think it's going to be important."

They were approaching the apartment and Greg was expecting her to turn down into the underground carpark, when she carried on past the entrance and then turned left into the first side street and immediately accelerated.

"What's up?"

"There's an SUV that picked us up as we came into the city. It might have been a coincidence as we went along the Passeig Marítim, but they followed us down into Portixol. Two guys and they're keeping just far enough back," said Terri.

"Good spot. Let's see what they want. Now you've got a little bit of space, see if you can find somewhere to park along here where they can also park and let's get them out on foot."

Moments later, she had pulled across the road and into a space and left enough gap behind that the SUV could park if they wanted to. They got out of the car and started walking forwards. Greg could see there was a junction at the end of the street that offered possibilities to get themselves in the shadows. He listened for the SUV's engine. He couldn't hear anything, but then again with these damn hybrids that switched to electric at low speeds, they may still be behind them. He chanced a glance behind and just caught the SUV pulling into the gap. He motioned to Terri to quicken the pace just a little. If he got these two having to rush to catch them up, then they might just be off their guard enough to help with the element of surprise. Terri spotted a small service bay on their right and they tucked themselves into the shadows and waited. Greg counted silently. He guessed they would be with them in twenty seconds and he hit nineteen as they came around the corner and Greg stepped out behind them.

"Guys, what can we do for you?"

The two who had been following them had been given the brief by Alex Krikorian. They were to look out for the open top Mercedes coming into the city from Illetas and see where it went. Being caught by the couple in the car wasn't in their plan and neither seemed sure where to go with this.

They were both dressed in dark trousers and dark shirts that were hanging outside the trousers and looked like they had just come from security duties at one of the clubs. Greg couldn't see if they were armed with anything. If they had a firearm then it would have to be in the back of their waistband or possibly, but less likely by their ankles, and he hadn't seen anything in their waistbands as he had stepped out behind them.

"Look, you seem unsure what to do. I'm assuming you were following us to see where we're staying. That doesn't look like something you're going to find out anytime soon. Now as I see it, you've got two options. One, you turn around and head out of here and report back that you lost us in the traffic with no harm done or, you don't turn around and that way you will end up on the floor and probably be hurting quite a bit," said Greg as Terri stepped out of the shadows and joined him.

The two men looked at each other and smiled. They thought they stood a good chance against the man in front of them. Admittedly he still looked in pretty good shape, but he was getting on for twice their age. Then the woman appeared. She was tall and blonde and looked more like a model than a fighter.

"Mister, now how about if you want to walk away unharmed, then you just tell us where you are staying?" the slightly taller one said as he pushed his shoulders back and chest out.

Greg didn't give him time to settle before he slowly moved forward, as though in an act of compliance before he launched an arcing right hook and hit the smaller man on the temple causing him to lurch sideways into the taller man who had been trying to react. Terri stepped forward and looking almost balletic, she kicked the taller one hard between his legs. He fell to the floor even quicker than the shorter man, who was at least trying to get back up. Greg grabbed the smaller man's arm and viciously turned it behind and up his back as he pushed him face first against the wall.

"Now, it's my turn to ask some questions. What's your name amigo?" said Greg.

There was a slight resistance, but this soon ended with a gentle application of pressure to the man's arm. Greg could feel the bone and tendons straining, but he was a little way away from breaking it just at the moment.

"Mister, mister, I'm just a door guy. My name's Vardan and he's Davit. We just got told to follow you, that's all."

"Who told you to follow us Vardan and why?" said

Greg.

"It was Alex. I don't know why. He just told us to look out for you coming in from Illetas and see where you went?"

"Ah, yes, but that wasn't all was it Vardan? You then thought you could take an old man and a young woman didn't you?" said Terri.

"I'm sorry, I'm sorry. It was his idea."

Davit was still groaning on the floor, so wasn't really in any position to say anything.

"Now listen Vardan, your friend is still hurting, so why don't you answer the next question. Where has Sonny had Anna Martínez taken?" said Greg.

"I don't know," said Vardan before he screamed as Greg exerted more pressure to his arm, "I swear on my mother's life mister, I really don't know. I think Alex took her."

"Who is Alex?" said Greg.

Vardan felt just a bit safer in answering this question.

"He's the boss's number two."

"Where did this Alex take her?" said Greg.

"I swear I don't know," said Vardan.

"Will your friend know?" said Terri.

His friend Davit was trying to prop himself up against the wall and he looked at Vardan. His eyes were telling him not to say anything.

"I can't say anything, he'll kill me," said Vardan.

"Don't worry mate, you just told me all I needed to know," said Terri.

Greg twisted again and heard the bone crack before he let Vardan slide to the floor whimpering. Terri was standing over Davit.

"So your friend thinks you may know more than him Davit? So do you? Now before you answer, this isn't one of those 'I'll give you a second chance' things. You two are already making too much noise and so we can't stay here too much longer. So one chance, got it?" said Terri.

"I can't tell you, he'll kill me," said Davit.

"And what, you think I won't!" said Terri quietly and with a flick of her body, she spun quickly on her left foot and caught Davit's head with her flying right foot leaving him unconscious.

"Those ballet lessons came in handy then my girl."

Terri smiled at him. "Yep, that and the Thai boxing I did in the Army."

She searched the two men. No guns, but two flick knives and both had a phone which she turned off and pocketed. She found a drain nearby, snapped the blades against the iron grate and dropped the knives through the drain cover.

Greg found their SUV keys and ran down and brought the car back and they loaded them into the boot. Davit was out like a light and Vardan was still moaning about his arm. Terri then ran back to her car and came back with a bunch of plastic ties.

"Best they don't get a chance to move around much in the back," said Terri. "I'll go and collect some extra kit and meet you at the finca. These guys might not know exactly where Anna is, but they can probably give up some possible sites we can get checked out."

"Yes, I'll get Tommy to meet me at the finca and we'll then have a little chat with our new friends here," said Greg looking down at the two bodies in the hatchback boot.

EIGHTEEN

Terri went back to her apartment and collected two boxes and loaded them into the Mercedes and set off to the finca.

At the same time Tommy and Simon were heading back to the finca where they met Greg and saw he was in a different vehicle.

"New car then?" said Tommy.

"They let me borrow it," said Greg, walking around and opening up the hatchback. "They wanted to know where we were staying, but now it's their turn to answer some questions."

The two men were stirring and found they couldn't move their hands. The one with the broken arm, Vardan, was flinching as he moved. Tommy wasn't too sympathetic but gave him an option.

"You can get out on your own or I can help you. What's it to be?"

Vardan started shuffling and got his legs over the end of the boot and his feet on the floor. Tommy stepped forward and took his broken arm and eased him up.

"See, if you co-operate, you won't get hurt, okay?"

Vardan nodded cautiously, unsure as to whether to believe the man in front of him. Davit was getting over the two kicks he had taken from Terri. He was angry and wanted to fight. He wasn't going to just give in like a coward, like Vardan. Tommy had been watching him and was waiting for what was likely to be a bit of a show of defiance. As Davit kicked his legs forward out the back of the hatchback, so the rest of his body came up and forwards, bringing his head up to. Too late he realised Tommy was waiting for this move and the resulting blow to his head smashed his nose and left him reeling back on the floor of the hatchback.

"Did I not warn you my friend? We don't give chances here. Comply and I won't hurt you. Mess with me in any way and it will hurt a lot. Comprendes?"

Davit could barely speak as he tried to clear the blood from his nose and mouth, but he nodded vigorously to Tommy in case it looked like he wasn't agreeing. Tommy then reached in and eased him out of the car and walked them both towards the finca.

They had planned for this situation and had identified one of the rooms as a suitable temporary containment area. They had fitted covert cameras and taken all of the non-essential furniture out, just leaving two single beds and Tommy led the way to the room with the two men, followed in by Simon and Greg. The men sat down on the beds and Simon gave them two small bottles of water. The both eyed the bottles suspiciously.

"Guys, just drink. Do we look like we need to drug you? We just need some questions answered. We will know if you are telling the truth and you know what will happen if you don't just give us what we want to know. Okay?"

"Yes, yes, but we don't know anything," said Davit.

"Sometimes you don't know what you do know amigo, so here's a starter question. Where are your accommodation houses where you guys all stay?" said Greg.

The two men looked at each other. Vardan was nursing his broken arm and wanted Davit, who was his supervisor, to answer the questions. Vardan was looking at Davit trying to tell him with his eyes to answer the questions. Davit thought that it seemed okay to tell them where they stayed as they could probably find this out anyway, just by following one of the doormen back home.

Davit said, "There's three apartments in the city mister and Sonny has his villa."

"Good and thank you. How many sleep in the apartments?"

Davit thought again. This didn't seem to be anything he would get into trouble about. Vardan was still looking at him. He could see the fear in his eyes. If they ever got out of this, he would make sure Vardan felt fear when he told Sonny what a coward he had been, but that didn't help now. He honestly didn't know where the woman was being held. He had heard there had been a kidnap, but he was too low down the command chain to know any more details. So he felt safe that he couldn't give away any information that might be a problem and get him in trouble with Sonny. He looked at the men in front of him. They weren't police. So he wasn't sure how far they might go. Would they kill him or Vardan or both of them? They had shown they wouldn't hesitate to hurt them, but he didn't want to answer any questions that might mean that, if they were released, he would have to answer to Sonny. He was brought back to reality when he heard Greg speak again.

"I can imagine you have been wondering how far we might go. Will you walk out of here? What can you tell us that may be okay if you do have to explain to Sonny what you have told us? So here's my advice for what it's worth Davit. You deal with the here and now. If you don't help me, then you will get hurt, no let me correct that, I will kill you. This is a very dear friend who your boss has kidnapped, so I am not in the mood for you messing about with me. No one can help you here, except me. Vardan here looks like he is just a foot soldier, so the responsibility lies with you. Let me ask you again. How many sleep in each apartment?" said Greg.

Davit didn't hesitate in his answer. "Between eight and ten in each one. The ones who stay at the villa are his bodyguards and Alex, his second in command."

Greg knew he had got him. It was time to ease back and gently encourage him to start talking freely as that was more likely to result in more information coming from him, rather than just question and answer.

"That's really helpful. Take some more water. You too Vardan. So what else can you tell us? You don't know where she has been taken do you?"

"No mister, I promise I don't. She could be at a number of places," said Davit.

"Yes, I understand Davit, that's fine. So just tell me the other places you have around the island and whether or not you have heard of any new places being found."

Davit had started to talk now and was still talking long after Terri had arrived. She had waited outside the room with Simon as there was no need to break the relationship Greg and Tommy had built with the two men. About twenty minutes later Greg and Tommy walked back into the kitchen area with a list of possible places where Anna may be being held.

"What do you think? Are we shooting in the dark here?" said Greg.

Simon spoke first, "Let's deal with what we have. The police have no idea where she might be. The Porsche hasn't moved and we've got five possible locations. We've got the thermal kit here to go and check them out."

Terri had opened the boxes she had brought from her apartment. Each contained a military grade drone fitted with cameras that Simon had described as having thermal imaging capability. Greg looked at Terri and Tommy, who both nodded.

"Let's do it. We'd better secure our two friends before we go, then we'll take two cars, the KIA and their hatchback. Tommy, you come with me and we'll do the first two on the list and you guys do three and four. Whoever gets finished first can crack on with the last one."

Tommy secured the two with more plastic ties, gaffer tape across the mouth and a warning they had cameras on them and any attempt to escape would not be wise. The two men nodded. They were broken mentally and were in no fit state to think of trying anything.

As they loaded up the vehicles with the drones, comms and assorted weaponry, Terri looked at her father.

"Are you going to hold off telling Lori anything about this?"

"Yes. To be fair, we're just scoping and I'm not intending any direct action. Not unless we see something happening that we don't like," said Greg, "and there seems little point telling her that Anna's villa was being watched either, as the guy will be long gone now."

"Okay, fair enough," and seeing Tommy come out of the finca she said, "Let's get rolling."

The two men left in the finca sat looking at each other. Vardan was thankful he hadn't been asked any more questions whilst Davit was wondering if what he had said had perhaps been too much.

*****

Tommy and Greg headed off in the hatchback and with little traffic on the road they made quick time getting towards the first place on the list. It was a finca located off the Ma1040 a few kilometres beyond the residential district of Establiments. They parked up about a kilometre away and got out on foot and started to make towards the finca. This is what would take the time. They needed to approach quietly and it was now almost 2am, so they needed to keep an eye on when the sun would come up. This was a farming area and some people would be starting to get up around the 5am mark. The flat terrain wasn't going to help them get a view on the place, so Greg decided to hold back and try the drone. Tommy got it up and flying and they looked at the images on his phone. There were no lights on in the place and no people or cars outside. Tommy switched on the thermal imaging camera to see if it could detect any heat source within the house. Greg knew enough about the technology to know that the drone couldn't actually see through walls, although he wished they could sometimes, just like in the movies, but they could give an idea on heat sources. So whilst it wouldn't look like body shapes on the screen, the blobs of heat might signify people being present within the building. There was a single blob coming from one of the rooms. Tommy shook his head and indicated they move back to the car.

"Good call Tommy," said Greg, once they were back in the car and en-route to the next address. "We can only go on what we're seeing and whilst it's a bit of a long shot, they've got to have people outside on watch, so that's what we've got to hope we see."

As they drove further up the Ma1040, towards Esporles, he texted 'NEG' to Terri and seconds later he got a similar message back from her. A few kilometres further on they came into a small village, more of a hamlet that was located in a dip of a valley and according to the SatNav the place was about three quarters of a kilometre away. They passed the side road that would take them to the place. It was another finca. Tommy drove on up an incline that gave them a line of sight over it. Tommy took a little while to find somewhere to get the vehicle off the road, but eventually he found a track that immediately swung behind a dry stone wall where they could keep the vehicle out of sight.

They approached the finca over a field of olive trees. They both smelled it at the same time. Pigs. They make really good guard animals, so if they picked up their scent it might start them off. Fortunately, what wind there was meant the pig smell was coming from behind them, so hopefully that would mean their human scent was blowing away from the pigs and not towards them. They took their time and therefore it took a little while to get over some more dry stone boundary walls that were topped with two strings of barbed wire they had to cut through, but after fifteen minutes they had found a position looking down on the finca that was surrounded by rows of old vines. They were still about a half a kilometre away and that was the closest they wanted to get. It was still dark, but it wouldn't be long before the first signs of light started showing through. Greg quickly found the finca in his Pulsar Accolade binoculars. There were lights showing on one side of the finca and he picked out the rear of a car, possibly a BMW.

"Let's get the drone up Tommy and see if that's the Beemer we're after."

Tommy launched the drone and Greg kept monitoring the outside of the finca. His binoculars also had thermal imaging and recording capabilities and even before the drone reached its searching height high above the finca, he had spotted two men outside the finca. Both were armed with what looked like machine pistols. One was sitting by the house in a chair, looking at his phone and the other one was on an outer point, about seventy five metres from the finca. Far enough out to be able to spot trouble before it arrived. This suggested these guys knew what they were doing, but then again there were only two of them. He had to therefore consider the possibility of alarm mechanisms around the site. He moved the drone forward to look at the building itself and turned on the thermal imaging camera. The lights that were showing on the left hand side of the house were giving off some heat, but there was possibly something in the dark unlit part of the premises.

"Tommy, we've got two armed tangos on the outside, one by the finca and one about seventy five metres out, at about six o'clock. See what else you can see from above and I'll call Terri."

Tommy nodded and Greg called Terri. It rang twice and then the call was cut-off. A sign that she was unable to talk and she would call back when she could. Greg watched the screen on his phone as Tommy flew the drone high and wide over the finca until it had a good view of the rear of the premises. He focused in on the car Greg had seen and it was a BMW. Hard to tell the colour in this light, but by the shading in the image it looked likely to be a dark colour. The camera was recording video of the fly past and Tommy was also collecting stills of the two men and the car. They were carrying machine pistols. Difficult to tell specifically but they looked something like Škorpions. Greg then saw him focus in on the building itself. The man at the front of the house was now standing up, so Tommy took the drone higher in the sky. There was very little chance he could see the drone, but Tommy wasn't going to take any chances. There were no lights on the drone showing as they blanked them all with gaffer tape, but there was still the outside chance the drone might be picked up against a cloud, so Tommy held the drone high above until the man sat back down again. He then manoeuvred the drone around to the other side of the finca and directed the thermal camera at the unlit part. There was something there, but it was difficult to be sure and with Greg sensing the first signs of light wouldn't be far off, he tapped Tommy on the shoulder and motioned to him to bring the drone back. He pulled away from where they had been watching the finca and a moment later his phone buzzed.

"Had any luck at number two?" said Terri.

He told her what they had seen and first of all she confirmed that her number two just seemed to be another accommodation block as there were numerous cars there and no guards on the outside.

"I'm going to get Tommy to dig in and then I'll pull back and meet you at the finca. We can maybe get an ID on these two guys and then I'll wake Lori up, although I doubt she's gone to bed yet," said Greg.

"Okay we're making towards the fifth address as I want to just to confirm that's a negative and then we'll see you back at the finca," said Terri.

Greg crawled back into position next to Tommy and checked he was set up with water and some nutrition bars and that he was happy with his cover. They checked his comms radio and his phone and agreed a thirty minute text. Tommy was an experienced CROPS guy (trained in Covert Rural Observation Post techniques) and Greg knew he would say something if he wasn't okay with staying out here on plot. Greg backed up again and left Tommy gathering various pieces of grass and fallen branches and twigs that he found lying around him to provide some additional cover to his position.

It would take about twenty minutes to get back to the finca, so with time being important, he sat in the car for a moment and cut and pasted the link to the drone and sent it to Lori and Sam's phones. He then rang Lori and she picked up immediately.

"What are you doing?" she said.

"Just doing some scoping work and now I've got something, I am telling you what I have got, okay?"

"Where is this?" She was looking at the finca and could see the two men and the BMW. "Greg, how the hell have you got this and don't do any more."

"That's two questions and a statement. I'll deal with the statement first and then answer the second question first as it's easier and quicker. I am doing nothing more. Right, I have someone watching this finca in a safe position. He is CROPS trained. I'm sorry I'm not sure what that is in Spanish, but he's covert rural trained."

"Yes, yes, I get that," said Lori. "So back to question two."

"How did we find the finca? We were being followed and I took a decision to see if they could identify the locations Sonny is using across the island."

"But what if they tell Sonny?"

"We've still got them," said Greg.

"So you've kidnapped two of his men?"

"And technically stolen one of his cars if you are worried about what offences I may have committed against him, but I don't suppose he will be reporting them to you will he?" said Greg.

"I don't know whether to be angry or pleased," said Lori.

"Well let's start with pleased shall we? Can you see the images?"

"Yes, I'll get the intel guys on those two images, although I think one is Alex, that's Sonny's number two. That definitely looks like the car doesn't it? But Greg, you must leave this to me. I will get the team out now and we'll be there in less than an hour."

"Good, I was hoping you were going to say that."

He gave her the location details and Tommy's frequency, so that she could use him to help direct their approach to the finca and then he set off to get back to meet Terri and Simon.

NINETEEN

S am hadn't been able to sleep and when Greg's text came through with the images he was on his way downstairs when he saw Lori in the hallway.

"You saw the text from Greg?" said Lori.

"Yes, it's looking good, but it's not 100% that my mother's there is it?"

"No, but the car and the two armed guys watching out the front makes it look very promising."

Garcia rang Pérez and briefed him on the finca and gave him an hour to get a team up to the area and get a plan scoped out.

"How did he find it?" asked Sam.

"He kidnapped two of Sonny's men."

"He did what!"

"I know," said Lori. "Apparently they were being followed out of the city and Greg and Terri took them down a side street and reverse ambushed them. He's now got them holed up somewhere and they gave up a list of five possible sites."

"Just a thought Lori. Something we have found in London is that the OCG bosses don't always trust their guys and they make them put a Tracker App on their phones."

She followed his thinking and rang Greg.

"Have you still got the phones and can you get into

them?" said Lori.

"Yes to both questions, they were happy to open them up with Touch ID and then we changed them to no password and turned them off. Why?"

She was going to ask why they were happy to help open the phones, but thought better of it.

"Check if they've got a Tracker App. Not teaching you to, what is it you say? Suck eggs, but obviously you'll need to get the phones well away from where you are, as they will be able to track you as you try to use the phone to track their OCG contacts. Sam says the OCGs in London are doing this to keep track of their people. Sonny may not be tracking Alex as presumably he trusts him to have him as his number two, but Alex might be tracking the rest of them. The finca is looking really good as the likely place but it wouldn't hurt to get some confirmation if we can."

"Yes, good point. We might as well get as much intel as we can and I'm sure our new friends will most likely have the phone details of all the team in their Contacts. I'll get Simon to head into the city and see what we come up with and get back to you," said Greg.

Lori cut the call and looked at Sam.

"What are you thinking?" said Lori.

"This is looking good, but I hope they can get something more to narrow things down. If you go for this and she's not there, Sonny will know and who knows what he might do then."

"Sam, you know as well as I do the risks involved in kidnap management. I'm going to wait to see what Greg comes back with on the phone tracking. We still have his man Tommy in place above the finca and he is our eyes for any new movement, plus we have the tracker on Sonny's Porsche, which at the moment still hasn't moved from the city, so it looks like he's maybe holed up in a hotel somewhere."

"Yes, you're right Lori. From where we were when she was taken to now we've made some good progress, better than I could have hoped for really," said Sam. He paused, "So he kidnapped two of Sonny's men?"

Lori half-laughed, "Yes, not sure how to write that one up in my Decision Book." Sam nodded as he knew she was talking about the process of SIOs managing investigations and how all decisions would be recorded with a clear rationale. "And then there's the small matter of their interrogation." She shook her head.

"Still rather be where we are though Lori and I know this isn't usual, but can I come with you when you hit the finca? And I promise I will hold back and let your guys do their thing."

"As long as your promises are better than Greg's, then yes. You can stay with me at the outer point until Pérez calls us in. Which reminds me, I should call him to get an update on his plan," said Lori.

*****

Simon had driven into the city to check the mobile phones and then he rang Greg.

"I've got a location confirmation on a number at the finca. The guys had a whole bunch of matching contacts, so I took those as being all OCG guys. I've got Alex's number listed, but he's not appearing on the Tracker App which is pretty much what we expected and as I've only got one number showing on the App at the finca, it suggests the other guy there is going to be Alex, just as your DI Garcia suggested."

"Simon, that's brilliant mate. What's the name of the other guy and I'll check him out with our two guests?"

"It's Tigran. I've now turned the phones off and I'm heading back to the finca."

Greg was by now back at the finca and he updated Terri.

"I'll find out what they know about this other guy,"

said Terri and headed off to the temporary detention room.

She entered with a cheery greeting, "So guys, how are you doing?"

Both men sat up and looked at her warily. Davit's head and testicles were still very sore, whilst Vardan was holding his broken arm gingerly. Neither looked like they would offer much resistance, so she decided on going easy with them.

"Quick question guys. Tell us what you know about Alex and a guy called Tigran," asked Terri.

Davit looked at Vardan. He could see again the fear in his eyes that he didn't want to be the one doing talking. Davit just shrugged, *'I might as well tell them. We're probably dead either way, so I might be able to do a deal if I try to help them.'*

'Total submission,' thought Terri.

"Alex Krikorian is in charge of us. He's Sonny's second in command. They are both ex-special forces, so we're always careful around them as they take no shit from anyone," said Davit.

"What's going to happen to us lady? Are you going to kill us?"

"No, of course not mate," said Terri as she turned to go out. "Not unless you make me that is."

The two men just sat there. If they did get out Sonny would probably kill them anyway if he suspected they had said anything, so maybe it was better to stay here and wait to see what happened.

Terri closed and locked the door and then rang Lori and briefed her on the information as to who Pérez's team could expect to meet when they approached the finca and that they should bring a signal jammer, just in case there were Wi-Fi alarms set out in the grounds surrounding the finca.

*****

Anna had managed to get some sleep. She had woken up hearing the sounds of birds singing. It was light and she could hear movement from the next room. She checked her body again and she had no physical injuries. She got up and went to the window and by standing high up on her toes she could just see out. There was a man in the distance. Maybe eighty to a hundred metres away, so too far to positively identify him as one of the men from last night. He had a machine pistol slung over one shoulder. She heard a kettle boil nearby and the noise of cups or mugs. She looked around the room for a bucket or a bowl. Nothing.

"Hello, hello, I need the toilet please."

"Wait."

"Okay, thank you, but I'm afraid I can't wait too long."

No response. But that was now two people she could say were there and she hadn't heard any other sounds to suggest there were more than two. If he came and took her to a bathroom then what she saw would be very telling. She hoped he would be wearing a face covering. That at least gave her hope of a safe release. If he wasn't worried about being seen, then things weren't looking good. She didn't have to wait long and the door opened and the second man stood in the doorway. He was wearing a balaclava. She felt herself breathe out with relief.

She christened him Dick and the one outside would be Harry. Dick was six foot plus with an athletic build. He looked like an ex-soldier and was dressed in black trousers and white shirt that he had obviously been wearing since yesterday. His clothes and his shoes looked expensive, which suggested Dick was reasonably high up in the organisation. She recognised his voice as he had been the first of the men who had come into her room and was therefore presumably in charge

227

of this operation.

She made a point of not looking directly into his eyes, but she saw enough to make her think he was a man not to mess with. She had already formed a strategy of compliance to avoid antagonising her captors. With no easily available source for a weapon of any sort and now given the size of this man, she dispensed with any thought of overpowering her attacker, even using the element of surprise as they were unlikely to expect an old woman to attack them. Escape was possible if there were indeed only two of them, but her only exit seemed to be through this door as the window was too small.

'Okay, let's find out what I can see if he lets me go to the bathroom.' With that Dick motioned to her to come to the door. The bathroom was immediately to her right and she tried to close the door behind her, but he pushed it back open. She expected him to do that. She put on a little show of being embarrassed, although it didn't faze her in the slightest as something like this was normal in her previous life in the field. She noticed that he didn't grin or snigger. He was above that. He had a job to do and that was to ensure she didn't escape and was held for as long as was needed. There was toilet paper which she was grateful for and she thought back to her previous experience when she had been held. This place was like a hotel compared to that. She was still only wearing her night dress, so he could see she wasn't going to be able to hide anything. She stood up and he stepped to one side to let her come out and as she did, he handed her a paper cup of water.

"Thank you," said Anna.

He said nothing. She turned left back into her room and he closed and locked the door.

TWENTY

They had arrived at an RV point about a mile from the finca. It was now 6.00am and there was some movement in the area.

Pérez had been getting new images from Tommy and his two teams of four were all briefed on the terrain and the movements of the two tangos. Lori, Nino and Sam were in a third vehicle and Nino had an investigative team held up five kilometres away, ready to move in for evidential searching after the place was secure.

Lori made a final call to Pérez and authorised him to deploy. The operational strategy Lori had originally set was still the one Pérez was working to and he was now in command of the tactical decisions from here on in. All of his decided actions needed to be routed towards delivering a positive outcome of her strategy.

It was to be a silent approach from both sides of the finca. He had identified routes in from studying Tommy's pictures and the topographic maps of the area. Nino was in control of the signal jammer and this was key to the teams making progress and neutralising the threat from both tangos. Lori, Sam and Nino would be able to see everything Tommy could see as he was relaying his images direct to their phones. There had been some discussion about sending up the drone, but with the light now having broken it was decided that it was too risky. The two men on guard seemed to know what they were doing and so Pérez was adopting caution in his approach, as they needed to be given a level of respect for their potential skill set, to minimise the risk to both his men and more importantly the woman who was currently held captive.

Tommy looked on the scene below and thought through the possible scenarios he would consider and compared those to the police team he knew were getting ready to deploy. The guy on the outside in the Point position needed dealing with quickly and he would have done this with a silent approach and a knife, followed by a headshot to the one by the finca.

'Guys, you need to be positive here and deliver a level of force appropriate to the risk to the victim,' he said to himself.

Pérez was delivering a similar message to his team. Whilst there was an inherent intention to save life, be it the victim, his officers or indeed the kidnappers, he was well aware that the risk to the victim, Anna Martínez, was at such a level that lethal force was justified. He had contemplated a sniper to do just that, however, whether it was defensible in a Court of Law was debateable if it could be shown that there was another way and as a police officer he knew he had to operate not just within the law, but also within the spirit of the law. He needed his teams in position and to then assess the likelihood that they could deal with the outer guy quickly and quietly without resort to lethal force. However, he made it clear that the back-up plan, Plan B, would include the option of a head shot using a supressed Sig Saur assault rifle and that would be on his order. He had been with these guys for two years and they accepted his direction without question. He checked his phone for the latest images from Tommy and called him on the radio.

"Alpha 1 Team leader to Charlie 1, sitrep please."

He heard Tommy respond in his gentle rolling Bajan accent.

"Charlie 1 to Alpha 1. Good to go."

Lori and Sam heard the radio communication and each took a deep breath. Sam found this the hardest part of command. Sending people in to dynamic action, with the associated risk when weapons, especially firearms were involved, whilst you sat safely back in an office or a car was still hard and he could see that Lori felt the same. Radio comms would be at an absolute minimum now until Pérez called the Operation over.

They watched on their screens as Tommy transmitted the pictures of first Pérez and the Alpha team moving into position, before switching to see the Bravo team track around the rear aspect of the finca. Two of the Alpha team broke off and moved forward in a crouched profile until they ran out of full cover and took to the floor and started crawling forward keeping to the rows of vines and taking cover when Point man looked down the row they were in. They had split up and were about six rows of vines apart. The images showed the Point man was looking around and at one stage was looking directly up at Tommy's position before he moved on. He had seen nothing and was just scanning for any change in the environment, but Tommy was well hidden and was very mindful of the lens on the binoculars not reflecting off the morning sun.

"In position," came the transmission from first Alpha 2 and then quickly followed by Alpha 3.

"Thirty seconds," said Bravo 1.

Nino sat waiting for the order from Pérez, Alpha 1.

"Bravo team in position," said Bravo 1.

"Jammer on," said Pérez.

Nino activated the switch that turned off all Wi-Fi

in a three hundred metre radius. Lori saw her phone go black and knew that Alex, the man at the finca would have just seen the same thing. Through his binoculars, Tommy could see Alex was touching the controls on the phone, trying to get the pictures back. Alpha 2 had a very small window of opportunity to move forward towards the Point man and Alpha 3 was on standby to go to Plan B if necessary. Tommy was providing short concise commentary on Alex as he would be the one to call the alarm if he realised it was a signal jammer affecting his phone. Alpha 2 got within yards of Point man and still had cover hidden under the old vines and waited for Tommy to give the call.

"Charlie 1 to Alpha 2, wait, wait, wait."

Alpha 2 raised himself to a kneeling position, breathing slow and easily and held the Taser lightly in his hand, ready to discharge.

"Wait, wait……, good, good," said Tommy to make sure he was heard.

Alpha 3 was ready and threw a stone to distract Point man who turned away from where Alpha 2 was rising up and in one motion fired the Taser directly into the man's neck, releasing the 50,000 volt charge, causing Point man to drop like a stone.

"Alpha 2 complete," said Alpha 2.

"Jammer off please," said Pérez.

Nino flicked the switch back and Alex saw his phone come back on and he looked up to see where Tigran was. As soon as he couldn't see him he realised what had happened and went to pull his machine pistol into position, when he heard a shout.

"Stand still, armed police. Do not move until I tell you," said Pérez rising from where he had been taking cover. He had the telescopic sight of his SIG to his left eye and Alex looked down and saw a red dot on his chest.

Alex had been in prison for a year before he joined the Army. He had taken the ultimatum they had given him. Join up or stay in prison for four more years. He had hated being locked up and knew that a kidnap charge meant a long sentence, something that he wasn't going to accept. He weighed up how far away the man with the gun was and his chances of a sudden move to escape the bullet. He knew the problem was that there would be others and they would move in quickly once they saw he was being compliant, leaving little opportunity for him to then try make a break for it. He made his decision and accepted that it could be the last one he would ever make.

Pérez saw the man standing still. He was looking at the red dot on his chest and he sensed that he was deciding what to do next. Pérez knew that this was Sonny's second in command and that he would be a potential valuable source of intelligence if he came quietly. Pérez was by now around forty metres away from the man. If it was him in Alex's shoes, then forty metres was a fair distance to take the chance of distance versus a moving target. The decision would come shortly and Pérez was ready.

"Don't do it, last warning," he said.

Alex Krikorian looked back towards Pérez and smiled. He went as though to release the Škorpion from his neck strap. He was anticipating that Pérez would relax, giving him a split second to drop to the floor and take cover. But he was wrong. Pérez didn't relax and as he saw Alex look up and smile he guessed what Alex was going to do and it wasn't surrender. The moment he saw Alex start to move and bring up his gun, he followed him with his telescopic sight and fired two single shots and Alex fell to the ground. Bravo 1 and 2 came from the rear of the finca and started shouting at Alex to lie still and release his weapon. He didn't move.

Bravo 1 moved forwards with cover from Bravo 2 and stood firmly on the Škorpion and then kicked it away and it moved without resistance. He lent forward and checked for a pulse. Nothing.

"Bravo 1 to Alpha 1. Target confirmed as neutralised," said Bravo 1 in Spanish this time, followed by the same message in English for the benefit of Charlie 1.

"Alpha 1 copied."

"Charlie 1 copied."

Alpha team secured Tigran in plasti-cuffs and Bravo 1 started to carry out a methodical search of the finca. Bravo 1 called out twice again, once in Spanish and once in English.

"Any persons inside the finca lie down on the floor and discard any weapons."

Anna had heard the shouting and was straining to see outside of the window, but couldn't see anything. She then heard the sound of Pérez's shots. The suppressor making them sound like muted whistles and then she heard what she assumed was a radio transmission as it was in a quieter voice. When she heard the same man calling out again, she answered both in Spanish and English.

"I am unarmed. I am Anna Martínez and I think there is no one else here."

"Wait where you are."

"Yes, understood. Entiendo," said Anna in both English and Spanish.

"Bravo 1 to Alpha 1 contact made with Señora Martínez. House entry commencing."

Lori looked at Sam and could see the relief in his face. They saw the Bravo team enter the finca on Lori's phone screen, but then they went out of sight as they went in through the door.

Anna heard them coming in and heard the shouts of "¡Despejado!", 'Clear!' in Spanish, from the team as they checked each room. The voices got nearer and she lay still on the floor with her hands and legs stretched out. She knew they were coming to rescue her, but she also knew that they wouldn't make any assumptions and needed to know she was unarmed. Bravo 1 opened the door and she smiled at him.

He quickly assessed the room and asked her to stand up slowly and turn around once, which she did. He could see she was in a thin night dress and was not holding or concealing anything. He called out again, "¡Despejado!" and then took his helmet and smiled at her.

"Señora Martínez, it is nice to see you," said Bravo 1.

"It is nice to see you too," she said and although she had held up really well until then, all of her strength suddenly disappeared and she started to fall back on to the bed, until he stepped forward and caught her.

*****

Lori and Sam moved quickly forward after Pérez confirmed the finca was secure and one of the Bravo team took them through to see Anna, who had tears in her eyes when she saw them.

Sam hugged her tightly.

"Mum, are you okay?"

"Yes, I'm fine. But it's so good to see you. Honestly I'm fine," she repeated as if to reassure herself as much as Sam. "How did you get to me so quickly?"

"It was Greg and Terri," said Sam. "They got a great lead and then Lori's team did the rest. I'll tell you all about it later, but can I just check again? Are you okay?"

"I can't believe you got to me so quickly. But yes, to answer your question. I'm fine. They knocked me out with some chloroform or something like that, but all in all they were very fair and they didn't harm me."

Lori had been waiting to be told that Alex's body had been covered up. As much as she knew Anna was an ex-spy, she had been through a hell of an ordeal and it was perhaps best she didn't see the body.

"Okay, let's get you back home Señora and I'd like you checked out by a doctor, just as a precaution," said Lori.

"Yes, I'll get that sorted Lori," said Sam. "Can we leave the statement till later?"

"Yes, of course. I suspect that our man Tigran will be more interested in helping us with information about the OCG than answering questions on the kidnap, so we'll be focussing on that to start with," said Lori.

She would need to stay there to await the doctor to certify Alex's death and there would be a senior officer en-route to manage the police shooting. Greg had texted her to say he was on his way with Terri and she would collect Tommy and he would take Anna and Sam back to her house. He had also been getting the images from Tommy through to his phone, so he had seen what had taken place.

"Greg is on his way and he will take you home and I'll catch up later," said Lori.

"Thank you. Sergeant Pérez and his team were first class. I can't believe what has happened in the last day or so," said Sam, "and to get my mother back within, what? Six or seven hours, is some going. Can I ask, is Pérez okay? I've been involved in the follow up to a number of police shootings and there can be a lot of pressure on the officers involved in the inquiry that inevitably comes afterwards."

"Thank you for thinking of him Sam. He's a good officer and a good man. I know what you're saying. Even when you have done the right thing, as he did today, the inquiry can sometimes make you feel like a villain. I will tell him you have asked after him and I know that will mean a lot to him, coming from an experienced firearms commander."

At that moment Tommy made his way down to see

them at the same time Greg and Terri arrived.

"Great job Señor Tommy," said Lori. "You made a really difficult job a lot easier with your comms and the images you were transmitting. Thank you."

"Just an everyday job Ma'am," said Tommy, smiling. "Thank you though, it's appreciated."

"Ma'am?" said Lori to Greg.

"Mam, as in ham. What do your team usually call you then?" said Greg.

"Boss, Señora, Inspectora. So that's a new one for me. I thought 'Mam' was only something you called your Queen?" said Lori smiling.

TWENTY ONE

Greg took Sam and Anna in the KIA and Tommy went with Terri, who was using the Armenians' hatchback.

"Tommy, you did a great bit of work back there mate," said Terri.

"Thanks. Those GEO guys did a good job. Their Sergeant, Pérez, is very good. You'd like him."

Tommy was in his mid-40s and looked upon Terri as a younger sister who he needed to look out for, although he knew he didn't really need to look after her. She was tough, bloody tough and she could really handle herself in a fight, but he wasn't shy in coming forward with suggestions on who she could go out with.

"Thanks Tommy, I'm sure he is very nice, but....."

"Here we go again with your 'buts'. I'm just saying he seems a nice bloke that's all. Anyway, before all this kicked off you said something about going out for dinner with your half-brother? I thought you were going out with Sam?" It suddenly dawned on him what he had said and he looked at Terri and she smiled back. "You mean, your dad, I mean Greg and Sam's mother, Anna?"

"Yep," said Terri.

"Did he know?" said Tommy.

"Apparently not. He hasn't seen her since he finished

training which was Sam's age plus 9 months ago."

Tommy just sat there. "Half-brother eh? Just as well you didn't....."

"Don't even go there Tommy," said Terri laughing.

On the way back to the house, they gave Anna an overview of what had happened after she had been kidnapped and then Sam called Dr Sanchez, their family doctor for as long as they had been on the island. He was waiting at the house when they arrived and despite Anna's protests that she was okay, he carried out a thorough check up of her before finally declaring her fit and well and just needing some rest.

They then sat in the kitchen with coffee and ensaïmadas. It was now 7.30am and Sam had given up trying to get his mother to catch up on some sleep.

"I've got that call coming in from Rob this morning and he was quite clear that he wouldn't talk to anyone else. I promise I'll get some rest this afternoon, when things have quietened down a little," said Anna.

"Okay, point taken. What about the two guys then Greg?" said Sam.

"Well, they're pretty low down the food chain I think and so I don't think they will be any more use to us. I'll check with Lori and see if she wants them, but they might just be an unnecessary distraction for her too. So if all else fails we'll just let them go and they can explain to Sonny what happened to them during the night. In fact thinking about it, why don't we just ring Sonny and tell him what's happened and see if that shakes him up a bit?"

*****

Sonny woke up and felt Jaz was still beside him. He liked her. She was her own woman in a culture that he knew was sometimes difficult for young women to keep their own identity. She was also no fool and she had sensed he had things on his mind. Taking the Martínez woman had seemed like a good idea last night, but he had Sergei's weekly call this morning and he still hadn't found who the damn grass was within his own team who was filtering information through to Sergei. He got up and showered and she was awake as he came out of the bathroom.

"Are you coming for breakfast?" said Jaz.

"I'm sorry I can't. I have a breakfast call with Sergei at nine, so I need to get back to the office, but let's catch up later, maybe lunch, but if not, then definitely dinner." He kissed her and held her hand gently.

"Are you okay Sonny?" she asked.

"Yes, I'm fine. I enjoyed last night. See you later."

He wasn't alright, but he needed to focus on this morning's call and make sure Sergei didn't embarrass him again. He texted his driver and two minutes later he stepped outside the hotel and into the waiting Porsche.

"Where to Boss?"

"The office and make it quick," said Sonny.

*****

The tracker had pinged in Greg's phone as soon as the Porsche had moved and Greg had been watching it since then. Sonny had been expecting an update call or even just a text from Alex and was surprised he hadn't had anything from him. He rang Alex's mobile but got no reply. This was the time when he wished Alex was on the Tracker App as well, but then he tried Tigran's phone. No reply again and the Tracker App showed the phone was still at the finca, so everything was presumably okay. He hadn't planned to go to the finca, but he wanted to check things out with Alex.

"Change of plan Narek. Take me to the finca that's on the way to Esporles."

"He's doubling back," said Greg. "I'll ring Lori before we ring him, as I did promise to tell her before we did anything."

She quickly picked up the call.

"Buenas dias. How is Señora Martínez?"

"Yes, all good. I'm sorry, but I need to be quick and tell you something. I've got Sam and Anna here and we're on speaker phone. The doctor's been and we're just having some breakfast. Two things. Did I tell you we have got someone looking at who the scammers are? He does some work for the British Intelligence Services and Anna managed to pull some strings and he is calling this morning with what he has dug up on the people behind the scam."

"Yes, you mentioned something, but nothing about the Security Services, but that's okay, I forgive you. What is your second thing?"

"We've got a number for Sonny and I'm thinking it might be interesting if we get Sam to ring Sonny and see what drops out of that?"

There was a pause before she answered.

"I hesitate to say this, but given the fact that we probably haven't got enough to charge Sonny with the kidnap, then this might actually be a good idea."

"Might be a good idea. That's high praise indeed Señora Garcia," teased Greg.

"Don't push it Señor," countered Lori. "Plus we have just had a blocked call come through to Alex's phone. It could have been Sonny. We turned Tigran's phone off and they are both now on their way to headquarters for forensics to look at their call history, so if Sonny checked the Tracker App it would still show as being at the finca."

"Have you still got some of Pérez's team there?" said Sam.

"Yes, why?" said Lori.

"We've just seen the Porsche double back along the Passeig Marítim and looking at the route he could potentially be heading for the finca. We should know in the next few minutes," said Sam.

Lori called up Bravo 1, who was still at the site with his team providing armed cover for the forensic team, to let him know what was happening.

"Okay Sam, Bravo 1's got the guys on an outer and inner cordon and if it's just Sonny and his driver then they have enough to deal with him. Now let's wait to see if he goes to the finca. If he gets cold feet, then let's put the call in then," said Lori.

"Agreed. Good plan," said Greg. The Porsche was still heading in the direction of Esporles. "It's looking very promising Lori, they have just turned off the Ma20 onto the Ma1040, heading north."

*****

Sonny tried Alex's phone again. Still no reply. He sent a text, *'Call me now*." Still no reply. He had known Alex Krikorian for over fifteen years and he had never known him to not respond to a call or text within a few minutes. This didn't feel good. He tried Tigran's phone again. It was just ringing.

"Stop the car!"

They were on a quiet country back road and the driver pulled over immediately and Sonny was out of the car and on the ground looking underneath the car. The driver realised what he was doing and went to the other side of the car. Sonny found it first, at the back of the car, where Tommy had attached it. He pulled the tracker off and got to his feet. The driver saw what he had in his hand. Sonny pulled his gun from behind his waistband and pointed it at the driver.

"Boss, Boss, I'm sorry, I don't know how it got there."

"And that's just the problem you clown. It's your job to keep me safe and you have spectacularly failed."

Sonny shot him in the head before the man could react. He then smashed the Tracker with the butt of his gun and threw the pieces in the field at the side of the road. The driver was lying by the side of the car hidden from view from the road. A car approached from the distance and slowed as it passed them, but only because it was a narrow lane and there wasn't much room to pass. Sonny felt his anger subside and almost regretted what he had done. Less so because he had killed the man, but more because it meant he would have to move the body and it was starting to get hot now and if he was being tracked then it might mean he was being followed. He decided he didn't have time to get the body into the field, but settled for pushing it into the roadside ditch. He removed all the man's belongings and then covered the body with dead branches and grasses, before getting back into the car and turning around and heading back towards the City, but taking a different route. He didn't see any suspicious looking vehicles for a couple of kilometres, by which time he thought it was more likely that he had only been tracked, rather than actually followed.

*****

Greg saw the signal go down and waited a few moments to see if it came back and when it didn't he rang Lori back.

"Looks like we've lost the tracker on the Porsche. He was about six kilometres down the Ma1040 when he stopped and we lost the signal."

"I'll get a team out there to check it Greg. In the meantime, why not let Sam make his call," said Lori.

*****

Sonny had got back to the office and was sitting waiting for Sergei's weekly call. He wasn't worried about his figures as they were looking good, but he was on edge. A feeling he didn't like. He called Arman and sent him to check out the finca, but warned him to be on his guard because something wasn't right. He was waiting for the video conference call to come through when his phone rang. It was a blocked caller. Very few people had this number outside of his team.

"Yes," said Sonny.

"Things aren't going your way are they Sonny?" said Sam.

He recognised the voice from outside the club.

"Detective Chief Inspector Sam Martínez, what a pleasure," said Sonny.

"So you were on your way to the finca then? Why did you stop?"

"Something came up, but presumably you know that already?" said Sonny.

"You shouldn't have kidnapped my mother Sonny. That was a mistake, a big mistake."

"Come now, I have no idea what you are talking about. If something has happened to your mother then I can only send my sympathies."

"You've no need to worry Sonny, this isn't being recorded and yes, I know you have covered your tracks pretty well by getting your second in command to do the kidnap. But the good thing is that my mother is now safe and Alex Krikorian, your number two, well he's dead and we also have two of your other men who you sent to find out where my friends are staying."

Sonny tried not to show in his voice that hearing that Alex was dead had shaken him.

"So tell me Sam, are you now just a simple bookseller, as you seem to be moving away from the rules and regulations of traditional law enforcement?"

Sam hadn't given any thought recently about whether he would be returning to London, or if he had decided to stay here and help his mother with the business, but Sonny's words made him come to a sudden decision.

"Well you're right actually Sonny. I am now just a

bookseller and that means I am coming for you." Sam didn't wait for an answer as he cut off the call and then looked at Greg and his mother.

"Bit of a sudden decision Sam?" said Anna.

"I like it," said Greg, "and there's plenty of opportunity to come and help me and your half-sister whenever you want."

"Yes, it was sudden, but we need to sort this guy out and by the way, thanks for the offer of work Greg. I might take you up on it, but I don't have to start calling you Dad or anything do I?" said Sam.

Both Anna and Greg looked at him.

"I'm kidding," said Sam. "But it seems the right thing to do Mum and for the first time in a while I feel good about things. Okay, so Sonny is probably going to run and hide somewhere and he might be difficult first of all to find and then second, to deal with. Greg, you were talking about approaching this another way before? I think you said something about cutting off the head of the snake? Well I have an idea and we need to go to Armenia. Mum, will you be okay here? Greg, can Tommy come here to the house?"

Greg nodded.

Sam continued, "Mum, if you take the call from Rob about the set up in India, and Greg, we're going to need transport to Armenia. I hope to be able to tell you whereabouts after I've phoned a friend in London."

"Okay, he's due to ring at ten," said Anna.

"And I'll get Terri thinking about travel and logistics," said Greg.

Greg then looked at Anna and they both smiled. It looked like the family side of the business had just got bigger.

TWENTY TWO

Sonny sat at his desk looking down at his phone. What had just happened? Suddenly the laptop was buzzing. It was the incoming conference call.

"Good morning Sergei my friend, how are you?"

"I am fine Sonny and I hope all is good with you too?"

"Yes, things are going very well down here in the Balearics. The numbers are good and we're looking to expand into two more clubs."

Sergei sounded friendly enough to Sonny and he had congratulated him on the numbers before he had carried on with the rest of the OCG managers on the call. He was waiting for Sergei to come back to him about something, but after giving the guy in London a roasting about falling numbers, Sergei just checked in with Sonny for any other news and Sonny wasn't about to tell him that he had lost a kidnap victim and five of his team were either missing or dead.

He came off the conference call and Arman was waiting in the office for him. Sonny had got him to go and scout around the finca and see what the hell was going on up there. He could see Arman was looking very uncomfortable.

"I know it's bad news, so stop shaking and just tell me what you saw."

"There were cops everywhere Boss. I went around the back of the premises and got to a position where I could look down and it looked like they had a forensics team in there and those GEO guys were guarding the site. I also saw them loading a body bag into an unmarked van. Boss, what's happened?"

"Never mind. Alex fouled up and so we need to regroup. As of now, you are my number two. Understood?" said Sonny.

Something had happened and whilst Arman didn't know what it was, it had created an opportunity that was too good to miss.

"Yes, Boss. What do you need me to do?"

"You know how most of the business is run. I know that. Alex told me you were smart and that you would soon be ready to take on more responsibility. Well, it's just come a bit sooner than you expected. Keep the business flowing, but there's one more thing. I'm worried we've got a mole in here. Someone who is feeding stuff directly through to Sergei and that's something I can do without, especially at the moment. Find me the mole and bring them to me. Make sure they are alive Arman, as I will want to talk to them. Okay?" said Sonny.

"Got it Boss."

Arman knew about the mole already. He knew, because he was the mole. Sergei had brought him into this dangerous game of cat and mouse with a promise of early promotion and a threat of permanent unemployment if he didn't. Sergei Grigoryan was not a man you said 'No' to.

He waited till he had left the office and was in his car before he felt calm enough to call Sergei.

"Yes."

"Alex Krikorian is missing Boss. Sonny's promoted me to second in command and we've got four other guys also missing. I don't know what the hell is going on Boss, but Sonny looks like he's losing it."

"Thank you for your opinion Arman, but never, repeat never, disrespect your immediate boss, do you understand?" said Sergei.

"Sorry Boss, I was just trying….."

"I know Arman, but just the facts will suffice thank you. What is he intending to do now?"

"I think he might be going to lie low from the police for a while. There's rumours going around that the woman Alex kidnapped has somehow been rescued by the GEO, even before the night was out. Maybe that has something to do with our missing guys?" said Arman.

Sergei went silent, taking in what he had just been told. Kidnapped a woman? What the hell was Sonny playing at doing something like that without reference to him? The murder of the British woman and now this. He was troubled. Sonny was a trusted member of his inner council and yes, a friend. They had been through a lot together, but what on earth was he doing kidnapping people without reference to him first?

"Okay, thank you Arman. This is helpful and good luck with your new role," said Sergei.

"Thank you Boss," said Arman, thinking it was just as well he hadn't mentioned that he had been there at the time of the kidnap, but by then Sergei had hung up and was already ringing Sonny.

"Sergei, good to hear from you," said Sonny.

"And you too Sonny. Just wanted a chat. Is everything all okay with you?"

"Yes, it is thanks. How about you?"

"Yes, I'm fine thanks. Things aren't going as well as I'd like across in the States, but other than that we're in pretty good shape."

"That's good Sergei, but tell me, what's the real reason for your call?" said Sonny.

"You were always very good at seeing through me Sonny. Look, I'm worried about you. You don't seem yourself and you come across like you're hiding something from me. We've known each other a long time and I'd like to think you would tell me anything. Anything at all Sonny, as I am sure we could sort out whatever the issue may be."

Sonny paused and it was long enough for Sergei to tell that there was something, but Sonny wasn't sure if he wanted to tell him.

Finally Sonny said, "Honestly Sergei, things are fine. You were right about the British woman. That was a mistake and it has brought some heat down on me that I could do without, but it is starting to go away as the police have nothing to go on."

A half-truth thought Sergei, is always a good way of hiding the full truth. Sonny was owning up to his mistake with the MacDonald woman, but he wasn't going to tell him anything about the kidnap.

"I'm glad that everything else is all good then my friend and there really was no need to worry about the MacDonald woman. It's a small mistake, but nothing that can't be rectified," said Sergei. "Right, I'll leave you now, so enjoy the rest of your day. Have you still got your Indian woman across there? I think you like her don't you?"

"Yes, I do. She's different and in a good way from other women. She's only here another few days and then she will be going home," said Sonny.

"Well enjoy her company whilst you can Sonny and we'll catch up soon."

Sonny came off the phone and immediately rang Jaz.

"Hi, what's up?" said Jaz.

"Listen, I can't explain, but when is your flight home?"

"It's tomorrow evening, but why?"

"Look, I can't explain Jaz, but try and get an earlier flight home. Those things I told you about? I might have some more problems with them, so I'd like you to get away from here and from me as soon as you can."

"Okay," she said slowly. "I'm sure I can get an earlier flight back to London and I can stay there an extra day if I need to," said Jaz. "But you will have to tell me what this is all about at some stage."

"Yes, I will, I promise," said Sonny.

*****

Terri had diverted to Anna's villa and dropped Tommy off to provide protection for Anna. She then left for the finca, followed by Greg and Sam and on the way Sam rang Jimmy.

"Jimmy, it's me," said Sam.

"You alright mate?"

"Actually, I've not felt as good as this for a long, long time."

"Don't tell me, you've met a tall leggy blonde, fallen in love and have decided to jack it all in and live in the paradise they call Mallorca?"

"Well, you got two out of three right mate."

"What? I was joking! What's been happening?" said Jimmy.

"It's a bit of a long story and I think you'll need to come out here with Di and the kids and then I'll tell you both all about it."

"She won't be able to wait till then Sam. She'll be talking wedding outfits, the lot."

"She'll have to hold off on the wedding outfits Jimmy. That was the only bit you got wrong. I have met a tall leggy blonde though."

"Go on," said Jimmy.

"Turns out I have a half-sister and I've met my bio-logical father."

"Bloody hell! Really? How on earth did all this happen? Did you know anything about them?"

"Co-incidence and no, I didn't know anything about Terri and neither did my mum of course, as Terri came into the picture long after my mum's relationship with Greg."

"So, let me get this straight. This guy Greg is your biological dad and Terri is your half-sister through him?"

"Yes and yes and she's Australian and he's a former spook and oh, by the way, so is my mum. A spook I mean."

"Listen Sam, this isn't some sort of late April Fool is it? Half-sisters, spooks and a biological father? Come on mate, are you having me on?" said Jimmy.

"Hard to believe chum and I haven't mentioned my mum being kidnapped and then rescued and here's another one for you. The bit about living in paradise? I've decided to resign."

"Kidnapped? What do you mean? Is she alright and what do you mean you're going to resign?" Jimmy paused, "I'm not being funny, but have you been on some strong medication or something?"

Sam laughed.

"I said I'd tell you all about it when you guys come out. The main thing is she's fine. A bit shaken obviously, but they didn't harm her and we got her back within eight hours."

"You got her back?" said Jimmy.

"Well, I was there alongside the SIO, DI Garcia. Greg had, how can I say this? He'd taken two of the OCG captive and had discovered some possible safe houses where they might be holding her. He then identified one that looked really promising, gave it to Lori who got her GEO guys to hit the place."

"Lori is the SIO, not the tall leggy blonde then?"

"No, Terri is the Aussie tall leggy blonde, ex-forces

and tough as nails. Lori is Spanish, a DI attached to the GEO, brunette, very good looking and has taken a shine to Greg."

"It all sounds a bit incestuous out there mate," laughed Jimmy.

"A lot, in fact a hell of a lot has certainly happened in the last few days. Keep the resigning thing under wraps for the moment will you? I'll tell you more later, but for now can you do me some research on an Armenian OCG boss called Sergei Grigoryan?" said Sam. "This doesn't need to be secret, secret Jimmy. This guy has fingers all over Europe and the States, so I think we need to know more about his outfit and what they are doing in London anyway. But for the time being I am particularly interested in what you can find out about his base. Where does he live? Where does he go? Does he have any favourite cafes or restaurants?"

"Sam," said Jimmy, "you don't have to tell me this, but what are you thinking of doing?"

"For your ears only," said Sam. "We're going to try and have a coffee with him and that's not code for anything Jimmy. I do mean, I just want to talk with him."

"Okay, I think," said Jimmy, as he typed the name Grigoryan Sergei into his intel desktop.

"Right, I've got your man here. I'll get on this and do a full trawl of the Euro-Intel sites and see what there is on him, but you wanted to know if we could place his base and it looks like it's Yerevan. That's the capital city and it seems like he takes his private jet out of Zvartnots International Airport whenever he needs to go anywhere."

"Private jet eh? Business must be booming," said Sam. "Jimmy, you're a star."

"I know," said Jimmy, "give my love to your mum and hey Sam?"

"Yes?"

"Don't forget the falling in love thing."

"Stop it and get on with your job Constable," said Sam.

"Right away, soon to be retired Detective Chief Inspector. I'll get back to you when I've got more on your new Armenian friend," said Jimmy. Sam retiring he thought. His best friend since joining the Met. He had worried about him ever since the shooting. He had never blamed him and never would. It was an operational incident and that was it, matter closed. He picked up his phone and started dialling his wife.

'She'll never believe all of this.'

TWENTY THREE

Rob phoned Anna at 10am. She had managed to get an hour's rest just sitting in her chair in the living room and felt better having recharged her batteries.

"Good morning Anna, how are you?" said Rob.

She quickly filled him on what had happened. She needed him to know the threat level and where it had come from.

"I'm glad you're alright Anna. It must have been quite an experience. Thanks for telling me. I'm happy it doesn't change the threat towards me, but it's good to know. Okay, so you wanted to know more about Intertech."

Rob then went on to tell Anna that what he had found showed that there were a number of shadow companies operating this particular scam. All were being managed by the same organisation, Intertech, a privately owned business where the major shareholder was the CEO, Jasvinder Kaur or Jaz Kaur as she chose to go by. She also owned and ran another legitimate call centre operation, Direct Solutions, but she kept them entirely separate. She also had a Facebook account that provided some more detail of her interests and that included some trips to Mallorca.

"She looks like she is or has been in Palma recently

according to pictures she has posted," said Rob.

"Can we see any of these images Rob?"

"Yes, don't worry, I have put all of this information on a file and I will send you a link to access it. The link will be open for two hours after we finish the conversation and then I will remove it."

"Okay, I understand," said Anna. "So where is this woman based?"

"It looks like her main office is in Mumbai, but she seems to be running at least five dodgy call centres that I can find at the moment. She's no mug Anna. She's Harvard educated and runs her business on very effective and efficient lines, pretty much what you'd expect from someone with a Harvard MBA. It took a little while, but I've tracked down some of the payments people have been making, to see where they end up. For example, Sheila MacDonald and Bill Patterson thought they were speaking to different companies, but it was actually the same call centre and although they paid their money, both by credit card incidentally, it was to different payees. The money all eventually loops back to this Kaur woman's Intertech holding company, but she's put together a very well protected financial network where money goes all around the place to get clean, before it eventually ends up in her main account in Mumbai. She looks like she has also been developing a strong social media profile for at least the past two years, with donations to various community projects and some high profile networking with big business and politicians. So she isn't afraid to get her face in the news, which is great for us, but not such a great idea for her. We've got her house in Mumbai, where she lives most of the time and then there is a secluded villa she uses for holidays down near the Goa coast. Just by looking at the number of payments going in to a couple of the shadow accounts for one day, she is making some serious money

Anna and I've found what look to be dividend type payments the holding company are paying direct to an account in her name and she's personally pocketed in the region of £2 million in the last two years from these scams, not to mention what she makes from her legitimate businesses."

"And how many vulnerable people does that add up to?" Anna hadn't realised she had asked the question out aloud.

"Trouble is Anna, Kaur is just one of many who I and the rest of my team come across and half the time, no, I mean most of the time, the authorities can't get near these people."

"And I don't know what we will be able to do either Rob, but we have a very angry and vengeful widower who wants blood," said Anna.

"To be honest, I don't blame him. I hate these people. Maybe not so much the ones in the call centres as I sort of get it that they are trying to do a job to put food on their family's table, but even saying that, I watched the guys in Kaur's call centre in Mumbai over the past few days and they were enjoying it. Enjoying making people like Bill and Sheila MacDonald part with their money and then they're cheering when they get someone like Bill, when he pays up something like £900."

Rob then completed his rundown on Kaur and the rest of the Intertech set up and then sent through the link with the information.

"Anna, it's been a pleasure. I will check back in a day by text, just to confirm you understand everything that's in the file, but after that you won't hear from me again, so I wish you well."

She thanked him for his help and then set about opening the link and downloading the file. She then rang Sam.

"Hi Mum, how did you get on with Rob?"

"He's a mine of information that young man. I've downloaded the file he sent me and I'll send it to you, Greg and Terri. First things first, Rob has identified a woman called Jasvinder Kaur as the CEO of the company who runs the call centres responsible for the scam. She's primarily based in Mumbai and in the last two years, she has made around £2 million from her scam business."

"I think we need to have a talk with this Jasvinder Kaur and see if we can't persuade her to make some sort of restitution," said Sam. "In the meantime Mum, how are you feeling? Are you okay?"

"Yes, I managed to grab an hour's sleep before the call and Tommy has just made a nice cup of tea." She smiled as Tommy came through the living room doors with two cups of tea.

"That's great. We're just going back out to the finca where Tommy and Simon have been staying. We've got a bit of tidying up to do and then we'll be back early this afternoon to go and meet the MacDonalds and I was thinking you would like to come to see John?"

"Yes, I would like that. He must still be in shock from losing Sheila. By the way, I've rung the hospital and Bill is doing okay and he should be able to come home in a day or so as well."

"That's great. Right, we'll see you later," said Sam.

*****

As Terri, Greg and Sam arrived at the finca, they saw Simon sitting in the porch area.

"I've been having a little chat with our friends and they've been very helpful about what they know about Sonny, so I have a list of addresses and businesses for your police lady friend Greg," said Simon.

Greg ignored Simon's little jibe about Lori and smiled instead. A little chat from Simon could well have left the two Armenians traumatised, but nicely warmed up for some more questions about Sergei Grigoryan.

"Sam, do you want to take this and see what they can tell us about Sergei?" said Greg.

"Sure, let's see what they know."

Sam went into the finca bedroom where he could see the two Armenians sitting on the two single beds.

"Guys, just so you know, it was my mother that was kidnapped and so I'd like you to tell me something about Sergei Grigoryan."

As soon as the two men heard the name they flinched.

"So you know who I'm talking about. Good," said Sam.

"We can't help you. We told your friend everything we know about Sonny," said Davit.

"And you've done a great job with that, but before we decide what to do with you, I need you to answer some simple questions," said Sam.

"Mister, we can't tell you anything about Sergei. He would kill all of our families if he ever found out we had said anything," said Davit.

Vardan just looked at Sam and nodded. Sam could see the fear in their eyes. He tried the sympathetic approach, to get them engaged.

"Look, I'm not after his secrets. I just want to know what he's like. I gather from what you are saying, that he can be very threatening. Is that right?"

"Yes mister. If you step out of line, even once, he might kill you and he does it himself if he feels he needs to show everyone that he is still the boss," said Davit.

It was good that he had at least got Davit talking. An old trick, but it had worked. Ask a simple non-threatening question that was pretty obvious, but if it meant that the person spoke, then it might mean they would continue to talk if you were clever in how you asked your questions.

"Well, I don't want to put your families at risk guys. So where do they live back in Armenia?" said Sam.

Davit said "Artashat" and Vardan mumbled "Aragatsotn."

"Are they anywhere near Yerevan?"

Davit said, "About twenty five kilometres."

"About the same, almost thirty kilometres," said Vardan.

"And Sergei operates out of the Yerevan area doesn't he?"

"Yes mister," said Davit. "But, honestly I can't tell you anymore."

"No, that's fine. I understand. So while you're working over here, does he provide any help to your families?"

This time Vardan spoke. They had given him some painkillers for his broken arm and he was feeling more comfortable.

"Yes, he's very good to them. We get paid an allowance for being away from home and he sends food hampers and flowers for our wives and mothers. He's a very good family man."

"Sounds like a good, fair man. So does Sergei have any regular coffee places he enjoys going to?"

"Why do you want to know that mister?" asked Davit warily.

Davit clearly didn't like where that line of questioning was going, so Sam eased back.

"Just interested. Our argument is with Sonny you see, not Sergei. So I just want to know what sort of boss he is."

"A very good boss mister. Like you said, a very fair man and a family man," said Davit.

"Does he have children then?" said Sam.

Before Davit could stop him, Vardan said, "Yes, he

has a daughter who he dotes on. She's eleven and he tries to meet her every day from school and take her for an ice cream or a drink in the main square."

Davit punched Vardan on his injured arm and shouted something in Armenian, presumably something to shut him up.

"Davit, you don't have to worry. You haven't told us anything Sergei would be unhappy with have you?" said Sam.

Neither man was necessarily sure how to answer that question. They both realised they should have just kept their mouths firmly shut and taken anything the Englishman might have threatened them with, but in the event, he had managed to get them to talk through some simple interrogation techniques.

Sam left the room, locking the door behind him.

"Impressive mate, very impressive," said Terri who had been listening at the door.

"Thanks. I've had a few years' practice and these two aren't the brightest spanners in the box are they?"

"No, think you're right there," she laughed.

Greg was sitting in the kitchen looking at the file Anna had sent.

"John MacDonald is going to be keen to know about all of this stuff, so what's our plan?"

Sam smiled. He had come to Mallorca to get away from a job that was weighing him down with the pressure and stress and yet, here he was talking about how to deal with an Armenian OCG with a man who he had found out was his biological father and a beautiful looking Aussie woman who was his half-sister.

"What are you smiling for Sam?" said Greg.

"Fate and the circumstances that brought me to be here with you guys."

"In a good way?" said Terri.

"Very much so. Okay, so first things first. I definitely

think we should go to Armenia," said Sam.

"And do what?" said Greg.

"With Sonny going to ground, it's going to take a long time for us to find him and we've already been through the fact that there may not be sufficient evidence for Lori to put a charge on him. Therefore, let's go about things differently and go and speak to his boss."

"What, just walk up and ask him for a chat? I don't think he's the sort of guy to go for that," said Terri.

"But if we can get his attention, he might be willing to listen. Terri, can you get hold of your charter plane guy again and see if he's available to take us to, which airport Sam?" said Greg.

"Zvartnots," said Sam.

"I think I might be all out of favours with pilot boy though. He can take us, but we might have to pay."

"I thought you had a thing going with him?" said Greg.

"A while ago, but it sort of fizzled out."

"Well confirm with him how much and let's talk to John MacDonald about a war kitty," said Greg.

Terri said, "What about these guys? What shall we do with them? They've about exhausted their usefulness to us haven't they?"

"Yes, I think so. With what they've told us about Sergei, together with the list Simon got from them with all the clubs and businesses they are involved in across the Balearics, they've given up a lot more than we could have hoped for, especially with the details of all the nightclubs, brothels, taxi companies and drug dealers the Armenians are running. I think that will be more than enough for Lori and she won't have to answer any difficult questions about how they came into police custody," said Sam.

"I'll take a run out with Simon and we'll drop them off somewhere near the hospital, so Vardan can get his arm reset if he wants," said Terri.

She walked back into the finca to the bedroom where the Armenians were.

"Time to go amigos," she said.

Both men cowered down when they saw her holding blindfolds.

"Guys, look, it's okay. We're the good guys and so we're going to let you go."

She saw the look of confusion on their faces.

"Don't worry, these are just so you don't know where you are. We'll even drop you off near a hospital, so you can get your arm fixed Vardan. Now you can't ask fairer than that can you?" said Terri.

They still weren't sure, but there wasn't much else they could do but comply. She secured them with plasti-cuffs on their wrists and ankles and flipped them both into the boot area of the hatch and added the blindfolds. Vardan couldn't stop shaking, convinced he was going to be taken somewhere and shot and he started muttering something that sounded like prayers.

"If you don't stop with your whining I'll shoot both of you. Do you understand?" said Simon, who was quickly losing patience with Vardan. Knowing from his interrogation methods that Simon was not someone to be messed with, Davit gave Vardan a sharp jab with his elbow that successfully shut him up.

"We'll be back with ice creams," said Terri, leaving Greg and Sam smiling as she set off down the drive.

TWENTY FOUR

Anna was walking around her garden, making a mental note of what she needed to be doing over the coming weeks to keep it all looking nice over the summer when her phone rang.

It was a blocked number, so she answered it cautiously with "Hello?"

"Hello, is that Mrs Anna Martínez?" said a young female voice.

"Yes, who is this?" said Anna.

"Are you free to take a call from Sir John?"

"Yes, of course."

"Hello Anna, I was concerned to hear you had been involved in a little bit of trouble and wanted to check that you are alright?" said Sir John Woodward.

"Yes, I'm fine thank you John. There was a little bit of excitement, but I'm back safe now. Thank you for getting the wheels turning. I've had a very able young man tell me all about the people responsible for the scam," said Anna.

"Good, good. I think you are understating your 'little bit of excitement' my dear, but then, you always did play things down and keep calm in a crisis."

"Thank you for calling John, but can I assume that you aren't just ringing to check on my well-being?"

"Astute as ever Anna. This business, it's raised some

eyebrows with our old company. They know that Greg is there with you and they're wondering what you have in mind to do next?"

"They aren't looking to interfere are they John? These people have murdered one British subject, beaten up another and kidnapped me. John MacDonald for one, is not going to be happy if he finds out HMG are trying to curtail any, shall we say, reasonable response to these attacks on British subjects," said Anna.

"Nothing could be further from the truth Anna."

"Well I'm very pleased to hear that John, so why are you asking?"

"Well as you probably realise, Her Majesty's Government cannot necessarily be seen to be engaging with individual crimes by organised gangs, however, they want to let you know that they can offer support which could come in the shape of many forms. So, please use Martin Carruthers as your contact."

"Goodness, I don't know what to say John," said Anna.

"No need to thank me. We have long memories within the Service and you were very much valued for your contribution to national security. My secretary will text you his private number and Anna, you need only ask if you want anything and I mean anything from Martin. If it is within his gift, he will make it happen. Give my best to Chambers too, I liked him, he was a damn fine field agent because of your training Anna. Now you take care of yourself."

She thanked him and thought for a few moments about what Sir John had just said. She had known him when he was just a young entrant to the Service. They then worked together on a number of operations and she had seen in him the characteristics required to reach the highest levels of the Service. Did he know about her and Greg? Maybe, as it wouldn't take any great deduction to realise she had to resign almost nine months from the end of Greg's training, but he had returned her calls when she had phoned to congratulate him, first for his knighthood and then his retirement, so she knew he meant every word of what he said about her reputation within the Service and that felt good. She then phoned Greg and explained about the call. He put her on speaker phone so that Sam could hear what the former Deputy Head of MI6 had told her.

"So he said we just need to ask?" said Greg.

"Yes, that was pretty much the gist of it. Ask and if they can, we will get," said Anna.

"What are you thinking then Greg?" said Sam.

"I think we may have just solved the issue of how we get the equipment into Armenia."

*****

When Greg called Lori, he could tell from her voice that she'd had a long day, no doubt having to explain how she came upon the information to raid the finca for a British woman who had been kidnapped.

"It's okay. It's just procedure Greg, but it can be so tiring when you have had such a successful outcome and then we all have to jump through hoops, especially poor Fernando Pérez who has been going through the usual post incident investigation for a police shooting. I feel for him but it's the same in many countries when a police officer shoots someone and yes, I know why, but for God's sake, the man had a Škorpion machine pistol and had kidnapped a woman. What the hell else was Pérez expected to do?"

He let her have her rant. She had no doubt been keeping it together for her team throughout the day and this was her chance to get things off her chest out of earshot of the team. He heard the out rush of emotion in her voice coming to a close.

"Thank you. I feel better for that."

"It sounded as though it helped," said Greg. "So how about dinner tonight? I can fill you in on some thoughts we've had to progress this forward."

"Yes, I'd love that. Oh and can I ask, when did you part company with those friends you were keeping company?"

She meant, of course, the two Armenians and he thought to tease her for a moment, but no, she was tired and she needed to know they weren't an issue for her.

"Yes, they left today. They were very helpful and you should have got some useful data from them via email," said Greg.

"Had one of them broken his arm?" said Lori.

"Yes, he had an accident, so we dropped them off at the hospital, the one north of the city, just off the ring road. Why do you ask Lori?"

"I got the email and it is very interesting. Unfortunately, it looks like your two friends were later involved in a road traffic accident and the car burst into flames, although they were both sitting in the back seat and there was no sign of the driver. However, early examination of the bodies suggests one of the men had a broken arm."

"Looks like Sonny didn't believe them when they said they hadn't told us anything," said Greg.

"No, but unfortunately it's just added to the concerns of the local authorities that we have bodies mounting up on their island paradise," said Lori.

"Guess you really need that dinner then."

"I do," said Lori.

*****

Anna hadn't seen John MacDonald for a couple of years. Sheila had been on the island and had come to Luis's funeral, but John had been away on business and wasn't able to get back. They had always got on well as couples, even though they came from completely different backgrounds, so Anna wasn't surprised when the first thing John did was to apologise for not getting to Luis's funeral.

"John, I understand. Sheila told me you couldn't get away, but now tell me, how are you? I'm so sorry about what happened to dear Sheila," said Anna.

John was still managing to hold things together quite well. He would find himself crying in his bedroom when he was alone and whilst he wasn't afraid to cry in front of his boys, it was more about not being able to stop once he started. However, Anna's kind and soothing voice reminded him so much of Sheila and he felt the tears spilling down his cheeks.

"It's okay John, let it out," said Anna gently.

She held him in her arms and then his boys both came and gave him a hug too.

"Thank you," he said softly before turning to Sam. "Well my boy, I haven't seen you in such a long time. It's a shame we are meeting in such circumstances, but I hope to see more of you and your mother in the future, as I've decided to spend more time out here."

"It's nice to see you again Mr MacDonald and I'm so sorry to hear about what happened to Mrs Mac," said Sam.

John smiled hearing Sam call Sheila 'Mrs Mac'. It was something he first called her when they got married. He knew Sam had heard him calling her 'Mrs Mac' one day, when he was round playing with the boys and so it was after that he would hear Sam using 'Mrs Mac' whenever he spoke to Sheila. Sam must have only been six or seven then and now, just like his boys, he was all grown up.

"Thanks Sam, that's kind of you and you can call me John you know, it's okay." John paused before carrying on, "So what the hell has been going on Greg? You said there had been a couple of issues you were looking at, but then you tell me Anna was kidnapped?"

Sam smiled. John was not a man to mince his words and he was back focused on the response to his wife's murder. *'Woe betide anyone who gets in his way,'* thought Sam.

"Yes, on reflection I should have seen it, but we got lucky. Terri and I got tailed by a couple of the gang who turned out to be not that great in terms of surveillance skills. We got the better of them and to cut a long story short, they gave up some possible locations and we got the police involved, DI Lori Garcia?"

John nodded.

"And she had a team go in and recover Anna," said Greg.

"Good. So presumably this was a response by the OCG boss? Where is he now?" said John.

"Yes, we called Sonny after we'd got Anna back and we've definitely got him spooked and he's run for cover. We could spend time looking for him, but we don't know if he might have already left the islands, but Sam has come up with a plan to tackle things by going to the head man out in Armenia," said Greg who looked across at Sam.

"It's something that's unofficially recognised as a useful and sometimes very effective tactic back in London, John, for example, where a local gang boss steps over the line of let's call it 'normal activity'. So when something like a murder or some other serious offence occurs, this will then result in the police engaging more openly with the OCG, bringing with it a lot of unwanted attention. However, if it then becomes apparent that there's little or no chance of a successful judicial outcome through the Court system, it has been known that a quiet word in the ear of the big boss can lead to the offending person being dealt with, shall we say, 'internally'," said Sam.

"Have you done this Sam?" said John, then stopped himself. "No, don't answer that. Silly question, but I gather it works?"

"Yes. It's a business proposition and they know we will then lay off with the more overt police attention. Obviously we're still going after them for any criminal activity, but they aren't stupid and they know our resources are limited and we have to focus on the most serious and pressing cases. So if they keep their heads down, they might just stay off our radar whilst we direct our efforts on other OCGs," said Sam.

Chris said, "Armenia isn't London though Sam. You won't have a SWAT team, or whatever you call them, hanging around the corner will you?"

"No, you're right, but we think we can cover our backs and get the message across. Lori Garcia isn't going to stop her investigation, so she will be ruffling the feathers of the OCG on the island, so they will be feeling the heat that will cut down on their income, something the big boss over in Armenia is not going to want. Any sign of weakness and another OCG, probably over here we're talking about the Russians, well they will step in and take over," said Sam.

"Bloody hell, it's just like in business," said Jack, John's youngest son.

"Yes Jack, it is," said Sam. "And the big boss, a guy called Sergei Grigoryan apparently runs things just like a business, with weekly performance meetings and quarterly targets and so on."

"And the best way to take a business down?" said John, who went on to answer his own question, "Is through hitting their cash flow. Now listen, I want this bastard sorted and let me tell you this, you now have access to a £2 million operating budget. We can also run this like a business, but Greg, you only have one performance target, no, make that two. Are you clear on that?" said John.

"Yes John, we are," said Greg looking at Sam, who didn't hesitate and gave a nod of his head.

Sam had now very firmly stepped over the line from law enforcement officer to 'doing the right thing'. Anna, his mother, looked at him with questioning eyes. He looked back and smiled and mouthed the words *'it's okay'*.

"Good that's settled. Let's have a drink and Anna and I can have a proper catch up," said John.

TWENTY FIVE

Miquel had the table in the front window already prepared for them. Five glasses of chilled cava were waiting as they walked through the door and Sam took time to greet the rest of the team as well.

"Señora Martínez, welcome back. It is so good to see you again," said Miquel.

"Gracias Miquel. It's been too long," said Anna.

She and Luis had been regular customers to Contrabando since it had opened, but she hadn't been since Luis became too ill to make the journey out of Palma.

"So Miquel, let me introduce you to Señora Lori Garcia," said Sam.

"Señora, es in placer conocerte," said Miquel. "It's a pleasure to meet you."

Lori, Miquel and Sam spoke quickly in Spanish going through brief introductions as to how they knew each other before reverting to English for Greg and Terri's benefit.

"I am trying you guys," said Terri. "As I really want to learn more of the language for when I am over here. So brother, will you teach me?"

"Of course little sister, I'd love to."

Greg looked at Anna. They weren't a real family. He knew that, but it felt good to see Sam and Terri getting on so well and she had taken to Anna like she was a long lost Aunt. His thoughts were interrupted by Miquel as he took them to their table.

"We have some fabulous specials tonight and Sam, I have a couple of bottles of one of your favourites, Ribas de Cabrera." He then left them to look through the menu.

Greg raised his glass and said, "Here's to love and friendship, family and someone I know you two miss very much. To Luis."

As one they said, "Salud" and Anna looked across at Greg and quietly said, "Thank you."

Miquel came back after a few minutes with the wine and six large red wine glasses.

"It's too good for me not to taste some of this as well amigo," said Miquel to his friend.

It was a 2014 wine and as usual, the Ribas de Cabrera didn't disappoint. It was as good as Miquel said it would be. They had all looked through the menu and after talking through the specials with Miquel, they went with his recommendations and then spent the rest of the evening relaxing much more than they thought about planning what they were going to do next. Sam sat listening to the conversation going on around the table and realised he was feeling completely at ease with the world and most of all, himself. He wasn't sure how it had taken the kidnap of his mother to help him get through the stress and pressure he had been feeling as a result of the PTSD, but somehow, he had made some giant steps forward. He knew it hadn't all just suddenly gone. No, it was still there, but he was now able to manage it and he had made up his mind to try counselling again. He looked across at Lori who was sitting diagonally to him and saw she was looking at him.

"Are you okay Sam?" said Lori. "Greg tells me you have decided to stay here in Mallorca. So, you are resigning from the Met?"

"Yes, I'm feeling really good actually Lori and you're right, I've decided to stay. It was something that I had pushed to the back of my mind, but knew that it was an issue I needed to consider. My parents have been great about it, with no pressure on me to come back, but I've given it a lot of thought and now is a good time. In fact, it's a really good time to do this."

"It's a big step for sure," she said, "but I get the feeling you will also be doing some work with Greg and Terri, yes?"

"Well, I'd be lying if I said there wasn't something in that Lori. I've had a great career in the Met and have loved being there to make a difference, to help people. I hope that doesn't sound too corny does it?" said Sam.

There was a chorus of, "No, it doesn't."

He looked around the table and saw they had all been listening.

Greg then said, "So on behalf of the shareholders of 3R, that's me and Terri, I'd like to welcome two new members of the team."

"Two?" said Sam, looking at Greg, who then looked at Anna.

"Yes, two new members. I'm delighted that we have also managed to secure the services, when required, of a certain, highly valued former member of the British Intelligence Services," said Greg.

Anna looked at Sam and grinned. "I couldn't resist it when he asked me. After all, you'll be looking after Sa Petita Llibreria and the rest of the company won't you?" she teased.

Lori said, "You are a very formidable team. The bad guys had better beware I think."

Miquel arrived at that moment with a tray of five glasses of Suau, with each brandy glass warming over a glass of hot water.

"I think I have come at a good time for another toast amigos," said Miquel.

"Here's to 3R," said Greg.

"3R!"

*****

They finished the night debating on who should go to Yerevan. The key issue was whether Anna should stay behind and if so, should they leave Tommy or Simon? Lori was happy to provide a team at the house, but Sam felt they would be better used in Lori's plan to hit the OCG businesses hard to try to flush Sonny out of hiding.

"Why don't we all go?" said Anna. "We don't know what we'll be facing out there and anyway, if I'm supposed to be part of this team, then I bloody well want to come."

Sam looked at his mother. He rarely heard her swear, so she obviously wanted to make her point. Greg didn't even have to give it a second thought.

"Yes, of course you're right Anna. We need lots of options to react to whatever happens out there. Terri, tell your pilot we're all going and ask him to make the flight plans for tomorrow," said Greg.

They finished outlining the plans and itemised the actions. Anna would make contact with Carruthers regarding logistics, visas and permissions. Terri would deal with all the resources they'd require and Sam would work on the intel for when they got there.

"Good. I think we have a plan. Now I think ladies and gentlemen, it is time we all got some rest," said Greg.

They said their goodbyes to Miquel and the rest of the team and Simon and Tommy were waiting outside in their vehicles to collect them.

As Terri got in next to Tommy she said, "Get your stuff packed tonight mate, we're all off to Armenia tomorrow."

"A holiday at last," said Tommy.

Terri grinned, "Not quite, but we should have fun, now don't hold back, I need my bed."

Tommy accelerated out of Llucmajor and headed for the motorway back towards the city.

TWENTY SIX

"**M**artin, good morning. I'll get to straight to it. We need some help getting some weapons into Armenia," said Anna.

"Okay Anna. Shouldn't be a problem as long as you aren't taking in enough for an army. Presumably you want this done soon?" said Carruthers.

"Yes please Martin, very soon. We take off today, so can you get it there late tonight or latest tomorrow morning."

"Let me see what I can do Anna. Can't promise tonight, but tomorrow is a distinct possibility. We'll get what you need into the country, whether it's through an official crossing point or if we have to smuggle it in, but it will get there. Send me a list of the equipment on this email. It's encrypted and so it's safe. I will have someone out there to meet you, but I'll text you details on times and places."

As Carruthers came off the phone he rang his contact in RAF Intelligence.

"Hello Peter, I've got a job for you. I need a package taking to Cyprus for an onward journey from there."

*****

The following morning, as Terri got the KIA ready to go to Anna's villa to collect Anna and Sam, Greg phoned Lori on the pretence of an update on Sonny. Tommy had given him a bit of friendly stick about being 'loved up' last night, after they had dropped her off at her apartment and he'd kissed her goodnight, so he knew in reality that he just wanted to hear her voice again.

"Hola Señor Chambers," said Lori who was standing in the open office with her team.

"Hola Detective Inspectora Garcia. I guess you can't talk then?" said Greg.

"Let me check those details for you. They're in my office."

Nino just looked at her and held his hands to make a heart between his thumbs and forefingers. She knew she wasn't kidding anyone and anyway, who cares? She was working with detectives for God's sake, so if they couldn't spot there was something going on between her and Greg, then they shouldn't be on her team, she smiled.

She got to her office and sat down and flipped off her shoes and put her feet up on the desk. They had agreed that it was probably better that she didn't know some of the detail of what he had planned, just in case she was asked by her bosses.

"So to what do I owe for the pleasure of this phone call Señor?"

"Just wanted to hear your voice."

"Señor, are you falling in love with me?"

"I think I might just be," said Greg and felt himself blushing and waiting for her to say something.

"Well I hope so," she said quietly, "because I think I'm falling for you."

Silence hung in the air. He felt like a teenager again. Hanging on the phone to a sweetheart and then neither of them saying anything.

"Greg, whatever you are going to do over there, I want you, no, I need you to stay safe and to make sure you come back to me. Do you understand?" said Lori.

He heard the emotion in her voice, "Yes, I do understand my love and I will."

"Good, that's okay then." He heard her breathe out with a rush, as though that had been something she had needed to say to him. "Now when you get back you can take me out for dinner, just the two of us."

"I'd like that. I'd like that a lot," said Greg.

He had no idea where this relationship might be going, but one thing was for sure. He liked it a lot. Was it love? It had been a long time since he had felt more than a strong affection for someone. He caught himself smiling. Maybe it was?

"What are you smiling for Dad?" said Terri, as she stopped the car where Greg was standing.

"Just thinking."

"Hmm, is this love I see before me?" said Terri.

"I don't know my darling daughter, but whatever it is, it feels.......nice, very nice," said Greg.

"About time if you ask me, but lap it up Dad, she's lovely, so she gets my vote."

He reached out as she was driving and gently squeezed her hand.

"Thank you, that means a lot."

She smiled and then said, "Right enough of this soppy stuff. 3R have got an Armenian gangster to sort out."

*****

Terri dropped Sam, Greg and Anna at VIP Departures and went and parked the KIA in the multi-storey carpark. She waited at the carpark entrance for Tommy and Simon, who were in the Armenian Nissan hatchback, before heading for the airport cargo area. She followed the directions Carruthers had sent through and saw a tall man with wavy blonde hair holding a clipboard.

"That's our man," said Terri.

"You must be from 3R. I'm Michael," said the man. "I think you have something you want transported?"

"Yes please Michael. Do we need to fill anything in?"

"No, we will handle all of that and someone will be there to meet you," said Michael.

"So, how do you get this kit in?" said Tommy.

"Probably best if I don't tell you that if you don't mind. We have a number of ways and…"

"The less people know about it, the better," said Tommy, finishing the sentence for him. "Sorry, it was a stupid bloody question, but a very polite way to answer it."

"Quite," said Michael as he smiled at him. "Okay, let's get to Bay 43 and unload the kit over there. We've got some other crates over there that we can use to pack it in."

It didn't take long to unload the equipment and they left Michael transferring the packages into the crates, together with another man who wasn't introduced to them, but who presumably was also from the same outfit as Michael. They parked the Nissan in the carpark and then met up with the others in the private jet terminal where Terri saw the pilot.

"Daniel, so good to see you again."

"Terri, you look gorgeous as always and it's my pleasure, especially as you are paying me for once," said Daniel with a smile.

"Ha!" said Terri, "I do sometimes pay you. It was only those trips back and forth to Palma where you helped me out."

"Just teasing. Now, hello everybody. As you've gathered my name's Daniel and I'll be flying you today, together with my co-pilot Frances." He turned and waved forward a young woman wearing the same uniform type of clothing as Daniel, but with epaulettes showing she was a senior first officer, rather than Daniel's four band Captain's insignia. Daniel and Frances then escorted the group forward through to the Security and Customs control and then they boarded a people carrier that took them out to a jet.

Greg sat down in one of the seats towards the front. It was obviously a fair bit smaller than Sir Henry's jet, but this Cessna Citation XLS was still a very impressive aircraft. He had been on this aircraft on a number of occasions when clients needed him somewhere and quickly. It had an eight passenger capacity and so it was perfectly comfortable for the six of them. Daniel came up on the radio and told them about the flight plan to Zvartnots International. It was just over 1900 nautical miles and with the Citation having a range of only 1800 nm, they would need a quick re-fuel at Athens, but with good weather they should arrive around 17.00 local time. As the plane was taxiing, Daniel stepped back into the galley and checked on everyone and sorted out cold drinks for those who wanted them.

"We'll do tea or coffee once we're airborne, but it's never a good idea on take-off or landing. Can you also hold off on any mobile calls just whilst Frances gets us in the air, but after that you can make and receive calls as you wish."

It was a silky smooth take-off and once they had levelled off, Sam, Greg, Anna and Terri sat around the table to go through the outline plans once again, whilst they had some peace and quiet, as they didn't know how much time they might have once they got to Yerevan. Sam took a call from Jimmy about what he had found out about Sergei Grigoryan. This confirmed what Sam had found about Sergei's daughter and the regular trips to the main square in Yerevan, but Jimmy was able to add in the crucial missing piece of the jigsaw, which was the actual location, as he'd found an otherwise irrelevant intel entry about the Meeting Point, a café in Republic Square.

Terri swopped seats with Tommy as she and Simon immediately started researching the area for the logistics of the planned interaction with the Armenian OCG boss, including access and exit points to the Square as well as line of sight into the Square from up to three quarters of a kilometre away. Tommy then joined the others looking at the seating plans of the Meeting Point and deciding on the final tactics to engage with Sergei. They weren't on the ground for long in Athens and Daniel confirmed they would be landing on time at 17.00 hours local time in Yerevan.

As they made their approach into Zvartnots International airport Daniel's voice came over the intercom.

"As you can see ladies and gentlemen, we are making our final approach into Zvartnots International. You should be able see the old circular Terminal 1 on your left hand side which sadly is no longer in use, as they closed it down around 2011, but in its day it must have looked pretty impressive. We'll be going through to the VIP Terminal where you can collect the two hire cars you've booked."

Daniel finished his update with the usual, 'Please ensure your seats are returned to the upright position and your safety belts are fastened'.

Within minutes they were on the ground and had taxied to the allotted space in the private jet area. As they stepped out onto the tarmac they could feel the heat. It was as hot as in Mallorca, with the same white glare of the sun bouncing off the runway. The VIP Lounge staff were waiting for them with a people carrier that took the six of them to the VIP Terminal, leaving Daniel and Frances to complete their check-in procedures and then make their own way into the city to their hotel. Daniel was being well rewarded from

John's operational fund and was well aware that they may need to depart at short notice, so he would ensure the plane would be ready for take-off within an hour of getting Terri's call.

The group proceeded through the customs check without any awkward questions, with Greg telling the Customs Officer that they were there looking for investment opportunities. They were all only carrying hand luggage, including some dummy material on investment opportunities in Armenia, just in case anyone should want to take a look in any of their cases. And the Customs Officer did just that, picking two bags at random and finding an assortment of business clothing and various documents relating to Future Investments, one of a number of shell companies Greg had in place to provide cover for team members when they were visiting different countries.

He knew that there was a fair chance that their presence would draw some attention and that someone, maybe even the Customs Officer himself, would be making a call to either the local police or the OCG or maybe even both. As it turned out, the call went into just the OCG and a message was passed to Miqayel, one of Sergei's Lieutenants that a group of British investors had just arrived in a private jet from Mallorca. Miqayel wasn't privy to anything that was going on in Mallorca with Sonny and so merely kept the information to provide to Sergei in tomorrow's morning briefing.

As they walked out of the Terminal, Terri saw the Hertz rep and she took care of signing for the cars and confirming the driver details. She then handed Tommy the keys to a blue Mercedes GLE, whilst she walked to a smart looking red BMW X5 series. As they loaded the cars, Terri and Tommy quietly checked the cars were clear with an anti-bugging device. Anna then got a text from Carruthers, *'Meet 10.30 tomorrow Tairov Street.*

Off M5. Take jct opp Kilicia Bus Stn. Turn left for 200 yds.'

"I've got the contact point. 10.30 tomorrow morning," said Anna.

They checked the location on one of their maps and calculated it was only about five to ten minutes outside of the city and was actually just off the main road they would be taking into the city, so they could do a quick recce on the way in.

It was twelve kilometres into the city centre, straight along the M5, one of their regional roads, so slightly better than most of the road system in Armenia. They were still in a poor state of repair compared to most European countries, but the cars were new and so the suspension systems dealt easily with the bumpy road surface. Terri led the way and after double checking that they weren't being followed, she turned off when she came to the Kilicia Bus Station and they drove slowly up and then back down Tairov Street. It was open ground and as the packages were relatively small, a quick exchange shouldn't be too difficult.

They got back onto the M5 and headed for the Marriott Hotel in the centre. Terri had put the pilots in the Europa Hotel that was a short walk across the other side of the Republic Square. She wanted to keep a bit of distance away from the pilots, so they weren't immediately associated with their passengers, plus there was the added bonus of the other hotel providing a different option if they needed to regroup somewhere. At the end of the M5 they turned right and crossed the Victory Bridge that spanned the Hrazdan River and followed the road around and into the city and pulled up outside the Armenia Marriott Hotel in Republic Square. It was housed in one of the impressive buildings within the square, with beautiful arches and the only open air café in the Square, the Meeting Point.

They had thought about whether they should split

the group into different hotels, but decided that as this wasn't a covert operation, they would stay together and use the cover of the Future Investment Company to explain the size of their group. The hotel front reception team greeted them and Terri and Tommy gave up their keys to two of the guys who took the cars off to park.

Terri had made the reservations under their own passport names and had booked three rooms. Greg was sharing with Anna, she was with Simon, and Sam was with Tommy, who hadn't stopped grumbling about having to share a room since he had found out on the plane. She had particularly wanted to share with Simon, so that they could talk through any operational issues about their role the following day. She had originally put Sam and Anna together, as mother and son, but changed her mind at the last moment. She wasn't actually sure why, but realised later that she must have subconsciously thought Greg and Anna might have things from their past they might want to talk about in private.

After checking into their rooms, they met downstairs and ordered coffee in the Meeting Point. Tommy was still making noises about sharing until Terri told him in no uncertain words to 'Shut up and move on'. They sat at a table with Terri, Simon and Greg facing out onto the street and Anna, Tommy and Sam facing inwards. They looked like any other group having conversation over coffee, whereas they were carrying out the first recce on the location where they intended to speak to Sergei.

"I'm getting a good visual on the Central Library at around 1 o'clock," said Terri.

"Yes, it looked good when we researched this and I like it even better now we've seen it. The trajectory is good too, especially with this sun blind they've got here," said Simon. "Do you see any problems with direction of the sun?"

"No, that should be fine. We can see where it is now and so thinking about where it will be, at what, three hours or so before the same time tomorrow, I don't think it's going to be a problem," said Terri.

"Okay, so what about his team? How many do you reckon he'll have and how do we deal with them?" said Greg.

Simon spoke first, "This is home turf for him isn't it? So, I'd be surprised if he has more than two close-by, plus two more with the two cars nearby. Thoughts?"

"Yes, I'd go with that," said Sam. "Certainly it would be the way I'd do it if I was arranging his protection."

The conversation then settled into finalising some of the detail as to who would be doing what. Sam had asked and Greg agreed that he would be the one to approach Sergei. Greg and Anna would be sitting in the Meeting Point keeping watch and Tommy would be within twenty five metres of the Café, ready to intervene if required. Terri and Simon would be providing long-distance cover from the roof of the building at 1 o'clock. They finished their coffee and after agreeing to all meet in the hotel in the bar at 8pm for a pre-dinner drink, Terri and Simon made their way across the Republic Square to check out the Central Library.

"Terri, can I just check, not that it bothers me either way, but I'm more thinking of the exit plan, are you planning on taking a shot?" said Simon.

"I'm not planning on it, but there's no point in offering up a bluff is there."

It was a statement, more than a question back to him. Simon just nodded. He might have said out aloud that he was okay either way, but he wouldn't have been happy with a bluff as that wasn't the way he'd been trained. He had worked with Terri on many occasions since she'd joined 3R and he knew how good she was in the field. She was a meticulous planner and she expected the same from her team, so if your plan included a possible action, then you needed to be prepared and ready to carry out that action and just as importantly, to have considered all the scenarios of whatever may come as a result of your action.

They carried on walking around the Square, like any other couple on the tourist trail and then spent the next thirty minutes checking out the block, where the Library was situated, looking for ways to get up onto the roof. After a few dead ends they found a fire escape with a pull down ladder in a back alleyway. They looked around for something to grab the ladder by and eventually found a pole that should have presumably been somewhere close to hand to the ladder, but had been misplaced behind some waste bins. Simon pulled down the ladder and checking no one was looking they went up one at a time. Once up on the roof they checked for any CCTV cameras and worked their way around them to a position where they could see Republic Square and then The Meeting Point on the other side of the Square.

Terri took out a distance finder and checked the line of sight.

"Okay, it's 442 to 446 metres depending on seating position."

"Nothing for a hotshot like you then," said Simon smiling.

"I reckon even you might hit a barn door from here," she teased.

They checked the view around them from where they were positioned to see if they would be overlooked from anywhere. They had good cover from some air conditioning units situated on the roof and Simon also found another fire escape ladder on the other side of the building, which gave them a second option if needed for their exit. Once back on the pavement below they walked around the perimeter of the building looking for possible locations to leave a vehicle in the event of a fast get away being required. It was mostly street parking, so they would play that by ear and if need be, use Tommy to pick them up. Satisfied with their work, they strolled back in the sunshine into Republic Square and then into the hotel to get ready for dinner.

TWENTY SEVEN

Sonny banged the table hard with his fist.

"What is that damn woman doing?"

Garcia's team had been busy and had been targeting the sites on the list that Greg had given her. Sonny had been told that another of his premises had been hit by the police that morning. He didn't know how the police were getting this information, but it was potentially the two idiots, Davit and Vardan, who Alex had sent to follow the white Merc seen leaving the Martínez villa. Whilst they didn't know everything about how the OCG worked, they knew enough to make things difficult for him at the moment if they had been giving up information.

He could deal with the police raids on the clubs as a business inconvenience, but this latest hit was on one of his drugs distribution warehouses. He had lost a significant quantity of good quality coke that was cut and ready for sale. This meant a loss of income that at some stage he would need to explain to Sergei. He had planned to stay away from the city for a day or so to let things quieten down after the kidnap had gone so badly wrong, but he was now having to rethink this strategy. Whilst he was pretty happy that the police couldn't pin anything on him, he was nevertheless concerned at what the Garcia woman was doing to his business, not to mention the London cop. The Martínez guy and the others were last seen by his sources at the airport and now he had no idea where they had gone. He knew they had left in a private plane, which also worried him. Where were they getting the sort of money required to pay for a private jet?

At least he had heard from Jaz that she had got to London safely and without incident and was now on board a flight back to India. What he didn't know was that after she had been identified by Rob, a notification mark had been added by Martin Carruthers, who was now tracking her movements in and out of British ports and he had seen Kaur had arrived in London the day before and had flown out today on the BA flight to Mumbai.

Sonny checked his watch. She would still be in the air, so he would ring her later to explain what was happening.

*****

They had spent an uneventful evening having dinner at the Marriott and had all gone up to their rooms by 10pm. Once back in their room, Greg went around checking to see if anything had been disturbed and looking for any surveillance bugs with the anti-bug device, but found nothing.

"This feels just like old times," said Anna. "Checking cars and hotel rooms for bugs."

"Are you okay with all of this Anna?" said Greg.

She thought for a moment before responding.

"Yes. I haven't missed it, at least not after the first six months or so which was probably because I had a baby to think about. But now with Luis gone, I'm thinking 'Why not?' Does that make sense Greg?"

"It makes absolute sense to me," he smiled, "and look, you only need to do whatever you want to get involved in. A lot of what we do isn't this secret squirrel stuff that you used to be involved in. Most of it is often routine and if I'm honest, a bit boring, which is why I like having Terri to look after the bulk of the business and she leaves me to schmooze the clients and cherry pick which jobs I want to be a part of."

"Well it sounds perfect to me Greg. I don't feel old and past it and I still want to do things with my life, especially now I have lost Luis, so I'd love to help out where I can."

"I'm glad and I can't believe we have met up after all these years. It's meant that I can tell you something now that I never got the chance to ever tell you," said Greg.

Anna flinched, thinking he was about to say something about the time they had spent in Cambridge and she wasn't sure how she would react.

"You were considered the best of the best and it is down to you that I am still here in one piece. Your training saved my bacon on so many occasions I can't begin to tell you," said Greg.

He saw Anna relax and smiled.

"Oops. Did you think I was about to say something about undying love and a love lost?"

"Well," she paused. "Yes I did and I wasn't sure what I'd say," said Anna.

"Oh Anna, I hope you're not disappointed, but it was the 'saving my bacon' bit I wanted to tell you. You have always been special but…," said Greg.

"Look, stop there, no apologies needed. What we had was really special but I haven't been pining for you ever since," said Anna smiling.

"Oh good. That was a bit awkward for a moment," said Greg and they both started laughing before he carried on, "Do you think Sam is okay with everything?"

"Yes, I do." He knew Luis wasn't his biological father, but he had a great relationship with him and I'm sure he looked upon him as his dad. I think he likes you, in fact I know he likes you as he's told me and he really likes Terri as well. He thinks she's such a breath of fresh air and very good at what she does with you and 3R, which is why I think he really would like to be a part of it."

"That's great. He is a good lad and the Met's loss is definitely 3R's gain and I know you're also happy he's going to be able to help out more with your family business too," said Greg.

"I'm so glad you like him and yes, I'm very proud of him," said Anna.

Greg lay down on one of the two large double beds whilst Anna was in the bathroom and he put a call in to Lori for a catch up.

"Do I need to be jealous about you being in the same room with Anna," she joked.

"No, but I do like the idea of you being just a little bit jealous," said Greg.

"So you've never dated a Spanish woman before have you?" said Lori.

"Er, no, why?"

"You don't want to make us jealous Englishman."

"Ah, yes, good point and noted my dear," he laughed.

He filled her in on the plans for seeing Sergei and that they were happy with the plan and the logistics to then get out of Armenia in quick time. She then told him about the raids her team had been carrying out on Sonny's business and the feedback they were picking up that he was feeling the heat.

"Things are going to plan then Lori. I'll touch base tomorrow when we hope to be in the air by around 18.00 local time here at the latest."

"Have you decided what you will do then?" she asked.

"I think it's probably going to be India, but I'm leaving things open until we see how tomorrow goes," said Greg.

They finished their call just as Anna came out of the bathroom and she mouthed to him to give her best wishes and after he came off the phone he told Anna about what Lori had said about not making her jealous.

"She seems like a really nice woman," said Anna.

"Yes, I think she is and one that I won't let slip through my fingers."

*****

Before breakfast Simon had retrieved the keys for the Mercedes and had parked it close to the Central Library in Vardanants Street. They all met up in the hotel breakfast room and to anyone looking at them, they appeared to be a business group discussing their meetings for the day. Afterwards Tommy and Simon quietly collected everyone's hand luggage and put it in the back of the BMW and at 10.00 Simon and Terri headed off for the meeting at Tairov Street a half an hour later. They took an alternative route, coming off a side road on the Victory Bridge and heading west into Tairov Street. They drove past the spot they had identified as the drop and completed a circuit of the area. Seeing nothing, they parked up with a view of the drop zone and waited.

There was very little traffic, other than a few cars passing them and some traffic that seemed to be heading for the Hotel Aramas, so it was going to be relatively easy to spot anything unusual. At 10.29am they saw a new looking Ford Fiesta park up on the side of the road close to the drop zone. A man and woman got out of the car and went and looked at the rear of the car. The man then opened the hatchback and then they saw him bring out a spare tyre and a car jack. The man looked in his 60's and the woman looked about half his age, possibly a daughter thought Terri. The man then checked his phone and sent a text. Less than a minute later Terri's phone pinged with an incoming text from Anna, *'He's there waiting for you.'* She texted back, *'Yes, got him.'*

"That's our man, Simon," said Terri pointing towards the Fiesta as she started the car and drove towards them.

As they pulled up alongside, Simon lowered his passenger window and said, "Can we help you with anything?"

The man turned and smiled.

"Yes, that would be most helpful," said the man in a broad Yorkshire accent. "And I assume you must be Terri? I'm Martin Carruthers. Pleasure to meet you both."

"Well I wasn't expecting you Martin, that's for sure," said Terri.

"I don't get out much these days sadly, so given the somewhat unusual circumstances of us helping you I thought it perhaps best if I delivered the package myself. This is Anamika from our local office."

They finished the introductions and Simon got down to changing the tyre for them whilst Martin took Terri to the back of the Fiesta and showed her three packages. Two looked like briefcases and the third was a long cardboard tube. When she took the tube out of the Fiesta it came up to just under her chin and was about 30cm or a foot in diameter. It had 3R markings on it and was marked up as a rollout presentation screen. She put the tube and the two briefcases into the back of the BMW whilst Simon finished off putting the spare tyre on the Fiesta.

"Good luck today Terri and we'll be here this afternoon ready to collect the packages from you as agreed with Anna. Just get her to text me when you're on your way and Terri, please give my very best regards to her and tell her I hope to meet her one day. She is a bit of a legend in the Service," said Carruthers.

"Will do Martin and we'll see you later," said Terri, as she engaged Drive mode on the BMW and drove away. "Legend huh," she smiled.

They got back to the hotel without incident and carried the briefcases and the cardboard tube into the hotel, declining the offer of help from the porter captain at the concierge desk and took them straight to their room. She then texted Sam and Greg that they were back and minutes later all six of them were standing in the room looking at the open packages.

"Okay, I've just brought Glocks for you guys as we'll be too close to think about using anything else and besides, these we can hide, whereas anything bigger would just stand out and the name of the game today people is low key remember?" said Terri.

"Yes," said Greg, "we've only brought these for a just in case scenario. If all goes to plan, Sam will make contact and then we'll be on our way after a brief, a very brief conversation with Sergei Grigoryan."

"Anna, by the way, Martin Carruthers sends you his best and says he wants to meet you when all of this is over. He's cute, maybe fifty, so a bit of a toy boy for you," said Terri.

"How nice of him to come all this way," said Anna.

"And he says you're a legend," said Simon.

"Well that's a lovely thing for him to say, but it was all a long time ago. Now can someone show me the ins and outs of a Glock, as it's a long time since I've handled one?" said Anna.

Simon took one and broke it down for her and then rebuilt it. She then took it from him and Sam watched on as his mother, who he had thought had been an administrator in the Foreign and Commonwealth Office held the Glock confidently in her hands and broke it down and rebuilt in not much more time than Simon had.

"Impressive," said Simon.

"Mum, you're amazing," said Sam.

"Not amazing my dear, just very well trained, but thank you anyway. Now I'm not wrapping you in cotton wool here Sam, but I used to do this for a living, so tell me again how you're going to make the approach today," said Anna.

"Jimmy sent me some pictures he has picked up from one of the Europol agencies that shows Sergei at one of the front tables with a young girl who is believed to be his eleven year old daughter," said Sam. "During the summer and when he's not away on business, he's pretty much regular as clockwork in picking her up from school and bringing her here to The Meeting Point to have an ice cream. The pictures show two men who stand a little way from him, as he doesn't like to be crowded when with his daughter and then there are two cars parked up close by with the drivers. He stays for around twenty minutes whilst she has her ice cream and then they leave and one car takes the daughter home and he goes to see his mistress. The latest intel Jimmy found was that he was in here yesterday with the daughter at the usual time, around 14.45 hours."

"So that's the intel. What are you going to do Sam?" said Anna.

The others watched as she took on a steely and commanding look that all but Greg hadn't seen before. Greg couldn't hold back a smile as he was remembering being in a training room with Anna when she cornered him with questions on his tactical options, whilst Sam was clearly taken aback at how his mother was grilling him on what he intended to do.

"He's on his turf here, so my thinking is that he won't be expecting any sort of a direct approach. The two guys watching him are seen standing towards the front pavement area, one either side of Sergei, to stop any approach from the front and the guys in the cars watch for any threat from the rear, straight out of the hotel. We've got an image of a waiter bringing a coffee and an ice cream on a tray, so I'm going to have you and Greg sitting at a table immediately behind where we expect Sergei to sit. Then as the waiter comes out from the hotel with the coffee and ice cream, you guys will leave the table and take up cover positions close by and I'll sit at the table you've just vacated. I'll then engage in a conversation with Sergei and whilst I don't think he will be overly concerned with seeing you guys, I am anticipating that if I have to make the point that we've got this covered, then Terri here will provide just that."

Anna looked at Sam for a second and then thought for a moment before she spoke.

"It's a sound plan Sam. Some risk, but with good contingencies and I think you're right with the element of surprise being in our favour," said Anna. "So some lunch first for us, but I expect you want to be on your way don't you Terri?"

"Yes Ma'am," said Terri smiling. "Come on Simon, the Boss wants us to shift out."

As they gathered up the equipment they were taking Simon turned to Terri and whispered, "Legend".

"She certainly is mate, I'll give you that. Now let's grab some water and sandwiches and get Tommy to drop us off so we can get into position," said Terri.

*****

"You enjoyed that didn't you," said Greg as they walked into the lift.

"Yes, I did actually. I realise now just how much losing Luis took the wind out of my sails and now I'm feeling fresh and alive again," said Anna.

"You were spot on with Sam as well and I think he

296

appreciated your feedback on his plan."

"I don't want to sound like an old timer telling the young ones how they should be doing things, so I'm glad that you think it came across okay," said Anna and thought to herself that after all these years she was seeing her student become the teacher.

"What are you smiling at?" said Greg.

"You, I knew you were good when I first saw you. It's going to be fun working together again."

"It certainly is," said Greg as they walked out of the lift towards the restaurant, "and now, as you said my dear, it's time for lunch whilst we leave the young ones to get themselves ready for this afternoon."

TWENTY EIGHT

T hey knew they had a wait ahead of them, but then again they were both trained in this type of activity. Therefore the three hours or so, until things would start to happen, was actually no time at all.

After Tommy dropped them off by the alleyway behind the Central Library, Terri and Simon had made their way up on to the roof via the fire escape ladder. They went through their usual routine of checking visibility of the target area, as well as their surroundings and the wind direction, to ensure they had suitable cover in which to operate without being seen.

Simon, as Terri's spotter, had the anemometer (otherwise known as a wind meter), together with a ballistic calculator, a device that automatically worked out the trajectory and direction based on the data fed into it. Terri checked the distance again. No change at 442-446 metres. The pictures she had seen showed Sergei sitting at a table that looked out onto the pavement area in front of The Meeting Point. It had to be highly likely that the staff knew exactly who Sergei was and that he would use the same table every day. Therefore she focused through the telescopic sight on the table she had seen in the picture and in particular on the chair that faced out on to the pavement.

"Distance is 442 metres with no perceptible wind."

"Check. I've got nothing either from the wind machine. I think we're good to go on this Terri. How about some lunch?" said Simon.

He opened his rucksack and brought out the sandwiches and water they had bought from a shop on the outside of the town, en-route to get to Vardanants Street at the back of the Library.

"Cheese and Tomato or Ham and some sort of pickle?" said Simon.

"I'll take the cheese please mate," said Terri.

It was another warm day and the sun at the moment was just above them, causing them to seek out the shade of the air conditioning unit they had seen the day before. The Meeting Point café was running in a SSW direction from where they were, so Terri had calculated that by 15.30 the sun could be a bit of a problem to her as it might be almost directly in her eyes. The good news was that she would be aiming down and so the trajectory would help negate any undue effect of the sun. So this, plus the fact that she only had to aim for Sergei's torso, rather than having to focus on a head shot, would make things considerably easier for her preparation.

She was an experienced sniper from her time in the Australian Army. She had specialised in long distance work after showing her prowess on the firing range in training, when she out-performed the instructor. She had a natural aptitude for handling firearms, especially rifles, after being shown how to shoot by her stepfather. Whilst he had no formal training, he'd been taught to shoot as a boy by his grandfather on the family farm.

Women soldiers had only just been allowed to engage in combat fighting in the Australian Army when Terri was deployed to Afghanistan in 2013 and she had led a patrol team which included a sniper capability when required. Early on she was challenged as to the level of her shooting skills until it became all too apparent that she was by far the best long distance shot in her unit. She knew she had the technique, but she had also talked to Greg about the pressure and psychological aftermath of taking a life from long distance.

Like many snipers, she never referred to the people in her sights as targets. There was a myth she was told early on that snipers dehumanise people, whereas the reality is often that they completely recognise the person they can see as being a human being, perhaps with a family.

She had learned to compartmentalise the threat the person in her sights posed her comrades and innocent members of the public. It was this risk to life that gave her the justification to engage with them, without her ever losing that sense that whoever was in her rifle sights was still a person and not just a target.

Nevertheless, when the ceasefire in Afghanistan came, she had felt a relief within herself. A relief that she would no longer feel the sniper's pain of taking a life.

Since working with Greg at 3R she had worked in some challenging areas and had needed, on occasions, to either take proactive action against a protagonist or indeed to defend herself, but she had not had to kill anyone.

Simon saw her in deep thought and recognised where she might be.

"Thinking about what you're about to do Terri?"

She looked at him and studied his face. She knew full well his background as a former member of the SAS with over ten years' experience, but she also knew him as one of the most compassionate men she had ever met, something which her father had also seen in him and why he chose to recruit him.

"Yes." She paused a moment. "Is that me getting jittery Simon?"

"No," he said softly and then he paused. "The day you don't think about it is the day you need to stop doing this shit. I know the primary objective here is to show this guy Sergei that we're not messing about by putting a red dot on his chest, but if it all goes belly up Terri, then you and me, we will do what we've both trained to do. So whilst you're not doing any of that long distance stuff where you just snuff someone out okay, you may still need to put a bullet in someone, because that someone is taking a pot shot at one of our amigos down there and we need to protect them."

"I know, I get it Simon and mate, thanks, I appreciate that."

"One final thing. You know how good I think, no, how good I know you are. But what you must do, if you are at all worried that you may freeze, is to step back and let me do this. Okay?" said Simon.

"I know and thank you for saying it to give me that opportunity. I think it's just been a while and I thought I could just get the kit out like I used to do and crack on. I suppose it brings back memories," she said.

"And not all of them are going to be good," said Simon. "Right, let's rest up. We've got about an hour to kill before we need to do the final prep and check comms and before we know it we'll be in the air with your nice pilot boy. So what is the story with you two? Any romance in the air so to speak?"

"Oh nice quip, mate," said Terri. "I do like him and we've had some fun, but I don't think our jobs make things easy for anything to happen."

"Oh that's rubbish!" said Simon. "If you want to make it happen, you will, so stop thinking about it and do something and here ends the lesson on building lasting relationships."

She smiled. He was about ten years older than her and she had always looked at him, a bit like Tommy, as an older brother who was forever trying to look after her. He was a good man. A hard man too, God he had made her blood run cold once when she saw him attacked by three men in Cairo. They thought they had an easy target with an unarmed foreigner. He taught her a lesson about ensuring you are the one left standing in any engagement with an attacker.

She had met up with him in a souk and she'd been looking at things in a carpet shop when she saw two men try to grab him from behind, whilst a third was in front of him waving a knife. Before she could even get to him to help, Simon had ducked his body down, turning one of the men into a battering ram that he charged into the man with the knife knocking him to the floor and he kicked the knife away to safety. The other man behind him tried to react but walked into Simon's thrusting elbow, which caught him just under the jaw and he staggered back creating room for Simon to follow up with an arcing right hook that left the man on the floor unconscious. The moves were short, efficient and highly effective and she saw how Simon seemed to be in slow motion, breathing easily and in complete control.

He used everything to his advantage and the one he had used as a battering ram came back at him, but as Simon feigned one way and then the other, the man was caught off guard and Simon used the man's momentum to propel him hard into one of the alley walls, leaving him moaning and bleeding from a head wound. 'Knife man and battering ram' were looking around, looking for a way out, but again the lesson for Terri wasn't finished. '*Find out why*' was what he said later.

Recognising the man with the knife was probably

the leader, he isolated him by despatching the other man, the 'battering ram', with a vicious kick to the man's right knee cap and she heard the sickening crunch of bone cracking before she heard the scream of pain. Then he was on 'knife man', holding his head under his left arm and he was applying pressure by twisting it very slowly in a rolling motion.

"Just tell me who sent you and you can go home with just a headache my friend," said Simon quietly.

The man was either brave or stupid, but he took the option of trying to shake his head. Terri saw Simon lift his right hand and bring it down in a fist on the man's nose.

"One last chance and then I break your neck."

The man started to scream as Simon applied more and more pressure on the man's neck. She didn't know if she should intervene, but before she could do anything she heard the knife man trying to say something. Simon eased the hold and then the man couldn't talk quickly enough as he gave up the information before Simon did as he said he would and let him go. Afterwards she had asked him what he would have done if the man hadn't spoken.

He had looked at her, almost quizzically and then said, "Broken his neck, like I told him."

'Yes,' she thought. *'He's a tough one is Simon.'*

*****

Sam had considerable experience both as a police firearms commander and as a firearms officer. However, he knew he was entering new territory here. Greg and the others were far more experienced in terms of this type of operation, so he was happy to seek their advice and take their guidance. He and Tommy had been carrying out a final recce of the area and deciding on where they would take up their positions when Tommy turned and looked at him.

"Are you okay going in here unarmed Sam?"

"Well I'm not sure 'okay' is the word I'd use, but I think it's the right way to do it," said Sam.

"Yes, I do too. Any sign of a weapon and he, if he's carrying, or if not, one of his guys, would probably take you out before they ask any questions. Just because you haven't got a weapon in your hand doesn't mean you're not protected. You can trust Terri with the long distance stuff and of course you've got three Glocks for company with me, Greg and Anna," said Tommy.

"Thanks Tommy, I appreciate that and yes, I know my back and for that matter, my chest is covered. I think the plan is sound and as long as his guys are good, which if I was him, I'd want my best blokes covering me, then I don't think they'll go firing off shots in a public place without good cause."

"Good, so don't go giving them any reason to shoot you and everything will be fine and dandy. Now let's eat. I never like going into battle without a full stomach," grinned Tommy.

Sam thought for a moment about Tommy's choice of words, but thought better of it. He knew what he meant. Time for food.

TWENTY NINE

Greg and Anna were finishing off their lunch, sitting at a table immediately behind the front table that they expected Sergei to occupy in about half an hour's time.

They had seen a waiter place a RESERVED sign on the table at 14.30, so everything seemed to be going to plan. They watched as Tommy and Sam went through their final checks and they had also been keeping a look out at the top of the Central Library for any sign of Terri and Simon and they had seen nothing, not even any unwanted reflections, as by this time the sun was facing back towards the Library.

Anna had already offered up to be in charge of Comms. She was carrying a Glock, but she also knew she would be rusty after having not handled a firearm in over thirty five years. So it made sense to her to control the Comms and only draw the Glock if things went badly awry. She spoke as though she was chatting with Greg as she went around each of the group checking they could receive and transmit before returning for final confirmation with Terri and Simon.

"All clear Anna," said Terri.

"Roger that Anna," said Simon.

"Anna, I'm just going to check the red dot in three, two, one," said Terri.

"Confirmed," said Greg, as he saw the red dot momentarily appear on Anna's summer dress.

"Sam, let me know when you are ready to take up position," said Anna.

"Yes, yes," said Sam in the usual police radio speak. "Five minutes."

"Okay, we're set to go. Comms transmissions to a minimum from now on please," said Anna.

She then dialled Daniel's mobile. He picked up immediately.

"Good afternoon Anna. We're going through our final checks at the moment, so we'll be ready to go when you get to us," said Daniel.

"Thank you Daniel, we'll see you in around an hour or so," said Anna.

She put her phone into her handbag and nodded to Greg. A few minutes later they saw Sam moving slowly towards them and they both got up and moved away. Sam looked around the café and to anyone looking, it would have appeared as though he had been fortunate to turn up just as a table became clear. Sam sat down with his back to the pavement and facing the café windows. A waiter approached the table and gathered up the plates and glasses, before returning to wipe down the table and offer Sam a menu.

"Just a coffee please," said Sam.

"Certainly Sir," said the waiter.

Sergei Grigoryan arrived as expected, at 15.25, when two black BMW M5s with blacked out windows pulled up outside the front of the café. Greg saw them appear and was concerned they might block Terri's view, but as soon as Sergei got out with a young girl, presumably his eleven year old daughter, the two BMWs moved away, one to either side of the front of the café and the drivers got out and waited by the vehicles, looking back into the café area.

Sergei walked into the outside terrace area and headed for the table with the reserved sign. One of the waiters arrived shortly after carrying a tray with coffee and a fancy bowl of ice cream. The back of Sam's chair was only a yard or so from the back of Sergei's chair, so he was almost close enough to touch him.

"Terri, to confirm, you are at my six o'clock," said Anna.

"Roger," said Terri, and then waited for Anna to describe the location of Sergei's men in relation to Sergei.

"The cars and drivers are at five and seven o'clock to the subject, about thirty metres away. Two guards are standing at three o'clock and nine o'clock to the subject," said Anna.

"Roger that again," said Terri.

"Sam, they're doing a visual sweep of the Square, so now is a good time," said Anna.

Sam double clicked his mic to confirm he'd heard before he moved his chair slightly backwards and to his right and spoke quietly to the man behind him.

"Good afternoon Sergei. Please do not be alarmed. I'm not here to harm you or your daughter, but I do want to talk," said Sam.

"We have engagement," said Anna.

Sergei Grigoryan barely moved when he heard the man's voice behind him, but he did look at his men and made eye contact and with a barely perceptible movement of his head he indicated the man behind him may be a danger.

"You are playing a very dangerous game here whoever you are. My men will shoot you if you do not tell me who you are and what you want in one minute," said Sergei.

"My name is Sam Martínez."

Sam then opened his mic so that his next words would be heard by the rest of the team.

"And before you tell your men to do anything I want you to look down at your shirt."

Terri had been holding her aim on Sergei's chest area since he had sat down. As soon as she heard what Sam said, she flicked the switch on her telescopic sights and a red dot appeared on his white shirt.

Sergei looked down at his shirt and couldn't help but flinch when he saw the red dot. How the hell had these people got into this position to put him at such risk and worse still, when he had his daughter with him?

"I thought you said you wanted to talk," said Sergei.

"Yes, but you just told me you would get your men to shoot me."

Sergei smiled.

"Sam Martínez? You're the Mallorcan Bookseller aren't you? So what brings you here to threaten me whilst I have my child with me? That is not what I would call a very nice thing to do Bookseller."

Sam was distracted for a moment. *'He called me Bookseller. Where the hell has that come from?'* he thought, before he refocused.

"What brings me here is that your man in Mallorca had my mother kidnapped, which again, is not a very nice thing to do, wouldn't you agree?" said Sam.

Sergei turned in his chair to look at Sam. He saw he was in just a shirt and didn't appear to be carrying anything. He motioned to one of his men to come across. Simon tensed as he was watching the wider view of the scene and put his hand on Terri's shoulder, a sign she understood to mean she may need to engage. The man at three o'clock walked across to Sergei with his hands at his side.

"Milena, I'm sorry my child, but I just need to talk to this man for a moment. Why don't you go with Grigor and eat your ice cream over there my darling?"

"Okay Papa," said the little girl, as she picked up her

bowl and walked across to an empty table with one of her father's bodyguards who looked back with confusion, uncertain as to what was playing out in front of him, but not seeing any message from his boss to engage. Simon took his hand from Terri's shoulder.

"So if you don't want to shoot me, which presumably you don't, as you would have done it by now, what do you want?" said Sergei.

"To suggest a business transaction. One that I think you will find acceptable," said Sam.

"This had better be good Bookseller, as I don't take kindly to be threatened in my home town," said Sergei.

"I think my mother would say the same, in fact she might just do that," and Sam nodded to his mother who got up from her chair and walked across and sat next to Sergei.

"Señora Martínez," said Sergei.

"Mister Grigoryan, I can understand how you might feel affronted at being threatened in your own town. Well so was I when your thug Sonny had me kidnapped. So did you know about this?" said Anna.

He looked at her. He guessed she was around sixty five. She could have been older, but she looked vibrant and was certainly attractive. Well dressed, but not in a rich extravagant way, she was wearing a beautiful flowing summer dress that showed she chose carefully. Yes, this lady had class.

"It pains me to say lady that I did not know about it. I allow my people a certain degree of latitude in how they run their part of my business, so perhaps there was a good reason for what Sonny chose to do."

He looked down and was relieved to see the red dot had disappeared.

"But I accept that whatever the reason, it must not have been very pleasant for you, so please accept my apologies."

Anna smiled. He was trying to understand what they were doing here in Armenia, in his town.

"Thank you and your apology is accepted," said Anna.

"So what do you want from me, other than an apology?" said Sergei.

"You seem to be the type of person who would want to ensure that what you were being told by your people was in fact all of what was going on. So can I assume that you have some insider knowledge and that you have someone telling you that there is a lot of police attention being directed at your operations?" said Sam.

"Ah yes, Señora Garcia. A charming woman, but what is it you English say, she is like a dog with a bone. So come now, we haven't got all day. I know your pilots left for the airport over an hour ago and so I imagine our meeting will not be long?"

Sergei looked at Sam and then his eyes moved towards Greg on the other table and he nodded towards him, before turning to look at Tommy who was across the other side of the road. Sam hoped he didn't show any reaction. They had talked about how much Sergei might know about their visit and they hadn't hidden the fact that they were in the country and this pretty much confirmed that the message had got back to Sergei.

What Sergei didn't let on was that he had only found out that morning at his daily briefing that some investors had arrived the day before. When pressed, Miqayel hadn't known as much as he should have. A mistake that he wouldn't make again. Sergei had anticipated something happening, but even he was taken a little aback at the brazen approach at The Meeting Point. He was annoyed with Sonny that he hadn't thought through the idea to first of all kill the MacDonald woman and then to follow it up with a kidnap.

These were two serious errors of judgement and he didn't want to see a third, but he feared he might.

"No, it won't be long Sergei if I may call you that?" said Sam.

"Why not? We are almost friends now Bookseller," said Sergei.

"You can make the problem go away if you change the management of your Balearics team," said Sam.

"And if I don't? What? The police carry on being a pain in the ass? I can live with that. They will get fed up eventually and then we will start the business up again," said Sergei.

"I understand you might be able to play a waiting game with the police, but it won't just be them you see Sergei. The other mistake Sonny made was to murder the wife of a very good friend of ours. A very wealthy friend with significant influence across the world. He has already provided a £2 million fund to use against your OCG and he will keep doubling that if he needs to. You may wonder how we managed to get firearms across the borders and into Armenia in such a short time. Only people with very extensive resources can manage to do that. People who operate in collaboration with the Security Services for example. This isn't a threat Sergei, but a warning. If you don't feel this is a transaction that is worth you taking on, then the alternative will take a lot more of your time and it won't just be in the Balearics. We will start on the rest of your organisation and leave what is then left of your OCG for the Russians to pick up."

Sergei pondered for a moment about what this Bookseller had just told him. It was a threat and he didn't like being threatened and certainly not in a café in his own town. But he did run the organisation like a business because he found it the most effective and efficient way of making money. Therefore, he needed to lose the emotion and focus on the problem he was being given. But he also wasn't going to let them get away with this too easily. If there was an opportunity he would let them know that they could not make Sergei Grigoryan look foolish without some sort of retaliation.

"Okay Bookseller, you have two hours to get out of my country. I do not take kindly to being offered such business advice when I have a sniper pointing a gun at me and by the way, how far away is he?"

"She, Sergei, is 442 metres away, but she shoots within a five centimetre spread from a mile, so this is pretty much like picking cherries off a tree for her," said Sam, and just for effect he had left the mic open again and Terri had flicked on the red dot and flashed it twice.

"An impressive display and I would like to meet your sniper one day in better circumstances, as I understand she is very beautiful," and he turned again and looked directly at Greg who felt the hair on the back of his neck start to bristle.

"Sergei, this isn't advice, this is a stone cold promise that if you ever go anywhere near any of my friends or family, you will regret it in ways you don't even want to imagine," said Sam.

The mic was still open and Sam motioned Sergei to look towards his daughter who was looking down at her school uniform wondering what the red dot was that seemed to be playing on the front of her dress as though it was something to do with the sun. Sam turned back to see Sergei was gripping the sides of his chair and his face was taut with anger.

"Bookseller, you don't fight fair," he said, trying to stay calm. "I love my friend Sonny, but I love my daughter more. So, I think your business idea may be of some interest to me. We will think about a restructure and I will let you know what I decide," said Sergei.

He looked Sam directly in the eyes and then back to

his daughter and then to Anna.

"Señora, I am truly sorry about what happened to you. Now I think it is best if you, your son and your friends get out of my country." He looked towards Sam and said, "You have two hours."

"We'll be gone in one," said Sam.

THIRTY

They met up half way towards the airport. Terri and Simon had waited until the others had got away from the Square without any problems before they made their way down off the roof and got back to the car.

They had seen Sergei leave in one of the cars and his daughter in the other. Terri rang her father as they made their way back to the drop off point.

"Do you think he will give us two hours Dad?"

"Let's put it this way. The sooner we're in the air the better and without over-egging things Daniel had better be prepared for a possible ground to air attack," said Greg.

"Okay, I'll brief him. Not a lot he can do if they've got the proper kit, but better he's forewarned," said Terri.

Simon wasn't hanging about as he drove and they got to the drop off point in just over five minutes and saw Carruthers parked up, but this time without the subterfuge of the punctured wheel. There was a different young woman with him this time and Simon looked at her again and recognised her from the café, where he had seen her sitting with a coffee and reading a book. Carruthers saw Simon looking at the woman.

"Yes, we had Laura here keeping tabs on you. So it all seemed to go very well. She particularly liked the red dot episode," smiled Carruthers.

"Glad we put on a good show for you Laura, and Martin, thanks again for all your help. Now could you get this stuff out of here and get it to India?" said Terri.

"India? Now what are you going to do over there that I need to know about? Is this to do with the Kaur woman?" said Martin.

Anna had heard the exchange between Terri and Martin and stepped in.

"Probably best we don't tell you too much Martin, but I suspect you may well know already. We're going to see her about a refund on a software support package her company arranged for one of our friends," said Anna.

"Right. Well that sounds all very reasonable Anna. We'll get these to where? Which airport? Mumbai?" said Martin.

"Yes, somewhere close to Mumbai would be just fine Martin," said Terri giving him a wide smile.

With the packages safely transferred into Martin's Fiesta, they set off again in the Mercedes and the BMW and within ten minutes they were entering the airport where they saw two Audi A7s parked up at the entrance with six men standing by them. As the men saw them arrive there was a movement by the man at the front to show them he was armed with a machine pistol.

"It's just a show of strength to let us know Sergei's pissed off with us," said Simon.

"Let's hope so," said Greg, "as we're sitting ducks now we've handed the Glocks back."

They drove on and parked up at the VIP terminal. Terri grabbed both keys and dropped them in the 'Leave Keys Here' box as they walked in to see Frances, who was waiting for them at the security desk with one of the VIP team. They walked them quickly through Border Control, where the officers gave their passports a cursory glance before they got into a VW Transporter that took them all out to the Citation which already had the engines running. Within two minutes of them getting on board, Daniel had been given clearance from air traffic control and five minutes later his passengers felt the wheels lift as the Citation made it into the air. Daniel climbed more steeply than usual straight after take-off as he and Frances looked around for any evidence of a man-pad, a man portable air defence system launch pad, or rather in this case, an air attack launch pad.

These types of surface to air missiles were usually fired from weapons on the back of vehicles but could also be from shoulder held weapons. Despite millions being invested in military research to find an effective tool to combat man-pad weapons, there had been nothing identified as being anywhere near economically viable. Therefore, Daniel's best defence was to keep a sharp lookout for anything suspicious and to climb quickly to 20,000ft and get at least four miles away and therefore beyond the effective range of most man-pads.

Greg and Terri had flown with Daniel on a good number of occasions and looked across at each other, realising they had never felt him take-off at such a steep angle. Tommy had cottoned on quickly and was looking out of the window at the airport below.

"Bit worried about man-pads are we?"

"Just being careful," said Terri.

"Bloody good job too," said Simon, who was also craning his head to see out of the window.

A few more minutes passed before they felt the Citation bank left and head west.

"Ladies and gentlemen, I'm pleased to advise we are now safely on our way to Chhatrapati Shivaji International Airport, otherwise known as Mumbai. Frances will be flying today and we'll be stopping off at Muscat in Oman for a refuel and a leg stretch," said

Daniel.

*****

Greg came off the phone after calls to both Lori and John MacDonald and turned to the rest of the group.

"Lori is fine. Her team have been giving Sonny something to think about and John's happy we're all in one piece."

"Have you told them we're now en-route to Mumbai?" said Terri.

"Yes, Lori will keep a watching eye out for Sonny in case she sees any fall out from our visit to Armenia and John is keen to know how we get on with breaking up Kaur's operation out there," Greg paused. "So young Rob told you Anna, that Kaur has at least four, if not five call centres operating didn't he?"

"Yes, the one he got into is situated in the north of the city. The file he sent has got pictures of the inside and outside of the premises," said Anna.

"I suppose one issue we have is how to get these to the police where they won't get hijacked in any court proceedings," said Sam.

"Yes, good point Sam. I'd hate for us to make real inroads into this woman, only for it all to fall flat because we've gained evidence through unauthorised means," said Greg.

"By unauthorised, presumably you mean illegal?" laughed Sam.

"Well, quite, but it doesn't sound as bad if we say unauthorised does it," smiled Greg.

"We may be able to use Martin for this. Anything coming in from MI6, the British Secret Service, will carry a lot of kudos and they may be able to get around questions of where and how the evidence came from with a 'national interest' response," said Sam.

"Okay, let's see if Martin is up for that. Do we have Wi-Fi up here Terri?" said Anna.

"Yes," said Terri and handed Anna her laptop to email Martin the file. "Now I think we've got about seven hours or so before we touch down at Mumbai to get some rest. Daniel is stopping for fuel in Muscat, Oman on the way if anyone wants any duty free?"

Simon smiled, "No, I think I'll just get my head down."

There was general nodding of heads from the others in the group. They would need to do some work when they arrived in Mumbai before the sun came up and so resting up now was a good idea. Frances came around with drinks and blankets and then she turned down the cabin lights. Greg was on his laptop catching up with some other clients and Sam got up out of his chair and went across to see Anna after she had finished sending the email to Carruthers.

"You all okay Mum?"

"Yes, my dear. I'm fine in fact. What about you?"

"I'm good too. Actually I feel really good. I don't know whether it's because I've made my decision to stay in Palma, or because I'm leaving the Met behind me and starting off on this new adventure with Greg and Terri, but whatever it is, I'm liking it," said Sam.

"I was so worried, actually we both were, I mean your father," she felt she had to correct herself and said, "Luis," when Sam stopped her.

"Mum, Dad will always be Dad okay? Greg might be my biological father but I know who has been my father all these years," said Sam.

She smiled. Luis would have dealt with all of this so well, just like Sam, so she needed to do the same.

"Dad would have liked that Sam. Very much, very much indeed," as tears welled up in her eyes. She hadn't cried for some time about him, so maybe it was the emotion of everything that had happened recently. He hugged her gently and felt her tears against his face.

Then he felt his own tears coming down his cheeks.

"You've got me at it now Mum. We're hardly the two ninjas facing off a mob boss now are we?" he whispered.

She gently eased herself away and she was back smiling.

"I think I just needed a bit of a release."

"I think I probably did too Mum," said Sam.

"That's good and I'm fine now, honestly and will be even better after a few hours of sleep."

He was such a good son and she couldn't help but to be excited at the prospect of him coming home to work with her and to eventually take over the business. Then of course there was Greg and Terri and whatever 3R may bring their way. Exciting times indeed. She put her seat back and within minutes Sam saw she was asleep. Greg saw him looking at her.

"What are you thinking Sam?" said Greg.

Sam turned and sat back in his chair.

"I've been in the Met for seventeen years Greg and for sixteen and a half years I have never really spoken to her about my job. You know, some of the ugly things I've dealt with and some of the close shaves I've had and all because I haven't wanted to worry her. Yet all along, she had as much knowledge and experience as me, if not more so, of operating in challenging and dangerous environments and being faced with life threatening situations."

"I know the feeling Sam," said Terri, "I thought Greg was in IT sales when I was growing up. Sneaky pair aren't they?"

*****

Martin Carruthers saw the file he had received from Anna Martínez. Rob had already sent him a copy as part of their agreement and he had looked through it with interest, but as it had little bearing on national security he hadn't taken much more interest in it initially. But after he had taken the call from Sir John Woodward he had begun to wonder what, if anything, there might be in terms of payback for the Service, other than helping out a former colleague from many years ago.

He knew Greg Chambers from his time as a field agent and he had been a very good agent. However, Anna Martínez or Anna Mitchell, as she was recorded in her personnel records was unknown to him, although it was clear she had been very highly regarded. The Service wasn't in the habit of doing favours or at least not favours without something in return, therefore when he had seen Anna's email about talking to the Indian authorities about undertaking some sort of law enforcement engagement on this Kaur woman, he had seen the potential opportunity. He hadn't responded immediately, as he knew she was on a plane with the rest of the 3R outfit and any mention of 'payback' was something best talked about without other listening ears, so he just sent a brief email saying that he would look at the file and get back to her.

He wasn't sure if Sir John would approve of what he had in mind, but he knew full well the current Director General would. He decided that this didn't need to be a *'I'll do this, if you do this for me arrangement'*, but it could be something to call in at a later date. After he had put a call into his opposite number in the Indian Central Bureau of Intelligence, the CBI, he rang Anna.

"Hello Martin, so do you think you can provide some help for us?" said Anna.

"Yes, absolutely and I don't even need anything from you at the moment," said Martin.

Anna heard the words Carruthers had used 'at the moment'. She may have been out of the spy game for a long time, but she still sensed something in his choice of words. She paused for a moment, but decided to let it go, as the primary objective was securing some enforcement action against Kaur.

"That's great Martin," said Anna. "Just putting you on to speaker phone."

"No problem at all. So I have spoken with the CBI, the Central Bureau of Intelligence who are based in New Delhi. They need Government authority to investigate, but the man I spoke to sees no issue with that since this is an economic crime with international impact and as such, comes within their jurisdiction. We should get the go ahead pretty quickly and so he is starting the planning phase to carry out raids on four of the call centres our friend Rob has identified for them in the file. He has stated however, that you cannot accompany them on the raids."

He paused, but Anna stayed silent, so he continued, "This is because they do not want, in fact, they cannot be seen to be operating with a private enterprise, but they are very happy to do this as a Government to Government thing."

Greg nodded to Anna and she replied, "I'm just glad they will help Martin, so we've got no issues at all with that. We'll focus on the main call centre and keep a watching brief and see what happens to Kaur when the raid takes place."

"Good plan. Right, that's that then Anna. We'll get the packages to you when you land in Mumbai. It won't be me this time as I'm heading back to London, but it will be Laura, who you all met on your way out of Armenia," said Martin.

"That's great and thank you again," said Anna.

"Don't mention it and Anna, I look forward to catching up with you for a coffee sometime if that's something you would like to do?" said Martin.

Greg looked at her. He knew exactly what was going on. Carruthers was trying to get her back in the system.

He guessed what she would say and he was right.

"Martin that would be lovely. Let's do that sometime soon," said Anna.

She came off the phone and Greg was still looking at her, but he was smiling.

"You're enjoying this, aren't you?" he said quietly so that Sam couldn't hear.

"Well I can hardly say no and it's just coffee isn't it," said Anna.

"I think we both know it's more than just a coffee. He wants payback for helping us out. I wonder if Sir John knows?"

"Hmm, maybe not. Anyway, a coffee won't hurt and yes, I am interested. I'm almost seventy, just lost my husband, but in the last week I've been kidnapped, sat next to an Armenian gang boss whilst carrying a fire-arm again and been offered a job by you with 3R, so what can I say? It's been huge fun to feel alive again after losing Luis."

He looked at her and smiled. "You're still the woman I knew all those years ago Anna Martínez," he said softly.

THIRTY ONE

Mumbai was an hour and a half ahead of Armenian time and so after a quick stop at Muscat to refuel, it was gone midnight local time when they touched down and taxied to the corporate terminal at Chhatrapati Shivaji International Airport.

Frances opened the hull door and she immediately felt the heat of the night air as it was still around thirty degrees centigrade. The airport had full fixed base operator (FBO) services for private jet arrivals and so as they walked down the plane steps and stepped out onto the warm tarmac they were met by the FBO staff and taken in a people carrier into the private passenger lounge.

Once inside the cool of the air conditioned lounge the FBO staff helped them through the security and border control checks before assisting them with their hand luggage to the outside of the Terminal. Terri saw Eshaan Achari standing by two Hyundai SUVs.

"Welcome back to Mumbai Terri," said Eshaan and shook her hand. "It is so good to see you again and you have brought your father with you too. Mr Chambers, a pleasure sir, as always."

"Good to see you again too Eshaan and I'm fine with Greg honestly."

"Okay Eshaan, where are we staying? It's been a long

day and I think we all want to get our heads down, although I've got one quick job for me and Simon before you disappear if that's okay?" said Terri.

"Yes of course and I have you all booked in at the JW Marriott at Juhu, so we're only about fifteen minutes away, probably less at this time of night," said Eshaan.

"That's great and thanks for getting things all set so quickly, as I know you've been busy with that Trent MacDonald stuff," said Terri.

"It's my pleasure Terri and things are going well with the job and we've had a good result today with five men being dismissed, so I think we have blocked that particular problem."

3R maintained a presence in India and Eshaan headed up the business for Greg and Terri with full time offices in Mumbai and Bangalore. They were primarily engaged with providing support for Trent MacDonald, but the Bangalore office also worked with clients specialising in software development, where security and confidentiality was vital for client relationships. Terri had asked him to look into some losses that were going on at one of the new Trent MacDonald sites that had recently opened up. He had reviewed the site with one of his team and they had installed some covert cameras in the areas they thought most vulnerable and within a week they had identified the five people responsible, the times and the method of how items were being stolen, as well as where the items were then being taken.

"Sounds like some great work Eshaan," said Greg. "Well done and Terri and I will make sure we make time in the near future to drop by the office and thank the guys in person too."

"Thanks Greg and I know they'd really appreciate that too. Okay everyone, let's get you all loaded up and we'll be on our way."

It was less than fifteen minutes before they were being checked in by the Reception team and shown to their rooms. They agreed a breakfast time of 08.15 the following morning. Two minutes later, Simon and Terri were back out of their respective rooms and headed down in the lift and met up with Eshaan who was waiting outside in the SUV.

"Okay my friend, let's go and have a quick look at this call centre," said Terri. "What can you tell us about it?"

She had sent him through the details of the call centres and asked him to plot them all up. He was ex-Indian Special Forces and she had met him in Afghan a few years back. As the work in India was expanding she had told Greg they needed someone to run things for them out here and she had identified Eshaan and he hadn't let her down, in fact he was excellent.

Eshaan produced a paper file of maps and photos of the four sites, with particular focus on the one they were now heading for. They moved off from the hotel heading north and then turning right at the top of Juhu Lake. Eshaan stayed on this road for just over half a kilometre before turning left onto the Swami Viveka-nand Road. Known locally as S.V. Road, it was the major arterial road in the western suburbs of the city.

"There are many, many call centres in this surrounding area," said Eshaan. "The one we want is another kilometre or so from here."

A minute or so later, he turned left off the S.V. Road just before the Barfiwala Flyover and into a small industrial area. He pulled over after seventy five metres and pointed at a building across the other side of the road. A two storey building with a glass frontage and other than the company name, Intertech above the main entrance, it looked like many of the other offices situated along the road. Terri could see lights were on in the offices on the second floor.

"Is that where we think the call takers operate from?"

"Yes, I'm pretty sure," said Eshaan. "There's a lot of people traffic around this area 24/7 and I've seen them going up the stairs that you can see over there." He pointed to a staircase on the left hand side of the building that could be seen through the full length windows. "I'm sorry Terri, but I haven't been able to sit up on the building because there's not a lot of cover and you said to make sure I wasn't seen."

"That's no problem at all. You've done a great job setting this up in double quick time. Simon, what do you think?"

"Yes the cover is difficult. I can't see them being overly surveillance conscious, but I agree, let's keep things safe and focus on getting eyes on the road coming into the estate. Can you get one of your guys to park up so they've got a view of the road coming in off the S.V. Road?" said Simon. "You got details of the Kaur woman too? Maybe get a watch on her place as well."

"Yes, we've got those. I'll get both watches on from 05.00, is that okay?" said Eshaan.

"Perfect mate," said Terri. "Right, back to the hotel, I need my bed."

Eshaan set off back to the hotel and dropped them off outside the main entrance and then picked two names from his contacts list and rang them with the details of the early start they would be on in just a few hours' time before he headed back towards his apartment.

*****

Jaz woke up with her phone ringing. It was Aditya Biri, her call centre manager at the Andheri West site. Just as she picked up the call she heard knocking on her bedroom door. She was about to say, 'Come in,' when Ekam burst in, something he would never do unless it was urgent.

"Miss Kaur, Miss Kaur, we have a problem, the police. They've raided four of your call centres," said Ekam.

"What!" said Kaur. "Wait a minute. Aditya, what's going on?" But the phone had cut off.

Aditya had been getting a coffee at the machine on the first floor. It was his usual seven o'clock start to his day in the office when he had heard shouting and noise from the main entrance. He hadn't clearly heard the first shouts, but the second came through loud and clear. 'Police, Police.' He ran down the stairs and saw them coming in through the doors. He turned around and ran back up as fast as he could to his office trying to ring his boss. He opened up his desk top and started the procedure he had been entrusted with when he was given the role of manager. He calmly went into the files and even as the police officer came through his door and pointed a gun at him, he pushed 'enter' and the program started.

"Step away, step away and drop the phone," the police officer shouted.

Aditya immediately pushed cancel on the phone and then held his hands in the air and started protesting his innocence and asking what was going on. The officer was distracted for long enough in dealing with Aditya to not notice the line on the screen building towards 100% when the program would be complete. It was only then that the officers in the main call centre started shouting as first one and then more of the desk top screens started to go blank. Aditya heard the commotion and smiled. The program was working and not just here, but across all of the other sites. He glanced back at his screen. 92%. One more minute and it would be complete.

A woman entered the room. She had a look of authority. She saw him looking at the screen and she went to his desk top and saw the number was now 97%. She cursed and started to push buttons trying in vain to stop the program. He thought she might say something or threaten him, but he realised it was too late. 99% and then 100%. It was done. He knew what would come next. He'd be arrested, but then she would get her lawyers to come and help him, at least that was what she had said. He hoped he could trust her. The worst Miss Kaur had said would happen would be a charge of obstruction and if he was unlucky a period of imprisonment. Something he wasn't looking forward to, but she had said she would give his family £200 for every day he had to spend in jail. The female police officer couldn't understand why the man in front of her was smiling. It had to mean that whatever he had managed to do had destroyed the evidence they were looking for. 'Shit,' she thought. That means a lot of explaining to her boss who had said this was a job that had been authorised at ministerial level and had international relevance.

"Shit," she said, but out aloud this time. "Cuff him and get him away from me."

*****

"Miss Kaur, we need to go and go now," said Ekam.

"I hope to God that Aditya activated the abort program Ekam. They've got nothing on us if he did, but if he didn't….." said Kaur, as she slipped out of her flimsy night dress and found some underwear, a pair of jeans and a top.

Ekam looked away immediately, more out of shyness than anything. She often changed in front of him, showing no signs of inhibition because she had been doing this since she was a child and thought nothing of it. But he had grown more and more embarrassed, as the years had gone by, of his reaction every time he saw her naked and he had to look away to hide the feelings he had for her. He pulled himself together and re-focused on the job of protecting her.

"He's a good man, so I'm sure he did what he needed to do Miss. I will ring the lawyers and get them in to see him and we'll know very quickly. We always knew this day might come Miss and if it has worked, then all will be well and you can quickly rebuild the business again."

"Yes, I know, you're right, but I don't like things going wrong. It was bad enough with what seems to be happening to Sonny without now getting this," said Kaur.

She paused for a moment and whilst she never sought his advice, she spoke her thoughts out aloud.

"You don't think any of this is connected with Sonny do you Ekam?"

He didn't really know what she had been doing in Mallorca, but he couldn't see how any connection could be made to her from anything to do with the Armenian thug.

"I don't see how that could happen Miss, but still, we won't take any chances, so let's head for Goa," said Ekam. "I suggest we use a private charter company?"

"Yes, you're right and good idea, we'll get there quickly and this can all die down whilst we're away. Let's go. I could do with a holiday. We can check in with the rest of the team from down there, to make sure they are okay. I've got the master files here," she said, opening her personal safe and taking out a USB, "so come on, let's go."

She followed him out of the villa and down to the Mercedes, but she still had a nagging feeling about a possible connection to Sonny.

Ekam eased the car out on to the main road and headed towards the airport. The man in the parked Hyundai SUV let another car pass him, to provide some cover, before he turned and followed the Mercedes.

Traffic was slow as the morning commuter traffic had started, so he had time to make a call on his mobile.

Eshaan had taken two calls so far that morning. The first was from his man at the S.V. Road who had said he had seen five police vehicles enter the business estate. He had followed them in at a distance and seen them carry out a raid at the Intertech offices. Only one man had come out under arrest and he had pictures of him. The second call was from the man watching Kaur's villa. He was now mobile and following Kaur and the bodyguard. It was too early to be sure, but his man thought they may be heading to the airport. Eshaan then rang Terri to update her.

*****

Martin Carruthers put the phone down on the call he had just taken from his contact at the Indian Central Intelligence Bureau. Perhaps they had underestimated this Kaur woman. The police had apparently under-taken an effective raid of the four premises, but one of the call centre people, believed to be the manager at the Andheri West site, had been smart enough to start some sort of program that seemed to have completely disabled, if not destroyed the entire Intertech IT sys-tem. Kaur hadn't been at any of the four sites and a fol-low up visit to her house had been equally unsuccessful and it now looked like she had left the city. As things stood at the moment, there was no evidence to suggest any criminal wrong doing by her or her company, sim-ply because the evidence had been erased or destroyed in some hi-tech abort program.

"Anna, I hope you're well? Presumably this is break-fast time for you and you may have heard that the po-lice have raided Kaur's four sites?"

"Yes, Martin, we've all just come down for breakfast and Terri has taken a couple of calls already. Did the po-lice find anything?" said Anna.

"Unfortunately not. Any evidence that was there is believed to have been destroyed by some sort of hi-tech program that wiped all the files across all four sites," said Martin.

"And presumably all the data Rob obtained would be inadmissible in a court of law?" said Anna.

"Unfortunately so." He paused and waited for her as he heard her tell the others what had happened. "Do you have any immediate plans Anna? Just wondering if you want those packages dropped off for you?"

Again a pause.

"Yes please to the packages Martin. If she is on the way to the airport we may be able to find out where she has gone. Wherever she goes, we will try to follow," said Anna.

"Okay, Laura will be with you shortly. She's bringing some fishing gear, but she will ring you first. Good luck and keep me posted if you get a chance," said Martin.

*****

"Disappointing about the IT system being sabotaged," said Greg, "but she must have a back-up and be looking to start up again once things quieten down. So where are we betting that she might go?"

"Well she's got lover boy back in Mallorca?" said Terri.

"Well she may be outside of India, but I just get the feeling that she's going to want to stay somewhere she feels safe, so I reckon she'll go to her place in Goa," said Sam.

"Okay," said Greg, "the bets are on Goa. Terri, let's see if Eshaan's man can get close enough to see where she goes in the airport."

"I'm on it and I've just phoned Daniel to get himself and Frances back to the airport in case we need to shift out in double quick time."

THIRTY TWO

It was only an hour down to Goa by plane, however, Jaz really didn't fancy flying with a plane load of tourists, so she dialled one of the local private jet companies she often used when she wanted to get away quickly.

The second one she rang could get her airborne in less than an hour, so they headed for the corporate terminal and within twenty minutes she was sitting on board sipping a glass of champagne. Ekam parked the car in a limited waiting area and rang one of his men to come and collect the car before he joined her on board. He could tell she was anxious, which was really unlike her because she was usually really strong when faced with any challenge.

"How long will you be?" she called out to any of the crew who might be listening.

"We are just finalising our flight plan with the control tower and we should be good to go in about five minutes Miss Kaur," said a voice from the cockpit.

"Have you got a car ready to meet us when we arrive Ekam?"

"Yes Miss, it's all arranged. One of the drivers will meet us as usual."

Jaz knew she was always collected at the airport and taken to the villa, so she couldn't understand why she was asking such irrelevant questions.

"Miss, is something worrying you that I don't know about? I don't mean to pry but is there anything I need to know to ensure I can keep you safe?"

"I'm not worried, so don't ask such stupid questions," she snapped, before turning to look at him. "I'm so sorry Ekam. I didn't mean to snap at you. I know you're just trying to help."

"There's no need to apologise Miss, I am just here to serve and to keep you safe," said Ekam.

She thought for a moment. She knew that Ekam knew about the call centre operations and the software scam, but she hadn't told him about the side line with Sonny in Mallorca. She wasn't hiding it, but equally she had never shared everything about the business with Ekam either. But he was right, if he was to be able to protect her then he needed to know where any possible threat could come from.

"Look Ekam, I have been doing a little side line with Sonny, you know the guy I met in Mallorca?"

Ekam nodded.

"Well it seems that he is having some difficulties with the police over there and some sort of private security company, who are acting for the family of a woman who was somehow killed in a burglary by Sonny's team."

"Do you think it is the Spanish police who are now looking at you?" said Ekam.

"I don't know. But they worry me less than this private outfit because Sonny doesn't know what they are capable of."

"This woman, how did she die if it was just a straight forward burglary?" said Ekam.

Jaz went quiet.

"I don't know. Sonny is so gentle with me, but I get the feeling he could be, well you know…" she tailed off and looked down. "I really like him Ekam, but I think he may have brought trouble on himself and now he's brought trouble on me."

"Where is he now?" said Ekam.

"He's keeping a low profile in Mallorca. There's not much the police can do with him as they haven't got any evidence apparently, but they are making things very difficult with his business and now his boss is asking some very awkward questions, so I'm thinking of telling him to come out here," said Jaz.

He couldn't hide it. He breathed out and she heard the rush of air and looked at him.

"What? What is it Ekam? Would that be so wrong to help the man I care for?" she said.

"Miss, I'm sorry. I was only thinking of you and if he comes here, then we don't know who he may bring with him who may present a threat to you," said Ekam.

"Well you can protect me can't you Ekam? Or are you saying you aren't good enough to protect me against whoever these people may be?"

Once again, she had snapped at him. He said nothing. He loved her with all his heart and would never put her in any sort of harm's way. But this Armenian thug, because that was what he thought of him as, had done just that. How could, or even how dare this gangster put her in any form of danger. Ekam would kill him himself if it meant she was unharmed, but he looked at her again. She saw straight through him. She knew he had feelings for her, but she had never encouraged him in all the years he had been with her. She treated him sometimes like an older brother, but other times and this was just one of those times, he felt like he was only another member of staff, a bodyguard who just needed to do what he was paid to do.

"You haven't answered me Ekam. What are you going to do to protect me?" she said.

"What I have always done Miss. I will lay down my life if that is what is needed."

She softened.

"I know you would Ekam," she said, as she sat back in her chair and felt the wheels start to roll as the plane moved forward towards the runway.

Standing inside the corporate terminal, the man from the Hyundai SUV looked out the window and watched the private plane as it moved away. He then rang Eshaan.

*****

"Where is he Nino?" said Lori Garcia.

"Still lying low I reckon Boss. We haven't seen him for days now and there's been little or no activity from any of the others in the gang hierarchy."

She sat back in her chair and thought about what Greg had said about what had happened in Armenia with Sergei Grigoryan and the mention of a restructure.

"How long do we think Sonny has been the boss of the OCG in the Balearics?"

"It's about three years give or take. He came in and took over from the previous guy. Rumour has it that he was permanently retired so to speak and by Sonny," said Nino.

Nino looked at her.

"Do you think that Sergei would do that?" said Nino.

"I don't know. They are or at least were, very close, but he talked about a restructure to Greg, I mean Señor Chambers, and if Sergei feels Sonny has compromised him he may forget his past loyalty to his friend and do what's right for the business. Sergei hasn't remained at the top of the OCG without being ruthless as hell has he?" said Lori.

"No, you're right there," said Nino, "and Boss, it's okay, I get that you like Greg Chambers, he seems like a really good guy."

She smiled. She knew they would notice, but she was glad all the same that Nino had given a sort of sign of approval. She didn't know why, as what had her life and in this case, her love life, got to do with Nino and the team anyway? She looked at him and saw him smiling.

"What are you smiling at Sergeant?" she said.

"Nothing Boss," he said.

"Well stop smiling and go and do something useful, like find Sonny," said Lori.

Nino looked back as he left her office, still smiling. She shook her head. Was she blushing? *'Oh, who cares,'* she thought and she smiled back at him.

*****

Sonny was sat by the pool drinking a cold beer at the villa he had rented by Port d'Andratx. Was he getting paranoid? He hadn't heard from Sergei in a day or so. No calls or texts when he usually had something from him, even if it was just sharing a joke. Had Sergei lost faith in him? If he had, that would mean only one thing. A restructuring is what Sergei called it.

That's what had happened just over three years ago when Sonny had turned up at the house of the previous In-Country Head of the Balearics and retired him with a bullet to his head. Well he wasn't going to wait around and see who Sergei sent. Besides, *'Who did he have anyway who was better than Sonny Sargsyan?'* Maybe he should go on the offensive? Why shouldn't he get rid of Sergei and take over the whole OCG? Next to Sergei, everybody was shit-scared of him, so why not? But whilst he still had this damn mole in his camp, who could he tell without risking it getting back to Sergei? He looked down and saw that his hand was shaking. *'I'm getting paranoid,'* he said to himself. He took a couple of long deep breaths and thought for a moment. His phone rang. It was Jaz.

"Hello handsome," she said.

"Just what I need," said Sonny.

"In a good way I hope?"

"In a very good way," said Sonny. "I think I'm going nuts here and I can't trust anyone."

She smiled to herself. She wanted to help and here was her chance, even though she knew Ekam didn't approve.

"Look, why don't you come and see me? I'm in Goa. I'm in the shit too and I've come out here to hide and I need some company."

"What's happened Jaz?" asked Sonny.

"The police raided four of my call centres. But we managed to shut everything down before they found anything that might be difficult to explain."

He listened and thought about what she had said.

"In the world of criminal gang performance it could be said that you and I aren't doing very well my sweet," said Sonny.

"You are right there hun," she said, laughing. "So, why not come out and keep me company?"

He paused for a moment. What would he say to Sergei? Maybe nothing. Leave him guessing where he had gone.

"Now that's a great idea. If I get a flight to Goa, can you get me picked up at the airport?"

"Yes, of course, tell me when and," she paused, "Sonny?"

"Yes."

"I'm glad you're going to come," she said.

"Me too," said Sonny.

*****

Terri was sat with the others, around a table in her room, when she took the call from Eshaan. His man at the airport had seen a private plane leaving the corporate terminal with the Kaur woman and a man believed

337

to be her minder or bodyguard. Eshaan's man had managed to find out where the plane was heading and it was, as Sam had guessed, going to Goa.

"I was going to meet Laura to get our gear but I'll get her to hike the stuff down to Goa and we'll tie up down there. Now before we do anything else, we need to decide who goes to Goa. There's good reason for us all to go, but equally, this may suit a smaller team? My preference is a smaller team, but I'm open to everyone's thoughts," said Terri.

Greg had seen her do this before. She was very democratic was Terri, especially if she got her own way and if she didn't, she'd just tell them what they were going to do. Simon and Tommy both understood this, but Sam and Anna obviously had no comprehension about how Terri operated and he wondered how they would respond to Terri's form of democracy.

Sam was taken in by Terri's offer to open things up and he set out a number of ideas, all of which she listened to carefully and then dismissed one by one. Anna had watched what was going on between Sam and Terri and Greg thought he saw a smile. *'Did she know?'* thought Greg.

"Terri, I'm inclined to agree with you," started Anna, and Greg saw Terri nodding approvingly. "However, let me turn this on its head. What would you need to see happening that would change your mind from a small team to a bigger team?"

To be fair, Terri acknowledged what Anna had just done with a nod towards her dad. Greg saw Terri push her shoulders back into her chair as she thought. This wasn't going to be railroaded through with just Terri's ideas. Anna had been a past master of planning and Terri knew she had been out-manoeuvred with a classic counter-punch question.

"Good question Anna. If I didn't know what we were

going into, then I might be persuaded to go to a bigger team."

"So a bit like with Armenia?" said Anna.

"Yes," said Terri slowly, before adding, "and that's check mate I think Anna," and she smiled at her. *'God, this woman is good,'* she thought to herself.

Sam looked across at his mother having just seen a master class of negotiation.

"Right, that's that then I think. We all go and then we recce her villa and then decide on the deployment," said Greg. "Terri, can you get Daniel set up for us to roll and we'll leave here once we're all packed up and ready."

"I'm on it."

As the room broke up to get ready to leave, Greg took his daughter to one side.

"Are you okay with all that?"

"What? You mean Anna taking my legs?" said Terri.

"Well I wasn't going to put it like that, but yes," said Greg.

"Yes, I'm fine, especially as she did it in such a British and ladylike way. What's to be offended at? She made a really good call and it was a good reminder that I can be a bit, well you know, bullish, can't I?" said Terri.

"Yes, my darling daughter. Sometimes it can be one of your best attributes and sometimes it can get in your way. But I'm proud of you, for the way you dealt with that."

She kissed him on the cheek and smiled.

"Love you Dad and see you later," she said.

*****

Daniel and Frances were waiting in the terminal when they arrived and they were soon all out at the Citation and ready to depart when Greg's phone rang.

"Lori, what's up?" said Greg.

"We've lost Sonny and by lost, I mean we can't find him. I was thinking what you were saying about a restructure and I'm wondering if he might have skipped the country?" said Lori.

"I'm assuming you've checked his villa, the one down by s'Arenal?"

"Yes, we went in this morning. It was on a slightly dubious warrant, but it got us in there. There was only the housekeeping staff in there, so Sonny has obviously cleared out of there and gone somewhere else on the island. There's no record of him leaving under his own passport, so I'm making a guess that he's either dead or he's left the island under a different name."

Greg thought for a moment. He had thought Sergei would be more efficient than this. Now they had Sonny running loose.

"You don't think he might try for a restructure of his own and take out Sergei?" said Greg.

"It had occurred to me. I mean, he must be thinking that Sergei has lost faith in him and that can only mean one thing. What do you think, because under the European Court of Human Rights I have a legal obligation to warn someone, even if it is a criminal, if a serious threat has made against their life? However, thinking about it, I'm only making a supposition, so I'm happy that as we haven't heard of any threat as such, we only tell Sergei if we think it may be a tactical option to consider?" said Lori.

"So we warn Sergei as a means of trying to secure some sort of response? Isn't that entrapment?" said Greg.

"It could be construed that way if I did it," said Lori.

"Ah, I get you," said Greg. "Have we got Sergei's phone number from the guy who was shot at the finca?"

"Yes, he was Sonny's number two, so he was high enough up the organisation to have access to Sergei if needed." She gave him the number and said, "I'll leave you to make the call. And Greg?"

"Yes," said Greg.

"Stay safe for me."

"I will my love, don't worry and I'll be back before you know it," said Greg.

"I can't wait," she said.

He turned to the rest of the team and updated them on the phone call from Lori.

"So what are you looking to achieve by putting a call in to Sergei?" said Anna.

"First of all, he'll know we're keeping tabs on him and I want to keep him feeling that pressure so that he goes through with his restructure. Second, if Sonny has left Mallorca on a false passport, we might never see him again. I don't think John MacDonald will want his wife's murderer going walkabout into a free and easy lifestyle, especially if he's shacked up with his Indian girlfriend. So Sergei just might be able to find Sonny more easily than we will," said Greg.

"What about if Sergei gets to Sonny before we do and then we never find out what's happened? John won't know then either," said Terri.

"Okay, there's some pros and cons here," said Greg, "but as we've lost Sonny, I'm thinking we go with the best current option and get you Sam, to speak to Sergei. Agreed?"

Everyone nodded and Sam dialled Sergei's number and put his phone on speaker phone.

"Yes? Who is this?" said Sergei Grigoryan.

"Sergei, it's Sam Martínez."

"Ah, Bookseller. What do you want now?"

"We've heard that Sonny has left Mallorca under a false passport. Did you know?"

There was just enough of a pause to tell Sam that Sergei didn't know.

"Why should I confirm or deny the movements of

my team to you Bookseller?"

"Because our business transaction still stands Sergei, that's why. You deliver on the restructuring we talked about in the Balearics or we make life for your OCG very difficult over a number of different locations," said Sam.

"Don't threaten me Bookseller. We both know there would be casualties on both sides and so how many of your loved ones are you prepared to lose?" said Sergei.

Sam heard the menace in Sergei's voice. He clearly wasn't someone to be intimidated. Sergei would fight fire with fire if necessary and then see who was the last one standing.

"It's not a threat Sergei. It's just giving you the opportunity to not have to fight fires on too many sides of your business and leave yourself vulnerable to a takeover. Presumably it has occurred to you that Sonny will suspect that you may be thinking of a change of management and he may be considering a reverse takeover."

"He wouldn't dare.....," said Sergei.

He hadn't been able to stop himself coming out with the words. Sonny wouldn't, couldn't think of doing something like that? But then again, he himself hadn't had any compulsion to arrange the death of Sonny, his long-time friend, who was like a brother to him.

"I can see that I've got you thinking Sergei," said Sam. "So what if he's on his way to you now? He knows you better than we do and we got to you easily enough."

Sergei let the words sink in before he said anything. Had he made a mistake in challenging Sonny? They had been so close for so long. Had he been too quick to condemn him? He had no qualms over the death of some English woman. That was of no concern to him. It was the business that mattered to him and any unwanted attention, from the police and now this pri-

342

vate security company who seemed to have significant funds and resources with which to make things difficult for him, was something he would do his utmost to protect against.

"Bookseller, you are right, I did not know that Sonny had left Mallorca. If he comes to me then I will deal with him personally. But if he goes elsewhere I will send someone who I know will find him. Now once again, I think our time together is at an end. Goodbye."

Sergei rang off before Sam could respond.

"He hung up," said Sam.

"He's certainly got a thing about you being a Bookseller hasn't he?" said Terri.

Sam laughed.

"But I suppose it's now an accurate description of my life," said Sam.

"Okay, let's get back on track shall we?" said Greg. "Let's leave things to play out now, but we need to be mindful that if we find Sonny, then there may be one of Sergei's team somewhere close behind."

Just at that moment Daniel's voice came across the intercom.

"Seatbelts everybody please, we've got clearance to take-off."

THIRTY THREE

Sergei picked up his phone and rang Arman.

"Boss, what can I do for you?"

"Where's Sonny?"

Arman paused. He hadn't seen Sonny for a day or so, but that wasn't altogether unusual. However, he wasn't sure that would be an acceptable answer to Sergei.

"I don't know Boss. I saw him the day before yesterday, but he hasn't been back into the office since then. Do you want me to go and call on him? I expect he's at the villa," said Arman.

"You won't find him there. He's apparently left the country on a different passport. Check the villa and then check your sources at the airport to see if they can help."

"Yes Boss, I'll get straight on it."

Arman cursed out aloud as soon as he came off the phone. Sergei wouldn't have been impressed with him not knowing where Sonny was.

It only took him twenty minutes to get to the villa. Sonny wasn't there and the housekeeping staff hadn't been told when he might be back. He made some calls into his contacts in the Airport Security team and took a call fifteen minutes later. They had his photo coming up on a passport in the name of Yuri Pavlovich who was shown as boarding a flight to Madrid and then bound for Goa via Doha. He rang Sergei.

"You should have known about this before I rang you Arman. Don't make a habit of this," said Sergei.

"No Boss, sorry Boss," said Arman, but Sergei had already cut the call and was dialling a new number.

*****

The Russian saw the name on the incoming call. She knew he wasn't a man to be kept waiting.

"I've got a job for you, in Goa. When can you leave?"

'Hello to you too Sergei,' she thought, but he clearly wasn't in the mood for pleasantries.

"I can leave today, so depending on flights, I should be there tomorrow."

"Good," said Sergei.

"Who is the target?"

"Sonny," said Sergei.

She paused. She knew Sonny was pretty much Sergei's right hand man.

"Sonny?" she said.

"Yes, is that a problem?" said Sergei.

"No, I just wanted to confirm. So he's in Goa. Do we know where?"

"I'm sending you an image. Jasvinder Kaur. She runs call centres in India and we've been doing some business with her in the Balearics. She has a villa somewhere just outside Goa. She's not a target unless she gets in the way. Is that understood?" he said.

"Yes, loud and clear. Anything else?" she said.

"There may be another team tracking the woman. They're British and a private outfit, but they're good, very good in fact, maybe ex-Special Forces. Again, they're not part of the deal, but if they get in your way, you know what to do," said Sergei.

"Intriguing," said the woman.

"It's not bloody intriguing. It's just a mess that needs tidying up."

"Okay, no problem," she said.

Sergei put the phone down. It might be the right thing to do for the business, but he still didn't like making the decision. He had used her before on a number of jobs where he wanted to put distance between himself and the person he wanted removed. The Russian was good, very good at what she did, so it shouldn't take long before he could get the Balearics back on track.

*****

They were actually in the air for less than an hour when Daniel announced they would be landing soon. They had Wi-Fi on the plane and so Terri had been organising cars and somewhere for them to stay. She had booked two nights as she usually did, with the proviso they could leave after one. She'd also messaged Laura to check on an exchange time. Ideally she wanted the gear by the evening at the latest, to allow them to make an early start in the morning as Sam's intel guy had come up with a location for Kaur's villa and it was about twenty kilometres away.

They landed without issue and were soon out at the front of the airport where the meet and greet team from the car hire company were waiting with two Ford SUVs. Terri checked the documentation and signed the papers before they loaded up into the two vehicles and headed for the hotel.

They had booked three rooms again. Firstly for ease, but secondly because three couples looked more natural in a holiday setting. After they checked in, they all headed for the hotel bar and sat down to talk through their next moves.

"So what's the objective in seeing this woman?" said Anna.

"I think we should be persuading her to give back some of the money she has made from people like Bill," said Sam.

346

"Do you mean some or all?" said Greg.

Sam thought for a moment and said, "Well thinking about it, I think it should be what we think she has made, so let's start with two million."

Simon let out a low whistle.

"Well that's what Rob reckoned she was making when he looked at her files, so let's go with that," said Anna.

There were nods of agreement from the rest of the group.

"Okay, so that's the 'what' we're planning on doing, but what about the 'how'? Looking at some Google Earth maps, her place looks like it is some way from anywhere. No neighbours close-by and there's a whole load of open ground surrounding the villa, so it's not like we can just sneak up on her unannounced," said Terri.

"We could do something like we did in Yerevan?" said Tommy. "You know, turn up at the front door, but have some back-up, with you and Simon hidden away."

"That could work," said Sam, "but we'll need to do a recce of the place to find out how many people she has there and what the surrounding environment is actually like."

"Agreed. Terri, it needs to be your call on whether you can give us the support we may need, so I'll leave it to you and Simon to sort out the recce after dinner, okay?" said Greg.

"Yes, no problem, we'll report back later."

*****

After dinner, Terri and Simon set off in one of the SUV's and found Laura waiting to do the handover near to Colva Beach.

"How did you get down here then?" asked Terri.

"Helicopter. Scared the hell out of me, but it was quick and easy to get your gear down here. I'll wait

347

around here for you to pick up your stuff," said Laura. "If you need to disappear in a hurry, just leave the stuff in the cars and text me where they are. I'll get those picked up and we'll get everything back to you in due course."

"I'm tempted to ask how you might do that, but I suspect you aren't going to tell me are you Laura?" said Terri.

"You're right on that. Anyway, I hope whatever you are planning goes well," and with that she turned and walked towards a waiting car.

They put the packages Laura had brought into the back of the Ford. It looked like a collection of fishing gear and unlocking one of the boxes, Simon took out two of the Glocks and handed one to Terri.

"Probably best we go prepared. No point wandering into the lion's den without having something to offer them," said Simon.

*****

They were already half way there at Colva Beach, so it didn't take long to get to the coordinates they had been given. There were no signposts, but from the co-ordinates it looked like it was going to be somewhere on their left. They wanted to look at the back of the property first. Simon was watching for a turning on the left and pointed when he saw an unmade road, that when they turned into it, led them into some dense woodland. The GPS map indicated what appeared to be some open ground about a kilometre ahead. The space was about a kilometre in diameter and in the middle sat a building, presumably Kaur's villa.

Terri continued driving until they saw a single track road to their right. She branched off and came to a stop when she could see lights in the distance through the branches of the trees. They got out of the vehicle and made their way to the edge of the trees. It was dark now, but Terri got a good view of what was before her with her night scope. The land sloped up from the woodland towards the centre of the open space, so that anyone in the villa could look out west across the top of the woodland and see the coastline. She handed the scope to Simon who took his time surveying the layout of the land.

"Okay, so this will make things just a little bit harder than having a straight forward downward view, but at least there are no obstacles in my way," said Terri.

Simon nodded as he looked through the telescopic night sight at what was the back of the villa. He could see a swimming pool, sun loungers and a patio table and chairs. The villa had what looked like a full width of glass across the back of the property which, from this angle, framed the pool and patio furniture like a picture.

"I can see a man and a woman inside the property, but I can't get a clear image of them because they've got low lighting on in the room. Wait, there's another man who has just entered the room and is talking to the woman. Maybe the bodyguard? But if so, who is the other guy? Another member of her staff?" said Simon and passed the sight back to Terri.

"Damn, you're right, the light is just blurring it. I can't see the faces. Come on, let's see what is around the other side of the property and then get back to the hotel," said Terri.

They made their way back to the SUV and then drove around the outer perimeter road, watching out for any protective measures. They stopped every now and then and checked through the branches for any sign of trip wires or surveillance cameras, but saw nothing.

"She must feel pretty safe out here, but then again they've got that free space in front of the villa as a defence, so who knows what they've got out there to greet any unwelcome visitors," said Simon.

The front entrance was sited on the main highway and there was still some traffic around. Terri waited until a car passed where she was parked and then followed it back onto the highway and as they drove past the villa entrance Simon had his phone on video record.

"Lots of lighting and by the look of it, there are cameras positioned to the front and then again back down the drive to the villa. Two men on guard. Neither seem to be hiding the fact that they are armed," said Terri.

"Okay, I've got it," said Simon, after checking the video he had taken showing the front entrance. "Thoughts on getting into the villa Terri? I don't think we know enough about what's in the open space to chance a silent approach across that, so how about we just rock up and knock on the front door?"

"Well what we haven't seen is lots of protection guys, so maybe we leave Greg and the guys to take out the two at the front and then get to the villa and we'll get in position around the back," said Terri.

"There's some risk, but it's four against two at the front, so pretty good odds," said Simon. "Let's take it back as Option One and see what they say when they've seen the video."

*****

It was close to eleven o'clock when they made it back to the hotel and met up with the others in a quiet corner of the hotel bar. They quickly went through what they had found out and passed Simon's phone around so that everyone had the chance to look at the front entrance. Greg waited until everyone had seen the video before speaking.

"So do we have an Option Two?"

"Not a safe one," said Simon.

"So Option One is safe?" said Tommy.

"Safer than Option Two, which would be to chance your arm and walk across unknown ground that if I was setting up security, I would have covered with all manner of movement activated alarms. We just don't know what these guys might use and I don't fancy finding out they've opted for land mines," said Simon.

"Aren't land mines now illegal in warfare?" said Sam.

"They are in over a hundred and sixty countries Sam, but some countries are still using them," said Greg.

"Can I say something?" said Anna.

"Fill your boots Anna," said Terri.

"Terri and Simon have given us what they determine is the best option, so I think we need to work around that and spend time focusing on how we get in the main entrance and up to the villa."

"As always Anna, the voice of reason. So, what are people's thoughts? Distraction? Puncture? Car broken down? Sickness? They are the usual favourites," said Greg.

"So there will be four of us at the front right? With you two going to the back of the villa to provide support?" said, looking at Terri and Simon, who nodded. "So, let's use Greg and Anna as bait because they are….," he paused.

"It's okay," said Anna gently, "you can say it."

Tommy squirmed a bit, but then finally said, "Well you're older than we are and look less likely to be about to start an attack on their stronghold."

"Nicely put Tommy," said Terri. "So you guys can bring down their guard and Sam and Tommy can take them out."

"Or," said Anna, "Plan B and we get them to bring down their guard and then we'll take them out."

It was Terri's time to squirm a little now and then she saw her dad laughing at her.

"Yes, okay, then you guys get to be the action heroes," said Terri.

"Ideally, we want you to try to get the cameras turned off, or at least directed elsewhere, before you start your way up the main drive," said Simon.

"We'll have to play that by ear as we won't know what we're faced with until we get there," said Greg, "but that's what we'll work on, so here's an idea and all thoughts welcome."

Greg then worked through the outline of a plan and after some tinkering they all agreed that, in principle, it stood a good chance of succeeding in getting them in through the front entrance. With that they broke up with some going to their rooms, whilst Sam and Terri stayed down at the bar.

"You okay with tomorrow Sam?" said Terri.

"Yes, I admit I'm feeling a bit on edge and I think it's because this is all a bit different to how I'd see operations rolling out in the police."

"How do you mean?" said Terri.

"We always had a primary goal of arresting someone or stopping someone doing something, you know, stop them committing the robbery or something like that. But here, well, we're going in and we're going to ask Kaur to transfer two million quid and she's going to say what? 'Of course, no problem'. It's the, *what we do to persuade her,* bit which is what I'm struggling with, as it's so up in the air."

"I do get where you're coming from Sam. We've both been used to working within the operational parameters of organisations that are subject to extensive legal scrutiny, whereas here we're dealing with people who don't play fair. They'll shoot first and not even bother asking questions, so yes, adapting to that might take you a while, but don't worry, you'll have Greg right by your side and when I say he's good at this stuff, I mean he's really good and I'm not just saying that because he's my, or should I say, our dad."

Sam smiled. He hadn't been just what you might call an ordinary cop, dealing with the everyday issues that came up in general policing. It had been a good few years since he'd entered the world of major crime and specialised firearms, however this was still feeling like a very different arena for him, where the law was not going to be at the forefront of his mind. He could see that Terri had moved from being a trained soldier, operating within the accepted rules of combat engagement, to being able to deal with the world she now found herself operating in with Greg and 3R.

"What do you see as the possible outcomes tomorrow?" said Terri.

"Honestly?" said Sam. "We kill the two men at the front entrance, then possibly the body guard if he gets in the way and then if she doesn't play ball, we kill Kaur too."

Terri didn't show anything as Sam went through his possible outcomes. She needed him to consider the worst case scenario and see how he dealt with it.

"So are you okay with taking these people out Sam?"

"Wow, that's a question?" said Sam.

"Better I ask it now than you start thinking about it tomorrow mate."

"Good point," he said, then paused. "Yes, I can deal with stopping someone if they're a threat to me, or any of our team and if stopping them means they lose their life then, yes, I can handle that. The bit I'm maybe still working through is when they aren't offering a specific threat at the time I engage them."

"Look Sam, we're not executioners. During my time with 3R, I've never taken a shot or done anything that has been terminal to someone that hasn't been as a direct result of them engaging with me first. Now if Simon was here, he'd call us a couple of wallies for even thinking this stuff. He's been trained to deal with threat and potential threat and by that, he'd see those two on the front entrance as a threat that couldn't be left to potentially raise the alarm or come back to attack us if they got loose. My dad is to an extent, of the same ilk and let's not forget your mum, that's how she would have been trained too. You and me? Well, maybe we were just trained to fight, well let's call it, 'politely' and you're now in a game where the gloves are off and we're not bound by the Queensberry Rules."

"I've never had a sister, but I'm glad I've got one now," said Sam, and got up and gave her a hug.

"And just to think when I first set eyes on you I thought you looked a bit hot. Now wouldn't that have been awkward?" she laughed.

"Oh, let's not even go there Sis," said Sam. "Right, time for bed and sleep and Terri," he paused, "thank you for that."

She didn't say anything but just hugged him again.

THIRTY FOUR

Simon and Terri set off around 9am and headed for the villa. It was warm, around twenty seven degrees, but already it felt hotter because of the humidity.

They went straight to the location they had first seen the villa, parking up and unloading their gear. In the daylight they could see the impact of the completely open space, surrounding the villa, made it look slightly eerie, like it was dead ground with no vegetation or animals.

Terri checked the scope and they were about half a kilometre from the back terrace. Whereas the night before she couldn't see into the living room area because of the background lighting, today the glass doors were wide open. They looked like concertina sliding doors and they were pushed to the right hand side of the aperture. The two of them sat quietly and watched for any movement around the villa or the perimeter. Terri could see occasional movement behind the windows in some of the rooms, but no one had yet come outside.

"You still okay with this location Terri?" said Simon.

"Yes, it's as good as we need it. I wish we had a camera on the front to see what's going on, but there's no chance of that."

"They'll be fine," said Simon. "So whilst you're finalising your set up, I'm going off for a recce on foot."

Terri texted Greg that they were in position and sent their GPS position. It was now just before 11.30am and the wind, what there was, was coming in from a WSW direction off the coast, so it was coming across her right shoulder towards the villa and the sun was around her two o'clock position, if the villa was at twelve o'clock. She then spent some time prepping her rifle and because of the sun's position she attached the anti-glint cap to the scope.

Used primarily to help keep it clear in wet weather, the cap also provided two other uses. One was to disguise the unnatural 'scope ring' of the telescopic sight, which is often the give-away of snipers as there are no perfect circles in nature, but secondly, it also helped to prevent any glint or flash off the scope lens and she guessed Simon would be checking for that whilst out on his recce. She then added the flash hider to the muzzle, a device designed to decrease the level of flash when she fired the rifle, thereby reducing the chances of her position being identified.

She checked her scope and used the x20 setting to get a good close up for setting the range and then reverted back to x12 as her shooting setting. She knew the distance wasn't going to be an issue. The chairs by the patio table were coming up as 512 metres, but with no elevation she was still a little uncertain about the wind coming in from the coast that might be swirling about in this open space. Simon, as her spotter, would give her the final data when she needed it using the anemometer, but if the wind was swirling she'd just have to deal with it as and when the time came and the fact that the distance wasn't excessive gave her a margin to play with.

She got up from her shooting position and took a pair of binoculars and then looked around the villa again. It was on two floors with what looked like a main bedroom on the upper floor, facing west towards the coast, with a large balcony over-looking the pool below. She thought for a moment that she saw someone through the bedroom balcony doors, but couldn't get a clear look. She then brought her sights down to the ground floor. The room that backed out onto the pool was presumably the living room and there were other rooms either side of it. The one to the left had a smaller set of french doors, so possibly some sort of dining room and the other room to the right just had a large window looking out towards the pool, so that might be the kitchen. She then caught sight of a man in light chinos and dark t-shirt walk from around the side of the building. Was that the bodyguard? She couldn't see any sign of a weapon. This was a big property, so she was expecting to see more evidence of security. She texted Simon, 'See anything?'

He was making good ground around the perimeter. He had gone to his right when he'd left Terri as they hadn't seen this part last night and so far he hadn't seen anything to worry him. He continued on and then quickly stopped where he was. There was a small building ahead that they hadn't seen from their position and he realised they wouldn't have seen it the previous night because it was hidden by a small copse of trees. Some sort of cover maybe to block it from the woman's view? He got as close as he thought safe and then looked through his binoculars. Yes, this was where the security team were holed up. At least three men, no four. Maybe the team that had been on the night before? A four man team gave them two at the front, one by the villa and one on wander patrol. That was how he would have done it, so presumably they should expect the same numbers for the daytime team. He saw Terri's text and messaged her back with details of the security house and then took one final check on her position for any sign of scope ring. Nothing. He then started to make his way back to her.

Terri took in the details in Simon's text. Eight security guys plus the bodyguard and then Kaur herself. The odds had gone up somewhat since they had planned the Op last night. She forwarded the text on to Greg and then rang him a moment later.

"Did you get the latest intel from Simon?"

"Yes, I'm thinking we may need to alter our strategy," said Greg.

"What about an upfront approach? She knows her organisation has been busted. She might realise it's connected to what went on in Mallorca, but she probably doesn't know how. It ups the risk a fair bit as she will be on the front foot when you sail into her lion's den."

"You're right about raising the risk, but Anna's had a thought about how Rob the IT man could balance things up a bit," said Greg. "She's calling him now."

"Okay, I'm intrigued, but it's still leaving you guys really exposed until you get around the back when I can give you some cover," said Terri.

"I know, but with what's gone on I think she will want to hear what we have to say," said Greg. "So we're heading out and will be with you in about twenty to thirty minutes."

Terri sat back and thought through the potential scenarios that might play out and a few minutes later she heard Simon's voice.

"Just me, back with the shopping," he joked.

They talked about the options of relocating to be able to see the security building as well, but they would lose the angle she liked of the back of the villa, where they could see both sides of it. They checked their equipment for a final time. Because they were being shielded by the trees, Simon still couldn't give any firm clarity on the wind as he couldn't get a true reading of the anemometer (which looks a bit like a mini weather vane with cups that spin). He could see dust in the open space was swirling about and stopping and starting, but going on local weather forecasts he knew that even at its maximum, it should still only be about 10-12km/h, so nothing too much to worry about and he was happy with the distance and the trajectory data he was seeing from the ballistic calculator. He'd done some sniper spotter training in the SAS, but most of it was self-taught and guided by Terri when working out in the field with her and the most important element he knew was to remain calm and focused and give the shooter the detail at the right time. Meanwhile, Terri was back in position lying down in her shooting position, checking her comfort level, whilst breathing slowly and moving her hands calmly and efficiently across the rifle, practising the reload, adjusting the sight and settling in behind her sight.

"You set for this?" said Simon.

She didn't look up, but just gave a thumbs up. Everything from now on would be with minimal communication. Simon would be the one talking and she would be listening and reacting. Simon got the text from Greg that they were just turning off the highway. Moments later they pulled up behind them and Simon passed the keys to their SUV to Greg.

"We'll pick you up in a while. Stay safe and we'll get this done as quickly as we can," said Greg.

Simon winked at him.

"Sure thing Boss, I'm looking forward to a nice pint of bitter back in London."

*****

Greg and Anna got into the SUV Simon and Terri had been using and set off one way and Sam and Tommy turned theirs around and went the other way. The plan was that Greg and Anna would approach the front entrance from one direction and Sam and Tommy from the other, although they would hold back and only go in if they were called or they got no response on three minute time checks. Anna checked her covert comms kit. It wouldn't stand up to close scrutiny, but her hair covered the ear piece pretty well and the mic was 4G W-Fi and hidden in her bra.

"Testing, one two three," said Anna.

"Loud and clear to Simon and Terri."

"Same to Sam and Tommy."

"Okay guys, let's do this. Nothing silly, just the stuff we know we can do," said Greg.

"Roger that," said Sam.

Greg saw one of the men at the front entrance get up from his seat as he realised the SUV was coming towards the gate house. The man was wearing a light grey suit and Greg could make out the tell-tale bulge of a handgun holster, against the inside shoulder of his jacket. He slowed down and stopped beside the man and lowered his window.

"We'd like to see Miss Kaur," said Greg.

"No appointment, no visit," said the man.

Anna was surveying the gate house and saw the second man coming out to see what was happening. She'd also seen the CCTV cameras by the gate house were fixed on a position behind their SUV and the other one was pointing back down the driveway towards the villa, so they had no camera currently on them. She looked at Greg and motioned to him to change their plan and quietly spoke into her microphone.

"Change of plan. Repeat. Change of plan. We have no cameras on us, we will revert to Plan B. Stand by."

Greg nodded and casually opened the door, as did Anna. Neither of the guards took any of their movements to be threatening and both continued to approach them. Anna deliberately moved away from her door causing her guard to change his direction to follow her and he called out.

"Lady, stop there. Please don't leave your car."

She turned around and feigned surprise that she was causing an issue.

"I'm so sorry young man. I was just stretching my legs." The man came closer and Anna continued talking, "Gosh it's a hot one today isn't it, now where did I leave my mini fan?" and she opened her handbag, just as the man got too close for him to be able to move for his gun.

He suddenly realised that it wasn't a mini fan she had taken from her handbag, but a Glock handgun which was now aimed at his stomach.

"Lady! What the…"

His partner heard him and instinctively turned towards him and away from Greg and didn't see the Glock that came crashing down against the side of his head, knocking him out cold.

"Slowly does it my friend. Do as I say and you will be okay. Do you understand?" said Anna.

The man nodded.

"Now carefully take your gun out of your jacket holster with two fingers and drop it on the ground."

She then motioned for him to walk towards the gate house. Greg picked up the other man and pulled him into the gate house. Sam moved their SUV forward and parked up behind the other car, before picking up the handgun off the ground. Anyone looking at the gate house from the security building would just think the guards were talking to someone. Tommy moved quickly forward and bound the hands and legs of the two guards with plasti-cuffs and taped up their mouths. As Greg and Anna pulled away in their SUV and made their way up the drive, Tommy went back in the Gate House and knocked the remaining conscious guard out with a punch to the side of the head.

"Best if you're asleep whilst all this goes off," he said out aloud to no one in particular, whilst Sam moved the SUV forward to a position where it looked like he was talking to someone in the gate house through the window.

"So far so good," said Anna into her mic. "That went better than we expected. Approaching the villa."

Terri still had sight on the man and woman.

"That's got to be Kaur and the bodyguard."

"Agreed," said Simon, who then passed the message across the comms.

"We have two people by the pool. Male and female," said Simon. "The woman looks like Kaur and the male is her bodyguard, dressed in dark polo shirt and light chinos. She is sitting at one of the tables to your left, nearest the pool. She's got a tablet. Looks like she has just opened it up. Can't be sure, but it looked like finger-print access. He's standing up. Can't see any weapons."

Anna clicked her mic twice to confirm as she looked at Greg.

"What do you think? Just knock on the door?"

"I think maybe we walk around the back. Sooner Terri gets us in view the better I think," said Greg.

"Yes, I like that idea," said Anna.

He stopped the SUV to one side of the front door of the villa and they got out and walked quickly around to the left side of the villa.

"I've got you," said Simon as he saw them come around the side of the villa.

Greg almost instinctively looked out towards Terri's location, but his eye was drawn to a glint at around his two o'clock. That couldn't be Terri as it was too far right of her position, but he was drawn back to what was in front of him, when he heard a woman's voice.

"Who are you? Ekam, how the hell did they get in here?" said Kaur.

Ekam had already moved between Kaur and the two people who he saw in front of him. Greg could see a radio on the table in front of him and Ekam was moving towards it, so he drew his Glock from his belt behind his back.

"I'd rather you didn't do that. We've just come for a chat with Miss Kaur and once we are done, we will leave and no one needs to get hurt," said Greg.

Ekam remained in front of the table where Kaur was sitting.

"I don't know who you are Mister, but this is a very big mistake that you don't want to be making. Leave now and you might just get away with your life," said Ekam.

"Brave words and I admire your courage and commitment to your Principal," said Greg. "However, we can all get through this if Miss Kaur, you will just hear us out?"

She had looked shaken when she saw the gun, but had relaxed when she heard the man start talking. If he had wanted to shoot her, he would have done that already, so what was it he wanted? If there was negotiation to be done, then she was a past master at that, so why not hear what he has to say?

"You have me at a disadvantage. Who are you and what are you doing here?" she said.

"Forgive me. My name is Greg Chambers and this is my business associate, Anna Martínez, but perhaps you know her name already as your boyfriend kidnapped her?"

She had heard his name and was already planning strategy to talk through whatever it was this man was here about, but when she heard Anna's name and about the kidnap she froze.

"I had nothing to do with that," she said.

"I know that young lady and that's not what we're doing here," said Anna.

"Before we go on. Ekam, tell your man in the villa to bring you a jug of water and some glasses and tell the other one patrolling the perimeter to go and check on the Gate House," said Greg in Hindi.

Ekam looked at Kaur, who nodded to him.

"You speak well Mr Chambers, presumably you have worked for some time in my country?" said Kaur.

"It was a while ago, but I sometimes needed to understand what people were saying about me, so it was important to get the basics," said Greg.

Ekam spoke to the two guards over the radio and passed the exact message Greg had asked him to say. Anna spoke quietly into her mic to let Sam know to expect a guard was on his way down to the gate house and got two clicks back from him. Moments later a guard walked out of the living area carrying a tray with a jug and glasses on it, unaware of the situation he was walking into. Anna walked behind him and checked for any sign of a weapon and as he put the tray down she jabbed her gun into his back and told him to sit down. Caught off guard, he looked in vain at Ekam, who just nodded and motioned for him to sit at the other table away from Kaur. Ekam thought this might just give him some opportunity as these people would need to be watching two tables now.

Greg then waved at Ekam to join his guard at the other table. Ekam didn't want to leave Jaz unprotected and he already felt a failure that he had left her exposed to danger. He thought they were safe out here and wondered how these two old, yes old people, had got through his security team at the gate house. He had four more men at the security house who he couldn't call and they were hidden from view by the copse of trees she had insisted on having planted. He sat back and felt the tension rising in his body as he decided what to do next. Would he have to give his life to somehow protect the woman he had loved since he had been a young boy?

"Now I need you to be aware that we haven't come alone," said Greg to the bodyguard.

Ekam snapped back into the moment seeing the man was talking to him.

"Please look down at your shirt. I appreciate your shirt is a dark blue, but I think it should hopefully still show up. It's a laser light attached to a rifle. So you will perhaps understand that we don't now need to be watching you two. Understood?" said Greg, as he opened his mic as he spoke and Terri turned on her laser light, as she aimed at Ekam's chest.

Ekam looked down at his shirt and looked up in the direction of the far trees, towards the coast, but could see nothing. Kaur again felt unsettled and now very much unprotected.

"Look, what do you want? You come in here threatening me. I've told you already, I had nothing to do with your kidnapping," said Kaur.

"But you see my dear, you did," said Anna. "It was your organisation that passed on the details of the scam victims to your boyfriend Sonny and it was his gang who murdered Sheila MacDonald, a very good friend of mine and then assaulted another very good friend of mine and then they kidnapped me. Now your business has already been subject to a number of police raids, but we know that you had a close down plan which worked very well and they weren't able to obtain any evidence."

"I have no idea what you are talking about. Scam victims. Murder, kidnapping? I am a business woman and

I run a successful call centre operation," said Kaur.

"The thing is that you do know about this Miss Kaur and that you have made a considerable amount of money from your IT scam from victims from all across the world. Now here's the deal. We will arrange for everything that could be brought against your company, both in an official and an unofficial capacity to be stopped, if you do something in exchange," said Anna.

Kaur looked at the woman and the man. Clearly they knew everything, but what was it they wanted? She knew she could get the business back up and running again, but not if she was going to get this continuing interference from the police and whoever these people were.

"Are you wired up or anything?" said Kaur.

"Just a local comms set up, nothing else," said Greg.

"So what do you want?"

"Two million pounds transferred to an account in London," said Anna.

Kaur was stunned. She was making a lot of money but that would almost clear her out. She had taken years to build up this business and it was now showing a really good return. She looked at Ekam. Why didn't he do something? Then she thought, 'Where is he? Where's Sonny?' She'd left him in her bed after they had made love that morning. Just at that moment he walked through the french doors with an AK47 assault rifle.

"Damn it, why can't you people just leave me alone?" said Sonny Sargsyan standing in a position where he had both Greg and Anna covered by the AK47.

"Oh shit," said Simon. "Sam, Tommy, if you've dealt with that third guard, be aware, we have an unwelcome visitor here, a very unwelcome visitor, Sonny Sargsyan."

"Bloody hell," said Sam, "we're making to the villa."

THIRTY FIVE

I t was a stand-off, but Greg couldn't tell if Sonny was fired up enough to the point that he would just start shooting.

He tried to gauge the look in his eyes, but saw only grey steely eyes looking back at him. One thing was for sure. Sonny wasn't frightened of anyone or anything.

"So I finally get to meet you Mrs Anna Martínez," said Sonny. "Now please tell me why you've been getting in my way and tracking me out to here?"

"It's no pleasure for me to meet you and to burst your bubble, we haven't come here for you. We've come to discuss a business transaction with your girlfriend Miss Kaur. Now did you hear that we have support both down at the front gate, who are currently on their way up to the villa, as well as some long range support?" and she nodded in the direction of the trees.

"Yes, I heard all that and Ekam here has another four men over there, so we could end up in a blood bath couldn't we?" said Sonny. "Or we could be sensible."

"If you had been sensible and not murdered Sheila MacDonald I probably wouldn't be standing here now," said Anna feeling herself getting rattled.

"No, but I would Sonny," said Greg. "You see Mrs Mac-Donald was the wife of a very important client of mine and let me put it this way, whether you come out of this little situation alive or not, your days are numbered as your boss wants rid of you."

Always confident in everything he did, Sonny couldn't help but be shaken by what he heard the Englishman say. Then he felt the anger rising inside him, just like it had when that stupid MacDonald woman hadn't done as she was asked. He'd see about Sergei getting rid of him. He would get rid of Sergei and take over the OCG. He started to raise the barrel of the AK47 and move into a firing position, but suddenly stopped.

He felt something on his chest before he actually heard the sound of a rifle firing. It was the last thing he heard, as he was dead before he hit the floor. All hell then broke loose as first of all Terri came up on the comms.

"Not me, repeat, not me. We have another shooter in the arena," said Terri.

Greg realised where the shooter was. That had been the glint he had seen. He should have noticed that.

"My two o'clock, the shooter is at my two o'clock, so Terri, Simon, they're about a hundred metres or so to your left. Repeat to your left," said Greg.

Simon started looking across the open space for any evidence in the bushes. But the second shooter was already up on her feet and packing up her gear, before she set off on foot to her Jeep, which was hidden away a half a kilometre to the north.

*****

She was just called the Russian. No one knew her real name, but it was well known within the circles she operated, that she had never failed to fulfil a contract and she wasn't about to start now. She had seen a man walking about in the main bedroom and although she couldn't get a clear look at his face, she presumed, by his build and height, that it was Sonny. She had seen Sonny well before Simon or Terri, because she knew he was there and he was the one she was waiting for. She had then seen another man and a woman appear, as they came around from the opposite side of the villa. Both armed with pistols, she assumed this must be the other team Sergei had spoken about. They seemed to be talking with the Kaur woman, so it didn't look like they had gone there to kill her.

The Russian had followed Sonny to Goa and as authorised by Sergei, she was to terminate Sonny whilst not interfering with anything to do with the Kaur woman, unless necessary. She had been watching the villa all morning, covered by camouflage cloth. She hadn't seen Simon or Terri and they hadn't seen her, so good was each other's cover, but it was her scope that Greg had seen when he came around the corner of the villa.

She had realised that shooting Sonny would cause confusion and give her an added advantage in getting quickly away from the area, leaving the others to deal with the resulting fallout with Kaur's security team. She was therefore in her car and driving away all within the space of five minutes of taking the shot.

*****

Meanwhile, the other guard, who had been sat at the table, had dived for cover at the sound of the shot and had gone scurrying off towards the security house, whilst Ekam, after seeing Sonny fall to the ground, had then heard his mistress scream. He got up from the table and ran towards her. Greg thought he was making for the AK47 and brought his Glock up and shot him, catching him in the shoulder and he fell to the floor. Kaur screamed again and seemed unsure as to who to throw her body on, Sonny or Ekam? Greg then scoured the area where he had seen the scope glint.

"Any sign Simon? I saw a glint as I came in, but didn't twig as I thought it couldn't be you as I knew where you two were sat up, so I dismissed it," said Greg.

Simon had made straight to the area Greg had indicated, but a quick search had revealed the shooter was long gone.

"Nothing, repeat nothing here," said Simon.

By this time Sam and Tommy had come around the corner with guns in hand.

"Two down and one escaped," said Anna. "Kaur is unhurt."

They nodded and moved to a position by the villa walls.

"Greg, Mum, get back in here now," said Sam. "We need to get some cover as we don't know what firepower the ones in the security house may have."

"Simon, Terri, we're moving back into the villa and once we're ready we will exit through the front door. I know we'll be blind there, but we'll be quick. In the meantime tell us what you can see," said Sam into his mic.

"You have four tangos coming your way Sam," said Simon.

"Roger that," said Sam, and motioned to Tommy, who had already seen the four emerging from their cover in the bushes. Judging by the guards they had overcome so far, these didn't seem to be particularly highly skilled, but they wouldn't take any chances, as any idiot with a gun can still do a lot of damage.

Anna had heard Sam and calmly walked across to Kaur and despite the difference in ages, she grabbed Kaur and hauled her into the living room whilst Greg checked on Ekam. He was alive.

"You'll live," said Greg, as he pulled off Ekam's t-shirt and held it to his shoulder and told him to press hard on it. He then picked up Kaur's tablet and followed Anna into the living area inside the villa.

"Hold your hand out Miss Kaur," said Anna firmly.

"No, why should…?"

She didn't get any further as Anna whipped her right hand, like a back hand in tennis and caught Kaur on her face with the back of her clenched fist. Kaur went to make a noise. But nothing came out as she fell back onto the couch, blood streaming from her nose.

"Hand," said Anna again.

Kaur held out her hand and Anna took it and pressed her index finger down on the tablet home button and the screen came to life.

"You won't get in there," snarled Kaur.

Anna looked at her and smiled.

"No, you're right, I won't, but I know a man who will."

She called the number that was already on her phone.

"Anna, how nice to hear from you. Are we set?" said Rob.

"Yes Rob, but we've got a bit of a problem here, so quick as you can please," said Anna, just as she heard shots from outside.

She watched the screen as she saw a pop-up appear from Rob.

"Anna, please press ACCEPT," said Rob.

"Done," said Anna.

Now having remote access to all of Kaur's master files, Rob then trawled through them and Anna saw the pages on the screen start to move faster and faster. Anna tried to follow what he was doing, but was also keeping an eye on Kaur who was glaring at her, so she couldn't really keep up with the speed of what Rob was doing.

"How are we doing Anna?" said Greg, "because I think we may need to be moving in the very near future."

"Rob? How soon?" said Anna.

"Couple of minutes should do it. Bit hairy out there then Anna?" said Rob.

"Just a bit," she said.

Greg saw an opportunity to slow things down and went and grabbed Ekam and the radio.

"Now look. We've got what we came for and the only one who needs to be dead is him out there. Call your dogs off and tell them to back off and your Principal stays safe. Okay?"

Ekam was about to pass the message over the radio when he heard Kaur's voice.

"Ekam, do something, they're stealing my money you dumb idiot. How could you let them do this to me?" said Kaur.

He looked crestfallen. He had guarded her all his life and had just taken a bullet in his side as he went to protect her and all she could think about was the money. Ekam looked at Greg who was still offering him the radio.

"Jasvinder," he said.

She looked at him amazed. He had never called her by her first name. She went to speak, but he put his finger to his mouth.

"Please do not say anything. My job has always been to protect you, rather than your money. I can get you out of this alive if you stop behaving like some spoilt little brat and let me do my job."

Ekam then took the radio and spoke quickly, passing a message that Greg could just about follow.

"Fall back to the security house and await further instructions. We are safe. Repeat we are safe."

He then handed the radio back to Greg knowing that he wouldn't be stupid enough to leave the radio with him as they left the villa.

"Sam, Tommy, go check the front and get both of the SUVs started and backed up to the house," said Greg.

"Looks like the guards are falling back. You guys all okay down there?" said Simon.

"Yes, yes, leaving in about two," said Greg.

"Dad, Kaur?" said Terri.

Greg knew what she was asking. Sonny was dead. He was the reason why John had lost Sheila, not Kaur. He looked at Kaur, who seeing his eyes seemed to understand what was happening and she started shaking. He paused for a moment and then shook his head.

"No, repeat No," said Greg.

"Understood," said Terri.

Tommy and Sam checked the front and saw it was clear and got the SUVs turned around and ready to go just as they saw Greg and Anna calmly walking out of the front door.

"Said your goodbyes then?" said Sam.

"Yes, she wasn't very happy, either with us or her bodyguard who seems to have got something off his chest," said Anna, as she and Greg got into the SUV with Sam.

Tommy accelerated away hard in front of them and turned left at the bottom of the drive and headed off to pick up Terri and Simon, whilst Sam, with Anna and Greg on board, turned right and drove hard back along the main road towards the coast line.

"Good decision back there," said Anna.

"Yes and I think John MacDonald would agree," said Greg.

*****

"Is Daniel ready to go as soon as we get back?" said Greg, after Terri had picked up his call.

"Yes, we can head straight to Goa International. Laura is also en-route and she'll pick up the firearms and get them shipped back to us. We just need to leave the SUVs parked up at the airport. Do you think Kaur will try to get her bodyguard to do anything to try to stop us?"

"I don't think so. By the look of her as we left, she did actually seem more concerned about him once she saw the extent of his injury. He really needs a hospital, so I'm banking on her concentrating on that. She did mutter something about, *'This isn't over,'* but hey, that's all for another day if she ever chooses to discuss the matter further," said Greg.

The rest of the journey was uneventful. Tommy caught them up before they reached the airport and they travelled in convoy for the final few kilometres of the journey before parking up outside the VIP terminal, where Terri could see Laura was already waiting.

"Hope we didn't interrupt your sunbathing?" said Terri.

"Nope, I was just finishing off my book. I'm going back by car as I can't stomach another go in a helicopter. Hope it all worked out okay for you?" said Laura.

"Like clockwork. Please say thanks again to Martin for us," said Anna.

"Yes, will do and Mrs Martínez? It's been a pleasure to meet you in person?" said Laura.

Anna just smiled and then looked at Terri, who was standing there.

"Are you really some sort of celebrity legend in the spy world Anna?"

"It seems I am my dear," said Anna as she walked off into the terminal smiling.

THIRTY SIX

They separated at the terminal as Tommy and Simon were going back to London via the next BA flight.

As regular air travellers, they had Lounge access and so they were looking forward to a couple of ice cool glasses of beer before getting on the plane. However, they didn't know until they checked in, but Terri had upgraded them to Business Class and as they boarded, they turned left for their seats and were greeted by the cabin crew team with a glass of champagne.

*****

Anna, Greg, Sam and Terri were going back to Palma de Mallorca with Daniel in the Citation. Once they were in the air, they could all feel themselves relax.

"Bit of a hectic one for you guys to start your new roles with 3R," said Greg.

"It was certainly different," said Sam, and when the others looked at him, he just smiled and said, "No paperwork."

"I don't know if exciting is the right word with people being shot dead in front of me," said Anna, "but I can't think of any other word for everything that has gone on. I just wish it wasn't as a result of what happened to poor Sheila."

"Yes, it will take John and the boys a good while to

get over this, but I think he'll at least have some small satisfaction that he has had some sort of justice for her with the result and that others may not suffer the same harm," said Greg, before adding, "I am assuming we all think the shooter was something to do with Sergei?"

"Did you initially think it was me?" said Terri.

"I wouldn't have minded either way, because he was damn close to getting the AK up and firing. My fault for not saying anything at the time as I saw the scope glint, but knowing you weren't at that location I put it down to something else. My mistake which I'm pleased to say didn't lead to any casualties on our side," said Greg.

"And when did you learn to speak Hindi?" said Anna.

"About thirty six years ago, not long after I had met you. My first mission ended up with an Indian connection and I had to go there, but today I was just glad that I remembered some of what I'd needed to know back then."

They settled back in their seats and once they got to their cruising height, Daniel came around with refreshments and gave them the flight plan. They would need to stop for fuel, but twice this time. Once in Oman, for a very quick top up and then straight onto Cyprus, where they would stay overnight before flying to Palma de Mallorca the following morning.

*****

Lori Garcia was waiting at the VIP Terminal when they landed the next day. Greg had called her when they had taken off for Oman and then again from the hotel in Paphos, Cyprus. She couldn't believe how excited she was to see him.

Greg had a similar feeling of energy building up inside him. He realised he really wanted this to work and he would find a way to get over the obstacles of where they both worked, even if it meant him moving to Spain to be with her and then using Madrid Airport for his business commitments around the world.

She hadn't waited for him to come through the Arrivals door. She had shown her GEO badge and was standing airside in the VIP Terminal, as they arrived in the people carrier from the plane. She ran and hugged him and they kissed like young lovers, before catching everyone looking at them and laughing.

Later, they sat at a coffee shop in Palma and he told her all about what had happened since he had last seen her. She listened and asked questions about certain details and then just sat back and looked at him.

"What?" he said.

"So is this what it's going to be like if you are part of my life? Never knowing what you might be getting yourself into?"

"Well no actually. Most of the time I'm sitting behind a desk these days and it's Terri who is out doing all the exciting stuff. I just meet the clients, enjoy a glass of wine or two and keep them happy on the phone," said Greg.

"Hmm, well I'm not so sure that's the man I want to be in my life. I like this one. The one who is flying across the world breaking up OCGs and tracking down murderers."

"Really?" said Greg.

"No, you idiot, give me the desk bound telephone man who will be safe and sound any day of the week," said Lori laughing. "Now when I retire and I know I can look after you. Then you can go and play again, okay?"

"Okay, I get it and I can't wait for you to join 3R," said Greg.

"Is that all you can't wait for Señor?"

He smiled at her. He knew what he wanted and he hoped she felt the same.

"I want to be part of your life Lori Garcia. A big part of your life and I understand if you think I'm rushing things, but that means more than just a few days and nights together before we go our different ways, much more," said Greg.

"I know," she said, "and I would very much like you to meet my two boys, so they can get to know the man who makes me so very happy."

She kissed him softly on the lips.

"I'd like that too."

They finished talking about work and he ended by saying he was going to meet John MacDonald that afternoon. She told him that she was staying on the island for two more weeks to see what happened with the Armenian OCG as a result of the new management. After paying for their coffees they got up and walked out hand in hand. They were now officially a couple.

*****

Greg and Terri went to the MacDonald villa that afternoon and collected Anna and Sam on the way. John and his sons listened attentively as the story unfolded. John nodded when he heard that Sonny had been shot and killed. Greg thought he might ask about Kaur still being alive, but he seemed content that justice had been done with the murderer dealt with and the instigator of the scam having been financially ruined.

"Greg, I hope you know how much this means to me and our, I mean my boys," said John.

"I do John, but I wish to high heaven that it was one job that I hadn't needed to be asked to do," said Greg.

"I know, but once it had happened, it was a job that damn well needed doing and I'm bloody glad it was you who was there for me. I want you to keep the rest of that £2 million and use it in any way you see fit."

"John, I can't. It's way too much. I only need to cover the cost of the plane and the incidentals. No one wants any sort of payment for this," said Greg.

"Look Greg, there will be another job like this, somewhere along the road where maybe the victim's family won't have the sort of money that I can lay my hands on, so keep it for then and don't say anything more."

John's voice had become firmer as he spoke and Greg was getting the message loud and clear.

"Okay, I understand. We'll use it when the situation comes around, just as you wish," said Greg.

"Good, that's settled. Now I've been thinking. I'm definitely going to keep the villa. Sheila would love it if my boys finally bring their kids out here when they get around to having some. Of course, you also have an open invitation Greg, as I understand that you may be spending more time in Spain and Mallorca from now on, seeing as I hear you have hit it off with a certain Spanish police officer?" said John.

Greg smiled. Nothing got past the old boy. He looked at Anna, then Terri and then Sam. They all shook their heads, so who knows how he found out, but found out he had and John was right. It was a beautiful place and whilst he couldn't see him and Lori having any more children, it would be great to bring Lori's boys here and their families too in due course.

As they were leaving the MacDonald villa Anna got a call on her phone.

"Anna, just checking in with you. I hope everything went okay on your travels?"

"Ah, Martin. Good to hear from you and yes, it was all very satisfactory. Have you been able to sort out the money we transferred through?" said Anna.

"Yes, £2.5 million. Rob found another half mill lying about and thought it best to take that as well as it was all no doubt from ill-gotten gains. We have set up a tri-partite team from London, Mumbai and Miss Garcia's GEO to manage the funds based on the files Rob was able to secure as he trawled her system. They are making great headway and have already earmarked about £100,000 to return to some very surprised people, many of whom had no idea they had even been scammed in the first place."

"Martin, that's excellent," said Anna.

"Well that's all for now, but you do remember what I said about giving you a call sometime?" said Martin.

"Yes for a coffee," said Anna.

"Well coffee, but also in case we need someone with your extraordinary talents, but that's it for the moment and so I'll leave you to enjoy getting back to Sa Petita Llibreria."

"Martin," she said quietly. "I have never mentioned Sa Petita Llibreria to you before."

"Oh, I'm sure you have Anna, anyway I must go," and he rang off.

"Greg, have you ever mentioned Sa Petita Llibreria to Martin Carruthers before?"

"No, why?"

She paused. So Carruthers had known where she was when she first spoke to him. Had they really kept an eye on her for all of those years? Again, she smiled.

"Oh, no reason. It doesn't matter," said Anna. "Now, what are we doing for dinner? Sam, shall we go and see Miquel?"

"Great idea Mum, I'll get it booked up. Let's go to his brasserie in the town square, Quina Brasa. How does nine o'clock sound to everyone?" said Sam, "and Greg, I take it you'll be bringing Lori?"

"Yes, that would be great. Terri, what about bringing Daniel?"

She looked at her father. Matchmaking again, but then again, why not? They had both rather given up a bit too easily last time and neither had been in any sort of serious relationship since.

"Yes, why not. I'll call him. Sam, shall I ask him to bring Frances?"

"No, and stop with the matchmaking. She's lovely, but I'm not looking for any sort of relationship at the moment," said Sam, and looked at all of them, especially his mother.

"Touchy, touchy dear brother," said Terri, and saw Sam in her rear view mirror, sitting there, shaking his head.

THIRTY SEVEN

Miquel was there to greet them as they arrived at Quina Brasa in the town square in Llucmajor.

Only Sam had been there before and so it was going to be a new experience for the rest of them and it looked fantastic.

Miquel greeted his friend with a hug and took them to a table he had reserved for them outside to take in the summer evening. On the table was a bottle of Cava sitting on ice, which he opened and poured as they sat down at the table.

"Amigos, welcome to Quina Brasa and what I hope is the first of many visits for you all."

"Muchas gracias amigo," says Sam. "Now you said you had some fantastic specials tonight. I can't wait."

They weren't disappointed with the fabulous food and delicious wines chosen by Miquel to go with each of the courses. The warmth of the summer evening didn't fall away and they continued talking at the table long into the night.

"Did you ever think what might have been Mum? If you and Greg had stayed together?"

"No Sam, it was never going to happen," said Anna. "It was and remains a wonderful week in my life, but that's how it was always going to stay. Just one week."

Greg looked about. Terri was talking quietly to Daniel. Was that a relationship that was going to rekindle? He hoped so as he liked Daniel and thought he would be good for Terri. He saw Sam talking with his mother and he knew Anna was so pleased Sam was feeling better and that he was looking forward to staying to live and work in Palma.

Finally, there was Lori, who was wearing a dark blue summer dress and looking just radiant with her hair down. The 3R management team had grown significantly this last week. In fact it had pretty much doubled in size, but it was still a family business and he liked that. He liked that a lot.

Greg then saw Miquel coming across to the table with a very attractive young woman. He nudged Anna who was next to him.

"More matchmaking?"

Anna smiled and then looked at Sam. She saw his eyes were fixed on the young woman before him.

"I want you to say hello to Carmen, my little cousin. You remember her from school Sam?" said Miquel.

During the evening Sam had seen a very attractive young woman working across on some of the other tables. He thought she had been looking at him during the night, but thought he must be imagining things.

"Carmen, of course, I remember you," said Sam, coming to his feet.

"Oh no you don't," said everyone at the table, and he turned and looked at them and smiled.

"Well I remember the little nine or ten year old girl who used to tag along with me and Miquel and get in the way when we were trying to play. You've er...".

"Grown up?" said Terri, standing up and giving Carmen a welcome hug.

"Lovely to meet you Carmen and yes, this is my brother. He's slightly awkward in front of girls, especially beautiful ones," said Terri.

Now it was Carmen's turn to look embarrassed, so Sam stood and took her to one side.

"I'm sorry, I hope we haven't embarrassed you?"

"No, I'm fine, but Miquel has talked so much about you and I was so looking forward to saying hello after all these years. But I need to get back to work now or the boss will tell me off."

She looked across at Miquel.

"Okay, but don't let him give you any trouble," grinned Sam, "and Carmen, maybe we can talk again soon?"

"Yes, I'd like that," said Carmen, looking down at her feet as she felt everyone at the table looking at her. "I've got to go now," she whispered, and she went back to the other side of the restaurant.

Sam sat back down and the table went quiet.

"What are you people like? I say hello to a girl and...," said Sam.

"And you're nearly officially part of my family now," teased Miquel. "Upset her and you know I will kill you, even though you are like a brother to me!"

Sam got up and embraced his best friend. He remembered how he had felt when he arrived back on the island a month or so ago compared with how he felt now. He was feeling great and he loved being around all of these people.

"Thank you amigo, for bringing me back to almost normal," said Sam.

"And thank you amigo, for wanting to come back," said Miquel.

The rest of the night just got better for Sam, as once Miquel had let Carmen finally finish work, he sat down with her and they just talked. She told him about her life after he had left for London and then about her Doctorate in California and then he told her about being in the police and then he surprised himself by talking about his PTSD. He felt so relaxed with her and they finished the evening sitting there holding hands and planning what to do together the next day.

*****

The next few weeks seemed to fly by. Sam was seeing a lot of Carmen and they both felt they were at the start of something good. She was actively looking for work and Sam was spending a lot of time with Alfonso, the company accountant, going through the books he had been so keen to show Sam a couple of months ago.

He saw Alfonso again one morning as he was walking towards Sa Petita Llibreria. It was an early start for both of them and they arranged to meet later to talk more about the property portfolio. It was 7.30am when Sam started going through a complete inventory check. After an hour, he stopped to make a coffee as he knew his mother would be arriving soon, when he heard the bell go as the shop door opened.

He looked up and saw a woman he recognised as one of his mother's friends. As she walked towards him, he could see that she had been crying. She looked at him and he thought she was about to turn around to go, but she stopped and composed herself.

"Is Anna in?"

THE END

BOOK TWO

"Is Anna in?"

The same three words that had been the start of a new life for Sam just a few weeks ago.

He looked at her and remembered her name.

"It's Mrs Green isn't it? I'm Sam, Anna's son."

She went to answer, but the tears started to flow again and she stumbled over her words.

"Here, sit down and I'll get some tea on. Mum will be in soon."

He grabbed a chair and helped her to sit down.

"He told me not to come. My husband I mean, but I don't know what to do. I'm so worried and I've been to the police, but they say it's too early to do anything and that she's a grown woman anyway."

"So tell me what's happened," said Sam.

"It's my granddaughter, Lily. She's not been home for two days."

Book Two in the 3R series is coming soon.

ACKNOWLEDGEMENT

This book would not have been possible without the absolute love and support of my darling wife, Julie.

Many thanks also for the support of family and friends and in particular for the specific contributions from Kevin Albin - fellow author, Elaine Penhal - another fellow author and book editor extraordinaire, Anamika Bansal - for help with my character names, Paul Read - for military tactical terminology, Lisa Simpson - for Spanish translation and Ian Hackett - for his firearms knowledge and advice.

Also a very big thank you to all my volunteer editors - those friends and family who have helped with the continuing editing process, especially the significant contributions from Elizabeth Lathwood and Sandra Symms.

Finally to my cousin, Brian, for his huge support in bringing to life the artwork for this book in depicting La Seu, the magnificent Gothic Roman Catholic cathedral located in the beautiful city of Palma de Mallorca. You can see more of Brian's work on brian-tarr.pixels.com

THE MALLORCAN BOOKSELLER LOCATION TOUR

There has been a lot of interest from readers in exploring the locations in the book.

The book was inspired by my love of the beautiful island of Mallorca. Therefore, whilst creating the story, I also wanted to promote many of the wonderful cafes, bars, restaurants and hotels I have found over the past fifteen years or so.

So why not see and experience the locations the 3R team have been to during their adventures in this story? And who knows, you may just see me there too!

I have listed most of the specific sites on the next page, however, you can also explore the island from the descriptions of the various locations, e.g. for the fincas used by 3R and for the kidnap, to identify for yourself the likely areas for these fictional fincas.

Locations

Cambridge
Running Track, Wilberforce Road

London
The Cittie of York Public House, Holborn
The Blackfriars Public House, Queen Victoria St

Madrid
Cafe Comercial
Universidad Complutense de Madrid

Mallorca
Bar 13%, Calle Sant Feliu
Cappuccino, Placa de Cort
Contrabando, Llucmajor
Hotel Cap Rocat
Hotel Gloria de Sant Jaume (Bar El Patio de Gloria)
Policia Nacional HQ, Passeig de Mallorca
Portixol Bay
Quina Brasa, Llucmajor
Rambla dels Ducs
Teatre Principal, Rambla dels Ducs

Armenia
The Meeting Point, Marriott Hotel, Republic Square

India
Business Park, Andheri West, Mumbai
JW Marriott, Juhu, Mumbai
Colva Beach, Goa

REVIEWS

Book Reviews are the life blood of all authors. Finding out what you thought about my book is really important to me.

Whether you have purchased this book new, or from a charity shop, or borrowed it from a library or a friend, please can I ask that you take a moment to submit a review on Amazon or goodreads.com

Please follow me on Instagram and find out more about the locations and how Book 2 is developing

the_mallorcan_bookseller

Thank you

Pete Davies

ABOUT THE AUTHOR

Pete Davies

 Retiring after a 30 year career within the British Police service, Pete had held a wide variety of operational and training roles, including being a firearms commander.

In 2012 he started a new successful career as an executive coach, working with clients within the public, private and voluntary sectors before committing to writing full time in 2020.

Enjoying the beautiful island of Mallorca for many family holidays over the years led him to base his first book on the island.

He lives with his wife and their labrador in Berkshire, England.

Printed in Great Britain
by Amazon